P9-BBU-875

Books by Isaac Bashevis Singer

Novels

THE MANOR

I. THE MANOR • II. THE ESTATE

THE FAMILY MOSKAT • THE MAGICIAN OF LUBLIN

SATAN IN GORAY • THE SLAVE

ENEMIES, A LOVE STORY

SHOSHA • THE PENITENT

Stories

A FRIEND OF KAFKA • GIMPEL THE FOOL • SHORT FRIDAY

THE SÉANCE • THE SPINOZA OF MARKET STREET • PASSIONS

A CROWN OF FEATHERS • OLD LOVE • THE IMAGE

Memoirs

IN MY FATHER'S COURT

For Children

A DAY OF PLEASURE • THE FOOLS OF CHELM

MAZEL AND SHLIMAZEL OR THE MILK OF A LIONESS

WHEN SHLEMIEL WENT TO WARSAW

A TALE OF THREE WISHES • ELIJAH THE SLAVE

JOSEPH AND KOZA OR THE SACRIFICE TO THE VISTULA

ALONE IN THE WILD FOREST • THE WICKED CITY

NAFTALI THE STORYTELLER AND HIS HORSE, SUS

WHY NOAH CHOSE THE DOVE

THE POWER OF LIGHT

THE GOLEM

Collections

AN ISAAC BASHEVIS SINGER READER

THE COLLECTED STORIES

STORIES FOR CHILDREN

The Image and Other Stories

Isaac Bashevis Singer

THE IMAGE

and Other Stories

Farrar Straus Giroux

NEW YORK

First printing, 1985
Printed in the United States of America
Published simultaneously in Canada by
Collins Publishers, Toronto
Designed by Cynthia Krupat

Library of Congress Cataloging in Publication Data
Singer, Isaac Bashevis.
The image and other stories.
Translated from Yiddish.
1. Singer, Isaac Bashevis.—Translations,
English. I. Title.
PJ5129.S49A2 1985 839'.0933 85–4487
The following stories appeared originally in *The New Yorker*: "Advice," "The Bond," "The Interview," "The Divorce," "A Telephone Call on Yom Kippur," "The Mistake," and "The Image." In *Partisan Review*: "Strong as Death Is Love" and "Loshikl." In *Playboy*: "Why Heisherik Was Born," "Remnants," and "On the Way to the Poorhouse." In *Cavalier*: "One Day of Happiness." In *The Jewish Chronicle*: "Strangers." Acknowledgment is made to Viking–Penguin for "The Enemy," which originally appeared in *Dark Forces*, edited by Kirby McCauley.

Contents

Author's Note

In the years I have been writing I have heard many discouraging words about my themes and language. I was told that Jewishness and Yiddish were dying, the short story was out of vogue and about to disappear from the literary market. Some critics decided that the art of telling stories with a beginning, middle, and end—as Aristotle demanded—was archaic, a primitive form of fiction. I heard similar degrading opinions about the value of folklore in the literature of our times. I was living in a civilization which despised the old and worshipped the young. But somehow I never took these dire threats seriously. I belong to an old tribe and I knew that literature thrives best on ancient faith, timeless hopes, and illusions. A writer should never abandon his mother tongue and its treasure of idioms. Literature must deal with the past instead of planning the future. It must describe events, not analyze ideas; its topic is the individual, not the masses. It must be an art, not pretend to be a science. Moreover, belief in God and His Providence is the very essence of literature. It tells us that causality is nothing but a mask on the face of destiny. Man is constantly watched by powers that seem to know all his desires and complications. He has free choice, but he is also being led by a mysterious hand. Literature is the story of love and fate, a description of the mad hurricane of human passions and the struggle with them.

I'm glad to see that the short story is very much alive today. It is still the greatest challenge to the prose writer and it becomes his highest achievement if he succeeds at being both imaginative and brief. As to Yiddish, it has not yet been liquidated in the melting pot of assimilation—an omen to me that the same is in store for other minorities, their languages and cultures.

Many of the stories in this volume were published in The New Yorker, *edited by Charles McGrath. All of them were edited by Robert Giroux, with whom I have been connected in admiration and friendship for the last twenty-five years, ever since I began publishing with Farrar, Straus and Giroux. My gratitude to them, as well as to my translators, who worked closely with me and spared no effort to give these stories the precision and clarity I hope for. The English translation is especially important to me because translations into other languages are based on the English text. In a way, this is right because, in the process of translation, I make many corrections. I always remember the saying of the Cabalists that man's mission is the correction of the mistakes he made both in this world and in former reincarnations.*

I.B.S.

The Image and Other Stories

Advice

In the years when I worked at a Yiddish newspaper in New York, giving advice, I heard many bizarre stories. As a rule, those who came to me were readers, not writers. But one time an advice-seeker happened to be a poet, an accountant by profession, whom I often met at meetings of the Yiddish Writers' Union, as well as at the literary cafeteria on East Broadway. His name was Morris Pintchover—a little man with yellow tufts of hair around a bald spot. He had sunken cheeks, a pointed chin, a short nose, and eyes the color of amber. Morris Pintchover dressed like an old-fashioned artist from Europe. He wore a broad-brimmed hat, a flowing tie, and spats over his shoes even in the summer. Pelerines—long capes for men—had been out of style for many years, but Morris Pintchover always wore one when he came to our literary gatherings. He had brought it from Warsaw near the beginning of the century. As he entered my office he said to me, "You are surprised, eh? I am also your reader and I'm entitled to ask your advice just like the others. Am I right?"

"Sit down. What can I tell you that you don't know yourself?"

"Oh, it is helpful to talk things over. After all, what is psychoanalysis? And why are Catholics so eager to make confessions? And what is literature? A number of great writers called their works confessions: Rousseau, Tolstoy, Gorky. I loved Strindberg's title *The Confessions of a Fool.* Actually, there is an element of foolishness in all confessions. I assume you've heard what's happened to me."

Morris Pintchover smiled sadly and showed a mouthful of yellowish teeth. I knew his case from the gossips in the Café Royal. His wife, Tamara, a poetess who could never find a publisher, had left Morris and gone to live with a man named Mark Lenchner, a well-known writer and a Communist, whose wife had tried suicide three times because of his constant betrayals. Mark Lenchner was known as a schnorrer and a cynic. Tamara was small, fat, with a high bosom. Her hair was set in ringlets and dyed the color of carrots. Over her upper lip she sprouted a fuzzy female mustache. She told little anecdotes at which no one laughed but herself. For years she waged war with the editors of Yiddish newspapers and magazines, cursing them with vile oaths behind their backs. What Mark Lenchner saw in her no one could understand. In the literary cafeteria some maintained that what he saw was a nest egg of a few thousand dollars that she had managed to save by peddling her privately published books of poetry in the Café Royal and in the hotels in the Catskill Mountains. The couple had no children. I heard myself saying to Morris, "Yes, I was told something about the matter."

"You probably know that Tamara is now living with Lenchner openly, before the whole world," Morris said.

"I heard that, too."

"It has come to the point where the humorists print jokes about me in the newspapers."

"Idiots. I don't read the humor section."

"My dear friend, I know very well how people see someone like me—a shlemiel, a cuckold, a husband with horns. You know as well as I that when someone commits an injustice people make mincemeat of the victim, not of the culprit. It is not the first time that Tamara has exchanged me for some charlatan. I have been suffering and keeping silent, not because I believe that one should offer the other cheek but because I have the misfortune to love her. Love is a sickness—some kind of pathology that cannot be explained. If a man has a tumor he is stuck with it—he must even nurture it. The fact is that since Tamara left me I cannot eat or sleep. I make serious mistakes in my work, and I'm afraid I'm going to lose my few clients. I haven't written a single line since all this turmoil started. What I want to tell you may revolt you, but I hope that you have more understanding for human weakness than the kibitzers in the Café Royal. Since she left me, my love for that treacherous woman has been burning with a fire I'm afraid may consume me physically. I am somewhat interested in the occult. There are cases where people have ignited spontaneously and burned to death. Naturally, the rationalists scoff at such events, because these don't fit in with their clichés. However, if emotions can drive the blood into the face, produce constipation, diarrhea, eczema, and high blood pressure, why can't they cause fire? Am I right or not?"

"I'm ready to agree to everything," I said. "But how can I help you?"

"My friend, I don't come to you to complain, but to ask advice," Morris Pintchover said. "When you hear what I want to ask you, you will be convinced that I have completely lost my mind. But insanity is also human. The story goes like this. That Mark Lenchner, the outcast, and his wife, Necha—a saint of a woman—had an apartment for which he never paid rent, except perhaps for the month when they moved in. Don't ask me how he managed this. The owner of the building was somewhat of a Yiddishist, and a leftist to boot. He played the part of a philanthropist and a Maecenas. It was always a miserable apartment. The ceiling leaked, and when it rained Necha had to put out pails and pots on the floor. But what did Lenchner care? He was seldom there—always running around with all kinds of sluts. The situation went on for as long as the landlord lived. When he died the heirs sued Lenchner for nonpayment, and now they are about to evict him with all his junky possessions. Vicious as he is, he cannot allow Necha to be thrown out into the gutter. Besides, he has his books and his manuscripts there. A few days ago I received a telephone call from Tamara. I was stunned. She has never called since she left me. I will make it short. Mark Lenchner, the rascal, proposed to her that he, Lenchner, and Necha and Tamara should all move in with me. I have a large apartment, and his idea was that all four of us should live together. He wants to be friends again, he said. He also would like to settle down finally and write his memoirs, or God knows what. I plead with you, don't look at me with so much irony. I know very well that Lenchner cannot be trusted. First he took my wife and now he tries to take my low-rent apartment—a real bargain. On the other hand, what could I lose? Since I cannot live without Tamara, let us at least be together under one roof. When a man stands before the gallows with a noose around his neck and they bring him the good tidings that the execution has been postponed, he does not ask any questions or impose conditions. Necha is a decent woman, a quiet dove. She will do as he tells her. What is your opinion?"

One eye of Morris's seemed to cry, the other laughed. I asked, "Why do you want to hear my opinion? You won't follow my advice anyhow."

"Possibly. Still, I would like to hear it just the same."

"My opinion is that a love of this sort is the worst kind of slavery. I still believe that man has free choice."

"Eh? I knew that you would say something like this. However, perhaps Spinoza was right that everything is predetermined. Perhaps the decision was made a billion years ago that Tamara, Necha, and Mark Lenchner should live together with me, no matter how preposterous and perverse the whole thing may seem to others. Perhaps free choice is exactly what Spinoza thought it to be, an illusion."

"If free choice is an illusion and everything is predetermined, why did he write his *Ethics*?" I asked. "What was the sense of preaching *amor dei intellectualis*, political freedom, and all the rest if we are nothing but mechanisms? That Spinoza was as full of contradictions as a pomegranate is full of seeds."

"And what was Kant?" Pintchover asked. "And what was Hegel? And what are all the other philosophers? You are right. Since I knew that I would be unable to listen to you, I shouldn't have come for advice. But a man in my state of mind cannot live according to logic. I'm sure you know that yearning is an excruciating pain. It is quite possible that hell is made up of yearning. The wicked don't roast on beds of nails, they sit on comfortable chairs and are tortured with yearning."

"For whom are they yearning?" I asked.

"For those whom they left on earth—everyone for his Tamara or her Lenchner. Be well and forgive me." Morris Pintchover extended to me a soft and moist hand. He smiled, winked, and said, "Thank you for your advice. Adieu."

•

A year or so passed and I heard that Mark Lenchner had been invited to live in the Soviet Union and that he had gone, leaving Necha behind. Stalin was still alive, but now in his interviews he maintained that Communism and capitalism could coexist. It was already known that he had liquidated most of the Yiddish writers in Russia, though the Communist Yiddish newspaper in New York assured its readers that all these accusations came from enemies of the people, the lackeys of Fascism. The Yiddish-speaking Communists still collected contributions for the nonexistent autonomous Jewish region, Birobidzhan. I was told that the writers in Moscow had arranged a grand reception for Lenchner, and that from there he had flown to Birobidzhan. This happened around the time when the Jewish doctors in the Soviet Union were accused of poisoning several Russian leaders. I had moved out of New York and had almost forgotten Morris Pintchover. I had lived in Israel, in France, in Switzerland. Someone in Tel Aviv or in Paris told me that Morris Pintchover had died, or perhaps he mentioned a similar name. When I returned to New York, years later, I no longer went to the office of my newspaper on East Broadway but sent my manuscripts by mail. I had ceased taking part in Yiddishist meetings and going to their lectures. Then one day I got a telephone call from the editor's secretary. The typesetter had lost a page of one of my articles, and I had to go down to East Broadway and fill in the missing page. I had to take three buses to get there from uptown. The third one ran between Union Square and East Broadway.

I passed a neighborhood where the population had changed—Puerto Ricans and blacks instead of the Jewish immigrants. Old buildings were being torn down. New ones went up. Here and there one could still see the walls of former apartments, with faded wallpaper or chipped paint. On one of these walls hung a picture of Sir Moses Montefiore. A wrecker's ball was knocking down walls with what seemed to be a light touch. Cranes lifted beams for new buildings. On one of the ruins stood four cats holding a mute consultation. I had a feeling that under the wreckage demons were buried—goblins and imps who had smuggled themselves to America in the time of the great immigration and had expired from the New York noise and the lack of Jewishness there.

After I corrected my manuscript in the typesetter's room I decided not to take the bus back but to walk to Union Square and go home from there by subway. I walked along Second Avenue. The literary cafeteria still existed, but the Café Royal, which had been a gathering place for writers and actors for many years, had closed and in its place was a dry cleaner's. I stopped at a window displaying a few long-forgotten Yiddish books with faded covers, as well as recordings of old Yiddish theater songs. After a while I continued up the avenue. And who walked toward me? Morris Pintchover—small, bent, shrunken, and in shabby clothes. The little hair that still remained on his skull had turned white. One could see a mere remnant of yellow in his eyebrows. He shuffled his feet as he walked, and leaned on a cane. So many of my colleagues had died in America or perished in Europe that I no longer knew who was alive and who was dead. He extended a bony hand and said, "I hope you recognize me."

"Yes."

"We haven't seen each other for years. Although we live in the same city, we have become estranged from one another. To tell the truth, New York is not a city but a whole country. Still, I was in contact with you—spiritually, I mean. I am reading you. After all, what is a writer? Only his works. I have published two books of poems—privately, of course. I doubt if you have ever seen them."

"If you'll send them to me, I'll read them. Almost no Yiddish bookstores are left anymore."

"Yes, we are in trouble, but the instinct to create remains as long as one breathes. I would have sent you my works, but I didn't know your address. When I send books to your newspaper they disappear. It seems there are still some people eager to steal a Yiddish book. This in itself is a miracle."

"Yes, true," I muttered.

"I guess that you don't remember my name. It's Morris Pintchover."

"I remember you very well. I have often thought about you," I said.

"Really? It's good to know."

I wanted to ask him about his wife, but I had forgotten her name. Besides, I had too often heard the same reply—"Died." As if Morris Pintchover could read my mind, he said, "Tamara is no more. She passed away two years ago. Got cancer and left me. In the old country there was such a thing as galloping consumption. Tamara died, I could say, from galloping cancer. One day she got sick and a few weeks later it was all over. Left this vale of tears like a saint. Perhaps it wasn't even cancer. When the doctors cannot find the correct diagnosis, they call it cancer. God sends more sicknesses to the world than the medics can name. Only yesterday I read that millions of viruses can live in one cubic centimeter of tissue. Yet they are made of many molecules. The microcosmos is even more fantastic than the macrocosmos. In the midst of all these wonders comes the Angel of Death and erases everything. May I ask where you are going?"

"Union Square," I answered.

"Are you walking there?"

"Yes, I am walking."

"May I accompany you?"

"Yes, with pleasure."

We walked, and Morris stopped every few steps. I wanted to ask him about Lenchner's wife, but I knew that sooner or later he would tell me anyway. He was talking to me and to himself: "A whole world has vanished, eh? When I was a boy the Yiddishist movement was only beginning. Our classics were all still alive—Mendele, Sholem Aleichem, Peretz. I remember quite well the Czernowitz conference. What optimism! It was like a new spring. When I came to America, New York had not one Yiddish theater but twenty. This whole neighborhood was boiling like a kettle with ideas and ideals. Now everything has changed, everything is different—people, houses, stores, styles. Some time ago I lay awake at night and it occurred to me: If there is a God and he exists eternally, how much could he have experienced in all this time? What would happen if he decided to write his memoirs? At what point would he begin? Would he go back one billion years? Ten billion years? A hundred billion years? It is eerie to think about such things—especially at night when one cannot fall asleep. Well, and who would be his publisher? He would have to publish himself, just as I do."

Morris Pintchover laughed, and showed a set of new false teeth. He said, "Perhaps you would like to walk along Avenue B. That is where I live."

"By yourself?"

"No, with Necha, Lenchner's widow."

"Aha."

"You most probably have heard that Lenchner went to Russia without her. He promised to bring her over to Stalin's paradise, but what did a promise mean to Lenchner? She received one postcard from him—not from Birobidzhan but from Moscow. The invitation had been nothing but a trap to do away with him. What they had against him I don't know. He served them faithfully. He defended all their evil deeds. To the last day in New York, he kept assuring everyone that the Yiddish writers in Russia lived in perfect bliss—Bergelson, Markish, Fefer, Charik, Kulbak. He called all of us here in America the worst names for suspecting the great benefactor Comrade Stalin. Lenchner knew quite well that he was lying, but he hoped that his brazen lies would save his skin if his comrades in Russia accused him of some deviation. Who knows what goes on in the brains of such villains? Since he knew what awaited him, why did he need to go there? There is something in Greek drama where the protagonist knows that he will fall into an abyss but is compelled by fate to choose death and cannot help himself. Perhaps you remember that I once came to you to ask your advice. Yes, Tamara and Lenchner and Necha moved into my apartment, and for a few weeks I imagined that I was happy. Yes, slavery. Our emotions are the rulers. They assail us like robbers, they mock all our resolutions. My neighbors ridiculed me and spat. Was I really happy? We delve into the worst suffering and we call it pleasure. When Lenchner left I became, so to say, the king. Tamara finally sobered up from her madness. How long can you be drunk? I forgave her. Did I have a choice? Nothing is as violent as the violence of love. My theory is that man is engaged in a clandestine love affair with the Angel of Death."

We stopped at a dilapidated building and Morris said, "Here is where I live. In this house, on the third floor. We have no elevator. I hope you don't mind climbing the stairs. Now that Tamara is in the true world, Necha has become everything to me—a wife, a sister, a mother. Of course, it is all platonic. She is a faithful reader of yours."

We went into a dark entrance and climbed the steps; at each landing Morris stopped and panted. He pointed to the left side of his chest. "The pump refuses to function," he said. "It has been doing it for eighty years. How long can it go on pumping? Enough is enough."

At the third floor Morris rang the bell of his apartment, but no one answered. He said, "Either she is not home or she doesn't hear. Wait. I have a key."

We entered a narrow corridor. Morris opened the door to the living room. It smelled of dust, medicine, and something rancid. Over a torn sofa with protruding springs hung a portrait of Lenchner—young, with curly hair, a black mustache, and shining eyes, which looked out with the arrogance and the complacency of those who have found the truth once and for all.

Morris Pintchover remarked, "This is he. What Tamara saw in this faker I will never know. But she defended him to her last breath. As for Necha, she was a real martyr. But now where has she run away to? We are only two old people and she buys food as if we were ten. Three-quarters of it is thrown out. She has a kind of buying mania. How much can we eat? A piece of toast and a glass of tea is enough for us for the whole day. Thanks to God and to Social Security, we have more than enough of everything. Sit down. What can I offer you?"

"Absolutely nothing," I said.

"Nothing, eh? A man must want something."

For a long while we sat still. Then Morris Pintchover said, "You were right then. I should never have taken them in. But what would I have done now without Necha? She is the only person who really knew Tamara and witnessed our great love."

Translated by the author

One Day of Happiness

In the three rooms, except for the kitchen, the shades were drawn. For Mendel Bialer did not like the sun. Now that he was older, he spent most of his time lying down. What did he have to do? He was already drawing his pension. And besides, his feet hurt him. At night he tossed sleepless on the bed, but all day long he dozed. The summer sun was so hot that afternoon it penetrated even the shades. One fly landed on his forehead. He brushed it off, only to have it settle again on his reddish nose. Though half asleep, he was worrying. The pension from the bread mill where he had been employed for thirty-five years as a bookkeeper was not enough to live on. He was behind in his rent. Moreover, he had an unmarried girl in the house, his daughter Feigele, or Fela, as they had called her in school. Though she was twenty-four, Fela still acted like a girl of sixteen, read foolish books, did not look for work. The matchmakers had tried to find a husband for her but she was choosy, behaving as if she were the daughter of a rich man and a beauty, whereas in fact she hadn't a groschen and was ugly besides. In the middle of his dozing, Mendel grasped his gray beard and frowned, as if to ask, "What will come of all this? What is she waiting for?"

Mendel's wife, Malkah, was in the kitchen peeling potatoes. The water plopped every time she threw one into the pot. In the bedroom, Fela was writing a letter. That morning she had bought herself a gilt-edged sheet of paper, an envelope, and a new steel pen with a fine nib that wouldn't blotch. For weeks, day and night, she had been thinking out the contents of this letter. She knew every sentence by heart. It read as follows:

Highly esteemed and beloved General, God-inspired Poet:

What I am doing now is madness or worse, but I cannot help myself. Some power stronger than I is driving me to write to you. I am almost sure you won't answer me. I am not at all certain you will even read my letter, for I know Your Excellency must receive hundreds and thousands of such letters from lost souls (ha ha!). I tell you right off that I am a Jewish girl, poor, and not beautiful (my picture is enclosed). But I love you with a burning love that I don't understand myself. I am literally being consumed by this tragic—you may call it comic—love. I think about you all the time and at night I dream only of you. I could tell you how all this started, but I am afraid of making you impatient. I save all your pictures from newspapers and journals. I have even stolen because of you, my love—tearing the pages out of magazines in cafés. You are my whole life. I know all your sublime poems by heart. I read and reread all your books, especially those about your heroism at the front. I live only for you: to be able to hear your metal voice on the radio; to watch you in parades.

Once, in the Café Rzymianska, you looked at me. The happiness which that look gave me, the inspiration which filled my whole being, no pen can describe—only someone with your talent would be able to. I realize my letter is too long already and that I must come to the point. I know that you are not only a national hero and a great poet but also a man with a heart for those able to admire your gifts. I ask you humbly therefore to grant me half an hour of your time. If you would bestow upon me the privilege of spending a few minutes with you, it would be my secret treasure to guard and cherish until my last breath. Unfortunately, my parents have no telephone, so all I can do is give you my address. Mostly, I am home all day. As I write this letter, I am aware how small my chances are, how terribly foolish I am, and perhaps also selfish. Adieu, my great hero, poet, and ruler of my soul.

With a love that will never die,

Fela Bialer

P.S. My parents are old-fashioned and mustn't know of their daughter's craziness.

The last word written, Fela let out a sigh. She had trembled all the time she was writing, fearful of blotching the page. In high school her handwriting had been good, but since then it had deteriorated: she made the letters too large, the lines crooked. At school she had excelled also in composition and spelling, but now she often made childish mistakes. It was all the result of her nerves. She had never graduated, having failed in mathematics. At first she had hunted for an office job but had not succeeded in finding one. Finally she had taken a sales job in a toy store, but had been fired the first day for making the wrong change. Her mother nagged at her constantly, and her father called her his "crazy princess." Fela was small and dark, with broad hips, crooked legs, a hooked nose, and large, bulging black eyes. In her diary she compared herself to an overripe fruit. Her bosom hung down; her arms were fleshy and loose with fat. Other girls would have tried to reduce, but the dishes in Fela's home were all starchy—potatoes, dumplings, kasha. And besides, she had an unconquerable desire for chocolate. Moreover, she was constantly hungry, as if afflicted with a tapeworm. Sometimes at night, lying awake, she could feel her body beginning to swell up like dough. Her skin burned, her breasts tightened as if filled with milk. And though Fela was a virgin, she was sometimes afraid she might suddenly begin to give birth. She felt fluids coursing through her like saps in a plant before blooming. Her breath grew hot, her insides clutched and twisted, and during the night she constantly had to go to the toilet. Of late she had begun to suffer from a strange thirst. Her mother often exclaimed, "What is the matter with that girl? A fire is burning in her, God forbid!"

Fela's love for Adam Pacholski had bewildered her. She saw everything around her through a fog. She couldn't cross the room without stumbling into chairs, the table, the commode. When her mother gave her a glass of tea, she would let it slip through her fingers. She couldn't heat a pan of milk on the kitchen stove without forgetting it and letting it burn. None of Fela's dresses fit her anymore. Her girdle cut her flesh. Her shoes pinched. And no matter how often she combed and washed her hair, it always looked gluey and disheveled. Her menstrual periods came irregularly, sometimes late, sometimes early, with a rush of blood that terrified her. To compose that letter without one blotch or mistake had taken an effort almost beyond her powers. Thank God, it had come out clean! Here and there, she had even managed to finish a word with a flourish.

Fela read the letter through once, a second time, a third time. After much hesitation, she finally folded it, inserted it, wrote out the address on the envelope, stamped and sealed it. Her hands quivered, her knees trembled. She could hear her quick breathing. In the living room her father had fallen asleep. Fela intended to cross the room silently, on tiptoe, but the door screeched behind her and her heels hit the floor rebelliously. Her father sat up with a start.

"Why do you make so much noise, you wild creature?"

"Oh, Daddy, excuse me. I'm so awkward. I didn't mean to."

"Why do you hang around idle? Other girls your age are mothers of children already."

The tears welled up in Fela's eyes. "Is that my fault?"

A sob clutched her throat like vomit. She covered the letter so her tears wouldn't get it wet and escaped into the bathroom. There she could cry, cough, compose herself. She dried her face on sheets of newspaper, set there for toilet paper. She flushed the water and said aloud, "Father in heaven, you see the truth."

2

Events moved swiftly. On Monday, Fela sent out the letter. On Tuesday just at dark, she received a telegram. Thank God, nobody else was home! She wanted to give the messenger boy ten groschen but could find no small change and gave him half a zloty instead. Striking a match, she read: "Wait for me tomorrow at four o'clock at the corner of Marszalkowsky Boulevard and Wspolna Street." Fela couldn't contain herself and had to run to the bathroom. There, lighting the candle stub attached to a shelf, she read the telegram over and over again. In the cramped apartment this was her only place of privacy. She wanted to laugh; at the same time she felt like retching. She had never expected him to answer so quickly. She wasn't ready. She had no dress, no shoes. Her hair was neither washed nor curled. "It's a dream, a dream," a voice in her head screamed. "You're an idiot. Any minute now you'll wake up." Fela pinched her cheeks and bit her lips. She had begun to sweat profusely, with a sweetish smell like that of a horse. How can I go to him? she thought. I'm unclean. Oh, I'm going to faint!

She fought against the dizziness. Her head swirled as if she were drunk. A nauseous fluid seeped into her mouth and she spat it out. She went into the kitchen. Bending down to the faucet, she half drank, half splashed her face with cold water to revive herself. She saw a bottle of vinegar on a shelf, opened it, sniffed it, and took a sip. "Don't let me poison myself with too much happiness," Fela implored the higher powers. As a rule her parents were always there, but today they had gone to visit a sick friend. What should she do first? What could she wear? All her dresses were torn, stained, faded, too tight, and out of style. The fishbones in her corset were broken. "I won't go to him. I can't. I will disgrace myself," Fela said aloud. She needed someone to help her, but who? She had once had girl friends, but now they were either students at the university or else had husbands. After her failure at the final examinations, she and her friends had grown apart. Some girls would have had a lot of cousins nearby, but Fela's parents had long ago left the provinces. "Just don't lose your head," Fela warned herself. "If you do, you'll fall to pieces altogether."

She would have to buy a dress. At Jablkowski Brothers one could get ready-made dresses. But where would she get the money? And would she be able to find a dress to fit her figure? And how could she undress before the salesladies when her petticoat and brassiere were torn? They would spit on her. "Oh, dreams of a chopped-off head!" Fela muttered. "It's impossible. I'm lost—lost!" Her belly began to expand until it was hard as a drum; she heard the seams of her shift splitting; she hiccuped. "God in heaven, help me," Fela prayed. "You have shown me one miracle, show another!" She was silent, as if waiting to hear God answer. Suddenly she remembered she had forgotten to extinguish the candle in the bathroom. A fire might start. She ran to put it out. Walking back in the dark to the bedroom, she knocked over a chair, hurting her knee. She threw herself down on the bed with such force that something broke under her, most likely the board supporting the mattress. She lay inert. Suddenly she jumped. Where was the telegram? She found it still clutched in her fist.

Lying there, Fela worked out a plan. She would have to commit a crime, certainly, and steal the gold chain her mother wore only on Rosh Hashanah and Yom Kippur. She would never find out Fela had pawned it. Long before then, it would have been redeemed. Fela stood up, fumbled for matches, and lit the gas lamp. Opening the drawer of the clothes closet, a heavy piece of furniture which had an elaborately carved top and lion heads for knobs, she took out the wooden box in which her mother kept her jewelry. On the very top lay the gold chain with the sliding catch, an inheritance from Grandmother Yetta. Fela lifted it and was astonished at its weight. I won't take a groschen less than two hundred zlotys, she decided.

The night was one long nightmare. Fela slept fitfully, starting awake, sinking back into sleep. She was hot one minute, cold the next. A leg throbbed, a hand twitched. Her throat burned and she went to get water; back in bed, she had to get up again immediately to go to the bathroom. Even before her eyes closed, dreams swarmed over her. She received not one telegram but a whole pile of telegrams, each with a different address, a different date, some of them signed Adam, others Pacholski, others simply General, others Poet. What kind of a game was this? Did he want to confuse her? Did it have something to do with military secrets? Fela shook and woke up. She searched for the chain behind her pillow, but it had disappeared. Had a thief been here? Had her mother discovered it missing? In her dream, Fela went on searching. She was caught, arrested, manacled, thrown into a dungeon. An old woman brought her a jug of water with a piece of black bread, but when Fela tried to drink, the liquid burned like poison.

At nine o'clock the next morning, Fela awoke. In the courtyard below, peddlers were already hawking cherries, peaches, smoked herring, fresh bagels. Through the open window came smells of pitch, fruit, garbage. Fela jumped out of bed. Nine o'clock until four o'clock—seven hours! In seven hours, she must do everything. To meet Adam Pacholski she must transform herself into an elegant lady—washed, bathed, combed, with a smile on her lips. A gift. What gift should she take? But no, it wasn't proper for a lady to bring a gentleman a gift at first meeting. Etiquette was against it. A lady must be dignified even if she has an appointment with an angel.

She heard her father scolding her from the other room, but about what she didn't know. She rushed in to him distracted. "Daddy, you know I love you. There's not a man in the world who could take your place." She caught his beard, clutched it, and kissed it as she had when she was a small child. On her way to the kitchen she heard him calling after her, "Crazy, crazy! Crazy girl." She turned around. "You may kill me, I worship you just the same." As usual, her mother began attacking her with complaints. Why had she slept so late? Why didn't she go out looking for a job? Why hadn't she washed the dishes last night? To all of which Fela answered only, "If you don't like me, find yourself another daughter. I only want you."

And she embraced her mother, kissing her cheeks, her nose, her forehead, even her wig.

"As I love God, the girl has lost her senses."

"Yes, yes, Mother. Your daughter is insane. I'm so happy I wish I could die."

"Let your enemies talk so!"

Fela ate, not knowing what, putting salt in her tea and stirring it with her fork instead of the little spoon. When she rose, she stumbled into the kitchen closet, bruising her shoulder. She stood for a while by the window. Outdoors, the sun was shining, the birds twittering. Magicians were performing in the courtyard. A man dressed like a clown swallowed flames from a torch and spun a glass of water around a hoop. A girl with cropped hair, wearing velvet breeches, lay on her back and rolled a barrel on the soles of her feet. "Oh, Mother, how wonderful it is to live," Fela babbled. "Why am I so happy? Oh, why? I'm so happy I could jump out the window!" Fela heard her mother mutter, "Either you are crazy or you're trying to make yourself crazy."

"I don't try, Mother dear, I am. Tell me the truth. Did you ever love Daddy? I mean with the kind of love that burns like fire?"

"Whom else did I love? The chimney sweep? But look, now it's all ended."

"Things will still be good, Mother dear. You'll have a lot of joy."

"When? Soon I won't need any."

3

Everything went so smoothly that Fela had to laugh. It was strange. For years she had been brooding. Now suddenly a day of action had come. She went to a pawnshop and pawned her mother's chain for a hundred and forty zlotys. She took a droshky to Marszalkowsky Boulevard, where she bought herself a new dress, hat, shoes, underwear. Passing a bathhouse, she went in and bathed. God in heaven, it was astonishing what could be done in seven hours if one had money. Wearing the new dress, the color of *café au lait,* Fela was unrecognizable. The straw hat trimmed with a brown ribbon gave her a ladylike appearance. The new shoes were tight but their high heels and pointed toes looked elegant. The corset was constricting but it made her figure firm and buoyant. The hot bath had taken away all the itches and smells. Fela walked as if on springs.

Her heart fluttered like a bird behind her left breast. She went into a coffeehouse and ordered a coffee. When she paid for that, only one zloty remained out of the hundred and forty, and that one would pay for the droshky to take her to the meeting. Fela opened the picture magazine the waiter had handed her and tried to read, but she couldn't understand the words; she couldn't even focus on the pictures clearly. Well, one day of happiness is enough, she said to herself. Every few minutes she glanced at her wristwatch. It wouldn't do to get there too early, but to be too late would also be dangerous. She must figure the time closely so that he would wait for her only a minute or two. Maybe the whole thing was nothing but a joke to him. The police might have been notified and would be waiting for her. Or he might bring a bunch of officers to laugh at her. On the other hand, maybe he would arrive with flowers. Anything was possible. This day was her fate. She sat there in a daze. Suddenly she looked at her watch again. It was late. She paid in a hurry and went out. The day which had been so sunny was now overcast and it looked as if it might rain. Birds flew low over the roofs, croaking. A droshky was coming by, thank God. Fela got in and said breathlessly, "The corner of Marszalkowsky and Wspolna."

The coachman turned the droshky and Fela felt herself spinning together with the buildings, pavements, passersby. The coffee had gone to her head like liquor. She was late already. He would have to wait for her not just one minute but at least five. Well, he's a man and I'm a lady. Let him wait. She was on the verge of tears or laughter. What an adventure! Perhaps her mother had discovered her chain was missing. Perhaps she had notified the police. What if the driver asked for more than one zloty? What would she do then?—bury herself alive!

God in heaven, now what. A long line of trolley cars had blocked the street. Fire wagons had stopped all traffic. The siren on an ambulance was screaming. Was there a fire? But where? A large crowd had collected. The driver turned his head in his oilcloth cap.

"Young lady, if you're in a rush, get out here. It's not far to Wspolna Street."

Fela handed him the zloty and got down. She almost tore her dress on the iron step. She made her way through the crowd as fast as she could and hastened toward Wspolna Street. She slipped in her high-heeled shoes and almost fell. That's all I need, to land in the mud, she thought. Adam Pacholski, out of uniform, was at the corner, a young fellow in a light suit, his blond hair cut in a brush. Could it be he? He smiled at Fela and waved a magazine. Reaching her quickly, he took her hand and deftly kissed the wrist above the glove, welcoming her as if she were an old acquaintance.

"You are late," he said. "But that is the privilege of the fair sex."

"There was a fire. The droshky couldn't get through."

"Follow me, please." He led her through a gateway and opened the glass door of the main entrance with a key. They entered a paneled elevator. As it rose, Fela, who had never been in an elevator, felt her brains rattling. She well knew that a girl should not go with a man to his apartment, but he hadn't given her a chance to say no. Her heart pounded; she couldn't utter a word. The movement made her dizzy. God in heaven, don't let me faint, she implored. Adam Pacholski opened a door into a corridor full of paintings. On a hanger hung a general's coat, a general's cap, and a sword. Flowers stood in a vase. Goldfish swam in an aquarium.

The room they went into was like a museum. Portraits of Polish heroes looked down from the walls, and there were medals, ribbons, all kinds of diplomas and citations. One wall was covered with the heads of stuffed animals, and with guns, pistols, sabers. The room smelled of leather and maleness. Adam Pacholski asked Fela to sit down and she thanked him. Opening a liquor cabinet, he poured out two glasses of a reddish liqueur. "In your letter, you wrote you were not good-looking," he said. "But you're a beauty."

"The general mocks me."

"Don't call me general. I am Adam and you are Fela." His tone was intimate. "Here's to your health." He clicked his glass against hers and smiled with that smile which was known all over Poland, perhaps all over the world. He was forty-two years old, but to Fela he looked no more than twenty-three. The liqueur was strong. A sweetness penetrated her limbs. The fumes made her nose smart and her eyes fill with tears. "You don't know how to drink," Pacholski remarked, getting a cookie for her and filling her glass up again. He glanced at his wrist-watch. In another room the telephone rang; he disposed of the call quickly. "Everyone calls me," he remarked, rejoining Fela. "Such bores."

"Perhaps the general has no time?" Fela asked.

"For a good-looking woman I always have time," he answered.

Pacholski gazed into Fela's eyes and began to speak like a fortune-teller. "You are a girl who knows how to love. You remind me of the lines in Heine's poem where he speaks of the tribe of 'Those who die when they love.' What do you find in my poems? Sometimes it seems to me they are worthless. You are Jewish but different from the other Jewish girls, completely different. They are realistic, mercenary, but you are romantic, a dreamer. You live completely in your fantasy. The nobility of the ancient peoples is in you. You're an Oriental beauty. It's quite possible that one of your great-grandmothers sat in the harem of King Solomon . . . What do any of us know about the generations? We Slavs are young and have just emerged from the forests, while you belong to an old race. Perhaps that's why there can be no peace between us. Except when we love, for then all boundaries disappear. Then we want to merge, to pour, one might say, our wine into your skin. Come, I can't wait any longer. I have to kiss you."

"Pan General!"

"Say nothing. You are mine."

He got up from his chair, kissed her, and pressed open her mouth. She sank as if her knees were giving way, and he half carried her, half led her into another room. Fela tried to resist, but Pacholski became wild. He tore off her hat, threw her on the bed, struggled with her dress. She wanted to scream, but he covered her mouth with the palm of his hand. Everything happened quickly, brutally, with a violence such as she could never have conceived. He pulled the cord of the drapes and the bedroom became dark. He threw himself on her.

"You harlot! You Jewish whore!"

4

The telephone rang and kept on ringing. Pacholski, half-naked, tore himself from Fela and lifted the receiver. It was some woman and he quarreled with her, finally shouting, "Lightning, thunder, and cholera strike you!" The phone rang again, apparently the same woman, because Pacholski threw down the receiver with a bang. His underpants were stained with blood. Fela was bleeding profusely, almost as if she were hemorrhaging. There was blood on the bed, on the carpet.

"I have had many virgins but not one of them poured like you," said Pacholski.

He kissed Fela and scolded her. Soon, he told her, a representative from the General Staff was coming and he had to receive him. He took off his soiled underwear and threw it on the floor. The doorbell rang. Pacholski opened the door a crack and accepted a telegram. He went to the bathroom for some clean linen, but the phone rang and he returned without even covering his shame.

Fela wept. Pacholski yelled, "Don't wail, you softie. On the battlefield we bled a great deal more. I once lay bloody in a foxhole with crows waiting to pick out my eyes." He had torn her dress. He brought her another that was hanging in the closet, but it was too long for Fela to wear. He started to look for a needle and thread, but again the telephone rang. When he had hung up, he turned to her.

"You've got to get out of here."

"Please leave the room for a few minutes," she answered.

"You don't have to be ashamed in front of me."

"Leave, I beg you."

He went out and Fela began to straighten herself up. Her dress was both torn and stained. Her underwear was useless and she shoved it into her pocketbook. She tried to get the corset back on but couldn't. Without even knocking, Pacholski entered the room, already dressed, a lit cigarette hanging in the corner of his mouth. He screamed at her, "Don't act like a tragic heroine. You will find a husband and that's all. *Basta!*" At the word "husband," Fela let out a wail. In a voice she didn't know was hers she yelled back, "Don't drive me. I'm not a dog."

"I cannot allow the generals to find you here."

Forcefully, he got her into her corset and found a safety pin for the dress. Putting his hand into his trouser pocket, he pulled out a heap of bank notes. Fela clutched at her hair, refusing the money.

"We will meet," he said. "I love you. But now you have to go. If not, I am ruined."

"How can I go out on the street like this?"

"Take a taxi. Go to a hotel."

"They won't let me in. Let me wait at least until it's dark."

"Pilsudski himself is coming here!"

Taking her by the shoulders, he pushed her along the corridor, kissing her hand and her face while he did so. He gave her his handkerchief. Opening the door, he gave her one last push and a kiss on the neck. He called after her, "I will always remember you," and slammed the door.

Fela walked down the steps, blood dripping on the marble and on the carpet strip in the middle. Crumpling the handkerchief, she pushed it into the open wound. She cried, unable to stop. Coming out through the gate, she looked around, uncertain in which direction lay home. In the dusk, Marszalkowsky Boulevard looked hazy and the pavement appeared to slant uphill. Crowds of people were pouring out of movie houses, stores, exhibitions. Trolley bells clanged; autos honked. Newsboys screamed out headlines. God in heaven, how long will this day last! Fela started walking blindly, not knowing if she was going toward the center of the city beyond which lay home or farther away toward the suburb of Mokotow. If only I had fifteen groschen for a trolley, she thought. People stared at her, but she narrowed her eyes and kept them fixed on the pavement. It seemed to her that men called out loudly after her and that women laughed. She heard a policeman's whistle and was afraid she was about to be arrested. She reached Jerusalem Boulevard. At least she had walked in the right direction. She wanted to sit down on a bench, but all the seats were taken. Her wound ached and the handkerchief had worked its way down and was about to fall out. The safety pin had come open and was pricking her thigh. Her feet hurt in the tight shoes and she could barely keep her balance on the high heels. Suddenly she slipped and almost fell. She stood still. Her stockings were coming down. The seams in her clothing were splitting. She couldn't shut her pocketbook and the stained underwear showed on top. If only I had poison with me—if only I could die right now, right here on this spot! She moved on. She must reach home.

The night fell, thank God! The street lamps were being lit. Fela walked half blindly. The important thing was not to fall down. Finally she reached Holy Cross Street and turned toward Panska Street, where she lived. What can I tell Mother? What can I say? There will be a scandal. Fela wanted to pray to God, but for what? God himself could not help her anymore. She saw a shop with its shutters closed and sat down on the threshold. Now she saw what she had done to her feet. The skin over one heel had rubbed off and the stocking was soaked with blood. She looked for a piece of paper to insert to ease the pressure but couldn't find one. A drunk lurched toward her, leering, as if ready to fall on her. She got up quickly and hurried off. She came to Panska Street. The gas lamps were burning. Children were playing in the half darkness. Though Fela had been born here, the street looked strange to her. She came to the building where she lived, went through the courtyard, and began to climb the stairs. Nobody stopped her! A small gas lamp cast a feeble light. Fela took one step at a time. Only now did she realize how worn-out she was. Her knees shook and she had to hold on to the banister. If only she had taken the key with her so that she could let herself in and go straight to the bathroom. She would have to knock, and her mother would know everything immediately.

Miraculously, the door stood open. The hallway was dark and so was the kitchen. Had somebody broken in? But no, her mother must have gone out leaving the door open. In the living room, Fela could see her father standing at the east wall in the dark, bowing, apparently in the middle of his evening prayers. She hurried to the bathroom. Only after she had locked herself in did she realize that hiding here was no escape. She would have to come out. She must take off the strange dress, conceal the stained underwear. Her mother might return at any minute. She had probably only stepped across to a neighbor, which was why she had left the door open. Fela felt sick. Her stomach heaved and she had to urinate. The handkerchief was gone. Warm blood was wetting her inner thighs and trickling onto the floor. She had no match to light the candle stub. She stood up and vomited. Fiery wheels spun in front of her eyes. Inside her skull a light blazed. Fela stretched out her hand to grope for paper on the shelf and touched a scissors. She knew immediately what she must do: she must cut open her veins. God himself had put the instrument there for her. Fela trembled. She had always known this would be the end. She had foreseen it, though whether in a dream or while awake she didn't recall.

Fela wanted to say a prayer, to recite some Jewish words from the Bible or from the prayer her mother used to read with her when she was still a little girl, but she remembered nothing. "God have mercy on my soul," she murmured. Seated on the toilet bowl, she cut her hand at the wrist as if it were a piece of cloth. Soon she cut at a second place and then at a third. It did not really hurt. Thank God, no one will ever see me alive!

Sitting on the toilet bowl in the dark, Fela leaned her head against the wall, ready to die. She could feel the blood running from her wrist and she was bleeding below, too. She became light-headed and felt herself swooning. Bells rang in her ears. Colors flared in front of her eyes. She was still here but already somewhere else. Fear had evaporated. A bellows pumped away inside her. Something inflated and then collapsed. Something inflated and seemed to be growing—some entity not of this world. She couldn't tell if it was more like a frog, a lung, a turtle . . . A crowd was nearing from somewhere. There was a drumming that echoed like hoofbeats. Then a loud noise and an outcry sounded close by.

The door was forced open. Fela's father screamed; her mother wailed. Neighbors came running. They dragged Fela out, lifted her, carried her. Towels were wrapped about her arm and somebody ran to get a doctor. Fela lay on the sofa while above her people screamed, waved their arms, bent down to examine her. Strange men lifted her dress, uncovered her. I cannot even be ashamed, Fela thought. But I'm dying happy. I forgive him. I forgive. She opened one eye and saw a soldier entering with a bouquet of roses, red as blood. Despite her agony, Fela's spirit grinned. Is he the Angel of Death?

She heard her mother asking, "Who are you? What do you want? They're not for us."

"For Panna Fela, with compliments," said the soldier, "from the general."

Translated by the author and Elizabeth Pollet

The Bond

e sat in a sort of combined café and garden. It was summer, when twilight in Warsaw lasts for a long time. The sun sets, but the sky remains light, retaining an early-evening glow. Birds still chirped in the branches of the trees. White-winged insects madly circled the globes of the lamps. The sweet smell of flowers blended with the aromas of coffee, cocoa, and freshly baked pastries. An August moon loomed in the sky, and near it a bright star.

We sat in a small group—several writers, a painter, and a sculptor. Soon they all left except for one Yiddish writer, Reuven Berger, and me. Reuven had early become known as a great talent but then stopped writing altogether. We drank coffee, ate buns with jam, and discussed women. Reuven told anecdotes and smoked one cigarette after another. In a remote corner of the café someone tinkled the keys of a piano. From the fields and orchards on the other side of the Vistula scents of late summer wafted in.

Reuven Berger flicked the ashes from his cigarette into an ashtray and said, "There are cases when a man is forced to slap a woman. No matter how considerate he may be by nature, he has no alternative. You know that I have a reputation for being overly gentle to the fair sex, but the story I have in mind is so crazy and unlike me that each time I recall it I must laugh.

Such a thing is only possible in life, not fiction. It is just too ridiculous to be believed."

"Enough suspense. Let me hear it," I said.

"All right. You know that from the age of fourteen I was involved with women. I loved them and they loved me. This event took place about eight years ago, perhaps ten. I lived with a woman who was terribly in love with me. With her kind, love becomes a total obsession. Her insane jealousy made a hell out of my life. Thousands of times I broke up with her and each time she came back. Her father was a pious Jew, an owner of a house. Her name was Bella. She used to move in our literary circles long before you began to come to the Writers' Club. She had studied in an exclusive Gymnasium for girls and had the manners of a well-bred lady. She was beautiful, too. But she began to drink on account of me. At that time I was still married. Bella would sit in her room alone, drink vodka from the bottle, smoke, and quarrel with me on the telephone if she could find me. I had to run from her. She grew worse from day to day. She tried suicide on several occasions.

"When she was in the midst of these fits, there were wild scenes. One thing alone could stop her delirious outbursts—slaps. I was forced to slap her repeatedly, and this immediately brought her to her senses. She would regain her composure, become logical and calm. I often drew an analogy to war. When a nation becomes destructively belligerent, there is only one way to bring it to its senses—defeat. If a pacifist heard this he would tear me to pieces, but it's true.

"Get rid of her? I did not want to leave her altogether. In my fashion I loved her. If not for these mad scenes, I could have been quite happy with her. But she was capable of tearing the dress from her body in the middle of the street or of trying to throw herself under the wheels of a streetcar. She would attack an innocent woman with whom I exchanged a word or two. On one occasion she was arrested for disturbing the peace. Her mother came to me to ask me to break up with Bella. But how does one end an affair with this type of woman? I would have had to run away to America or commit suicide myself.

"Now, I guess you know that for years I made a living from lecturing. But it had come to such a pass that I could not go anywhere without her appearing out of nowhere and rushing to see what I was up to. If I had to go to a lecture, she would follow me. I learned every trick in the art of conspiracy. I had a secret address, an unlisted phone number. Once I discovered a private detective lurking at my gate. Her father was quite rich."

•

Reuven paused and tried to balance a little spoon on the edge of a glass. He continued, "At this particular time, I was scheduled to lecture in Jedrzejow. It was a cold, rainy day. I was certain Bella knew nothing of my plans, but the moment I entered the train she was there. I will never know how she discovered I was taking this trip. The car was empty. I was too enraged even to scold her. We sat down in complete silence. After a while, she started, as I knew she would, with bitter reproaches and warned me not to attempt to put her out of my life. She was ranting and raving, as always. She became louder and more offensive from minute to minute and resorted to every type of threat and insult. I knew I had to slap her or there would be no lecture. I was so wrought up I didn't notice that at a stop other passengers had entered the car. She was, in fact, begging to be slapped. I gave her a smack across the face—one, two, three. It had the miraculous effect. One minute she was mad. The next minute the hysteria was gone. She smiled, became loving, coherent. Those who have never witnessed a sudden change like this could never imagine how complete it was.

Bella leaned against the train window, still weeping a little and pressing my hand to her lap. I was so confused that I didn't notice that directly across from me sat a woman looking furious, ready to swallow me alive. She seemed a small-town woman—not young, not old. Perhaps in her late twenties or early thirties. She reminded me of the suffragettes one saw photographs of in illustrated magazines, or possibly of the sort of female who would help manufacture bombs to be thrown at the Tsar. She carried a library book, the jacket carefully protected by a paper cover. Once or twice she opened her mouth as if about to blast me, but she seemed to control herself. More people entered the car and momentarily I lost sight of my angry co-passenger. Bella by now was absolutely normal, again and again apologizing, kissing me and promising to behave forever and after.

" 'Why did you follow me?' I asked her. 'This is a business trip, not a vacation.' She said meekly, 'Since I'm already here, allow me to stay with you the rest of the way. I'm dying to hear your lecture! You need not introduce me to anyone. I will stay away from you when we get off, and in the evening I will just come to hear your speech. I will find out when you are leaving and arrange to go back with you.' In short, she was not the same Bella but a quiet and humble lover. This change in personality always perplexed me anew. I thought, Who knows, perhaps slaps could be a cure even for some organic maladies. In these moments, rare though they were, she regained her old allure and I fell in love with her again. However, peace never lasted longer than a few days.

"We arrived at our destination and I took my suitcase from the shelf; I said goodbye and we kissed. A committee was scheduled to meet me at the station and I didn't want them to see her. She might have created a new uproar. I got off the train and there was the welcoming committee. They were the typical provincial intelligentsia. Once they get an opportunity to attach themselves to a writer from Warsaw, they cling and do not leave him for a moment. I don't need to tell you that every one of them had ambitions to write. I was sure that each had ready a poem, a novel, or a play. What else can they do in their godforsaken villages?

"The village itself looked to me like a miniature Siberia—dreary, muddy, with small cottages and one two-story hotel, where there was a reservation for me. The rain had stopped, but the sky was boding snow, hail, a blizzard. Nowhere, not even in the open fields, is the sky so wide and so otherworldly as in these bleak villages—the kind of sky that hovers over cemeteries.

"They began with the usual amenities—'Honored to greet you,' 'How was your trip?'—and the usual quasi-literary talk, with its errors and mispronunciations. The young men escorted me to the hotel and on the way they plied me with questions: How do you write? When do you write? Where do you get your inspiration? One of them started to criticize me for not being progressive enough and for not caring about the future of the masses. In those places you have to be prepared for all this nonsense. It was almost time for the lecture and I had to ask the committee to leave me so I could change my shirt. I had practically to put them out by force.

"Thank God, they finally left me alone. I bolted the door and had started to undress when there was a knock on the door. Who could it be? A female voice called, 'Open the door. I am the one who will introduce you tonight.' I quickly put on my jacket again, opened the door, and who do you suppose was there before me? The woman who sat across from me on the train.

"I have experienced all sorts of surprises, but this surely was the biggest of them all. She, too, seemed startled. She looked at me and her eyes seemed to turn over. I asked her to come in, but she stood rooted to the spot, not believing what she saw.

When she finally entered the room she began to speak. I don't remember exactly what she said; the sum of it was that she had read me and considered me one of the most romantic and gentle Yiddish writers in Poland. She had gone to visit a sick sister in a nearby town but came back a day sooner to introduce me. She was the Jedrzejow librarian and the chairman of the committee. She cried out that she had always been fascinated by the deep insight and understanding of women which my books revealed. 'God in heaven, how is it possible you are the same man I saw on the train? No, it isn't possible. Tell me I am in error,' she pleaded dramatically, with solemn face and clasped hands. She repeated, 'Is this really you? Is this true? Please tell me that I am mistaken!'

" 'I am sorry, you are not mistaken,' I told her, 'but I will explain everything to you later.'

" 'What? You are capable of such behavior?' she shrieked. 'If that is so, then everything is false. If that is possible, then the whole of literature is a sham and a fake and nothing but the meanest hypocrisy.'

"She kept on berating me, screaming louder and louder, until I managed to break in: 'Miss or Madam, whatever you may be, I must prepare for my lecture and I am already late. I will talk to you at the reception.'

" 'So! You are throwing me out?' she squealed. 'Don't you have any decency or shame? You who should be the pacesetter, the example for our lesser people! This is prostitution, sheer prostitution!'

"Her voice rose to a more hysterical pitch, while my watch showed that any moment the committee would come to escort me to the lecture. I knew from experience that they always arrive earlier than they say. I fell into real despair. Just a short while ago, I had had to rid myself of Bella's onslaught and here I was beset by a second one. I realized that in some uncanny act of female imitation she sought to create the same scene Bella had—a tirade of threats, abuse, tears, name-calling that could go on forever. I let out a mighty shout: 'Are you leaving, or do I have to throw you out?'

" 'Throw me out!' she yelled. 'Let the whole world know what a charlatan you are! You and all writers! You and all men —one bunch of liars, cheaters, seducers, murderers! Let the whole world know what a foul game you play to deceive the honest reader—to fool us, trick us with your falsehoods and cynicism. You devil, you monster. You demon!'

"Yes, you guessed it. I rushed over to her, seized her, and started to drag her toward the door. She let out a terrible howl, tried to resist violently, and I began to slap her just as I had Bella in the train. It all happened so fast I could hardly believe it myself. I threw the door open and pushed her out. I expected to hear her bang on the door and bring the whole village to the show. For a while I was ready to catch up my valise and run for dear life, but instead there was complete silence outside the door.

"I imagined she was lying in a faint. Perhaps I had killed her. How ironic it would be if this idiotic lecture of mine ended with a murder! I opened the door, but the corridor was dark and empty. She had left. It was only then that I realized what had happened to me. My hands trembled, my legs buckled under me, and no matter how I tried I could not button my shirt collar.

"I had prepared a manuscript for that night but could not remember where I had put it. Perhaps it would be best to flee from the village after all. At that moment, I heard steps and voices. Two young men were coming for me. One of them asked, 'Was Zipporah here?' I understood that Zipporah was the librarian. My throat had constricted and I couldn't bring out a single word. The two men gathered how upset I was, and one of them helped me with my collar button. The other asked, 'Why have you strewn your manuscript on the floor?' He picked up the pages and put them together. We then walked down the steps. There was no sign of the woman anywhere. Outside, it had become dark and a wet snow was falling.

"We finally arrived at the hall, and there was quite a large audience awaiting us. The committee representative, or whatever he was, inquired as to Zipporah's whereabouts. She was not in the hall. There were those who wished to wait for her. She had worked on her introduction for weeks. Others pointed out that it was getting late. Finally, a young man appeared and planted himself before the speaker's table. I could not make out what he was saying. One word stood out sharply in his oration—'which,' a word he repeated again and again, probably because in the provinces this word denotes high language. When he finished, I started my lecture. My words resounded hollow and remote in my ringing ears—almost as if I spoke in some foreign tongue. I expected jeering to break out from the audience at any moment, but there was complete silence in the hall. After my lecture, I went on to read one of my stories, but the letters danced madly before my eyes, and the print changed color. Luckily, I knew this story almost by heart. It was about the encounter of a boy and girl on a moonlit night—as tender and romantic a story as I have ever written. My reading was interrupted by applause many times, and I began to regain control of myself. My vision cleared, and the first faces I recognized in the audience were Bella's and Zipporah's. They sat side by side in the first row, cheering me and applauding. Their eyes shone with enthusiasm. I started to laugh out loud. My audience seemed momentarily puzzled, because this was a serious story, not a humorous one. But laughter is infectious, and soon the entire crowd joined me. Never before had I made an audience laugh like that. Oh, I must laugh again . . ."

Reuven giggled into his handkerchief and wiped the perspiration off his high, lined forehead. "I could write a story about it," he said, "but I have lost my appetite for the dirty scribbling profession."

"What happened to Bella?" I asked.

Reuven became serious in an instant. "She died. No, not suicide—not really. She killed herself gradually. She got jaundice. She ruined her kidneys, her liver. Everything. I will never know how she held out so long."

"And what about Zipporah?"

"She is still the librarian, as far as I know. From time to time she used to come to Warsaw, and on each visit she would call me on the telephone. She began each call with 'This is the woman you slapped.' She invariably asked for some small favor—for my opinion of a book, for a pair of complimentary tickets to a lecture, for an autograph. I would always accommodate her. She remained a friend of Bella's in all the time of her sickness. She visited her whenever she was in Warsaw. She sent her little presents for her birthday and for other occasions. Many times she asked me to lecture in the village. I just could not go there again. But I always promised. I would say to her on the telephone, 'Yes, my dear, I will come, and I swear to you by everything that is holy to me that I will not slap you this time. The opposite—I will kiss you if you will allow me.' And she would say, 'You had no choice. It was all my fault. As a matter of fact, what you did has created a kind of secret bond between us.' She has not called me for a long time. I hope she is all right."

"Was she ever married?" I asked.

Reuven shook his head. "Never. Sometimes I suspect that what happened between us was the closest contact she ever had with a man."

Translated by the author and Lester Goran

The Interview

I have met in my time a number of female rebels, but the first one engraved herself in my memory. I was only nineteen years old and I was the proofreader of the Yiddish literary magazine *Literarishe Bleter.* The editor sent me to interview an important visitor to Warsaw—an old philosopher, essayist, and aesthete, Dr. Gabriel Levantes, who had resided for the last twenty years in Berlin, where he was the co-editor of a Jewish encyclopedia. I had the opportunity to observe him a few days earlier at the Writers' Club. He was small and stooped, with shoulders too broad for his size, and his stomach stuck out like a pregnant woman's. He had a huge head of white hair. His beard and mustache were also white. Only in his bushy eyebrows were there a few black hairs. From under them peered out black, piercing eyes, like those of a porcupine. He wore a pelerine that reached to his ankles, and a plush hat with a broad brim. An article about him in a Warsaw Yiddish newspaper said that no one had ever seen him without an umbrella or without a cigar in his mouth. There were jokes about him that he even slept with the cigar between his lips.

This interview was my first effort at journalism, and I prepared for it days in advance. The night before, I could hardly sleep. About eleven o'clock in the morning I called up the

Hotel Bristol, where Dr. Levantes was staying. He seemed to be hard of hearing, because I had to repeat every word three times. He roared at me, as if I were the deaf one, "Young man, be here punctually at four o'clock—not a second later."

At fifteen minutes after three I began to walk to the Hotel Bristol from my lodgings on Nowolipki Street, and I got to the hotel at twelve minutes to four. It was cold outside, and now snow began to fall as thin and prickly as needles. I walked to and fro before the entrance, so as not to arrive, God forbid, too early. My winter coat had lost its cotton batting and I was shivering. In my haste and my fear of being late, I had forgotten my scarf and my rubbers. The hotel doorman, in a uniform with gilded buttons and the epaulets of a general, looked me up and down with suspicion. Droshkies, and even some motor taxis, which in those days were still somewhat of a rarity, pulled up at the curb. The gusty winter day was short, and the street lamps were lit early. The sky reflected the violet of an abortive sunset. I continued to look at my wristwatch, which had misted over. At three minutes before four I tried to enter the hotel, but the doorman stopped me with his white-gloved hand. "Hey, you, where are you going?"

"To Dr. Levantes."

"I think a woman is visiting him."

After some hesitation, the doorman gave me permission to visit Dr. Levantes, but I had to climb four flights of stairs, since I could not take the elevator, which was reserved for more prominent visitors. The doorman told me to wipe my shoes and not to dirty the carpet on the marble steps inside.

Exactly at four o'clock, I rang the bell and Dr. Levantes opened his door. He wore a long dressing gown with a braided sash and a pair of huge slippers. I immediately saw the woman the doorman had mentioned. She sat on the sofa across from the doctor's desk and was wearing a short, knee-length skirt in the current fashion. She seemed to me in her late thirties, perhaps even forty. She had on a hat that resembled an inverted pot, and boots that came up to her broad calves. She wore no makeup, and I imagined that I saw signs of pockmarks on her high cheeks. Between the fingers of her right hand she held an extinguished cigarette.

Dr. Levantes showed me to the sofa, and he himself sat down on a plush chair so as to face both of us. On the edge of his desk I saw a slender unbound book, a brochure. I could read the title and the name of the author on the first page: *The Naked Truth,* by Machla Krumbein. Dr. Levantes lifted the booklet with his thumb and index finger, looked at it for a moment, then mincingly put it back on the desk.

He said to me, "You'll have to wait awhile for the interview. This woman came to me unannounced. She considers herself a poetess." He turned to the woman. "Where did you say you came from?"

The woman mentioned the name of some village.

"Where is this godforsaken shtetl?" Dr. Levantes asked. "My dear lady," he said angrily, "this young man is a mother's child, most likely a former yeshiva boy, just hatched from the egg, and I don't want to spoil him by quoting your kind of poetry. I can already see your approach. So holy is art that everything is kosher in its name, even a pig's knuckle boiled in tallow. Let me tell you clearly: pornography is not literature. The purpose of literature is to lift up the spirit, to bring out for the reader what is beautiful and lofty, not to tease his lowest instincts. I know that since the war there has been a new strain in literature—in Germany, France, and especially in Russia, among the Bolsheviks. They have turned everything topsy-turvy. Evil is good, ugly is beautiful, crooked is straight. We have in Berlin a certain Rilke, who carries his poems in a sack like a peddler. You cannot understand a word of what these poets write. Their slogan is 'Back to chaos,' but I'm too old for that and this young man is too young. There is in Russia a madman, a certain Mayakovsky, who wrote a poem about a cloud in pants, and they quote him with great admiration. How can a cloud wear pants if it is all vapor? It could just as well wear spats and a fur coat. Some of these so-called poets are Jews. What is the name of that crazy woman? Something like Lasker. Well, I can still understand all this taking place in Berlin or Paris—even in Petersburg, Petrograd, or whatever they named it lately. These places always teemed with futurists, Dadaists, nihilists—all kinds of other 'ists.' But how is it possible that a woman from a decent Jewish hamlet should use such abominable language? Do you try to imitate the maniacs of Sodom and Gomorrah?"

"I don't try to imitate anybody," the woman said, in a voice almost masculine. "But since every human being, without exception, thinks about sexual relations from the cradle to the grave, how can poetry ignore the subject?"

"Every human being?" Dr. Levantes cried out. "I don't think about it even one hour in a week. Neither did my great friend Professor Hermann Cohen. If the human brain were always occupied with thoughts of lechery, men today would still crouch like apes and live in caves. There is in Vienna a certain Dr. Freud, a half-charlatan and full-fledged dilettante, and he tries to persuade us we are all a band of sex fiends. He's trying to become the Newton of human behavior. He has a whole coterie of hangers-on. May I ask you a personal question?"

"Yes, Doctor, of course," the woman said.

"Do you have a husband or are you unmarried?"

"I had one."

"What happened to him?"

"We are divorced."

"May I ask you why you are divorced?"

"You can ask anything. I left him because he did not satisfy me. Before he said good evening it was already good night. He was as quick as a rabbit."

Young as I was, I grasped what she meant, and I felt flushed. I had already read Professor Forel's book about sex, and I think I had even looked into Krafft-Ebing. Dr. Levantes began to growl and cough. He took a large handkerchief from his pocket and spat into it.

The woman rose. "Dr. Levantes," she said, "there was an article about you in the newspaper, and the author called you an independent thinker. This is the reason I came to you. Now I see you have all the prejudices of the fanatics. You probably recite thanks every day to God that he did not create you a woman. Let me tell you, Doctor, you've studied many books, but I've studied life. Our village was occupied by the Austrians in the war, and they brought with them first the cholera and then a famine. Many girls and young women became smugglers. They wrapped meat around themselves, under their clothing, and smuggled it into what used to be Galicia. On the way back they smuggled tobacco and other articles, which they hid in their underwear. There were gendarmes, called *Finanzer,* who lurked at night in the woods around the frontier. When they caught one of these women they forced her to undress and did with her whatever they wanted. I can tell you, Doctor, one fact—"

"I don't want to hear it, I don't want to hear it!" Dr. Levantes screamed. "If you want to tell me that most people are still animals, I will have to agree with you, but poetry is written for better human beings, not for the rabble."

"Your better human beings are as interested in sexual matters as the rabble," the woman said. "Everything you, Doctor, call culture has to do with it. What is the theater? What do the painters paint? What do the sculptors sculpt? Breasts, bellies, behinds. Give this young man a choice between the most wonderful book and a voluptuous female and you'll see what he'll choose."

"Madam, be so good as to go your way!" Dr. Levantes shouted.

It had become so dark that the woman's face had turned into a bundle of shadows. Only her eyes sparkled in the wintry twilight. I wanted to say that I would choose the book rather than the female—perhaps to please Dr. Levantes—but my throat became dry and I began to sweat. The woman moved backward and hesitated. Suddenly she ran to me and caught my wrist so hard that I almost cried out in pain. "I will wait for you downstairs," she whispered, and kissed me behind my ear. She slammed the door with such strength that the windowpanes rang.

Dr. Levantes called after her, "Whore! Harlot! Piece of dirt!" He shook, and said, gasping, "I don't recognize my Polish Jews anymore."

•

I had written a long list of questions for Dr. Levantes, but as soon as I asked the first he delivered a lengthy speech. He blew the smoke of his cigar directly into my face and spoke of many things at once—Spengler's *Decline of the West,* Bergson's *Creative Evolution,* the Balfour Declaration, the Bolshevik revolution, even Einstein's theory of relativity. He again and again attacked Freud. Even though steam hissed in the radiator, frost trees formed on the windowpanes. I wrote down as quickly as I could the doctor's clever words, but my brain was occupied with one thought: Would Machla Krumbein really wait for me? It was too cold for her to wait outside. As if Dr. Levantes could sense that I was thinking of her, he tried to refute her arguments. He compared the "human affects," as Spinoza called them, to a volcanic eruption. One must avoid the glowing lava, not try to swim in it. "There's only one question," he said. "Why did God or nature bestow on *Homo sapiens* such an abundance of emotions? What is their biological function? Neither Plato nor Spinoza nor Schopenhauer could really answer this."

Almost two hours had passed and Dr. Levantes was still pouring out his erudition. The room became filled with coils of cigar smoke. I imagined that the smoke came not only from the doctor's mouth and nostrils but also from his hairy ears, his beard, and even from behind his vest, as if he were burning in his interior. When I finally left, my knees had become shaky and I was dizzy. I opened the door to the street and breathed in deep the frosty air, and there was Machla Krumbein. She stood at a store window that was warmed by small gas flames to keep it from freezing over. I touched her shoulder and she started. I asked her if she had been waiting outside the entire time.

Her face was white from the cold, but her eyes lit up with the joy of a young girl. "So what?" she said. "I am accustomed both to the cold and to waiting. I smuggled things on days and nights when it was as cold as Siberia. Why did your interview last so long? Let's go somewhere. I'm a chunk of ice."

"Why didn't you wait in the lobby?"

"The doorman chased me out. He probably didn't like the way I'm dressed. One pauper snubbing another. Do you have some money with you? I'm without a penny."

She took my arm familiarly. The restaurants and coffeehouses in this rich neighborhood were not for the likes of us. We walked in the direction of Senatorska Street, and from there to the Jewish quarter. The whole time Machla continued to talk. "What kind of interview was this? Where's it going to be published? I went to the Writers' Club, but the receptionist would not let me in. If they had seen what I write, they would have hurled me out the window. What did you say your name was? I've never seen it in print anywhere. I had to publish my little book with my own money. That's why I'm bankrupt now. What do you write?"

"I want to write stories."

"Stories, huh? Will you at least tell the truth, or will you gloss over and prettify everything, as the other liars do? You look like an honest lad still, but when these scribblers take you into their establishment you'll become a cheater like them."

"What do you call the truth?"

"The naked truth. When those Austrian gendarmes told me to strip mother-naked I thought I would die from shame. But when you must do it you do it. Thank God, it was summer and not winter. They did to me what they wanted—four men, one more virile than the other. Then they spat at me and left as if nothing had happened. I lay there and wept for a long time, until it occurred to me that what had happened was not such a calamity after all. I realized then for the first time that this is what a female was created for."

"To be raped?"

"Yes."

Her words made me shudder. We came to a little coffee shop with a picture of a cow out front to indicate that it served dairy products. Even though I was not a vegetarian yet, I used to eat there frequently, because everything was cheap. We entered and took the one table that was not occupied. I had some money with me. The owner, an elderly Gentile woman, brought us buckwheat with milk, bread, herring, and coffee with chicory.

Although I was extremely bashful with women, Machla Krumbein, who looked old enough to be my mother and who spoke like a whore, made me daring. "What would have happened if the gendarmes had made you pregnant?" I asked.

"It couldn't have happened—I can't have children. I lived seven years with my husband and I remained barren. He was good for nothing, and after a few years I took lovers."

"Who were they?"

"Whomever I could get—a Jew, a Gentile, a coachman. Once I made love with a boy not long out of the cheder, about twelve years old. I had begun to read novels, and realized the writers were all brazen liars. They kept on beating around the bush and they never came to the point. They babbled without end about love. There is no love. It's all invented, a horse fair in the sky."

"I myself was mortally in love with a girl," I said. I could hardly keep myself from trembling.

" 'Mortally,' huh? And what happened?"

"Nothing."

"This is how all loves end. Love is nothing but a dragged-out sickness. A man should immediately get what he wants, not be fed with a lot of sentimental twaddle. Do you have someone now?"

"Not really."

"You can have me tonight if you want. All we need is a bed."

"I board in a private apartment."

"Do you have a room to yourself?"

"I have to cross their living room. There's a girl there, and we two—"

"You are in love with her?"

"We read books together."

"What books?"

"Various subjects—biology, psychology. Lately we've been reading Flammarion."

"Who is he?"

"A French astronomer."

"Is your girl a virgin?"

"Yes, but we never talk about such things."

"Take me home," Machla Krumbein said, "and I will speak to her clearly. These kosher virgins are as afraid of me as the Devil is of incense."

"I cannot do that."

"In that case you're not a man but a lamb. I would take you to my place, but I stay with an old aunt and she has only one room and one bed. She's as pious as a rebbetzin. All night long she groans and mumbles sacred words. She doesn't let me sleep. Her husband, my Uncle Nahum, died twenty-two years ago and she's never touched another man—she's still faithful to my uncle. That's what the liars and bigots have done to women."

I wanted to answer her, but my throat was constricted. She took a brochure from her purse and said, "Here, read this. It's my book, *The Naked Truth*."

It had thirty-two pages of poems, each line not more than four or five words. In about fifteen minutes I had read it to the end. I had never before read such obscenities. I didn't know what was stronger in me, my passion or my nausea. I glanced at the author. She smiled, and showed a mouthful of broad, strong teeth. She asked, "Have you ever read such hot stuff?"

"Never."

"My father was a Cohen. In ancient days they would have sentenced me to be burned. This is how it's written in the Pentateuch."

"Yes."

"If you have ten zlotys you can take me to a cheap hotel."

"You need to show a passport. I don't have ten zlotys, and besides, I have to pay for our dinner."

"There are little hotels where they'll let you in without a passport," she said. "Perhaps you can borrow some money."

"Now? At night?"

We sat in silence. I looked around at the other tables. At each sat a young man and a girl. They were talking about the political situation in Poland, about the news from Soviet Russia, Palestine. Some of them I knew. There were Communists, members of the leftist Workers of Zion, even an anarchist—a vegetarian. Machla Krumbein smiled and winked at me. "I have an idea," she said. "Borrow some money from the girl with whom you read books. When the interview appears you'll repay her."

I knew this was nonsense, but I stood up and paid the bill. We walked together to Nowolipki Street, and came to the building where I lived. I knew that my girl, Ilka, had gone to the movies with a girl friend. I could not ask her mother for a loan, because I already owed her three months' rent. I told this to Machla Krumbein and she said, "All the powers are against us tonight. If that old idiot Levantes weren't such a zealot, we could have made love all three of us together."

"With that old man?"

"I love old men. Some of them are lustier than the young. A threesome with you and him would have been fun, but it wasn't destined."

"Do you believe in God?" I asked.

"Everything comes from him."

•

We stood at the gate of my building, and Machla Krumbein said, "Perhaps your girl will soon be back from the movies. Sometimes if they don't like a show these girls leave immediately. I myself stopped going to the movies—they bore me stiff. A man meets a girl and the moment he kisses her he's in love forever. The heroines are all beautiful beyond words. Those who are not beautiful don't exist at all in these inventions. The men are all immensely tall and rich and eager to marry. Lies,

lies. In all literature I found only one writer who writes the truth—Strindberg. He's translated into Yiddish. What he says about us women is real. In my village they are all my blood enemies. They curse me with the vilest oaths. Why can't you take me up to your room? If you live there, you're entitled to bring in any guest you want."

"My landlady doesn't let me. Once, a girl visited me and the old woman ordered me to leave the door open."

"They are jealous, that's what they are. They are like dogs watching a stack of hay: they can't eat it themselves and they won't let others eat. How can I ever sell my book? The printer has put together five hundred copies. Would any bookstore take them from me?"

"I'm afraid no bookstore would sell them."

"This means I'm already excommunicated in Warsaw, too. The printers in Lublin refused to print it, but I found an old bachelor, and he became my publisher—anonymously, of course. I gave him what a man wants, and he turned romantic and did it all for me. He even proposed marriage to me, but I will marry the Angel of Death."

"Why do you say that? You are still young."

"Not so young."

"What do you do in that village?" I asked.

"I am a seamstress. The women won't give me any work, but the men come to me and let me take measurements for their shirts and underwear. While I take their sizes I tickle them. Oy, I must laugh."

"What's so funny?"

"Those hypocrites! A few days ago I became forty and I decided to live five years more, not a day longer. But for those five years I've promised myself to indulge all my whims. Women such as I should never get old. The warden of the burial society warned me that when I die he will bury me behind the fence, among the suicides and whores, and I told him that as far as I'm concerned he can cut me to pieces and throw me to the dogs. All they write in the holy books is balderdash. There is a God, but he never split the Red Sea. He never gave the Torah. Moses wrote it all from his head. He himself played around with a black female. When do they close the gate here?"

"They may do it soon."

The moment I uttered the words, the janitor came out from his cubicle with his big key and with his old dog limping after him. He gave us both an ugly look and asked, "Are you two going in or out? I'm closing."

Machla Krumbein started to give me her address. She planted a kiss on my mouth. She actually bit me. The janitor slammed the gate before her, and instead of going up the dark steps I went over to the garbage bin in the courtyard and wiped my mouth with a handkerchief. In the light of a single lantern that glimmered over the entrance I saw blood.

Someone rang the bell, and the janitor went to open the gate. It was Ilka—small, with a head of cropped hair as shaggy as a sheep's. Ilka's father had died in the typhus epidemic. Her mother sold secondhand clothes in the Karcelak Place bazaar. Ilka had gone to the Gymnasium, but she flunked the final examination. Lately we had read together a book entitled *The Life of an Amoeba.* We often spoke of chromosomes, centrosomes, and cytoplasm. I sided with the vitalists and Ilka with the mechanists. We also discussed Bukharin's work about historical materialism and Otto Weininger's *Sex and Character.* When Ilka entered the courtyard and saw me standing at the garbage bin she asked, "Why are you standing out here in the dark? Did you have the interview?"

"Yes, I had it."

"What did he say?" she asked.

"He said that a girl wasn't created to read about amoebas but for a man to sleep with," I said, baffled at my own words.

Ilka seemed more astonished than I was. We both stood speechless for a while. Then I heard her say, "At least you found the courage to tell the truth. A woman is nothing for you but a lump of flesh. Is that correct?"

"Yes, correct."

"In that case we must sever all our relations."

"If you think so."

"What is the sense of our standing at the garbage bin? Let's go up."

We walked up the dark steps to the first landing and stopped. I embraced Ilka and she did not resist. I kissed her and she kissed me back. I felt her face burn. She pushed me away and said, "You're a pig, like all the other men."

"That's what I am."

"You've disappointed me bitterly."

We went up another flight and we again stopped and kissed. From behind a door I could hear a baby crying and the mother singing a dirgelike lullaby.

"What a night," Ilka said. "First a disgusting movie that turned my stomach, then your strange behavior. Sometimes I feel that death is the only way out."

"Yes, let's die together, but before we die let's give in to all our desires."

"Why do you want to die with me?" Ilka asked. "Since you don't love me."

"There is no love," I announced.

"What is there?"

"Just lust."

"You kill everything."

We knocked at our door and Ilka's mother opened it. She

cried out to me, "Who bloodied your mouth?" She clapped her hands and screamed, "Yours, too, Ilka! Woe is to me and to my dismal life."

Ilka rushed into the bathroom. I ran into my room. As a rule, we used to drink tea and eat bread with jam before we went to sleep. Now I threw myself on the bed in my clothes. I could hear from the other side of the door the old woman's nagging words and Ilka's answer: "Leave me alone. Don't bore me. Be still."

The door opened abruptly, and the old woman put her head in. She had taken off her wig and covered her shaved head with a kerchief. She had already taken out her false teeth and put them in a glass of water, and her face sagged. "Be so good as to move out immediately tomorrow," she said.

"Yes, I will."

"And pay what you owe me."

"Not before my interview is published."

"You wild beast!" She spat, and slammed the door.

I extinguished the gas lamp and lay quietly in the dark. I could still hear the old woman's grumbling and her daughter's annoyed responses. I fell into a deep sleep. In the middle of the night someone nudged my shoulder. I woke up and it was Ilka. She murmured, "Here's your lump of flesh."

I stretched out my hand to pull her closer, but she resisted. I kissed her and swore love to her, and she said, "Shameless liar."

•

About fifty years passed, and I never heard the name Machla Krumbein, either in Warsaw or in New York, where I lived after I emigrated to America. I looked for her little book in Yiddish libraries and bibliographies, but both the writer and the book had vanished without a trace. Whenever I met someone from her region, I asked if he had ever heard of such a person and the answer was always no. I began to doubt whether this episode had ever happened. I knew from experience that certain occurrences of whose reality I was certain proved later to be nothing but dreams or fantasies. For years I used to dream I was in Siberia. I saw Siberian towns and forests. I traveled over Siberian taigas and tundras. Whenever I woke up at night I believed for a while that I really had been there, but after some pondering and consideration I realized that I couldn't have been, unless in a former reincarnation. Perhaps my meeting with Machla Krumbein was the same kind of figment.

In 1974, I was invited to speak at Oxford University, in England. The day after the lecture the librarian of the Jewish section gave me a tour of arcane Hebrew and Yiddish books and manuscripts in the Bodleian Library. I found a number of small storybooks that I had read in my childhood and that I was sure had been lost in the Holocaust. I recognized the faded covers, the typography, even the misprints in those flimsy and worn pages. Suddenly my gaze fell on a booklet that lay on a metal shelf without a library stamp, without a cover—an unbound remnant of a book which no one seemed to have catalogued. My God, I saw the name Machla Krumbein and the title *The Naked Truth*. When I lifted it, the pages crumbled between my fingers. The librarian had been called away to the telephone, and in some ten minutes I read the book again from the beginning to the end. No, it was not a dream or an illusion. There it was, with its crooked lines, provincial expressions, amateurish style. It again perplexed me, and ignited my imagination with the same uncanny power that it had in the little vegetarian restaurant on that winter night. Every poem proclaimed the erotic heat of a woman who didn't know and didn't care about any literary conventions. That village seamstress had wished that all human females would perish in some biological catastrophe and that she, Machla Krumbein, would remain the only woman in the whole world. All men would stand in rows from Spain to Vladivostok, from Alaska to the Antarctic, and she would copulate with every one of them—young and old, Chinese and Turks, Zulus and pygmies, lepers and perverts, murderers and maniacs. No, Machla Krumbein was not an idealist. She wanted all males for herself and no one else.

For some reason the librarian dallied at the telephone, and I kept reading the booklet forward and backward. I don't remember the librarian's returning or my leaving for the car that was supposed to be waiting for me. In all those years I had been convinced that Machla Krumbein and her work, if they ever really existed, had been burned in Treblinka, Majdanek, in one of the ghettos or concentration camps. But one last copy had been left for me to read and appreciate before total oblivion. Or perhaps some friendly demon, imp, or hobgoblin had restored it magically and brought it to me on this special visit from a mountain of ashes.

Translated by the author and Lester Goran

The Divorce

Many divorce cases were handled in my father's court. The court was nothing more than our living room, where my father kept his religious books and the ark for the Torah scrolls. As the rabbi's son, I never missed an opportunity to listen in on the petitioners who came for a divorce. Why should a man and a wife, often parents of children, suddenly decide to become strangers? I seldom got a satisfactory answer.

My father never began a divorce proceeding until he had attempted with all his power to make peace between the couple. He always asked the assistance of my mother, his rebbetzin. The couple often spoke to her first and then to my father. In almost every case, my father quoted the saying of the Talmud that when a man divorces his first wife even the altar of the Temple sheds tears. When I was a boy, the Holy Temple and the altar had been destroyed for about two thousand years. Just the same, in our apartment, at 10 Krochmalna Street, the Holy Temple, the altar, the priests, and sacrifices were more actual than the news in the daily Yiddish newspaper. Once, when my father spoke about the altar shedding tears, the woman who came to get a divorce cried out, "My dear Rabbi, if the altar knew how much I suffered from this tyrant it would cry day and night."

This time, the couple who came to us were not from our street but from Twarda Street. They had a store in a bazaar called Ulrich's Yard. Neither of them appeared to be over thirty. The husband wore a long gaberdine, a small cap, and an open-collared shirt with no tie. From behind his vest his fringed garment hung out. He was quite tall, with a long nose, a yellowish little beard, and barely any sidelocks. His eyes, too, appeared to me yellow. I could see that he was a decent man but not exactly a Hasid or a scholar. He said that he owned a store that sold dry-goods remnants—a bargain store. His wife seemed to be somewhat enlightened—she wore no wig, but she covered her head with a kerchief, so as not to offend the rabbi. Her shoes had high heels, and her skirt reached only to the middle of her calves and was held up at the waist by a black patent-leather belt with a brass buckle. She had large gray eyes, an angular nose, and a wide mouth. She seemed to me girlish, proud, and resentful at having to come to a rabbi's court with her private troubles.

When my father asked why they came to him, the young man said to his wife, "Since you summoned me to the rabbi, not I you, you answer first."

"Rabbi, we came to be divorced," the woman said in a clear and sure voice.

As a rule, my father avoided looking at a female, especially if she was married, to keep from falling into sinful thoughts. But now he glanced for an instant her way. With his left hand he grasped his red beard, and with his right hand he touched a large handkerchief that lay on the table. The touching of this handkerchief by the petitioners would symbolize a silent consent to my father's decree.

"Divorce?" he asked. "How long have you been married?"

"Over five years," the husband answered. "A week after Hanukkah it will be exactly six years."

"Divorce is not a small matter," my father said. "It is not to be taken lightly. The Talmud says that when a man divorces his first wife even the altar sheds tears for them."

"Rabbi, I know all this, but we can't live together," the woman said in a decisive tone.

"Do you have children?" my father asked.

"Three beautiful little girls," the husband cried out. "The oldest one is not yet four years old."

"For what reason do you want a divorce?" my father asked.

For a long while husband and wife kept silent. Then the woman cleared her throat, as if she were about to swallow the words she was going to utter: "Rabbi, he's a fool."

My father raised the brows over his blue eyes. He did not seem less astonished by this answer than I was. After a while he said, "King Solomon, the wisest of all men, deals in his Proverbs with wisdom and foolishness. According to him, only a sinner is a fool. Nothing can be more foolish than to spite God and his commandments. In the first chapter there is the saying 'The fear of the Lord is the beginning of knowledge: but fools despise wisdom.' As you see, the wicked are the fools. But your husband does not look wicked to me, God forbid."

The young man's yellowish eyes became full of laughter. "Rabbi, *she* is wicked."

"Don't say this," my father reproached him. "Anger, too, is silliness. The same King Solomon says in Ecclesiastes, 'For anger resteth in the bosom of fools.' "

"Rabbi, there are also good-natured fools," the woman said.

"No, goodness is the very essence of wisdom," my father answered.

My father quoted a few other passages from the Bible as well as from the Talmud. The young man must have been encouraged by all this indirect praise, because he said, "Rabbi, she only waits for an opportunity to call me names. The moment I open my mouth to say something she is already scolding me. She shames me before the customers. If I say it's day, she immediately says it's night. How can one dwell with a sharp-tongued person like her? She makes my life miserable. She has tortured me for so long that our being together is nothing but Gehenna."

"Did you say that you have three children?" my father asked.

"Yes, Rabbi," the husband answered. "One more beautiful than the other and all of them as sweet as sugar. Just from looking at them one's spirit is uplifted. But when a woman calls her husband ugly names and insults him in front of the children they, too, begin to lose respect. What does a child know? If their beloved mother says that Daddy is a shmegegge, they repeat it."

"This is wrong," my father said. "The Gemara says that a righteous wife cherishes her husband. In the 'Woman of Valor,' which all Jews recite on the eve of Sabbath, it is said, 'She doeth him good and not evil all the days of her life . . . She openeth her mouth with wisdom and on her tongue is the law of kindness.' "

"Rabbi, you listen only to what he has to say," the woman complained. "Why don't you listen to me?"

"I will listen to you, too," my father assured her. "It is my duty to hear both sides. Please, let me hear yours."

"Rabbi, he's a simpleton and a ne'er-do-well. He has as much sense in his head as I have in my left shoe. When you have a store you must be able to recognize who comes to buy and who comes just to browse and examine things and make a mess. There are many such customers. They go from store to store because they have nothing else to do. When I look at one of them I know immediately that she has no intention to buy and I get rid of her quickly, but this pinhead will strike up a long conversation. When a real customer comes and has to wait and listen to their silly chatter, she loses patience and leaves. We worked out a code. I would rearrange the comb in my hair when this annoying kind of person entered, and this would serve as a sign for him not to bother with her. But somehow he never notices anything. There is a saying that women have nine measures of talk, but he has eighteen measures. A woman tells him what sort of matzoh balls she cooked on Passover three years ago, and he talks to her for a whole hour about his Aunt Yachna's noodle pudding. When it comes the first of the month and I have to pay the rent, I have to borrow money from a usurer at high interest. Is this true or not?"

While the woman spoke her husband gazed at her lovingly. He even smiled at me, the rabbi's boy. I could see that he was amused by her ridicule. Even her insults seemed to please him. She is right—he is a big fool, I thought.

"Young man, I forgot to ask your name," my father asked.

"My name is Shmuel Mayer, but everybody calls me Shmelke," the man said. "Actually, I have three names—Shmuel, Mayer, and Alter. The third name I was given when I was two years old and sick with scarlet fever and—"

I had never seen my father interrupt anybody in the middle of a sentence, but this time he didn't let him finish. "Reb Shmelke, what do you have to say to your wife's complaints?"

"What is there to say? She has a polished tongue. Rabbi, she can always convince anybody that she is right. I am a simple man, not a mind reader. How can I know whether the woman comes to buy or just to browse? It is not written on anybody's forehead. At home I was taught that when a person speaks you listen. And when I am busy with someone I can't see what my wife is doing with her comb. Once, her code was that she would begin to cough. But how do you know whether she's coughing as a signal or whether she's really coughing? When the winter comes, with its snow and frost, everybody is coughing. Immediately after the Succoth holiday we get throat lozenges for our children, but they cough anyhow. The truth is that my wife—Salka is her name—was born with a bad temper. Her mother, may she rest in peace, told me that as a baby she was always crying. Some unexplained wrath burns in her. She must take it out on someone. We have three wonderful little daughters but she screams at them all the time, and when they do something that displeases her she beats them and pinches them. To beat a little child you must have the heart of a highway robber."

The door opened and my mother put in her pale face. "Young lady, be so good as to come to me in the kitchen," she said.

"The rebbetzin wants me?" Salka asked.

"Yes, you. I hope you don't mind."

"Yes, Rebbetzin. Just wait one moment. I know quite well, Rabbi, that when I leave he will say terrible things about me. But I really don't care anymore. I have to free myself from him somehow. I would rather rot in my grave than live with this blockhead." And the woman left for the kitchen.

•

I had a great desire to go and listen to the conversation in the kitchen, but I was afraid my mother would yell at me. Both my father and my mother had warned me not to listen in when petitioners came to our house. My father may have forgotten his warning, but my mother had a good memory.

I remained in my father's courtroom, and Shmelke said, "Rabbi, she is clever, beautiful, and charming. But she is a bitter piece. She is always frustrated, because of our struggle to make a living. A few steps from us there is another store like ours, and it teems with customers. The owners are drowning in money. The truth is that Salka's anger drives away the customers. In our business those who come to buy do a lot of haggling. No matter how cheap a price we ask, the customer always tries to bargain us down to a half. Who comes to buy remnants and secondhand material? Only those who like to get something for nothing. My competitor has a shrewd wife. She always wears a sweet smile and knows her business inside out. If I tell my wife to act friendlier to the customers she attacks me violently. Her eyes are as sharp as knives. Sometimes I think that the Angel made a mistake. She should have been born a man. One way or another, things go badly."

"Peace brings success," my father said. "If you two could live more peacefully, then . . ."

I wasn't eager to hear what could happen if the couple lived in peace, and made my way into the kitchen. I stood in a corner, hoping my mother would not notice me in the dim light of the little kerosene lamp. I had left a storybook there on a stool, and pretended to be reading as I cocked my ears. I was interested in people's talk—their expressions, their excuses for wrong deeds, and how they twisted things to suit themselves. I heard the woman say, "Rebbetzin, he is a fool, and there is no remedy for that from the apothecary. It is written somewhere that when the Messiah comes all the sick will be cured but the fools will remain fools. Why is this so, my good lady?"

"It is very simple," my mother replied. "The sick know that they are sick and they pray to God to be healed. But since a fool thinks that he is clever he never prays for help, and therefore he is doomed to remain what he is."

"Golden words. It is really as my grandmother used to say: 'Where there is Torah there is knowledge.' The moment he opens his eyes in the morning, even before he recites 'I Thank Thee,' he begins to pour out nonsense. I say to him, 'What is your rush? The day is only beginning. You will have plenty of time to make an ass of yourself.' He loves to tell me his dreams. I dream, too, but when I open my eyes it all evaporates. He remembers his dreams from beginning to end. His dreams are as silly as he is. He wakes up and says, 'I dreamed that I swallowed a saltshaker.' Only an idiot can have a dream like this. I hope I won't be punished for my words, but even his boots seem silly to me."

"His boots?" my mother asked.

"Yes, his boots. Isn't that strange? Once I looked at his feet and I thought, A foolish pair of boots. Forgive me, Rebbetzin, I now talk like a fool myself. But when you live six years with a fool it rubs off on you. On a clever man everything looks clever, even his clothing. Even when a smart man tries to be silly, somehow it all comes out smart. With a fool the very opposite is true."

"Salkele, forgive me," my mother said, "but such hatred for a man is not good, either for the soul or for the body. God forbid, you may get sick from that. It can affect your livelihood."

"You are right, Rebbetzin, a thousand times right. I don't hate him. He didn't do me any evil. I know it's not his fault, but when he starts to talk and to praise me I feel nauseated. I am ashamed to visit people with him. You know very well that a woman likes to look up to her husband, and if she looks down on him she cannot submit to him."

I decided to return to the men, eager to see Shmelke's foolish boots. He was now sitting at the table, which obscured his feet. I heard him say, "Rabbi, I am giving her everything—the apartment, the store, the merchandise. How will she be able to manage a store with three little children? But this is what she wanted. I will earn my piece of bread. I will contribute for the children as much as I am able. She wants me to come to see the children only on the Sabbath. I know beforehand that I will miss them terribly."

"Reb Shmelke, I don't know if the law is clear to you, but once you are divorced you are not allowed to stay together under one roof."

"Why not?"

"This is the law. Man and wife are accustomed to one another and the temptation is great. They may fall into sin. If she remarries, the sin would be even greater."

"Rabbi, how can I ever see the children? Every house has a roof. And in the winter one cannot take the children outside."

"Someone must be present when you come to see them. It is human nature that a man is more ashamed before other people than before God."

I put my hand into the pocket of my gaberdine and began to play with the groschen I had received as pocket money in the morning before going to cheder. I took it out, and accidentally it fell from my hand and rolled under the table. I crawled under the table and saw Shmelke's boots. In the bright light of our hanging lamp I saw that they were muddy, unusually large and clumsy, made of coarse leather, with low, broad uppers and worn-out heels. I imagined that they smelled of horse dung. Yes, these are really foolish boots, I thought.

My father bent down and asked, "Did you lose something?"

"It is my groschen. I found it already." I could barely restrain myself from laughing.

When I got up, Shmelke asked, "Where did you get the groschen? Did you find it in the street?"

"My mother gave it to me."

"What can you get for a groschen nowadays? Wait, I will give you a kopeck."

"Reb Shmelke, don't give him any money," my father said. "It is a big-city custom to give children money every day. We in Tomaszów never heard of it. When Jethro counseled his son-in-law Moses in the desert, he told him to provide from among the people men of truth, such that fear God and hate covetousness. Those who love money can be bribed easily. Many transgressions stem from the greed for money."

"Rabbi, you should have told this to my Salka. Sometimes I think that she would kill herself for a groschen. As I told you, we have a competitor and he is successful. Since it is a matter of luck, what is the sense of being envious? But she eats her heart out when she sees how well he is doing. She curses him and his wife with deadly curses. She comes home every evening sick. Rabbi, permit me to give a kopeck to the boy. This one coin will not make him covetous."

"Really, he doesn't need it."

Shmelke got up and searched long in his pockets, but he couldn't find a kopeck. Instead he took out a button, a piece of string, and a huge key—probably to the door of his store. "My Salka takes everything away from me," he said. "She cleans out my pockets. Forgive me, boy. There will be another chance."

"It doesn't matter. Thank you," I said, and I ran back to the kitchen.

I heard my mother say, "You cannot rely on maids and nannies. They are strangers. Whatever they do is for money. They don't have a mother's devotion. Every moment something can happen to a child, God forbid. It can fall, bang its head on a chair, climb up on a windowsill, get burned on the stove. There is not a day when I don't read of terrible things that happen to children when they are left to themselves."

"Rebbetzin, and what do grownups do to themselves? When I told my mother—she should intercede for us—that I was going to marry Shmelke, she said to me, 'My daughter, you are chopping off your own head.' "

•

The divorce took place in our home exactly four weeks later. I was there when the scribe wrote out the divorce paper with his quill and two witnesses signed their names. My father read to Shmelke out of a large volume, saying, "Listen, thou, Shmuel Mayer Alter, the son of Eliezer Moshe. Did someone force thee to give this divorce to thy wife, Sarah Salka? Say no."

"No."

"Art thou willing to give this divorce to her in thy name, in her name, and according to the divorce laws? Say yes."

"Yes."

When it came time for Shmelke to put the divorce paper into Salka's cupped hands he broke down, crying in a hoarse voice. My father said to Salka, "You are not allowed to remarry before ninety days."

And Salka said, "Of course I am about to run to the wedding canopy immediately. Who would take me except the Angel of Death?" And she, too, burst out crying. She ran to the door with her head in her hands and my mother ran after her. Salka had left her pocketbook and the divorce paper on the table. I got a lump in my throat, and for the first time I understood why the altar sheds tears when a man divorces his first wife.

I never saw either Shmelke or Salka after the divorce. But a woman neighbor of ours who knew the couple told my mother the events that followed. Shmelke had given his store to Salka, but weeks passed without anyone's buying anything. Salka was forced to sell out her stock for less than nothing and close shop. Shmelke remarried. His new wife was an old maid, and they opened another store. Just as everything Salka did failed, everything the newlyweds did succeeded. His store was always so packed with people one couldn't put a pin between them. His new wife did not consider Shmelke a fool. In comparison to her, he was a sage, our neighbor said. She was far from a beauty—small as a midget and broad as a cholent pot—but she was as good as a bright sunny day. She savored Shmelke's every word and kissed the ground he walked on. "I wish a life like hers to every decent Jewish daughter," our neighbor said.

"What about the children?" my mother asked. "Does he go to see them?"

"He sees them three times a week, perhaps every other day."

"This is not the right conduct," my mother said after some hesitation.

"Rebbetzin, he loves them more than his own life. He would kill himself for their sake."

"Why doesn't Salka remarry?" my mother asked.

"She's looking for a clever one, but why should a clever man take a shrew like her, and three children to boot?" the neighbor said. "But don't worry. Shmelke provides for them and for her nicely. He keeps bringing her gifts. I never see him in the street without packages and bundles. How does the saying go? 'A good cow lets herself be milked.' "

"Does Salka have a maid?" my mother asked. "Is there anyone present when he visits?"

"As far as I know, she has no maid. Since she has no store to attend to, she stays home and takes care of the little ones."

"It's not the right conduct," my mother repeated. "Human beings are not strong in their faith nowadays, and the Evil One is only too eager to put them to temptations."

The neighbor bit her lips and shrugged. "True, but maids are expensive, and one cannot trust them. How does the saying go? 'Everyone kindles his own fire in Gehenna.' "

The woman winked, sighed, nodded, and left our kitchen. She kissed the mezuzah twice.

Translated by the author

Strong as Death Is Love

My Aunt Yentl and her cronies were talking about love, and Aunt Yentl was saying, "There is such a thing as love. There is. It even existed in former times. People think that it's new. It is not true. Love is even mentioned in the Bible. Laban gave his daughter Leah to Jacob, but Jacob loved Rachel. Imagine, a saint like this. Still, he was flesh and blood. One glance at a person and you see his or her charm. The only difference is that in olden times once you liked someone you got married. Nowadays, couples get engaged but still look for others.

"Not far from Turbin there was a squire and they called him the crazy squire. Actually, all the nobles were somewhat pixilated. They lived in so much luxury that they didn't know whether they were coming or going. This squire, Jan Chwalski, was completely befuddled. He didn't speak, he screamed. He kept warning his serfs that he would whip them to death but he never laid a finger on anybody. When a peasant became sick, he sent in a doctor or at least a healer to cure him. He had a court Jew named Betzalel whom he often threatened to hang and shoot. Still, on Purim he sent him a Purim gift. When Betzalel married off his daughter, the squire sent her a wedding present. He came to the wedding and danced a Cossack dance with the Jews and made himself so ridiculous that the people almost choked from laughter. Chwalski never married because he was in love with a noblewoman who had a husband. Her name was Aliza and she was not really such a beauty as he imagined. Not bad, gentle and slender. Gentiles, as a rule, are blond but she was a brunette with black eyes and with a most charming smile. Her husband, Count Lipski, was the biggest drunkard in the whole of Poland. No one had ever seen him sober. He drank away his entire fortune. He knew that Chwalski was in love with his wife, but these things did not bother him. It was said that he used to wake up in the middle of the night and drink vodka from a pitcher through a straw. If this Aliza had been a loose woman, she could have committed the worst sins. But she was a dignified lady. She used to plead with Chwalski not to chase after her since she was married, but Chwalski loved her too much to comply. He wrote daily love letters to her and sent them by messenger. Maybe once a year he received a reply. It always said the same thing: 'I have a husband.' On Sunday Chwalski used to go to church just to be able to gaze at her. When both of them were invited to the same ball, Aliza accepted only one dance with him. It seemed she liked him, too, but she did not want to betray her husband. The priest often beseeched Chwalski to leave Aliza in peace. But Chwalski said, 'From all the women in the whole world there is only one Aliza. All week long I live with one hope, to see her on Sunday.'

"Count Lipski, her husband, was a tall fat man with a perpetually red face and broken veins covering his nose. He drank until he burned out his lungs. The doctors forbade him to drink but he drank to the last day. A doctor in our town said, 'If a man drank as much water as Count Lipski drank spirits, he would become mortally sick.' Chwalski, on the other hand, never got drunk. He was drunk from Aliza.

"Count Lipski had the eyes of a madman. He never knew

what was going on with his estate. Everything was handled by a manager who stole as much as he could, and the rest was lost through bad management. As to Aliza, she kept to herself and did not interfere with business matters. She liked to read books and to take long walks through the orchards. She never had any children. Who knows, Count Lipski might have been too drunk for anything. In his last months, he could no longer walk. The liquor had gone to his legs. He had also developed diabetes, since vodka contains a lot of sugar. One way or another he died without last rites, without confession, without a will. I was told that after his death his body blew up and became like a barrel. Almost no one from the gentry came to the funeral because he had insulted all his neighbors and blasphemed God and all the Christian saints. The hearse passed by our windows. I was still a young girl and I watched the procession. It is the custom among the Gentiles that two men lead the widow. Aliza had a brother somewhere whom I saw for the first time, and the other man was Jan Chwalski. Just as Count Lipski was tall and broad, so was Jan Chwalski small and lean, with a long yellowish mustache which reached to his chin. Aliza was dressed in black. Chwalski held on to her arm as if in fear that she might run away. Love is a kind of madness.

"Lipski died, he was buried. Everyone thought that the widow would immediately marry Chwalski, but she insisted that he wait a year for the period of mourning. When Chwalski found out that he would have to wait, he raised heaven and earth. Hadn't he waited long enough? But Aliza contended that she would never marry him before a year passed. Lipski did not leave a will, and a gang of would-be heirs emerged. They came, God knows from where, and took everything away from Aliza. On the other hand, there was not much to take. Whoever could, grabbed a piece. This is how people are. They imagine that they themselves will live forever. When Chwalski heard what was going on, he took a gun and came running, ready to kill all of them. But Aliza said to him, 'You don't interfere.' And her word was holy to him. There are such people who will silently allow others to rob them. Perhaps it was gentleness or perhaps foolishness. It was known that she came from very high nobility and with some of them money has no meaning. Their main passion is their honor. One way or another, she remained with nothing. All they left her was the empty walls. Lipski had had a court Jew by the name of Yankel. But how can a Jew fight off Gentiles? He came to her and said, 'Your Excellency, they take away everything from you.' And she answered, 'They cannot take more than I possess.' She had suffered all these years with Count Lipski, but no one ever heard her complain. Some people are wolves, others are sheep. But ultimately no one takes anything with them. They brought her a document and she signed it without blinking an eye.

"Not a month had passed and a marshal of the court came with some officials and they told Aliza to move out. Neither the house nor the furniture belonged to her anymore. Again Chwalski came running, ready to defend her: a little man and yet hot-blooded. If Aliza had asked him to jump into a fire for her sake he wouldn't have hesitated for a moment. But Aliza told him to leave matters alone. He wanted to bring her to his estate but she refused to go with him as long as they were not married. To make it short, she found some wealthy peasant—a village elder. He had a little hut beside his house where he kept flax and other objects and he cleared them away for her to live in. Her husband's relatives had left her a single bed and her books. That was all she needed. She had managed to hide some of her personal jewelry, which Yankel had later sold for her, and on this she supported herself for the year. On Sabbath afternoons the tailors' and shoemakers' apprentices and the seamstresses took a walk to the village to peer into her window and see what the haughty countess was doing. She didn't even leave herself a maid. On Sunday the elder took her in his britska to church. Chwalski again and again tried to persuade her to move to his estate but she did not let herself be persuaded. A pure soul, you should forgive the comparison, almost a rebbetzin.

"A year passed and she became a squiress again. All the nobility of the neighborhood came to the wedding. It is not the custom that a bride, even if she is a widow, should be dressed in mourning when she remarries. But Aliza insisted that she dress in black for the wedding. They showered her with flowers and gifts. The priest gave a sermon. One has never heard of peasants attending a noble wedding on their own volition. But peasants came from many villages. Since she lived in a peasant's hut, they considered her one of their own. She came to the wedding in the elder's britska. But from the church to Chwalski's estate she rode in a carriage drawn by eight horses and peasants dressed like dragoons rode in front. They had erected a gate hung with plants and flowers at the entrance of Chwalski's estate. A Jewish and Gentile band played a 'good night' melody for the couple. Chwalski was not especially rich, but he guarded his possessions and nobody could steal from him. It seemed that Aliza's bad luck had begun to shine. But wait a minute, I need a drink."

I brought Aunt Yentl a pitcher of water, and she murmured a blessing and drank. "Don't laugh at me," she said. "I feel like crying." And she blew her nose into her batiste handkerchief. Then she continued.

"Shortly after the wedding, Jan Chwalski gave the type of ball which was considered rare even for a king. It was a few weeks after Passover and the weather was balmy. Aliza was against it. She was quiet, proud, and no longer young. But Chwalski wanted to announce his joy to the world. He invited hundreds of nobles, who came from faraway cities. Carriages rolled in early in the morning and the ball lasted all day. The stores in Turbin profited. There was a band from Zamość and another from Lublin. For years people spoke about that ball: the food, the wine, the dances, the music. Reb Betzalel revealed later that Chwalski was forced to sell a portion of his forest for less than nothing to pay for all this. Of course Jews and peasants were not invited. But many young people stood outside and listened in, and even danced. The servants treated them to wine and food. The next day the nobles went hunting and killed God knows how many animals. When they left, the estate was in shambles. Aliza had pleaded with Chwalski not to squander his fortune, but he was insane from happiness.

"My dear people, all this good fortune lasted not longer than a year. Suddenly one heard that Aliza was sick. What the illness was I don't know even today. But Aliza slowly began to waste away. Chwalski again sold a part of his estate and sent for the biggest doctors, but no one could help her. Our own healer, Lippe, was called in, and he heard one of the doctors say that her blood turned to water. God forbid, when the time comes, the Angel of Death will find a way. The sickness lingered for months, and although everyone had given up on her, Chwalski kept bringing new doctors, professors, various quacks. He even went to the rabbi and offered him money for charity to light candles for Aliza's sake in the synagogue. Nothing availed. Aliza was dying. The priest came and she made her confession. He poured holy water on her and soon Aliza was no more. Reb Betzalel told us that she passed away like a saint. Who knows? There are good souls even among them. It is written in a holy book that good Gentiles go to Paradise.

"The way Chwalski cried and moaned and howled cannot be described. But dead is dead. They took her to the church and there her body stayed until the funeral. Chwalski had bought plots for her and for himself. He grew pale and emaciated, as if he had consumption. His clothes hung on him. His mustache became white. He walked and spoke to himself like a madman.

"But if one has years, one lives. He tried to poison himself, but someone forced two fingers into his mouth so that he should vomit. Whatever was left from his fortune was lost, although Reb Betzalel tried to save as much as possible. A year or two passed and Chwalski still lived. He had a portrait of Aliza and he stared at it day and night. He spent more time at the cemetery than at home. Every day he laid flowers on her grave. He ordered a headstone with the figure of an angel carved to resemble her. He kissed the stone and spoke to it. He no longer concerned himself with business matters. Reb Betzalel had practically taken over. A number of years passed. There is a saying that what the earth covers must be forgotten. But Chwalski could not forget. The priest reproached him, saying that it is forbidden to mourn too long. Chwalski was visited by other squires and relatives who tried to cheer him up, but he could not be comforted. He also took to drink. There was no lack of beautiful women in the neighborhood, but he wouldn't even look at another female.

"Now listen to this. After Aliza was buried, Chwalski locked the bedroom and no one was allowed to enter, even the chambermaid. He also kept her boudoir locked. Every stitch of clothing —even things she simply touched—became sacred to him. He himself slept in her nanny's bedroom. The cook prepared food for him but he barely touched a thing. He became even smaller than he had been and his mustache appeared even longer. In time he dismissed all his servants. And only the nanny remained, an old woman, deaf and half blind.

"That winter was one of the coldest. The seeds in the fields froze. So much snow fell that many houses became snowed under and the people had to dig themselves out. In the midst of this cold spell, Chwalski did not miss a day at the cemetery. One day Chwalski took a spade to the cemetery, most probably to shovel the snow away from the grave and the headstone. It was strange to see a squire carrying a spade over his shoulder, but people had become accustomed to his idiosyncrasies. He often spent all day at the cemetery and sometimes late into the night. Gradually, it became warmer and the snow melted. The water flowed over the village like a river.

"One time after Passover the cemetery watchman came to the police and reported that the earth around Aliza's grave had been tampered with. There were thieves at that time who stole corpses from graves and sold them to doctors who used the bodies to perform autopsies. But those vandals only stole fresh corpses. Who would perform an autopsy on a corpse which is already decayed? In Turbin people said that Aliza rose up from the grave and roamed the city at night. When such talk begins, witnesses immediately emerge: this one saw her, that one heard her. She was standing on the bridge, she was washing linen by the river, she was knocking at someone's shutter. The rumors reached Chwalski and he only shouted, 'Idiots, I refuse to listen to such superstition.'

"*Nu,* but when an entire town talks it is not baseless. The Russian authorities ordered a few soldiers to dig under the headstone and to open the coffin.

"When Chwalski heard this, he became wild with anger, but he seemed to have forgotten that Poland was no longer independent. The Russian soldiers pushed him back, dragged out the coffin, unscrewed the lid, and the casket was found to be empty. Half the town came running together to look at the black wonder. Somebody had stolen Aliza out from the grave. You could never imagine the things that went on every day in Turbin. They ran to tell Chwalski the news, but he hollered like a madman. Reb Betzalel was still alive, but he was no longer a court Jew. For a few days the whole town was boiling like a kettle. Jews were afraid that false accusations would be brought against them. There were already those who barked that the Jews used her blood for matzohs.

"In the middle of all this a new commotion broke out in the town. It happened like this. The old woman who served the squire was cooking grits for him and lit a fire. Her hands were shaky and a piece of burning kindling-wood fell. It soon became a blaze. The old woman began to scream and peasants came to see what was going on. The firemen came running with their half-empty water barrels. Someone burst open Aliza's locked bedroom door. It gives me the creeps to talk about this. The squire lay in bed snoring—it seemed he was drunk—and next to him lay a skeleton. Yes, Chwalski himself had stolen Aliza from the grave. He yearned for her so, that one winter night he dug her up, pried open the coffin, took out her remains, and carried them home. The night was a dark one and nobody saw. He admitted to everything when the police officials took him in for a hearing. She was already decayed, he said, and he peeled off the flesh, leaving only the bones. The Russians did not believe their own ears. 'How is it possible that a person can do such a wild thing?' they asked. And he answered, 'I just could not bear the longing. Better bones than nothing. If you want to hang me, hang me, but bury me near her.'

"Nobody among the Russians knew what sort of punishment to give for such a crime. They wrote a report out to the gubernoton in Lublin. In Lublin they didn't know what to do, either, and inquired in Warsaw and from there to Petersburg. Meanwhile, they allowed Chwalski to remain free. The skeleton they buried again. Chwalski lived only one year more. He had become like a skeleton himself. They buried him with all honors right near his Aliza.

"What I mean to say is: a person gets some idea in his head and it begins to grow and take over the brain. It becomes an obsession. You can even call it a dybbuk. Both he and she were people with souls. If there is a Paradise for Gentiles, I am sure they will rest there together forever. How is it written in the Holy Book: 'Strong as death is love, cruel as the grave is jealousy.' Well, the Sabbath is over. I see three stars in the sky. A good new week to all of us."

Translated by the author

Why Heisherik Was Born

In my first years at the Warsaw Yiddish Writers' Club, I became known as an editor of manuscripts. Working as a proofreader for the *Literarishe Bleter,* I had published a few stories and reviews and had edited a book or two for the Kletzkin Publishing Company. They paid pennies, but I could live on pennies. I was a boarder in a private apartment where the rent was cheap, and I had no need for clothes; year in and year out, my clothes lasted. I had still not found my way as a writer, and I spent most of my time with beginners like myself.

One day, at the Writers' Club, the hostess told me that someone was asking for me. I went to the door and saw a little man with a black beard, dressed in shabby clothes and patched boots. He looked to me like a street peddler. He carried a large package tied with much-knotted string. He said this bundle was his manuscript; he had written a book. Someone had told him that I could edit Yiddish writing.

I had to persuade the hostess to let the man in. Strangers were forbidden entrance. After some hesitation, she allowed him to join me for fifteen minutes. I sat with him, and he slowly untied the knots on his package. His manuscript contained at least a thousand scrawled sheets. I could see immediately that he could neither spell nor punctuate.

He told me that he had served in the Polish Army in 1919 and 1920, in the time of the Polish-Bolshevist war. He marched with the army as far as Kiev, and then he ran back from Kiev to the Vistula, chased by the Red Army. The Reds had been about to take the whole of Poland, but at the famous battle of the Vistula, Pilsudski's army managed to stop the Bolshevist attack. The man told me that he was a pious Jew, that in all those battles he had never missed a prayer or eaten anything that wasn't kosher. Whenever his division came into a town where Jews lived, he went to the synagogue or the studyhouse to pray in a minyan. He also attended the ritual bath for men, even though the water was always cold.

The Christian soldiers mocked him, called him names, and played mischievous tricks on him. His decision to eat only kosher food bordered on the impossible. Sometimes he had to fast for days or live on only a dry slice of bread. He was running and starving. He had to eat with the other soldiers, and the smell of their soups and meats made him almost insane. Some of the soldiers tried to push a piece of pork into his mouth. They laid him out spread-eagled and tried to pry open his jaws to thrust strips of bacon into his mouth; but he struggled with all his might, and after a while, they let him go. A miracle happened to him. There was a Catholic priest in his company who defended him. Not one miracle but a thousand happened to him. Bullets flew over his head; near him people lost hands and legs, their lives as well, but somehow he remained alive.

"I describe it all in this volume," he said. "I want Jews to read this and to know there is a God in heaven. I went to some newspapers and publishers, and they all told me I'm in need of an editor. My spelling seems to be not quite right. I have great difficulties with the Hebrew words. I have studied in the cheder the Pentateuch with Rashi, even the beginning of Gemara, but my father—he should intercede for me—died of typhoid fever, and my mother could not pay the tuition. She became sick with consumption, and I had to peddle merchandise behind the city markets to provide for my brothers and sisters. Every day was a struggle to bring home a few groschen. From this alone, one could write a thick book. Already then the miracles began to happen to me. Later, when I became a soldier and lay in the trenches where the Angel of Death appeared constantly, I vowed that if I had the merit to survive this slaughter, I would describe all of it in a book so that people should know that Providence keeps score of all human beings each minute and each second. I kept a little book of Psalms in my bosom pocket, and by the light of the bursting shrapnel I used to recite a passage or two in the trench."

I said, "You didn't write your name on the manuscript. What's your name?"

"Heisherik. Moishe Groinam Heisherik. The Gentiles, the bigoted ones, made fun of my name, but a name is a name."

"How do you make a living?" I asked.

"I buy up tripe—entrails, liver, kidneys—in the slaughterhouses as well as in the kosher butcher shops, and I sell it to soup kitchens. This is hard work but, thank God, I have a wife with seven children, and they need to eat. In the day I have no time; but at dawn I wake up and I write. How much will you charge me to go over my manuscript?"

I knew quite well that I would have to rewrite the entire book. Not only couldn't he spell, but he had no notion of sentence structure. After three words, he put a period, an exclamation point, or dashes. For no reason, he put quotation marks around words. Some of his smearings and smudges I could never hope to decipher. The truth is, I should not have squandered my time on such works if I wanted to become a writer myself, but for some reason, I was overcome with compassion for this shlemiel who had suffered so much and had remained faithful to his Jewishness.

I offered him a rate that was cheaper than cheap, but he winced and began to bargain and haggle with me. He called the pittance that I had asked for a fortune. He began to scold me and to scream.

"You sit here in this luxurious salon without a hat, without sidelocks, your beard shaved, and you try to rob a poor writer. Where shall I get so much money? Every groschen I make comes out of the marrow of my bones. I would have to take away the last bit of food from my children to pay you such sums. God punishes for exploitation. Who do you think I am —Rothschild? I live in a single cellar room with my whole family. Every month, when I pay rent, it is a miracle, like the parting of the Red Sea."

The man's voice became louder and shriller. A few young writers stopped to listen and to mock. I became so embarrassed that I said, "In that case, I will correct your manuscript with no payment at all."

"I don't ask you to do it for nothing. I'm not a schnorrer, God forbid. When this memoir is completed, all the newspapers will compete to publish it, and I'll pay you for your efforts— but you must give me a deadline on when you'll finish it. I cannot leave the manuscript without completing arrangements. I don't have a copy. If you lose some of it, God forbid, it will be a catastrophe. You must guard it like the apple of your eye."

For a while, we remained silent. I could see that besides his piety, Heisherik had a lot of chutzpah. I knew quite well that no matter how good a job I did, no paper would publish it. The Polish-Bolshevist war was already remote. I could see from thumbing through the manuscript that there was no tension to attract a simple reader, nor were there descriptions to please a more sophisticated one. I wanted to return his manuscript immediately and tell him to find some other victim but, again, I was swept away by pity. If this creature who had suffered so much for his Jewishness could wake up at dawn and work on his manuscript for hours, why shouldn't I give him some of the time that I spent with gossipers and jokers at the Writers' Club?

I said to him, "All right, I will do what I can; but I can't give you any guarantees in the event of a fire or some other disaster. According to the Talmud, a person who undertakes to take care of someone's property without reward is not obliged to be responsible in case of theft or loss."

"What? Since it was ordained in heaven that I should write it, God will not allow any evil to happen to it—"

He was about to say more, but the doorkeeper came over and said, "Mister, your fifteen minutes are over. You must leave now."

"What is this, a police station?" Heisherik asked. "I'm a Jew and a writer, and I will not be driven out of here. I have some business with this young man."

"You have to leave right now," the woman insisted.

Heisherik argued for a while. I was in the presence of something I would term religious arrogance. The Talmud has a saying about it: "Insolence helps even in heaven." How else could this little man withstand the hunger, the cold, the mischief that the other soldiers had inflicted on him? I had taken upon myself to do a virtuous deed, and I was resolved to do it as well as I could.

•

Many weeks passed, but Heisherik never showed up. From time to time I tried to do some editing on the manuscript. I often had to laugh at his writing. This Jew who knew little of Jewish lore was convinced that submerging in the ritual bath on Friday was no less important than the Ten Commandments. He had often risked his life to perform some ritual that a talmudic scholar would have ignored altogether. Heisherik had actually broken the talmudic law by endangering his life for such minor rituals. He had been beaten by the corporals and the sergeants. He had been put into a military prison. He could easily have been court-martialed and shot for insubordination. While the nations had waged war with one another for their worldly ambitions, Heisherik had waged war against man's intolerance. When it came to his numerous battle descriptions, he used an identical cliché: "Blood was flowing like water." Like many of the other soldiers, Heisherik had had no idea of where he was marching and what he was fighting for. Both the Poles and their enemies, the Bolsheviks, were to him the same Gentiles whose goal it was to restrain a Jewish soldier from attending religious services on time. I edited some fifty pages, but Heisherik never appeared. He had not left me his address.

One day, when I was sitting in the lounge hall of the Writers' Club with a few young writers, discussing literature—who had talent and who did not—a young member of the club came over, his face full of laughter, and said, "Isaac, your girl friend is looking for you."

"My girl friend?"

"Yes, your girl friend—a great beauty she is. Piff-paff!"

I went to the entrance hall, and an ugly, shabby woman stood at the door. She was wrapped in a tattered shawl and wore scruffy men's shoes. In each hand she held a basket covered with rags. She said, "I'm Heisherik's wife."

When she spoke, I saw that she hadn't a tooth in her mouth.

"Yes?" I said. "What can I do for you?"

The woman immediately burst out crying, and her wrinkled face became abominably distorted.

She screeched, "My husband deserted me and left me an

abandoned woman without a crumb of bread for my seven swallows. Father in heaven, what shall I do? The little ones are hungry. Woe, what happened to me! Such a misfortune, such a calamity, such an ordeal. What shall I do and where shall I go? Merciful God!"

The woman wailed and wiped her tears with her sleeves. She put down both baskets and pinched her cheeks. The hall was full of writers, young and old, and they all came over. Some gaped; others laughed. I asked the woman, "Where did he go? How can a pious Jew do something like this?"

The woman said, "To the Holy Land."

"To the Holy Land? Do they let Jews in? You have to show a thousand pounds sterling. You also need a foreign passport and a visa," I said.

"What do I know? For weeks, he went around telling everyone he had to go to the Land of Israel. I said to him, 'Murderer, what will happen to me and your children?' But he remained stubborn. A dead saint came to him in a dream and ordered him to go there. I'm only a female and I'm not versed in books. He's a writer, a great man, and I can barely read from the prayer book; but I need to eat and my children are without bread. How can a saint tell a man to desert his wife and children? How can a writer be such a cruel beast?"

The woman howled and clapped her hands as if she were at a funeral.

I said, "I'm sorry, but what do you expect me to do?"

"You work for him—you took his money. He took away the last food from me and his infants and gave it to you."

"My dear woman, he hasn't given me a single groschen."

"He gave you, he gave you. He stuffed you with money and left us naked and starving. God Almighty, you see everything. You wait long and your punishment is severe. Give us back the money that you grabbed from him. This was not money but sweat and blood. People, have pity on us. Don't let my kittens die from hunger."

And she beat her head with both her fists.

The older writers frowned. The younger ones laughed. I said to the woman, "I swear by God and by everything holy to me that I haven't taken from your husband a single groschen."

"You took, you took. People like you overeat and let a mother with her children expire from hunger. The landlord threatens me that he will throw us and our belongings out into the gutter. We owe him three months' rent. A fire should consume him, his fever should jump as high as a roof, and then he will taste my bitterness."

The hostess took the woman by the elbow and tried to push her out, but she would not go. Someone said, "Call the police."

"The police, huh? You call yourselves writers; bandits you are, not writers," Mrs. Heisherik howled.

I put my hand into my pocket and found a bank note there. It was ten zlotys. I gave it to the woman and said, "That's all I have; take it and never come again. I've taken nothing from your husband, and there's no reason for you to create scandals."

The woman snatched the bank note and lifted both her baskets. She uttered a long roster of curses and left, slamming the door. One should not do favors for anyone, the Evil One advised me. From now on, if anyone asks a favor of me, I will tell him to go to hell, I thought. I was hungry and had no money to eat supper that night.

The older writers shrugged their shoulders and went back to their tables, but the younger ones joshed me. One of them said, "Confess, you made her pregnant. We know, we know."

Another one said, "If she sues you, you'll have to pay alimony, like they do in America."

On the way home, I swore to myself that I would cast Heisherik's manuscript into the garbage. But somehow I could not bring myself to do it. I decided to wait until he arrived and give it back to him. However, for weeks his wife came to me at the Writers' Club—always on the same day, at the same time—and I had to hand her a ten-zloty note through the aperture in the front door. Each time she screamed that I had become rich from her husband's payments. My colleagues, the younger writers, never missed a performance.

A few months passed, and I began to believe that Heisherik's wife would remain deserted forever and I would continue to pay her "alimony" for the rest of my life. But one day Heisherik returned. I could barely recognize him. He looked sunburned and as swarthy as a gypsy. His clothes were in tatters. A part of his beard had become dirty gray. I asked him how he, a religious Jew, could have left a wife and children without any support, and he said, "I had to do it. A great yearning drew me to the Land of Israel, so great that if I didn't do it I would die. The Patriarchs—Abraham, Isaac, Jacob—and Mother Rachel came to me in my dreams. What I went through could not be written in a thousand books. As a matter of fact, I began to add new sections to the manuscript you hold."

I told him that I would not do any further work on his manuscript, and he said, "When the editors of our newspapers read the new chapters, it will cause a tremendous sensation, and you'll be richly rewarded for all your efforts."

He sat with me for more than an hour and told me all the details of his adventurous wanderings. He had walked hundreds of miles on foot. He begged alms. He found a way to smuggle himself into the Holy Land. He slept in fields and deserts, sometimes in city gutters. He walked the length and the width of the Holy Land barefoot. He prostrated himself on all the holy graves, slept in ruins and caves. Snakes bit him. He was attacked by Bedouins and jackals. But the pleasure of breathing the sacred air healed his wounds. Sometimes weeks passed and all that he had to nurture him was water and prickly plants of the scorched earth.

I knew that he was not lying. I was especially impressed by his story of how he had burned the soles of his feet by walking on the hot sand. It had burned him like blazing coals, and he had had to tear off his shirt and wrap his blistered feet. He did all that to reach the grave of a saint whose name I had never heard. I was so touched by the man's love for the Holy Land that I promised to continue editing his book.

As far as I can remember, I never finished that work. Heisherik began to send fragments to the Yiddish newspapers, and two or three were published in some provincial magazines. The Warsaw editors scolded me for troubling them with this illiterate maniac's ravings, and I had to swear to them that I would never again burden them with such scribblings. Needless to say, I have never received a penny for my efforts.

•

I could finish the story here, but life added an important chapter to the Heisherik story, and I cannot avoid reciting it.

As we know, from September 1939 until the end of World War II, many families in Nazi-occupied Poland were broken up. Many men managed to escape the part of Poland that Hitler had invaded and found sanctuary in the Soviet-occupied territory. Since there was no postal service between those two regions, an illegal messenger service developed. Those messengers were called holy messengers. They not only risked their lives but also were subjected to the most savage torture when they were caught. Most of them—or, perhaps, all of them—were motivated by a desire to hold the split families together, since no money in the world could have compensated them for their terrible hazard. Eventually most of them perished.

After the war, I learned that Heisherik had been one of those messengers, and he had been the most diligent of them all. He had finally been caught smuggling letters on the road from Bialystok to Warsaw and had been tortured to death. While Heisherik bothered me with his woebegone tales about the war of 1920 and, later, with his roaming, I often wondered, Why was Heisherik born? But it seems that martyrs, like soldiers, have to be trained for the mission that fate has in store for them. He could never have become a holy messenger without having gone through all the ordeals he had described in his pathetic book and had recited to me at such length. I believe that there must be, somewhere in the universe, an archive in which all human sufferings and acts of self-sacrifice are stored. There could be no divine justice if Heisherik's story did not grace God's infinite library for time eternal.

Translated by the author and Lester Goran

The Enemy

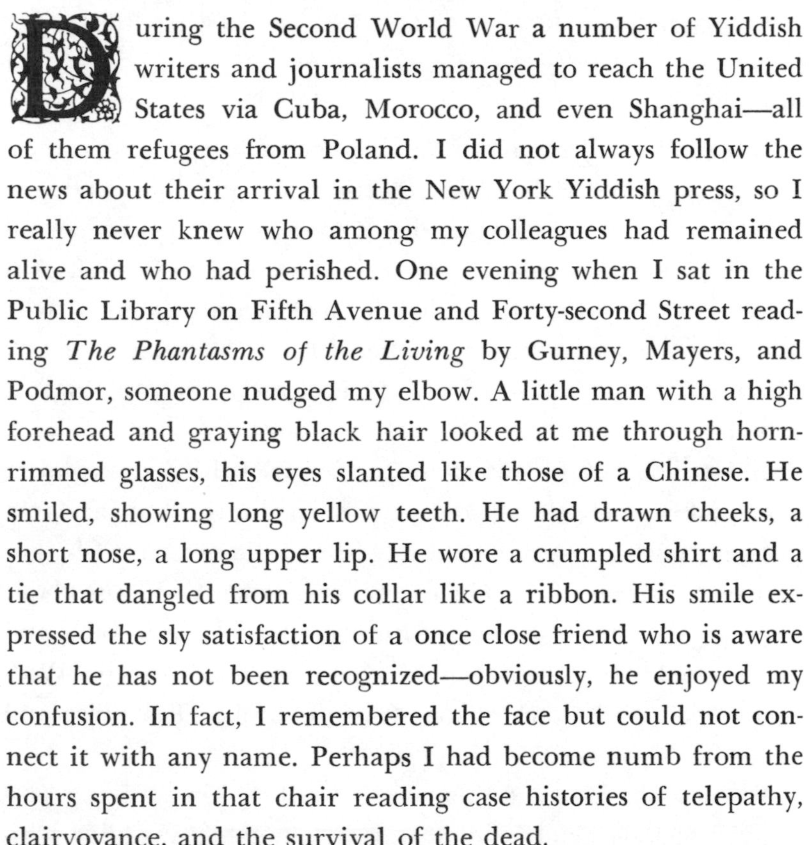

During the Second World War a number of Yiddish writers and journalists managed to reach the United States via Cuba, Morocco, and even Shanghai—all of them refugees from Poland. I did not always follow the news about their arrival in the New York Yiddish press, so I really never knew who among my colleagues had remained alive and who had perished. One evening when I sat in the Public Library on Fifth Avenue and Forty-second Street reading *The Phantasms of the Living* by Gurney, Mayers, and Podmor, someone nudged my elbow. A little man with a high forehead and graying black hair looked at me through horn-rimmed glasses, his eyes slanted like those of a Chinese. He smiled, showing long yellow teeth. He had drawn cheeks, a short nose, a long upper lip. He wore a crumpled shirt and a tie that dangled from his collar like a ribbon. His smile expressed the sly satisfaction of a once close friend who is aware that he has not been recognized—obviously, he enjoyed my confusion. In fact, I remembered the face but could not connect it with any name. Perhaps I had become numb from the hours spent in that chair reading case histories of telepathy, clairvoyance, and the survival of the dead.

"You have forgotten me, eh?" he said. "You should be ashamed of yourself. Chaikin."

The moment he mentioned his name I remembered everything. He was a feuilletonist on a Yiddish newspaper in Warsaw. We had been friends. We had even called each other "thou," though he was twenty years older than I. "So you are alive," I said.

"If this is being alive. Have I really gotten so old?"

"You are the same shlemiel."

"Not exactly the same. You thought I was dead, didn't you? It wouldn't have taken much. Let's go out and have a glass of coffee. What are you reading? You already know English?"

"Enough to read."

"What is this thick book about?"

I told him.

"So you're still interested in this hocus-pocus?"

I got up. We walked out together, passing the Catalogue Room, and took the elevator down to the exit on Forty-second Street. There we entered a cafeteria. I wanted to buy Chaikin dinner but he assured me that he had already eaten. All he asked for was a glass of black coffee. "I hate granulated sugar," he said. "Do you think you could find me a lump of sugar I can chew on?"

It was not easy for me to make the girl behind the counter pour coffee into a glass and give me a lump of sugar for a greenhorn who missed the old ways. But I did not want Chaikin to attack America. I already had my first papers and I was about to become a citizen. I brought him his glass of black coffee and an egg cookie like the ones they used to bake in Warsaw. With fingers yellowed from tobacco Chaikin broke off a piece and tasted it. "Too sweet."

He lit a cigarette and then another, all the time talking, and it was not long before the ashtray on our table was filled with butts and ashes. He was saying, "I guess you know I was living in Rio de Janeiro the last few years. I always used to read your stories in *The Forward*. To be frank, until recently I thought of your preoccupation with superstition and miracles as an eccentricity—or perhaps a literary mannerism. But then something happened to me which I haven't been able to cope with."

"Have you seen a ghost?"

"You might say that."

"Well, what are you waiting for? There's nothing I like better than to hear such things, especially from a skeptic like you."

"Really, I'm embarrassed to talk about it. I'm willing to admit that somewhere there may be a God who mismanages this miserable world, but I never believed in your kind of hodgepodge. However, sometimes you come up against an event for which there is absolutely no rational explanation. What happened to me was pure madness. Either I was out of my mind during those days or they were one long hallucination. And yet I'm not altogether crazy. You probably know I was in France when the war broke out. When the Vichy government was established I had a chance to escape to Casablanca. From there I went to Brazil. In Rio they have a little Yiddish newspaper, and they made me the editor. By the way, I used to reprint all your stuff. Rio is beautiful but what can you do there? I drank their bitter coffee and I scribbled my articles. The women there are another story—it must be the climate. Their demand for love is dangerous for an old bachelor. When I had a chance to leave for New York I grabbed it. I don't have to tell you that getting the visa was not easy. I sailed on an Argentine ship that took twelve days to reach New York.

"Whenever I sail on a ship I go through a crisis. I lose my way on ships and in hotels. I can never find my room. Naturally I traveled tourist class, and I shared a cabin with a Greek fellow and two Italians. That Greek was a wild man, forever mumbling to himself. I don't understand Greek, but I am sure he was cursing. Perhaps he had left a young wife and was jealous.

At night when the lights were out his eyes shone like a wolf's. The two Italians seemed to be twins—both short, fat, round like barrels. They talked to each other all day long and half through the night. Every few minutes they burst out laughing. Italian is almost as foreign to me as Greek, and I tried to make myself understood in broken French. I might just as well have spoken to the wall—they ignored me completely. The sea always irritates my bladder. Ten times a night I had to urinate, and climbing down the ladder from my berth was an ordeal.

"I was afraid that in the dining room they'd make me sit with other people whose language I didn't understand. But they gave me a small table by myself near the entrance. At first I was happy. I thought I'd be able to eat in peace. But at the very beginning I took one look at my waiter and knew he was my enemy. For hating, no reason is necessary. As a rule Argentines are not especially big, but this guy was very tall, with broad shoulders, a real giant. He had the eyes of a murderer. The first time he came to my table he gave me such a mean look it made me shudder. His face contorted and his eyes bulged. I tried to speak to him in French and then German, but he only shook his head. I made a sign asking for the menu and he let me wait for it half an hour. Whatever I asked for, he laughed in my face and brought me something else. He threw down the dishes with a bang. In short, this waiter declared war on me. He was so spiteful it made me sick.

"Three times a day I was in his power, and each time he found new ways to harass me. He tried to serve me pork chops, although I always sent them back. At first I thought the man was a Nazi and wanted to hurt me because I was a Jew. But no. At a neighboring table sat a Jewish family. The woman even wore a Star of David brooch, and still he served them correctly and even chatted with them. I went to the main steward to ask for a different table, but either he did not understand me or he pretended he didn't. There were a number of Jews on the ship and I could have easily made acquaintances, but I had fallen into such a mood that I could not speak to anyone. When I finally did make an effort to approach someone, he walked away. By that time I really began to suspect that evil powers were at work against me. I could not sleep nights. Each time I dozed off I woke up with a start. My dreams were horrible, as if someone had put a curse on me. The ship had a small library, which included a number of books in French and German. They were locked in a glass case. When I asked the librarian for a book she frowned and turned away.

"I said to myself, 'Millions of Jews are being outraged and tortured in concentration camps. Why should I have it better?' For once I tried to be a Christian and answer hatred with love. It didn't help. I ordered potatoes and the waiter brought me a bowl of cold spaghetti with cheese that smelled to high heaven. I said *'Gracias,'* but that son of a dog did not answer. He looked at me with mockery and scorn. A man's eyes—even his mouth or teeth—sometimes reveal more than any language. I wasn't as much concerned about the wrongs done to me as I was consumed by curiosity. If what was happening to me was not merely a product of my imagination, I'd have to reappraise all values—return to superstitions of the most primitive ages of man. The coffee is ice cold."

"You let it get cold."

"Well, forget it."

2

Chaikin stamped out the last cigarette of his package. "If you remember, I always smoked a lot. Since that voyage I've been a chain smoker. But let me go on with the story. This trip lasted twelve days and each day was worse than the one before.

I almost stopped eating altogether. At first I skipped breakfast. Then I decided that one meal a day was enough, so I came up only for supper. Every day was Yom Kippur. If only I could have found a place to be by myself. But tourist class was packed. Italian women sat all day long singing songs. In the lounge, men played cards, dominoes, and checkers, and drank huge mugs of beer. When we passed the equator it became like Gehenna. In the middle of the night I would go up to the deck and the heat would hit my face like the draft from a furnace. I had the feeling that a comet was about to collide with the earth and the ocean to boil over. The sunsets on the equator are unbelievably beautiful and frightening, too. Night falls suddenly. One moment it is day, the next is darkness. The moon is as large as the sun and as red as blood. Did you ever travel in those latitudes? I would stretch out on deck and doze just to avoid the two Italians and the Greek. One thing I had learned: to take with me from the table whatever I could: a piece of cheese, a roll, a banana. When my enemy discovered that I took food to the cabin, he fell into a rage. Once when I had taken an orange he tore it out of my hand. I was afraid he would beat me up. I really feared that he might poison me and I stopped eating cooked things altogether.

"Two days before the ship was due to land in New York, the captain's dinner took place. They decorated the dining room with paper chains, lanterns, and such frippery. When I entered the dining room that evening I barely recognized it. The passengers were dressed in fancy evening dresses, tuxedos, what have you. On the tables there were paper hats and turbans in gold and silver, trumpets, and all the tinsel made for such occasions. The menu cards, with ribbons and tassels, were larger than usual. On my table my enemy had put a fool's cap.

"I sat down, and since the table was small and I was in no mood for such nonsense, I shoved the hat on the floor. That evening I was kept waiting longer than ever. They served soups, fish, meats, compotes, and cakes, and I sat before an empty plate. The smells made my mouth water. After a good hour the waiter, in a great hurry, stuck the menu card into my hand in such a way that it cut the skin between my thumb and index finger. Then he saw the fool's cap on the floor. He picked it up and pushed it over my head so violently it knocked my glasses off. I refused to look ridiculous just to please that scoundrel, and I removed the cap. When he saw that, he screamed in Spanish and threatened me with his fist. He did not take my order at all but just brought me dry bread and a pitcher of sour wine. I was so starved that I ate the bread and drank the wine. South Americans take the captain's dinner very seriously. Every few minutes there would be the pop of a champagne bottle. The band was playing furiously. Fat old couples were dancing. Today the whole thing does not seem so great a tragedy, but then I would have given a year of my life to know why this vicious character was persecuting me. I hoped someone would see how miserably I was being treated, but no one around me seemed to care. It appeared to me that my immediate neighbors—even the Jews—were laughing at me. You know how the brain works in such situations.

"Since there was nothing more for me to eat, I returned to my cabin. Neither the Greek nor the Italians were there. I climbed the ladder to my berth and lay down with my clothes on. Outside, the sea was raging, and from the hall above I could hear music, shouts, and laughter. They were having a grand time.

"I was so tired I fell into a heavy sleep. I don't remember ever having slept so deeply. My head sank straight through the pillow. My legs became numb. Perhaps this is the way one dies. Then I awoke with a start. I felt a stabbing pain in my bladder. I had to urinate. My prostate gland is enlarged and who knows what else. My cabin mates had not returned. There was vomit all over the corridors. I attended to my needs and decided to go up on deck for some air. The planks on the deck were clean and wet, as if freshly scrubbed. The sky was overcast, the waves were high, and the ship was pitching violently. I couldn't have stayed there long, it was too cold. Still, I was determined to get a breath of fresh air and I made an effort to walk around.

"And then came the event I still can't believe really happened. I'd reached the railing at the stern of the ship and turned around. But I was not alone, as I thought. There was my waiter. I trembled. Had he been lurking in the dark waiting for me? Although I knew it was my man, he seemed to be emerging out of the mist. He was coming toward me. I tried to run away, but a jerk of the ship threw me right into his hands. I can't describe to you what I felt at that instant. When I was still a yeshiva boy I once heard a cat catch a mouse in the night. It's almost forty years away but the shriek of that mouse still follows me. The despair of everything alive cried out through that mouse. I had fallen into the paws of my enemy and I comprehended his hatred no more than the mouse comprehended that of the cat. I don't need to tell you I'm not much of a hero. Even as a youngster I avoided fights. To raise a hand against anybody was never in my nature. I expected him to lift me up and throw me into the ocean. Nevertheless, I found myself fighting back. He pushed me and I pushed him. As we grappled I began to wonder if this could possibly be my arch foe of the dining room. That one could have killed me with a blow. The one I struggled with was not the giant I feared. His arms felt like soft rubber, gelatin, down—I don't know how else to express it. He pushed almost without strength and I was actually able to shove him back. No sound came from him. Why I didn't scream for help, I don't know myself.

No one could have heard me anyhow, because the ocean roared and thundered. We struggled silently and stubbornly, and the ship kept tossing from one side to the other. I slipped but somehow caught my balance. I don't know how long the duel lasted. Five minutes, ten, or perhaps longer. One thing I remember: I did not despair. I had to fight and I fought without fear. Later it occurred to me that this would be the way two bucks would fight for a doe. Nature dictates to them and they comply. But as the fighting went on I became exhausted. My shirt was drenched. Sparks flew before my eyes. Not sparks—flecks of sun. I was completely absorbed, body and soul, and there was no room for any other sensation. Suddenly I found myself near the railing. I caught the fiend or whatever he was and threw him overboard. He appeared unusually light—sponge or foam. In my panic I did not see what happened to him.

"After that, my legs buckled and I fell onto the deck. I lay there until the gray of dawn. That I did not catch pneumonia is itself a miracle. I was never really asleep, but neither was I awake. At dawn it began to rain and the rain must have revived me. I crawled back to my cabin. The Greek and the Italians were snoring like oxen. I climbed up the ladder and fell on my bed, utterly worn out. When I awoke the cabin was empty. It was one o'clock in the afternoon."

"You struggled with an astral body," I said.

"What? I knew you would say something like that. You have a name for everything. But wait, I haven't finished the story."

"What else?"

"I was still terribly weak when I got up. I went to the dining room anxious to convince myself that the whole thing had been nothing but a nightmare. What else could it have been? I could no more have lifted that bulk of a waiter than you could lift this whole cafeteria. So I dragged myself to my table and sat down. It was lunchtime. In less than a minute a waiter came over to me—not my mortal adversary but another one, short, trim, friendly. He handed me the menu and asked politely what I wanted. In my broken French and then in German I tried to find out where the other waiter was. But he seemed not to understand; anyway, he replied in Spanish. I tried sign language, but it was useless. Then I pointed to some items on the menu and he immediately brought me what I asked for. It was my first decent meal on that ship. He was my waiter from then on until we docked in New York. The other one never showed up—as if I really had thrown him into the ocean. That's the whole story."

"A bizarre story."

"What is the sense of all this? Why would he hate me so? And what is an astral body?"

I tried to explain to Chaikin what I had learned about these phenomena in the books of the occult. There is a body within our body: it has the forms and the limbs of our material body but it is of a spiritual substance, a kind of transition between the corporeal and the ghostly—an ethereal being with powers that are above the physical and physiological laws as we know them. Chaikin looked at me through his horn-rimmed glasses sharply, reproachfully, with a hint of a smile.

"There is no such thing as an astral body. I had drunk too much wine on an empty stomach. It was all a play of my fantasy."

"Then why didn't he show up again in the dining room?" I asked.

Chaikin lifted one of the cigarette stubs and began looking for his matches. "Sometimes waiters change stations. What won't sick nerves conjure up! Besides, I think I saw him a few weeks later in New York. I went into a tavern to make a telephone call and there he was, sitting at the bar—unless this, too, was a phantom."

We were silent for a long while. Then Chaikin said, "What he had against me, I'll never know."

Translated by Friedl Wyler and Herbert Lottman

Remnants

Nearly all the members of the Yiddish Writers' Club in Warsaw, where I went in the twenties, considered themselves atheists. Free love was an accepted way of life. The younger generation was convinced that the institution of marriage was obsolete and hypocritical. Many of them had become Marxists and proclaimed something they called "Jewish worldliness."

A different kind of writer altogether was Mottele Blendower, a little man, a descendant of famous Hasidic rabbis. He had a dark, narrow face, a pointed beard, and large black eyes that expressed the gentle humility of generations. He was the author of a book about Hasidic life in Poland. One of Mottele's grandfathers had separated from his followers in his later years and had become a sort of divine recluse. After his death, his disciples destroyed his writings, because they hinted at blasphemy. Although Mottele had done away with his long gaberdine and his rabbinical hat and had cut off his sidelocks, he spoke like a rabbi, used their solemn style of language, took on their exaggerated politeness, always on the watch, God forbid, not to insult anybody. Mottele attempted to combine Yiddishist modernism with the lore of the cabala. He undertook to translate into modern Yiddish such mystical works as the Zohar,

The Book of Creation, The Tree of Life, and *The Orchard of Pomegranates.* In his essays, he preached that love and sex are attributes of the godhead and that the proper use of them can be a means to penetrate the illusion of the categories of pure reason and to grasp the thing in itself and the absolute.

Some time after I met him, Mottele had fallen in love with a woman named Zina, who was known for her beauty. She was blond, tall, and the daughter of a rich Warsaw family. One year, she was elected the Queen Esther of the Yiddish literary masked ball. She had married and divorced a rich young man, a lawyer. From her parents she had inherited a large sum of money, which evaporated with inflation. Zina was a distant relative of Mottele's. They had a big, noisy wedding.

Those who knew the bride and the groom foresaw that the match wouldn't last long. Mottele was gentle and weak, while Zina was robust. Her first husband, the lawyer, said openly that his ex-wife was a nymphomaniac. There were rumors in the Writers' Club that she had invited all her former lovers to the wedding. An intimate friend had learned that Zina confessed all her sins to Mottele, but he contended that he was not jealous about the past and that he would give her full freedom in the future. Mottele was supposed to have told her, "The roots of both of our souls are in the *sephira* of splendor, and in those spheres, sins are virtues."

One of Zina's lovers, whom she was supposed to have cared for most, was the writer Benjamin Rashkes. She told Mottele that she could never forget Rashkes. When he was forced to move from his bachelor's furnished room because he had impregnated the maid in his boardinghouse, Zina offered him a study in her new, spacious apartment. She put in a sofa, a writing table, and even a Yiddish typewriter imported from America so that Rashkes could work there whenever the Muse granted him inspiration. The trouble was that he was less and less inspired to write. He poured all his energies into so many would-be love affairs that he had no time for anything else.

There was constant talk in the Writers' Club about the triangle of Mottele, Zina, and Rashkes. Even though Rashkes promised Zina to avoid the Writers' Club and do his work, he came to the club every day and spent all the time on the telephone. Closing the door of the phone booth, he went on whispering his unending love declarations. Rashkes maintained that monogamy had destroyed eroticism. Men and women are not jealous by nature; the only thing they dislike is to be deceived. Also, they prefer the truth to come to them in small portions and as a part of the love play. Rashkes was telling his colleagues that many men enjoy sharing their wives with the right kind of lovers and that his ideas were based on his personal experience. The husbands of his paramours were all his friends and admirers, he said. They often reproached him for neglecting their wives. Rashkes claimed that he kept peace between his lovers and their husbands.

A year did not pass before the gossips in the Writers' Club had a new sensation to talk about. Zina had become seriously enamored of a known Communist leader, Leon Poznik. The Trotsky purges had been in progress in Russia for some time, but Poznik remained an ardent Stalinist. He was the editor of two Communist magazines, one in Polish and one in Yiddish. The *Defensywa*, the Polish political police, had arrested Poznik a number of times, but they always released him. They were not interested in keeping the leftist leaders in prison too long. Poland was officially a democracy. One could not jail people on the basis of their convictions. Besides, the leaders of the *Defensywa* did not want to root out Communism in Poland

and put themselves out of jobs. As for Poznik, he needed those short imprisonments to add to his prestige in the party and in the Soviet Union. He boasted about his courage during the interrogations, describing how well he lectured to the Polish Fascists about Leninism. However, the comrades called him, jokingly, the "Polish Lunacharsky"—a Communist of talk, not of deeds.

Poznik was broad-shouldered, small, and wore shoes with elevated soles and heels. His eyes, behind the horn-rimmed glasses with their thick lenses, seemed to sparkle with a light of their own. I often imagined that all the victories of world Communism shone through those glasses.

That Zina should fall in love with Poznik seemed unbelievable. He had a wife, a Communist functionary who had been sentenced to five years in prison. He bragged about his affair with an important woman in Moscow, where he was invited every few months. Besides, Zina had never shown any interest in politics. She had been at one time a disciple of the celebrated medium Kluski, who specialized in materializing spirits of the dead. It was her fascination with the occult that initially attracted her to Mottele. But who can fathom the ways of love? It became known in the Writers' Club that Zina now took part in all of Warsaw's leftist activities. The leftists published interviews with her in their magazines. She put on a leather jacket, the kind worn by the functionaries of the *Cheka,* the Soviet political police. She sold her jewelry for the support of political prisoners. Zina had revealed to someone that the *Defensywa* had summoned her for an interrogation and that she had been kept overnight in the arrest house on Danilowiczowska Street where suspects were held. There was a saying in the Writers' Club that Communism was like influenza: everybody had to go through it sooner or later.

In the spring of 1927, Poznik and Zina left for Russia. They disappeared suddenly, without any notice to anybody in the club. I was told that not even their comrades were informed. Neither Poznik nor Zina could have acquired a foreign passport. Those who were invited to the Soviet Union had to smuggle their way across the border at the town of Nieswiez. For a long time, one heard nothing in the Writers' Club about Poznik or Zina. Then the rumor spread that Leon Poznik had been arrested in the U.S.S.R. and put into the infamous Lubyanka prison. Rashkes had received a single Yiddish postcard from Zina with an altered name—he recognized only the handwriting. She used the conspiratorial code language: "Uncle Leon is mortally sick and they put him into the Lubya hospital. The doctors give scanty hopes." She signed the card "Your despairing Aunt Charatah," which is the Hebrew word for regret. Later, it came out that in Kharkov a Yiddish magazine had published an attack on an anthology Poznik had edited two years earlier. The writer of the article, a Comrade Dameshek, had discovered in Poznik's introduction to the book traces of Trotskyism.

•

Not long after Poznik and Zina left, the news spread in the Writers' Club that Mottele Blendower had become a penitent —not of the modern type that compromises Jewishness with worldliness, but one who returned to extreme orthodoxy. He grew his beard and his sidelocks, exchanged his modern clothes for a long robe, and one could see his fringed garment hanging down from behind his vest. He published a letter in the Orthodox daily condemning all his former writings as heresy and poison for the soul. He forbade all the Yiddish dramatic circles to use his play and sent back his membership card to the Writers' Club. The owner of a Yiddish bookstore made it known that Mottele had bought from him all the copies of his book, spat on them, and threw them into the garbage. Rashkes had gone to Mottele's apartment to get back some of his manuscripts, but Mottele told him that he had thrown them into the stove. Mottele's marriage to Zina was annuled, and he was allowed to remarry after collecting the signatures of one hundred rabbis. It was published in the Yiddish Orthodox newspaper that Reb Mottele had married a pious Jewish daughter, a descendant of renowned rabbis, and had become the head of a yeshiva. The curious in the Writers' Club found out that his new wife was an eighteen-year-old girl who, according to the Hasidic law and custom, had shaved her head the day after the wedding and had put on a bonnet, like a rebbetzin. Mottele had changed his telephone number so that heretics and mockers could not contact him. Once, when I met him in the street, I greeted him, but he turned his head away. It was hard for me to believe that only a year ago Mottele had spoken with me about Kant, Nietzsche, Kierkegaard, and Ouspensky. Previously he had been inclined toward Zionism. Now he called the Zionists betrayers of the Jews.

One winter evening, perhaps two years later, I received a telephone call at the furnished room I rented. I could not recognize the woman's voice until she told me that she was Zina. I had never been one of her friends—I used to greet her in the Writers' Club, but we seldom spoke. Now she spoke to me as if I were an old friend. She told me that she had made her way back to Poland illegally. While in Russia, she had learned that Mottele had remarried. Here in Warsaw, she had tried to call Rashkes, but it seemed he had moved out of the room where he boarded lately. She had asked for his address in the Writers' Club but no one knew it. She expected me to know Rashkes's whereabouts, but I couldn't help her. Zina's voice had changed. It sounded hoarse and old. She asked me if I could meet her in the street, at the corner of Solna and Leszno. I told her that I was afraid to be seen with her, because I might be arrested.

Zina assured me that the Polish authorities knew that she had escaped from Russia and there was no danger for me to be seen with her. She said, "My dear, I'm not the same Zina. My own mother wouldn't recognize me if she were alive. I lost everything in the Red Gehenna—my beauty, my faith in the human race. A living corpse is speaking to you."

I let myself be persuaded and went out to meet her. A mixture of snow and rain had fallen. An icy wind was blowing. At the corner of Leszno and Solna I saw Zina. I would never have known it was she. She looked emaciated and aged. Her hair had turned dark and was disheveled and stringy. She had on a gray padded jacket—the kind market vendors wore. She extended her moist hand and said, "I'm hungry and half frozen. I haven't slept for three nights. When we went to Russia, I left all my clothes in the apartment I had with Mottele. I tried to recover them, but his wife slammed the door in my face. The little money I had, I spent on telephone calls, but none of my former friends seems to be home. Where is Rashkes? Where is he hiding? They all run from me like from a leper. You won't believe it—the receptionist at the club didn't let me in. Well, I deserve it all."

Zina spoke and coughed. She spat into something that looked like a dirty napkin. She said, "My lungs are sick. I suffer from consumption or God knows what."

"What did they have against Poznik in Russia?" I asked. "He subscribed to all their lies."

"What do they have against anybody? They swallow one another like wild animals. Have pity on me and take me somewhere where it is warm."

After some hesitation, I took her to a café at 36 Leszno. The waitress frowned when she saw Zina. I ordered tomato soup for her and a glass of tea for myself. Zina had abandoned all manners. She dunked the bread in the tomato soup. She spoke loudly, and the patrons around us winced. She tilted the bowl, drank the last of the soup, and said, "I don't recognize Warsaw. I don't even recognize myself. What I went through from the day they arrested Poznik until now cannot be described. I literally lived in the streets. I hoped they would imprison me just to have a roof over my head. But when a luckless person wants something, the very opposite happens. I told them in clear words, 'You are murderers, not socialists, worse than Fascists. Your Stalin is a criminal.' They just laughed. They were even unwilling to commit me to an insane asylum. When I crossed the border on the way back to Poland, they let me go without asking for documents . . ."

Zina began to cough again. She took out the dirty napkin and blew her nose. "Don't gape at me," she said. "It's me—Zina, the ball queen of the Yiddish Writers' Club, the crowned Queen Esther. Woe to me!"

She smiled, and for a second, her face looked young and beautiful once more.

•

Years passed. I had left Warsaw and gone to the United States. The Hitler war broke out, and then the atomic bomb came, and afterward the peace. Between 1945 and 1950, we found out, more or less, who remained alive in Europe. I had heard that Poznik had died in prison in Moscow even before the war began. Others said that he had been sent to dig for gold in the north and that he died there from starvation. As far as I knew, both Mottele and Zina had perished in Poland.

In the fall of 1954, I made my first trip to Israel. There I got more details about those who had vanished in the ghettos, in the concentration camps, or in Russia. I heard gruesome facts about my own family. One day, in my Tel Aviv hotel, I was trying to read a book by the dim light that filtered through the shutters of the window. I had closed them for protection against the thin desert sand that would be carried in by the hot khamsin wind.

Someone knocked at my door. I had already become accustomed to unannounced visitors, since the telephone was seldom functioning. I opened the door and saw a little man with a white beard, dressed in a rabbinical hat, and beside him a tall woman in a wig covered with a shawl, her face golden from the khamsin sand. I looked at the couple and thought that they must be a pair of schnorrers out to collect alms for some cause. I noticed that the woman carried a box in one hand and an umbrella in the other. She looked me over from head to toe and said, "Yes, it's him!"

"May I know with whom I have the honor?" I asked.

"Little honor," she answered. "My name is Zina, and this is my husband, Mottele Blendower. Don't be afraid; we didn't come from the grave to strangle you."

I should have been shocked, but since I had undertaken this journey, I had become used to the most astonishing encounters. The little man said, "A surprise, heh? Yes, we are alive. I know that I was counted among the dead. They even published my obituary here, but I'm still in this world. Zina and I met in Lublin in 1948. My other wife and my children were killed in the ghetto, and what happened to me is a story of a thousand and one nights. We came here to the Jewish state only two months ago."

"Come in. Come in. This is really a startling event," I mumbled. Zina immediately crossed the threshold, and after some hesitation, Mottele followed.

He asked, "Why do you sit in the dark? Because of the

khamsin? I have experienced all kinds of storm winds, but a hot, sandy wind like this I see for the first time. The winds in Russia are always cold, even in the summer."

"Everything there is cold," Zina said. "In 1939, when the war began and the Polish radio announced that all men should cross the Praga bridge to Bialystok, I went with them—first to Bialystok and later to Vilna, which belonged to Russia. I was sure that the Communists would know my record and send me to Siberia or to the wall of the firing squad; but somehow no one paid any attention to me. What I endured in the Red paradise for the second time is not something to talk about now. I survived the siege of Leningrad and later found myself in the Caucasus Mountains, among Persian Jews. They had been there for the past two thousand years and spoke a mixture of Parsee, Hebrew, and Russian. In 1945, all the refugees attempted to return to Poland or reach the DP camps in Germany, but I said to myself, 'Since Poland is nothing more than one big cemetery, what is the rush?' But I became deadly sick with asthma. When I finally reached Warsaw, I walked among the ruins like that prophet—what was his name?—Jeremiah. I saw a young man there digging up the earth with a spade. I asked him what he was trying to find and he told me, 'Myself.' He was not exactly mad, but queer. Later, I met some of our former Communists who used to visit the Writers' Club. They had lost everything but their chutzpah. From there, I made my way to Lublin. One day, as I walked on Lewertow Street, I saw this helpless creature, my former husband. He had also managed to stay alive; isn't that funny?"

"Why are you standing?" I asked. "Sit down, both of you. I don't have any refreshments . . ."

"What? We didn't come for refreshments," Mottele said. "We came to see you. You don't look much older. We followed your work, even in Russia. In Poland, I found a book of yours. As you can see, my beard is all white. You must be wondering how we can be together again after what happened between us. The answer is that the signatures of a hundred rabbis cannot really annul the spirit of a marriage. Anyhow, our re-encounter was an act of Providence. There is a lot in the Zohar about naked souls, and we two are naked souls."

"Why do you stare so at my wig?" Zina asked me. "This was Mottele's condition, that I should put on a wig and behave like a pious matron. I told him openly that I don't believe in anything anymore. But since this was his will, I gave in. What is a wig? Just some hair from a corpse. The truth is that I'm almost left without hair. I got typhoid fever while in Leningrad and became bald. I read somewhere that hair grows even on the heads of the dead in their graves. But my hair won't grow. This means that I'm worse than dead."

"Zina, don't exaggerate," Mottele said.

"What? I don't need to exaggerate. The truth is weird enough."

"Where do you two live?" I asked.

Mottele grabbed his beard. "Promise me that you won't laugh at me and I will tell you."

"I will not laugh."

"They made me a rabbi," he said.

"Nothing to laugh at. You are a son and a grandson of rabbis."

"Yes, yes, yes. We came here without a penny. The Joint Distribution Committee paid our expenses. Someone announced in the newspapers that I was alive. There are quite a number of my father's Hasidim here, and they all came to me—from Tel Aviv, from Jerusalem, from Safad, even from Haifa, though Haifa is known as a town of radicals. They began to call me rabbi immediately. 'What sort of a rabbi am I?' I said to them. 'And what about Zina?' But they answered me, 'You are a child from our school. You are the image of your saintly father.' I will make it short: I became a rabbi and she a rebbetzin right here in Tel Aviv."

"In my eyes, you are more of a rabbi than all the others," I said.

"Thank you. Jews come to me on the Sabbath, we eat at the table, and I recite Torah. What is there left to preach to them? Nothing but silence. They rented an apartment for us and they provide for us. What could I do here? I lost my strength. They offered me compensation money from Germany, but this money to me is an abomination."

For a while we were silent. Outside, the wind howled, cried, laughed, like a bevy of jackals. Zina said, "Don't be amazed that I wear makeup. I know that it does not suit a rebbetzin. But I suffer from eczema. A man can let his beard grow and cover his cheeks. Everything shows on a woman. In a wind like this, my face swells up."

We were silent again for a long while. Then Zina said, "Guess what I have in this box."

"Zinele, he's a writer," Mottele said, "not a mind reader. Tell him what is there."

"Rashkes's unfinished novel," Zina said.

"Yes, I understand."

"No, you don't. That day in September when the Warsaw radio ordered all men to run to Russia, I went over to Rashkes and tried to persuade him that we should go together. But he refused. He was as pale as death. The first day of Rosh Hashanah, he lay down on the bed and never wanted to get up again. From all his admirers, only one woman remained faithful to him—Molly Spitz, a bad writer, a psychopath."

"I knew Molly Spitz," I said. "She used to come to the Writers' Club."

"Yes, she."

"I didn't know she was Rashkes's lover," I said.

"Who wasn't his lover?" Zina asked. "He ran after all women between fifteen and eighty. When the war broke out, they all forgot him—but Molly Spitz, that monkey, remained with him. The truth is that a Nazi bomb had exploded in the house where she lived and she was homeless. I had finished with him once and for all; still, I tried to save him. I pleaded with him, but he said, 'Zinele, go wherever you want. I have lived my life and this is the end.' He told me to open a drawer, and there I found what I am carrying now. He said to me, 'Take it if you insist. The Nazis don't need my writings. Neither do the Reds. They can use these pages for cigarette paper.' These were his last words."

"You carried it for all these years?" I asked.

"Wherever I went—to Bialystok, to Vilna, to Leningrad. This is not just a novel. This is the story of our great love. I tried to get it published in Vilna, but they had all become flatterers of Stalin. The mountain Jews in the Caucasus didn't know Yiddish. Here is his novel. I dragged it with me over all the frontiers, all the ruins. I lay with it in cold railroad stations. I took it with me to the hospital when I got typhoid fever. When I met Mottele in Lublin, I gave it to him to read and he said, 'It's a masterpiece.' "

Mottele slowly lifted up his head. "Forgive me, Zina; I never said this."

"Yes, you did. It was your idea that I should bring the novel to him," Zina said, pointing at me. "Now that we are in the Land of Israel, I want to publish it. I want you to write an introduction to it. This, too, was Mottele's idea."

Mottele shrugged. "All I said was that he knew Rashkes better than the others did."

That day I promised Zina to read the novel and write an introduction. The night after, I lay awake until three o'clock and I read the entire manuscript. I was reading and sighing. From time to time, I slapped my forehead. I had always considered Rashkes a genuine talent. But what I read that night was the worst kind of mishmash. Had he become prematurely senile? Had he forgotten the Yiddish language? The protagonist of this novel was not Zina but a man who indulged in drawn-out polemics with the Warsaw Yiddish critics in tedious pseudo-Freudian analysis, misquoting all sorts of writers, philosophers, and politicians. I never would have believed that Rashkes was capable of writing this bewildering hodgepodge if I had not recognized his handwriting. He had even forgotten how to spell. Rashkes had a reputation for being a humorist, but there was not a trace of wit in this pathetic monologue.

A few days later Mottele called me, and I told him what I thought of Rashkes's last work. He began to stammer. "I never praised it. I said one thing and she heard the opposite. If Hitler could hypnotize Germany and Stalin Russia, something is the matter with the human race altogether. Zina is sick. She was twice operated on for cancer. They cut off her left breast. I cannot tell her the truth about Rashkes. She will soon have to go to the hospital again. I myself suffer from angina pectoris. I shouldn't have visited you in that sandstorm, but she actually dragged me. What can I tell her about your introduction? Please find some excuse for declining."

"Tell her that I will send her the introduction from America."

"Yes, a good idea. There is great wisdom in delaying things. I would like to meet you alone, without her."

I made an appointment with Mottele, but a day before we were to meet, someone called me on the telephone and told me that Mottele and Zina had both been taken to the hospital. The man introduced himself as one of Mottele's Hasidim and an ardent reader of mine.

He said to me, "This may sound to you like a contradiction, huh? However, after Treblinka, one should not ask any questions."

Translated by the author and Lester Goran

On the Way to the Poorhouse

The inmates of the poorhouse all wanted to get rid of her. First of all, it's a shame to share sleeping quarters with a whore. And second, she didn't even come from this area. The authorities had confined her in the Janów prison, and while there, she became paralyzed. So what is her connection with the residents of Janów? Still, the Jewish community could not throw a Jewish daughter out into the street, no matter how depraved she was. So they put a straw pallet in a corner of the general dormitory, and there she lay. She was dark-skinned, with a youthful face, black burning eyes, brows that converged over the bridge of her nose, prominent cheekbones, a pointed chin, and black hair hanging straight to her shoulders. The paupers cursed her and she replied with ten curses for one. They spat at her and she spat back, hissing like a snake: "Pox on your tongue, black in the head and green before the eyes, a behind swollen from sitting shiva . . ." Adept as she was at name-calling and profanity, she was also capable of turning on the charm and telling lewd stories about herself to the men. Even though she could not use her legs, the women of Janów were fearful she might seduce their husbands. Whenever there was an epidemic of smallpox, measles, scarlet fever, or croup, the pious matrons of the town went running to the studyhouse, screaming at the elders that it was all a punishment for keeping the whore in a house belonging to the community. But what could they have done with a cripple?

Her name was Tsilka, and her Yiddish had the accent of those who lived on the other side of the Vistula. The residents of the poorhouse avoided her like a leper and she ignored them, too. But when the men from the town came to visit her and brought her groats, chicken soup, or a half bottle of vodka, she smiled at them sweetly and suggestively. She wore a string of red beads around her neck. Long earrings dangled from her earlobes. She pushed the quilt down to expose the upper part of her breasts. Occasionally she let her visitors touch her sick legs. She soon had a group in town who rallied around her. The town toughs warned Zorach, the poorhouse attendant, that if he mistreated Tsilka they would break his neck. They asked her many questions about her past and she answered them, shamelessly boasting about her sins. She remembered every detail, leaving out nothing. After a while, some of those who were living at the poorhouse made peace with her, because through her they, too, got better food and even some liquor. Those who lay on straw pallets near her began to enjoy her tales. Although they wished her the black plague and eternal hell, they had to admit that her stories shortened the monotonous summer days and the long winter nights. Tsilka maintained that when she was eight years old a horse dealer enticed her into a stall and there he raped her on a pile of hay and horse dung. Later, when she became an orphan, she began to copulate with butcher boys, coachmen, and soldiers. Her town was near the Prussian border and the smugglers of contraband made love to her. Tsilka named all the towns where she was in brothels, spoke about the madams and pimps. Cossack officers preferred her to the other harlots. They danced and drank with her. A crazy squire made her bathe in a wine-filled tub and later drank from it. A rich Russian from Siberia proposed marriage to her if she would convert to the Orthodox faith. But Tsilka refused to become a Christian and to betray the God of Israel. She had no desire to marry that Ivan and bear little Ivans for him. What could he have given her that she didn't have? She wore silk shirts and underwear. She ate marzipan and roast squab.

For many years, she was fortunate. She never became pregnant, she never got the clap. Other whores who began their profession later than she rotted away in hospitals, but she remained young and beautiful. Suddenly her luck turned. In a brothel in Lublin, a girl poisoned her procurer. At the investigation, she accused Tsilka of the crime. Tsilka was charged with murder and sent to the Janów prison because the women's section of the Lublin jail was overcrowded. There she spent nine months in solitary confinement in a damp cell full of bedbugs and other vermin. The Lublin investigators had forgotten her. Her papers were misplaced somewhere. The trial never took place. They had to free her. But a few days before her release, her legs lost their power and became like wood. Tsilka bragged that the prison guards had affairs with her. In a cell next to her sat a bunch of thieves. One night they gouged out a large hole in the wall, and through this, they copulated with her. Hodel the widow, whose pallet was close to Tsilka's, began to wince, raised her fists in a fury, and shouted, "Shut your foul mouth. Your words are deadly venom."

"Sweet venom."

"God waits long and punishes well."

"For my sake, he can wait a little longer," Tsilka answered mockingly.

There was quarreling in Janów because of Tsilka. The community leaders held a meeting as to what action was to be taken. She defiled the town. Even the boys in the studyhouse discussed her. After lengthy debates that lasted until dawn, it was decided to send her to the poorhouse in Lublin. The Janów community was ready to pay for her upkeep there. Lublin is a big city and they have many like her there. The old Janów rabbi, Reb Zeinvele, admonished his congregants that one leprous sheep can contaminate the whole flock. He remarked that Satan's aides were everywhere—in the marketplace, in the tavern, in the studyhouse, even in the cemetery. The situation in Janów had come to such a pass that respectable tradesmen, fathers of children, stood for hours around Tsilka's bed listening to her obscenities. They brought her so much food and so many delicacies that she gave gifts to those who flattered her. The children in the poorhouse she treated with cookies, raisins, sunflower seeds. She no longer lay on a straw pallet but on a bed with linen. In Janów it was unheard of for a female to smoke. Tsilka asked for tobacco and cigarette paper, and she rolled her own cigarettes and blew smoke rings through her nostrils. How long can a town like Janów stand for such loose conduct? After prolonged negotiations, a letter came from the community of Lublin stating that Tsilka would be given a cot in the room where the moribund are kept. A screen was to be placed near her bed, so that the others wouldn't have to see her insolent face. Besides the expenses for her maintenance, the Lublin community asked the Janów community to pay for her burial fees in advance, even though Tsilka would be buried behind the fence. When the contents of this letter became known in Janów, the Tsilka followers also gathered at a meeting and one, Berish the musician, who was known as a scoffer, a woman chaser, a vituperator, instigated the rabble. "The so-called upright citizens," he ranted, "are supposed to serve God, but actually they serve only themselves. They have appropriated the best of everything—the brick houses, the eastern wall in the synagogue, the stores in the marketplace, the fat women, even the best-located graves. However, the moment a shoemaker, a tailor, or a comber of pig bristles tries to raise his head, he is immediately threatened with excommunication and a bed of nails in Gehenna. We will not allow them to send Tsilka away to Lublin, where she will rot away while alive. We can take care of her here. It's true that she's a fallen woman. But who are those who fall into sin? Not the pampered daughters of the rich, may they be consumed in fire. It's our children who are fair prey to every lecher. Our daughters work as servants in the houses of the wealthy, and their sons, who are supposed to study all day long, creep into their beds at night. The mothers of these privileged boys pretend not to see. Sometimes they even encourage them." Berish spoke with such zeal and with such violent gesticulations that the crowd began to howl, to stamp their feet, and to denounce the rabbi, the elders, the leaders. One of them called out, "We have suffered long enough from these hypocrites."

"Brothers, let's go and break windows," shouted Beryl the barrelmaker. A pack of ruffians marched into the street, lifted rocks, and hurled them through the windows of the important Janów citizens. A Talmud student on his way to midnight study was beaten. A girl who came to pour out the slops was attacked and her braid cut off. From there, the rioters went into the tavern, bought a jug of vodka and a bagful of salt pretzels, and proceeded to the poorhouse. The old and the sick were already asleep, but Tsilka was awake. She had been informed about the meeting. She supported her head on two pillows, and in the darkness, her eyes glowed like those of a she-wolf. Lights were lit and drinks were passed around. Tsilka downed a full glass of the liquor, bit off a bit of salt pretzel, and began to malign the best people of Janów. Even though she knew the town only from peering through the prison bars, all the gossip and scandal had somehow reached her. The sleeping mendicants were awakened and treated to drinks. Yosele Bludgeon, who worked in the slaughterhouse, became so drunk that he tore off Tsilka's quilt, lifted her out of bed, and tried to dance with her. There was screaming, laughter, clapping of hands. The children of the poorhouse became wild, and began to jump and hop as on the day of the rejoicing of the law.

Hodel the widow went into a frenzy, "People, the world is being destroyed!"

Someone went to wake Zorach the attendant, who was also the Janów gravedigger. He tried to calm the mob, but he received a blow. He went to the rabbi. It was Reb Zeinvele's custom to wake up every night to study Torah and to write commentaries while drinking tea from the samovar. The outside door was bolted, the shutters closed. Suddenly someone banged at the shutters with a stick. Reb Zeinvele trembled. "Who's there?" he called.

"Rabbi, please open!"

The Messiah had come; the thought ran through Reb Zeinvele's mind, although he soon realized that the redemption would not begin at night. He went to unbolt the door. Zorach was panting. "Rabbi, we don't live in Janów but in Sodom," he cried.

"What happened?"

"There's lechery in the poorhouse."

•

The community won. A Janów salesman who delivered merchandise to Lublin paid thirty guldens to the Lublin elders, who signed a contract to keep Tsilka there until the day of her death. The Janów community was ready to send Tsilka to Lublin, but she took out a knife concealed beneath her pillow and threatened to stab anyone who tried to move her.

Berish the musician, her defender, swore that he would set fire to the houses of the community busybodies and that blood would be shed in Janów. Both sides bribed the authorities. It would have resulted in warfare if the women of the town, even those living on Bridge Street and Butcher's Alley, hadn't sided with Tsilka's enemies. Tsilka managed to instigate husbands against wives and broke up engagements. When women are determined, men lose the upper hand. Furthermore, Tsilka's pals fought among themselves and some exchanged blows. The community was now all set to execute its plan, but the coachmen's wives would not trust their husbands to take her in their wagons. Regular passengers refused to travel in her company. After much bickering, it was decided that Leibush the scabhead, who transported hides to Lublin tanneries, would take her in his cart. Leibush was already a man in his fifties and a grandfather. Other than Tsilka, he took with him a wandering beggar and two orphan sisters who went to Lublin for domestic service.

Tsilka's imprecations and knife waving were of no avail. Leibush, a small man, broad in the shoulders, with a thick red beard that began in the middle of his throat and reached his bulging eyes, stormed into the poorhouse, tore the knife out of Tsilka's hands, grabbed her like a calf destined for the slaughterhouse, and threw her among the hides. The beggar and the maids were already in the cart and Leibush headed straight toward the Lublin road. Street urchins ran alongside the wagon, screaming, "Rachav the harlot." Girls peered from behind the curtains. Tsilka poured out the most violent curses. She spat at Leibush and at the two orphans. One of them mumbled, "You should spit with blood and pus." Tsilka flung herself at the girl to scratch her eyes out. Suddenly she burst into laughter.

"I won't spit blood, but you will carry the chamber pots of your employers. All day long, you will work like an ox. At night, your mistress's precious son will force you to sleep with him and give you a belly. Later, you will be thrown out into the gutter, together with your bastard."

"You should get a boil on your behind for every decent maid

there is in Lublin." Leibush spoke from the driver's seat, not turning his back.

"How do you know they are decent?" Tsilka asked. "Did you try to lie with them?"

"My own wife was a hired girl in Lublin. At the wedding, she was a kosher virgin."

"Kosher like a pig's knuckle. Greater sages than you have been tricked."

Tsilka was now pouring out vituperations. She bragged about her abominations. The two sisters, perplexed, pressed even closer to each other and remained silent. The mendicant leaned on his bag, which had been filled with food and old clothing by the charitable women of Janów. Leibush emitted a whistle, brandished his whip, and spoke inquisitively. "You have discarded your last shred of shame, haven't you?"

"Those who are ashamed don't do what I did. I wouldn't be ashamed in front of my own mother."

"Don't you have any regrets?" the beggar asked. "After all, one gets older, not younger. You see already that God has punished you."

"My profession and regret don't blend. The poorhouse is full of cripples who constantly have God on the tip of their tongues. The pious also have a taste for the flesh. I should have many good years since so many yeshiva boys were my patrons. I was even visited by an itinerant preacher who specialized in sermons about morality."

"You should live so long, if you are telling the truth," Leibush said.

"Leibush scabhead, you should have so many blisters and carbuncles for the number of times this preacher had me."

"Shut your mouth or you'll soon find your teeth in your hand," Leibush cried out. The beggar tried to quiet him.

"It doesn't pay to fall into a rage, Reb Leibush. God does not listen to a whore's swearing."

"He listens, He listens, you nasty schnorrer. If you say one more word, I'll tear out your beard, with a piece of flesh in addition."

The two sisters, twins, let out one short shriek. They came from a decent home. Both had round faces, snub noses, lips that curled upward, and high bosoms. They wore the same shawls and their hairdos were identical. Tsilka stuck her tongue out at them. "Two stuffed geese."

The night began to lower. The sun was setting; large, red, with a ribbon of cloud through the middle. The moonless night was humid; there was lightning not followed by thunder. The horse walked at a slow pace. In the darkness, one could see the glitter of glowworms, the outline of a windmill, a scarecrow, a haystack. Dogs barked in the villages. Horses spending the night in the pasture stood motionless. Once in a while, a humming could be heard, but it was difficult to know if it came from a beast or a bird of prey. After a while, the cart traveled on a road through a forest. From the thicket wafted smells of moss, wildflowers, swamp. Tsilka's talk became even more abandoned. She reviled and blasphemed. According to her, rabbis, scholars, important people had one thing on their minds only—lechery. She told of an episode with a rich young scholar who was boarding at his father-in-law's and who stayed three days and three nights in a hayloft with her. Occasionally the horse stopped for a while, pricked up its ears, as if curious to listen to these human vanities. Suddenly Tsilka cried out, "Leibush scabhead, take me down."

"What's the matter?"

"I have to go where even a king goes on foot."

Since Tsilka was paralyzed, Leibush had to carry her. He

lifted her with ease, as if she were a bundle of rags, and carried her behind the bushes. One of the twins uttered a laugh and grew silent again. The beggar rummaged in his bag, pulled out an onion, bit into it, and spat it out. "By what merit does such an outcast remain alive?" he asked.

A quarter of an hour passed, perhaps more, but the two did not return. The horse kicked the ground once. The beggar remarked, "What are they doing so long?" and he answered himself, "They don't sing psalms."

Steps were heard. Leibush emerged from the thicket with Tsilka in his arms. She giggled, and one could see by the light of the stars that she was tickling him and pulling at his beard. Leibush carefully sat her in the cart. He then ordered, "Everybody else get out of the cart."

"What for?"

"I have to rearrange the hides."

The three of them alighted. Leibush jumped up onto the driver's seat, whipped the horse, and shouted, "*Heyta.*"

"Where are you going? Where are you leaving us? Oy, mama!" the sisters cried out in unison.

"Thief, brigand, whoremaster! Help, people, help!" the beggar wailed hoarsely.

They tried to run after the cart, but the road led downhill. The wagon soon disappeared. Leibush had taken the beggar's bag and the baskets belonging to the girls with him. The beggar beat his breast: "Children, we are lost."

"Oy, mama!" The two girls sank down and remained sitting on the needle-covered ground.

The beggar screamed with all his might, "There is a God! There is!"

The words reverberated and resounded with the mocking echo of those who rule in the night.

All three slept in the forest. The next day they headed back toward Janów. In Zamość, Bilgoray, Frampol, and Turbin, the news spread about Leibush the hide dealer, who left a wife, children, and grandchildren and ran away with a trollop. Messengers were dispatched, but they found no trace of the pair. Some people thought that Leibush crossed the border into Galicia with her. Others were of the opinion that the two sinners went to a priest in Lublin and were converted. Yet others maintained that Tsilka was a she-demon and that she carried Leibush away into the desert of Sodom, to Mount Seir, to Asmodeus' castle, into the dominion of the netherworld.

Leibush's wife was never permitted to remarry. The mendicant swore on the Bible that he had kept sixty guldens in his bag, a dowry for his daughter, who was already past thirty. He asked the community to reimburse him for his loss.

During the winter nights, when the girls of Janów got together to pickle cucumbers, pluck feathers, or render chicken fat for Passover, they would tell the story of Tsilka the wicked and Leibush the adulterer, who vanished into regions from which no one has ever returned.

Loshikl

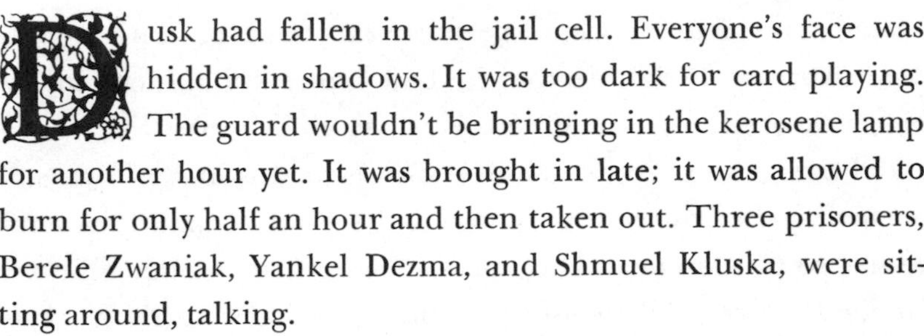

Dusk had fallen in the jail cell. Everyone's face was hidden in shadows. It was too dark for card playing. The guard wouldn't be bringing in the kerosene lamp for another hour yet. It was brought in late; it was allowed to burn for only half an hour and then taken out. Three prisoners, Berele Zwaniak, Yankel Dezma, and Shmuel Kluska, were sitting around, talking.

Berele Zwaniak said, "They know, they know, but they play dumb. Not all husbands are alike. One is ready to stab you if you so much as give his wife a smile or a wink. But some other sucker takes you in as a boarder and leaves you with his wife all day long and sometimes all night to boot. I knew such a couple. His name was Getzel and his wife's name was Malka. He rented an alcove in his apartment to a good pal of mine, a safecracker, Hershel Shmirer, a giant of a man. Getzel himself, a small fellow, had a little workshop two blocks away where he made paper bags. All day long he sat at his workbench and glued together the paper bags. In the evening, instead of coming home, he would grab a bite in the corner café and take off with his chums to play cards. He wouldn't get home until two o'clock in the morning, and sometimes he played till daybreak. How much could you possibly win at cards? Monday he would walk away with a ruble, Tuesday he would lose it back. But it's a kind of obsession. Something gets in your head and sticks there like a nail. Look at us. Stealing will never make you rich. But you get used to it and you think that without it you couldn't survive. It draws you like a magnet. The other day I swore to my mother by all that's holy that I would go back to shoemaking. She took a Bible out of her dresser and made me swear on it. But as soon as I walked out on the square I forgot everything I promised her. A friend of mine came along and he had a deal for me. He gave me no time to think it over. We pulled it off, slick as butter. Hard cash, not merchandise that needs to be sold through a fence on Wolowa Street. Then we dropped into Lazar's tavern and hit the bottle. But why do I tell you all this? Once you become addicted you see nothing else. At two o'clock in the morning, when Getzel, the husband, finally dragged himself home dead tired from a whole day's work and half a night's gambling, he fell into bed more dead than alive. You want to tell me that he didn't know? Card playing just came first with him."

"What would have happened if Hershel Shmirer had made her pregnant?" Shmuel Kluska asked.

"The sky wouldn't have fallen," Berele Zwaniak answered.

"What happened to them?" Yankel Dezma asked.

"It just so happened that Hershel Shmirer was caught red-handed stealing and they threw him in jail. Malka used to bring him packages to the cell."

"In love with the safe safecracker, huh?" Shmuel Kluska asked.

"A female, if you keep her happy, she latches on to you," Berele Zwaniak said.

There was in the same cell another prisoner, Itche the Blind, or Itche the Accurate. He was called Itche the Blind because he had only one eye; the other one had been gouged out many years back. The name Accurate was given to him because of his proper bearing. Itche the Blind didn't go out on the street himself anymore. He taught young punks the trade and got a percentage of every take. He was also part owner of a bordello. For almost fifteen years Itche the Blind had stayed on the loose. But he was arrested because of a run-in with a police commissar, and got entangled in a trial. He was soon supposed to be freed on bail. The guards in the jail held Itche in high esteem. He received from the outside packages of chocolate, cigarettes, even cans of sardines, to which he treated everyone.

For Itche the Blind it would have been degrading to involve himself with the petty thieves who were his cellmates. He was now stretched out on a bunk, smoking one cigarette after another. But the conversation apparently had captured his interest. From time to time he mumbled to himself. Suddenly he drew himself up to his full height, a huge man, wide-shouldered, with a shock of hair beginning to gray at the temples. He took a stride toward the others and asked, "May I say something, too?"

For a while all three thieves were speechless. Berele Zwaniak was the first to find his tongue. "Have a seat, Itche, you're like a rabbi to us."

Itche the Blind sat down.

"Have a smoke."

He offered each of the prisoners a cigarette. He took out a lighter and passed it around for them to light up. In a deep voice he said, "A rabbi, huh? We in Warsaw had only one rabbi, Chazkele, may he intercede for us. His word was gold. A day didn't go by without his hitting on some scheme. He had a mind like a trap. The chief of police himself respected him. If Chazkele hadn't become what he was, he could have been a big shot in Petersburg. I was listening to what you were saying. Men, women, whores, not-whores. Each woman has her own ways of hooking a man. In my youth I had my share of loving, I can't complain. I slowed down when I realized that one good female can satisfy a man better than five dozen tramps who are only after a pair of stockings or a mug of beer. You all are still bagel-snatchers, wet behind the ears, and what can you know? We have no Chazkele these days. No, and does anyone today remember Red Reitzele? That was what they called her. You've probably never heard of her. But there'll never be another Reitzele, either. Reitzele was a smart cookie. She had a husband, a businessman, not a crook. His name was Antshel, a real-estate broker. Those were the days when Warsaw was being built up with paved sidewalks, marketplaces, high buildings. The banks had a lot of money and extended credit. If you could show that you had five thousand rubles in cash, you could borrow an additional twenty or thirty thousand rubles on a mortgage. Our Jews began wheeling and dealing, and the time was ripe for a lot of brokerage business.

"Overnight, paupers became millionaires. Antshel knew how to open up doors, where and whom to offer bribes. He was a shrewd bastard. But he wasn't any good with women. For Reitzele he was barely enough for a snack, not a full meal. The likes of him have to be helped along. He wasn't one to begrudge others, like a dog on a haystack who can't eat it himself and who won't let others near it. As to Reitzele, she wasn't just a tease. When I met her I was eighteen and she a good thirty-six and maybe even a bit older. My parents had at first wanted to make a yeshiva student of me. But I didn't have a mind for the Gemara. When they saw that I would never turn out to be a scholar, they wanted me to become a tailor. However, in those days an apprentice had to spend three years in his master's house pouring out the slops and rocking the baby. It took a long time before he was allowed to sew on a button or make a buttonhole. When I found myself with my back up against the wall, I left everything and ran off to Warsaw. I found my way to Chazkele, who was the leader of all the toughs in the city. As I told you, I'm from the provinces, not from Warsaw. The Warsaw wise guys used to needle us newcomers and call us yokels or Litvak swine. In Warsaw if you were born on the other side of the city line, you're a Lithuanian. Here comes the guard with his lamp, a fire in his guts!"

A guard brought in a kerosene lamp with a blackened globe. A reddish glow spread over everyone's face. When the guard saw Itche the Blind sitting with the other inmates, he shook his head as if to say, This is beneath you.

Itche the Blind began to blink with his good eye. He spoke to the guard, "Stach, we don't need the lamp. It gives no light, only smoke."

"Mr. Itche, I'm not the boss here," the guard answered. "I'm just following orders."

"Here's a cigarette," Itche said, "but don't tell the other guards. They'll descend upon me like locusts."

"Thanks, I appreciate it."

"We're having a little chat to help us forget the stench from the can," Itche the Blind said, as if trying to excuse himself.

"Yes, I understand. I have to follow the rules. How does the saying go? 'The small fry are hanged and the big ones are thanked.' "

•

The guard left and Itche the Blind continued: "Chazkele talked to me for about half an hour. I told him that I couldn't find a decent night's lodging and he sent me to Red Reitzele. He said, 'Tell her Chazkele sent you and she'll open up doors for you. She likes young men, not old.' In my first half hour with him he gave me more wise counsel than the biggest lawyer could deliver in a year. If only I had listened to him, I would still have both my eyes.

"Reitzele lived on Smocza Street, in a large apartment, three rooms and a kitchen, a new building with gas and an indoor toilet. How I got the nerve first to approach Chazkele and then to go to Reitzele's is beyond me. I climbed up the painted steps, knocked, and a little woman with red hair like fire and green eyes like a cat's opened up. I stood at the threshold and she looked me up and down and inspected me as if I were to become her butler. Her teeth were sparse, but stronger than a dog's. Later on I saw her crack walnuts with those teeth. I told her that Chazkele had sent me, and a little smile lit up her face. I looked at her hands and felt a twinge of desire. Some men boast that they can tell a woman by her eyes, others claim that you can tell it all by the shape of the mouth. I can tell everything from hands. In the theater, when they want to flatter a woman, they rave about her long fingers. Nonsense! I like short fingers and short nails, too. She stood before me in a knee-length apron, a short housedress, and in slippers with pom-poms. Her knees were pointed like those of a boy. I took one look at her and knew that she'd be mine.

"Half an hour later we were kissing. We fell upon each other with thirst. She pressed her mouth to mine as if she were trying to swallow it. In bed, she asked, 'What's your name?' I told her, 'Itche,' and she said, 'I don't like Itche. I'll call you Loshikl, because you are young and strong and you jump like a colt,' and that's how it was. It lasted eight years. I would say to her, 'Reitzele, I'm an old horse already, not a colt, and she would reply, 'To me you'll always be a *loshikl* even if you're ninety.'

"That she was a good piece and that she loved men Antshel her husband knew quite well. For a couple of years he played dumb with me. Once, when he ran into me at Lazar's tavern and we had a drink, he became talkative. He said to me, 'What do you call two husbands of the same wife?' I said to him, 'Brothers-in-law,' and he said, 'That's a silly name. We're more like brothers.' He went on: 'Loshikl, now that the cat is out of the bag, what do you say to our little wife? Have you ever had anything better?' And I said, 'Never had, never will have.' He said, 'She talks the same about you. There's only one God and one Loshikl. Last year when they threw you in the slammer, she wanted to teach me your tricks, but I have no patience for such games. Jealous? How can I be jealous? She told me at the very beginning, "I'm not a rebbetzin, I like men." We are not her only ones. When she meets a man, right away she wants to try him out. If King Solomon, she says, could have a thousand wives, Reitzele can have a thousand husbands.'

"That evening, we became so close that we drank to brotherhood. Just the same, when you're in love with someone you can't be above it all. A man is not a stone, no matter how much of a front he puts up. It burns you up when you know that your beloved is sleeping around with others. But if you have no choice, you grin and bear it, as they say. You can get used to anything. You can live and love with an ulcer in your gizzard. You can dance with a toothache.

"Antshel was such a man. When Reitzele and I quarreled, he made peace between us. He wanted her to have her Loshikl.

"Yes, we all want pleasure, but what kind of pleasure is it to stretch out across someone's knee and be thrashed with a cat-o'-nine-tails till your butt swells? That's what some of my sweethearts wanted me to do to them. They would beg of me: 'Whip harder, Itchele, pull my hair! Bite my shoulder!' Reitzele had her own quirks. It started with her taking it upon herself to marry me off. I asked her, 'What good would it do you?' And she said, 'When a colt grows older he needs his own mare.' I said to her, 'What do I need my own mare for? So that she should run around with every thug while I rot in jail?' And she said, 'I have a husband and I want you to have a wife. It'll be more fun that way. We'll go to the theater together or to the circus, all four of us. We'll chat over a mug of beer.' I told her in no uncertain terms, 'It's not for me.' When she heard that, she set out to supply me with lovers. She would lie next to me on the sofa and say, 'Loshikl, I want to be your mother. I don't have any children, only one Loshikl, and I want to provide for his future. You are younger than me,' she said, 'and when I'm gone maybe you'll keep me in mind and say the Kaddish or light a candle for me.' I said, 'You're not about to croak yet, you'll outlive all of us,' and she said, 'No, Loshikl. My mother died young and my father passed away when I was a little girl of three. In our family, they barely make it to fifty.'

"I'll make it short. She wanted to set me up with some woman —if not a wife, let it be a lover. I asked her, 'What's in it for you?' And she said, 'It's interesting. It'll amuse me.' 'I could have,' she said, 'as many men as my heart desires. They still turn their heads after me in the streets as if I were a young girl, but for now, one husband and one Loshikl are enough.' Something is always nagging women on. Men go to war, or go on strike, throw bombs and get themselves banished to Siberia. A female has only one string to her bow. It's even written in the Bible.

"She wasn't just babbling," Blind Itche continued. "One day I came in for lunch and sitting there was a little female—slight, with orange-yellow hair, with a string of pearls around her neck. I saw right away that this was no ordinary piece, but well-bred, from a wealthy home. Reitzele introduced her: a doctor's wife. We had lunch and when Reitzele cooked you licked your fingers. We talked and I found out that the doctor's wife employed a cook and a maid. She had everything, but she was just about fed up with her husband, a skin doctor. He practiced at St. Lazar Hospital, and there they treat only cankers, psoriasis, lupus, what have you. All day long she didn't lay eyes on him, and when he came home in the evening, he buried himself in books and journals about people with little worms in their blood. 'He knows,' she said, 'everything. But how to satisfy a wife, that he didn't study.'

"When a woman speaks like that to a stranger, the first move is already made. After she left I asked Reitzele, 'Where did you meet this fancy lady?' And she said, 'At Lours's Café.' That's Reitzele for you. She could dress up like a countess and go to the theater, the opera, to Lazienki Gardens. She leaves Smocza Street, and right away she's a lady. The whole thing seemed crazy to me. I wanted Reitzele, not the skin doctor's wife. But Reitzele had already made up her mind. The first time it happened I couldn't believe it myself."

The jail door opened and the guard came in to retrieve the lamp. "By law, you should be asleep already," he said, "but I'll let it pass."

"We got a little involved in a conversation," Itche the Blind said. "We'll make up the sleep tomorrow."

"I know nothing. Just doing my duty," the guard said.

•

"What's the sense in fixing up your lover with another woman?" Berele Zwaniak asked.

The cell had become dark. Only the ends of the lit cigarettes cast a glow on everyone's face. Itche the Blind paused a while. "It doesn't have to make sense," he said. "Why did Leah in the Bible present Jacob with her maid? Why are we sitting here behind bars? I could easily have had a store on Miodowa Street just like the shlemiels who came here from the provinces and made fortunes. But you begin something and you can't get out of it. Once there was a professor and he spent much time pondering lofty thoughts, until he came to the conclusion that all men are crazy. Maybe it's really so."

"I'll bet you that Reitzele got a fee from the skin doctor's wife," Berele Zwaniak said.

Itche the Blind didn't answer right away.

"I don't know," he finally said. "I didn't know then and I certainly don't know now. If she did, she was welcome to it. Why did such a cute little woman have to pay for it? Some men would have paid *her*. On the other hand, if a lady like her were to start up with one of her own kind, right away it would turn into a complicated matter. He might want her to divorce the doctor, or whatever they do in high society. For people like that checking into a hotel is dangerous. All the hotels are full of snoops. At Reitzele's, everything went smoothly. Reitzele would go out and leave us alone. She always made up some excuse. She had to go to a store or to a relative. Reitzele didn't need the money. Her husband gave her more than enough. But how does it go? People have big eyes. They are greedy for all kinds of silly thrills. The doctor's wife called herself Fania, but whether that really was her name, I don't know. She never told me where she lived, and I never asked. In those days I didn't brood about things too much. I gorged myself, guzzled it up, had my Reitzele and the other one. When I needed money, I headed toward the city markets and I always returned with a little cash. I don't know why, but women always walk around with unlocked purses. That's how it was then, that's how it is today. We talked about things making sense. Does that make any sense?"

"The reason is," Shmuel Kluska said, "that they stuff so many gadgets into their purses they can't get them closed. My own sister does it. The buckle loosens and the purse opens by itself."

"How long did you have the doctor's wife?" Yankel Dezma asked.

"What? It didn't always go as smoothly as with Fania. One time Reitzele set me up with a queer piece. She was so besmirched with makeup that it made me sick. She spoke only Polish and refused to eat with us. If you offered her a glass of tea, she wiped the rim with a handkerchief. She started to interrogate me like a doctor: Did you ever have this? That? She'd brought a pink vial of disinfectant with her. It was all so nauseating that I began to vomit, and that was the end of that. I can see her even now, with a thick nose and a mouth like a snout. Another one wore a hat with a huge brim and a veil so heavy that you couldn't see her face. When push came to shove, she scurried off. But there were those who attracted me somehow. One was a poor girl from the provinces, a hatmaker. She worked in a store on Zabia Street. She always arrived hungry. If Reitzele gave her a bowl of soup, she asked for more. With Reitzele, it was a madness of sorts. After they left I had to report everything to her: what she said and what I said. Every little thing. She would shriek, 'Tell me more, Loshikl. Don't leave anything out.' I thought that as she got older she would cool off, but she became more and more embroiled. I had nothing to complain about really, but I was getting fed up with the whole kit and caboodle. I didn't need her meals or her lodging anymore. The cops were after me and it wasn't good for me to have a steady address. I moved to Poczajow and there I got myself younger and prettier women. Later the misfortune with my eye happened. All I did was make a joke with some jerk and the brute pounced on me with a knife. It was nothing but bad luck."

"Did you stop seeing Reitzele forever?" Berele Zwaniak asked.

"Not completely," Itche said. "Whenever we met, the fire for her was rekindled and I swore that everything would be the way it had been. But I saw her less and less. Chazkele died, and when that happened Warsaw was no longer Warsaw. As long as he lived we were his pupils. When he passed away we all became orphans. Quarrels began. Gangs formed. During the strikes in 1905, when the Reds attacked us, there was no one left to fight back. Everyone ran his own way. After Bloody

Wednesday the Reds, too, scattered like mice. Many escaped to America. In the midst of it all, Reitzele died."

"Got sick, huh?" Shmuel Kluska asked.

"Who knows what she had. Her time was up. She was fifty to the day. I could sit with you three nights and tell you stories about her and it wouldn't be enough time. Children, it's getting late. Soon they'll come in to wake us."

Translated by Rena Borrow and Lester Goran

The Pocket Remembered

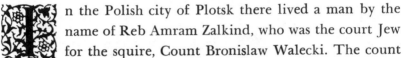

In the Polish city of Plotsk there lived a man by the name of Reb Amram Zalkind, who was the court Jew for the squire, Count Bronislaw Walecki. The count was not an enemy of the Jews; he traded with them and often consulted them in business. It was the custom among the Polish squires that when they gave a ball, the court Jew made the guests merry. He disguised himself as a bear, growled, crawled on all fours, and the guests had something to laugh at and to mock. But Squire Walecki looked down on this barbaric custom. He sat Reb Amram among the other guests at a ball, and had the cook prepare vegetables in a special pot to assure the Jew that the food was kosher. The squire owned many forests in which the trees were logged and floated on rafts down the Vistula to Danzig, where German merchants bought the lumber. Reb Amram spoke Polish and German well, and the squire frequently sent him to fairs in Danzig and Leipzig. He bought all kinds of jewelry there: rings, chains, bracelets, brooches, earrings, and precious stones for the squiress, the Countess Helena Walecki, and for her daughters. Reb Amram was not a learned man, but he remembered the law that if you owe but one groschen, even to someone overseas, you must go there and repay the debt, since only the sins committed against God, not against man, are forgiven on Yom Kippur. Reb Amram could have easily become rich the way many dishonest stewards, marshals, and usurers did, but he was by nature an honest man. In handling the squire's money, he accounted for every groschen. Even Reb Amram's enemies acknowledged that in money matters he was upright. In those times, traveling salesmen wrote everything down on a small chalk board, but Amram had purchased a pen and a notebook to keep records of his accounts. His coat had two deep pockets, one for expenditures and another for income. He kept all his personal earnings in a separate leather purse. At every opportunity Squire Walecki praised his court Jew for his honesty.

In time Reb Amram became quite wealthy. Envious townspeople gossiped behind his back and hinted that he only feigned honesty but was actually cheating the squire. They maintained that a Jew who works so closely with a squire could not avoid drinking non-kosher wine or looking and lusting after the female gentry, because Alte Trina, Amram's wife, was as small as a midget and slightly hunchbacked. Reb Amram was tall, straight, with blue eyes and a blond beard. Only a few white hairs could be seen on his head and beard, even though he was approaching sixty. He had a strong singing voice, was the leader of the morning prayers on the High Holidays, and was also the blower of the shofar, the ram's horn. The young matrons in the women's section of the synagogue savored his voice. Their mothers-in-law used to reproach them, "Look into the prayer book, not at Amram,"

As small and as frail as Alte Trina was, she bore Amram four sons and three daughters, and they all married well. It seemed that affluence was Reb Amram's lot. He did not, God forbid, say, "It was the might of my own hands that brought me this great wealth." He often contributed to charity. On the Sabbath or on a holiday he never returned from the synagogue without a poor guest. He gave generously to the society which married off orphaned maidens, to the watchers of the sick, toward purchasing sacred books for the studyhouse, and for redeeming innocent prisoners. Alte Trina often sent chicken soup to the sick in the poorhouse.

One summer a fair took place in Leipzig. Reb Amram Zalkind was sent there to meet with foreign merchants, to claim the debts which they owed the squire, and to negotiate down payments for new orders. Squire Walecki was marrying off his youngest daughter, the Countess Marianna, to the son of Count Zamoyski, one of the richest noblemen in Poland, and the squiress asked Reb Amram to buy for the bride-to-be a strand of pearls, a variety of gold utensils, as well as silk, velvet, fine linen, and various other costly materials. Reb Amram carefully wrote every item down in his notebook. He would be handling large sums of money and he made sure that every purchase was recorded clearly; he wanted no mistakes, God forbid, in the account. He told Alte Trina not to worry about him and not to expect him back too early, since business trips like these took much time. He said to her, "With God's help I will be back for the High Holidays."

Outside, Markel, his coachman, was waiting for him in a britska harnessed with two horses. Because he traveled so often, Reb Amram knew the prayer before embarking on a journey by heart. The maid, Reishe, brought him a basket of food, and Reb Amram rode off onto the highway which crossed the Prussian border into Leipzig. The journey was not without danger. Robbers lurked on the highways, as well as wild animals. The Poles and the Prussians constantly waged wars and minor battles. The customs officials harassed the traveling merchants, especially the Jews, who carried no swords and could not defend themselves. But, thank God, there was no mishap on this trip. They knew Reb Amram in the inns and prepared comfortable lodgings for him with strictly kosher meals. He always kept loose change—gratuities for the servants. Reb Amram had often visited Leipzig, but the city was never as full as this time. Traders had come not only from Germany and Poland but also from Russia, Italy, France—even from Spain, Portugal, and England. The inns were packed, foreign languages were heard. People could barely push their way through in the marketplace filled with covered wagons, carts, and carriages. Commodities were displayed which Reb Amram had never seen before. He was surrounded by lumber dealers and those who imported grain, flax, and hides from Poland. In addition to all the commotion, a traveling circus had come to town, with bears, lions, elephants, and horses, which were trained to dance to the sound of music. Despite high taxes and the vicious decrees imposed on them, the Jews engaged in many trades and had almost all the banks at their disposal. With letters of credit written in Hebrew or in Yiddish, they could borrow all the money they needed. The majority of Jewish bankers kept their capital in their pockets or in hollow belts strapped around their waists. The Jewish merchants lodged and ate together where everything was strictly kosher. Generally, the Gentile tradesmen got drunk toward evening, sang wild songs, and danced in the taverns with women. Leipzig attracted shady females who entertained the men. Prostitutes from all over came to the fairs. Although Reb Amram was a pious Jew, a man of the Torah, he somewhat envied the libertines who indulged all their passions. Alte Trina was always weak. Even on her clean days she had often dismissed him with various excuses: a headache, a toothache, a burning at the pit of the stomach, a chill in the bones. In her older years she became a broken shard. Reb Amram had entirely secluded himself from her, because no matter how he approached her, she immediately began to cry that he was hurting her. The evil spirit which lurks in each man and waits for him to become greedy for the pleasures of the flesh often chided Reb Amram: "Amram, you suffer needlessly. You wait for awards in the world to come, but they don't exist. What people don't grab for themselves in this world is lost forever. For almost two thousand years the Jews have anticipated the coming of their Messiah and He has still not arrived. They will go on waiting until the year 6000. There is no Paradise, no hell. The righteous do not feed on Leviathan, they don't drink the holy wine stored up for the saints, they don't wear crowns on their heads or enjoy the radiance of the Shechinah. They rot in their graves and are devoured by worms. The sinners are clever. As long as they can, they live it up." The Evil Spirit exhibited erudition: "If there was a hereafter, why is it not mentioned in the Bible? On the contrary, it is written in the Book of Ecclesiastes: 'But the dead know not any thing.' Even one of the Amorites denied the coming of the Messiah. Our ancient patriarchs—even Moses—were lecherous. Judah, whose name all Jews carry, went to a harlot."

Night fell. There was such a crush of people in the streets that Reb Amram could barely squeeze his way through. Music shrieked from taverns. The sounds of fiddles, trumpets, whistles could be heard as drummers drummed, hands clapped, feet stamped. The shouting of drunken males was mixed with salacious female laughter. From the open doors rose a heat like that from an oven and odors of wines, liquors, mead, beer, as well as from roasted chickens, geese, lamb, pork, all kinds of herbs and spices. Reb Amram had eaten a large dinner: chopped liver with onions, tripe, calves' feet, noodles with gravy, beef and horseradish, and later compote with plums and apricots. Nevertheless, the unkosher smells aroused a fresh appetite and a thirst in him. He sensed a mighty strength in his limbs. He felt he could wrench a tree out of the earth with all its roots. As he was passing an iron street lamp, a boyish need arose in him to show off and try to bend it. As he stood there contemplating his own prowess, a small woman with fiery red hair came over to him. She had green cat's eyes, a round face, and cheeks caked with rouge. She wore a short yellow dress and green high-heeled boots with black stockings. She gave him a sweet smile, revealing a full mouth of small teeth, and asked with a young voice, "Where are you from, buddy? From Poland?"

Reb Amram became so confused by her presence that for a moment he lost his tongue. Many whores had stopped him on his way, but they all spoke German, not Yiddish. He had heard that there were also Jewish whores in the big cities, but he had never encountered any. After a while he came to himself and answered, "Yes, from Poland."

"I am also from Poland," the woman said. "But I've been away for a long time."

"From where in Poland?" Reb Amram asked.

"From Piask."

"From the Piask thieves?" Reb Amram asked, and soon regretted his words. He feared she might curse him or spit at him. It was not in his nature to insult anyone. How do they say it? As long as a word is in the mouth, the mouth is the ruler; when it leaves the mouth, the word is the ruler. Thank God, the woman did not become enraged but answered him good-naturedly, "Not all Chelmites are fools and not all Piaskers are thieves. There are honest people in Piask, too."

"Forgive me, I was only joking," Reb Amram apologized.

"The truth is that there were a lot of thieves in Piask, but my father was an honest man, a tailor."

"How did you end up here?" Reb Amram asked.

The woman paused and then said, "It's a long story. I fell in love with a bear trainer—actually, not as much with him as with the bear. I was barely twelve years old, but I was already yearning to sow my wild oats. Both the bear trainer and the bear died a long time ago, but since then I have been dragging around with this circus. They pay me water on kasha so I have to earn a few extra gulden after the performance. The other women do it, too."

"Do you have a room here?" Reb Amram asked.

"I rent one for a few hours. Come."

She started to go, and Amram followed her with hesitation. He heard the Evil Spirit say, "There is no God, there is none. Even if there were a God, He would not remember every sin in every city at every fair in every land from India to Ethiopia. This whole game of piety is not worth a sniff of tobacco."

The woman led Reb Amram into a dark alley to a structure which looked like a stable and opened a door. A wick was burning in a shard with oil. A straw mat was spread on the floor.

"This is it?" Reb Amram asked.

"Yes. Two guldens!" And saying these words, the strumpet extended one hand for the money; with the other she opened her blouse quickly and displayed two stiff breasts with fiery red nipples. With one yank she tore open the buttons of her skirt and was mother-naked except for her shoes and gartered stockings. She did something like a somersault on the straw mat. "Come!" Reb Amram was about to throw himself on her, but at that moment he heard a terrible cry, "You are losing the world to come."

Reb Amram shuddered. He recognized the voice of his father, who had died over twenty years ago. Reb Amram started running, and he beat his head against the door. He almost tripped over the threshold. The woman screamed as if possessed, but Reb Amram ran through the darkness in a state of confusion and fear, as if he were being chased by murderers. The alley was full of potholes, stones, and unharnessed wagons. He crashed into the pole of a wagon, immediately receiving a bump on his forehead. His knee was scraped. He didn't know whether he was fleeing toward the residential area of Leipzig or to the outskirts of the city. He raised his eyes and the sky was seeded with myriads of stars. One star tore away from its constellation and swept over the sky, leaving behind a luminous trace. The heavens seemed ablaze with a divine conflagration.

As Reb Amram was running, he remembered the commentary of Gemara on the Joseph story in the Book of Genesis: When Potiphar's wife grabbed Joseph by the sleeve and requested that he lie with her, Joseph was ready to fall into depravity, but his father's image appeared and helped him resist the temptation. "The dead live!" a voice screamed into Reb Amram's ears or into his mind. "There is Special Providence. They see everything On High, every move a man is about to make, they read his mind, they weigh his deeds, they watch his steps."

Dogs barked at Reb Amram and tried to bite him, but he pushed them away with his boots, murmuring the words from the Pentateuch: "But against any of the children of Israel not even a dog will whet its tongue." Although he knew it was dangerous, he ran through the forest, where thieves and highwaymen loitered. They could have killed him there and no rooster would have crowed. He was escaping from a harlot, a demon, followed by the Angel of Death. His feet became strangely light. He skipped over fallen trees, puddles, heaps of garbage. The sweat ran over his face, cramps gnawed at his stomach, and he regurgitated a nauseating sour-sweet fluid. His belly blew up hard as a drum. In his distress it occurred to him that for the first time in his life he had forgotten to recite the afternoon prayer. He spoke aloud to the sacred soul of his demised father, thanked him for guarding him against the pitfall of lechery. He asked his father's spirit to protect him from robbers, since he was carrying the squire's money, and if he returned with empty hands, they would suspect him of theft.

Thank God, he managed to return to the city of Leipzig. Only now did he feel the pain in his forehead and in his knee. One of the dogs had bitten his leg and its teeth had torn through his pants. Reb Amram knew he was saved from many perils, those of the soul and of the body. He would have to recite the prayer for escaping danger twice and to redeem himself through much charity and many virtuous deeds. He arrived at the guesthouse where he was staying. The entrance was dark, but he heard talking and laughter from the kitchen and the chambers upstairs. What should he tell the owner of the guesthouse, the guests, his own coachman? They would see that something terrible had happened to him and ask questions. He was limping, his face was swollen, his boots were covered with horse dung and mud. He had to think up a lie quickly. Reb Amram recalled the saying from the *Ethics of the Fathers*: "One sin drags another sin after it." He stood in the darkness frightened by what had happened to him, baffled by his miraculous rescue, disgraced by his evil passions. He didn't dare to utter the name of the Lord with his defiled lips. He wasn't crying, but his eyes were burning and his cheeks were hot. He was on the verge of utter degradation and the fires of Gehenna.

2

Thank God, the trip back to Poland went without any mishap. Reb Amram brought back everything the squire and squiress had ordered, along with lumber contracts and a considerable amount of down payments. He had written down every groschen he had spent in his book. After the squire and the squiress thanked Reb Amram profusely for his diligence and good judgment in business, the squire and Reb Amram went into a separate room. Taking out heaps of golden ducats from his belt and various pockets, Reb Amram began to count the money.

He had kept the bank notes and contracts in an oak box with brass fasteners and a steel lock. As always, he hoped the accounts would balance out to the last penny. But strangely, five golden ducats were missing from one account. "How is this possible?" Reb Amram asked himself. The squire, who trusted Reb Amram explicitly, dismissed the matter with a wave of the hand. He insisted that Reb Amram surely forgot to write down some small expense. When he remembered it, the account would straighten itself out. Reb Amram offered to give the squire the missing ducats from his own purse, but the squire refused to hear of it. He argued, "It doesn't pay to be so concerned over such a petty sum." The squire was familiar not only with the New Testament but also with the Old Testament, and he quoted the words Ephron said to Abraham when he bought the Cave of Machpelah from him: "What are four hundred silver shekels between you and me?"

Reb Amram promised not to worry about it, but when he went back home, his spirit remained troubled, partly from the ordeal with the lewd female and partly because of the lost ducats. He sat up half the night and made calculations. He remembered every groschen he had spent in Leipzig, even the alms he had distributed among the beggars in the marketplace. But these five ducats seemed to have slipped between his fingers. Had somebody robbed him? Did the Piask trollop steal them? He was sure she had not stood so close to him that she could put her hand into his pocket. While pondering the lost ducats, he realized he had forgotten to bring his wife, Alte Trina, a gift, as he always did when he returned from a journey. She had not mentioned a word about it, but he imagined that she greeted him less warmly than usual when he came home. He had also neglected to bring a gift to the maid.

Reb Amram awoke in the middle of the night and lay awake until daybreak. While undressing, he had discovered a knot in the sash of his pants. He often made such a knot as a reminder to pay a bill, to answer a letter, or to give money to a needy charity. It had slipped his memory when, and for what reason, he had made this particular knot. He fell asleep at dawn, and the Piask woman came to him in a dream. She stood before him naked, her red hair loose, and she was singing a song which he had once heard in a tavern:

Oy vey, give me tea.
Tea is bitter—
Give me sugar.
Sugar is sweet—
Give me feet.
Feet are wet—
Come in bed.
In bed no sheet—
Come in street.
The street is dark—
Come in park.
In park no light—
Hold me tight.
In mud and mire
Burn like fire.

Reb Amram awoke with a start and with passion. The month of Elul was approaching, but he was wallowing in lewd fantasies. "Woe is me, I am sunk in iniquities," he mumbled. Normally Reb Amram waited impatiently for the Days of Awe to recite the morning prayers at the pulpit at the synagogue, dressed for the occasion in a white robe and a gold-embossed miter. Weeks before, he usually went over the tunes and the liturgies and practiced on the shofar, which he would blow. But now Reb Amram no longer yearned to lead the community in prayer. None other than Poorah, the Angel of Forgetfulness, must have accompanied him that fatal evening when he encountered the harlot in Leipzig. He could not even remember the explanation he offered the people at the inn for the bump on his forehead and for his torn trousers and filthy boots. And what should he tell the squire about the missing five ducats? Although Reb Amram was prepared to repay him from his own money, the danger of being disgraced was far from over. It was possible that the coachman had already relayed the strange event to the squire. Gossip travels quickly. Reb Amram did not want to contradict himself and be labeled a liar.

He fell asleep, and immediately the red-haired female appeared anew. He saw her descend the stairs of the Plotsk ritual bathhouse. She immersed herself three times, and her hair spread over the water like a red web. She began to climb out, winking at Reb Amram. "What happened?" Reb Amram asked himself. "Have I married her and she is making her ablutions? Is she cleansing herself for my sake? And where is Alte Trina? Is she, God forbid, no longer among the living?" He shuddered and awoke. "This female is one of Lilith's demons, whom she sends at night to seduce God-fearing men to pollution," Reb Amram said to himself. "I must not lead the congregation in prayer any longer. The prayers from one such as I will not reach up to heaven. They might even, perish the thought, bring evil decrees on the town—pestilence, famine, bloodshed." Reb Amram felt compelled to give the trustees of the synagogue advance notice to find a replacement.

As in the Book of Job, one evil tiding followed another. That morning after Reb Amram woke up from his troubled sleep, even before he went to pray, he heard the sound of a horseman approaching his house. It was a messenger informing Reb Amram that the squire had sent for him. Reb Amram was shaken up. Who knows, maybe the coachman saw him with the wanton female and reported it to the squire. Even though the squire was himself guilty of adultery, he probably expected right conduct from his subordinates. "*Nu*, my seven good years are over," Reb Amram murmured to himself. He let the britska be harnessed and went to the squire. Thank God, the squire received him in a friendly way. Reb Amram began to speak about the vanished gold ducats, but the squire interrupted him.

"Don't be foolish, Amram, what are five ducats to me? I trust my entire estate to you and you make a fuss over a pittance. If it had been a matter of a thousand ducats, I would not worry. I have sent for you because I have to ask you a favor."

"The squire wants a favor from me?" Reb Amram asked in astonishment.

"Yes. A big favor. I find it distasteful to request this of you, but I have no choice. A few days ago I met with my future in-laws, Count Zamoyski and his wife, the countess. You certainly know how influential they are in Poland and what a great honor it is for my wife and me to marry off our beloved daughter to their son. The countess stems from an even higher lineage than her husband. She is a descendant of a king of Poland. As you know, we are preparing for a wedding which will not be equaled in the history of Poland. The count told me that his court Jew, Reb Nissel, who is learned in the Bible and in the Talmud and is an experienced merchant to boot, is also a talented actor. Whenever the Zamoyskis give a ball, Reb Nissel disguises himself as a bear and amuses the guests. I had told him about you and I praised you to heaven. The count mentioned in passing, 'If your Amram is as clever and as witty as my Nissel, why don't they perform together at the wedding of our children and entertain us?' I tried to explain to the count that you are of a different breed, that it is beneath your dignity to act as a comedian. I told him that I have never requested a service like this from you. But the count became adamant about the idea. He literally demanded that you perform with his court Jew. This is how the Zamoyskis are: strong-willed and adventurous. They could always have anything under the sun. No one has ever refused them anything. I will make it short. I was practically forced to promise the count that I would ask you to consent. I assure you that this will be the first and last time. I have persuaded the count to agree that Reb Nissel will perform the role of the bear and you will be the bear trainer. You can lead Reb Nissel by a rope and converse intermittently. All the high-class guests will admire your facetious dialogue. I know that you are familiar with Jewish humor and wit. It is not such a shame to play the role of a bear trainer. I promise you that if you ever need a favor from me, no matter how great, I will do it for you with pleasure."

As the squire spoke, Reb Amram felt as if a fist clutched at his heart and crushed it with a mighty force. Reb Amram knew that some court Jews performed at squires' balls and made the guests merry, but he never wanted to stoop to that level. Reb Amram realized that this request of the squire's was a punishment from heaven for dallying with the redheaded whore even for a few minutes. He felt like crying out, "Your Excellency, everything yes, but this is too much of a blow." Instead, he asked, "When will the wedding take place?"

The squire told him the date. Reb Amram quickly figured out that the wedding would fall on the first day of Succoth. While other Jews were sitting in the Succoth under the wings of the Shechinah, being hosts to the souls of such saints as Abraham, Isaac, and Jacob, Aaron, Moses, and David, he, Amram, would be leading another Jew dressed up like a bear, and making a mockery of himself and of the scholarly Reb Nissel before a band of murderers and pagans. What in essence were all these squires? How did they manage to rule the land if not by the power of the sword alone? How did they reduce all the peasants to slavery and force the people of Israel, whom God had chosen above all other nations, to become their underlings?

"What is your answer?" the squire asked with a trace of impatience.

"If I am able to, I will do it," Reb Amram answered.

"Why should you not be able to?"

"Everything is in God's hands."

For a while they were both silent. Afterward, the squire said, "I understand very well how difficult this task is for you at your age and in your position. But I am afraid of opposing this powerful family. Today they are my friends, tomorrow my bloody enemies."

"Yes, true."

"You seem tired, Reb Amram. Go home and rest."

"Yes, I will do so. Thank you, Your Excellency."

"Why does God allow people to tyrannize over one another? What does your Talmud say about this?" the squire asked.

Reb Amram thought it over. "Everything is created so that people can choose between good and evil."

"Not always," said the squire, and made a gesture which meant that the audience was over.

Returning home, Reb Amram saw Alte Trina sitting on the bench in front of the house knitting a sock. He was surprised, since she seldom sat on the bench outside at this time of the day but was usually busy in the kitchen preparing a meal. He looked at her for a while. They already had grandchildren together, but it seemed to him that only yesterday he and his wife were still young. In those years he could barely wait for her to go to the ritual bath so that he might approach her. Now she was an old woman, her face withered and wrinkled. A few white hairs had sprouted under her chin, a little female beard. With the knitting needle she scratched her earlobe, which protruded from her bonnet, and asked, "What did the squire want with you? Why did he send for you so early in the morning? I worried myself sick over your safety."

"Nothing, Alte Trina. It had to do with his daughter's wedding."

"What does he want now?"

"Oh, something about the jewelry which I had bought for her."

"How many trinkets do they need? She will be bedecked with gold and diamonds from head to toe. They forget, the fools, that people don't live forever. You look pale, Amram. This trip has exhausted you." Alte Trina changed her tone.

"No danger."

"Why did you run there so early? You hadn't even prayed."

"If the squire sends a courier, you can't keep him waiting."

"I will give you a glass of milk. This, one is allowed to drink before praying."

"No, Alte Trina. Let me first put on my prayer shawl and phylacteries."

"Amram, wait, I must have a word with you."

"What do you want?"

Alte Trina brought over a chair and made Reb Amram sit down. "Amram, maybe I shouldn't say this, but you are traveling down a crooked path. If a stranger said this, you might suspect him of being your enemy, but I am your wife, the mother of your children, and I want only the best for you. Believe me, if someone asked me to lay down my head for your sake, I would gladly do it."

"Speak clearly. What am I doing that is wrong?"

"First of all, you work too hard. A man of your age—you should live to be a hundred and twenty—doesn't need to drag himself off to fairs in distant lands. You know very well that the roads are teeming with thieves and assassins. Does it pay to risk one's health so that some shiksa can dangle her jewelry before an impudent idolator? Recently I heard that Count Zamoyski was hunting during the harvest season along with a band of noblemen. Their horses and dogs trampled and ruined hundreds of acres of fields ready for the harvest, and when the peasants pleaded with the villains not to turn God's blessings into a shambles and bring famine to the villages, they fell into such a rage that they shot off their pistols and killed a number of them. Imagine, Amram, it is their peasants, their estates, but these drunkards think they are entitled to do anything they please. People have told me that the young count set fire to stacks of wheat which had been prepared for the threshers. Your squire is planning a wedding which will cost him a fortune. He is already in debt over his head. The end will be that he will go broke. And when they get into trouble, they come to borrow from the Jew. Then if you don't give it to them willingly, they take it by force."

"For the time being, our squire is not to blame," Reb Amram said.

"This is one thing," Alte Trina went on. "Second, you had told me that, God willing, after we gave away our youngest child, we would put all business aside and devote ourselves only to Jewishness. You even mentioned going to the Holy Land."

"To the Holy Land? Old people go there, not people our age. I don't remember saying that."

"You don't remember, but I do. And God certainly remembers."

Reb Amram had a desire to scold her, as always when she interfered too much in his affairs, but he recalled the squire's humiliating proposal to him and restrained himself. He shrugged. "Alte Trina, we'll talk about this later."

"Again later?"

"Let me finish the prayers first."

Reb Amram entered the room where he kept his bookcases and prepared himself for prayer. He put on the prayer shawl and the phylacteries, wound the thongs around his arm, and began to murmur the appropriate prayers. But he was distracted by confusing thoughts and he prayed without concentration. He even overlooked certain verses. To become a buffoon for the squire's sake? Lead Reb Nissel by a rope and crack jokes? Reb Amram stood up to recite the Eighteen Benedictions, but he omitted some passages and others he repeated. He resorted to addressing God in Yiddish: "Father in heaven, I am in a terrible predicament. Save me or take me away."

Reb Amram then realized that prayer of this nature is a sin. A human being has no right to dictate to the Almighty or to admonish Him. After a while, he took off the prayer shawl and the phylacteries. A great fatigue had come over him, and he felt a weakness in his knees. He locked the door which led to the corridor, collapsed onto the sofa, and fell into a deep sleep. As if the lord of dreams could scarcely wait for Reb Amram to fall asleep, he immediately brought him to Leipzig. It was again night, and he was standing with the redheaded harlot by a lamp post. Again, the Evil One cajoled him to damnation. This time Reb Amram saw Satan's fiendish image: taller than the lamp post, dark and sheer as a spiderweb, with horns like a he-goat, two holes instead of eyes, with the mouth of a frog. He whispered to Reb Amram, "Take her, the whore. Go into her. Have no fear. There is no law below, there is no judge above. And even if there were a God somewhere in the Seventh Heaven, He would not remember all the petty prohibitions, all the silly restrictions and interpretations from the times of Moses until some half-witted rabbi in a muddy village."

In his dream, Reb Amram followed the harlot, who led him into the dark hallway and opened the door of the murky shed. A wick burned in the shard with oil, a straw mat lay on the floor. The whore threw down the colorful rags and called out, "Two gulden. Come!" Reb Amram again heard his father's cry: "You are losing the world to come!" He started to run, and as he ran, he pushed his hand into his pocket and threw a handful of gold coins to the raging harlot. Reb Amram woke up instantly. The hand which threw the coins was still shaking, and his feet were scampering as if running. For a moment Reb Amram took the dream for reality. He was both in the study where he had prayed and in the shed with the whore. He fell on the floor, his teeth chattering. He lingered a while until he could fully grasp where he was. In all his anxiety Reb Amram realized that the dream had solved his riddle. In his consternation he had taken the harlot's fee from the pocket where he kept the squire's money. He had forgotten this, but the pocket, a little piece of lining fabric, had remembered and computed the balance accordingly—a silent witness that could testify against him on the Day of Judgment. Reb Amram felt like laughing and crying. If a pocket is able to remember, what about the Almighty, of whom it is said: "There is no forgetfulness before Thy Throne of Glory."

"Merciful God, have pity on me," Reb Amram called out. "My Father in Paradise, you are not dead, you live. Your sacred soul protected me in Leipzig. You hovered over me, kept a vigil during the entire journey, guarded my every step, and did not allow me to fall into the net of debauchery, to sink to the lowest abyss. There is a God, there is. There is a hereafter, there is," Reb Amram shouted in his mind to Satan the spoiler. "How could I have forgotten all this, and let myself go with a prostitute, about which King Solomon says, 'None that go unto her return again, neither take they hold of the paths of life.' God sees and the saints see and there is no death, there is none!"

Somebody knocked at the door—Alte Trina. How strange, but the moment he saw her, he also recalled the meaning of the knot in his sash: to buy for her the new edition of *Tzenah u-Reenah,* the Yiddish translation of the Pentateuch and its commentaries, since the binding of her old volume was torn and some pages had fallen out.

That day Reb Amram sent back the five gold coins to the squire by messenger. Later, he told the elders of the community that he was sick to his stomach and must see a doctor in Warsaw. In case, God forbid, he didn't recover, they would have to find another leader for the morning prayers on the High Holidays and another man to blow the shofar. He harnessed the britska himself, took Alte Trina with him, and left only Reishe, the maid, at home. He gave her a large sum of money to cover all her expenses in case of a long absence.

Reb Amram did not come back for the High Holidays. He never returned to Plotsk. After some time his sons and daughters came to town and brought a letter from their father saying that he was giving his house and his books to preachers and talmudic scholars who came to the city. Reb Amram's sons and daughters brought additional money for Markel the coachman, for Reishe the maid, as well as a letter signed by Alte Trina which transferred ownership of her clothing and utensils to Reishe.

The wedding between Count Zamoyski's son and Walecki's daughter never came to pass. A few days before the wedding the young count went hunting in the forest, and one of the hunters mistook him for an animal and shot him dead. Walecki's daughter, the bride, fell into melancholia after this dismal event and decided to enter a cloister.

Nobody heard from Reb Amram for over two years. Some believed that he was still visiting important doctors and healers in far-off cities. Others concluded that Reb Amram and his wife were no longer among the living. One day a rabbinical messenger from Jerusalem arrived in Plotsk and brought a letter from Reb Amram. Reb Amram wrote that after many months of wanderings and tribulations he and his wife miraculously managed to arrive by ship in the Land of Israel. They found a place to live in Jerusalem. From the money which he saved and which Alte Trina had received from selling her jewelry, they now could afford to devote their old years to Jewishness. He now studied the Mishnah in the studyhouse of Rabbi Yehuda the Hasid, and recited psalms at the Wailing Wall in the corner where the Shechinah has always been present. In the month of Elul, he and Alte Trina visited the graves of Mother Rachel, Rabbi Simon son of Yochai, and other saints. They traveled to the city of Safad, and he immersed himself in the ritual bath of the holy Isaac Luria. The sky in the Land of Israel is higher than in other countries, the stars are brighter, and the air is as clear as crystal and as sweet as wine. Reb Amram asked the townspeople of Plotsk to help this messenger collect money for a yeshiva, because in heaven are kept records of every groschen contributed to charity or, God forbid, used as means of transgression. He ended the letter with the puzzling words: "A man forgets, but his pocket remembers."

Translated by Deborah Menashe

The Secret

She was a tiny old woman with freshly dyed black hair, a little wrinkled face, and black eyes which gleamed with a youthful zeal. She leaned on a cane, gave me a coquettish smile, and revealed a mouthful of small false teeth. Her Yiddish was rich with all the mannerisms and intonations of the Lublin region. She was saying, "I read every word you write. I never miss your advice on the radio. I've been trying to contact you for weeks, but you're impossible to reach on the telephone. Where do you run around to the whole day? Excuse me for being so familiar with you. You don't know me, but I know you like a brother."

I thanked her and offered her a seat. She handed me her cane and I stood it in a corner. The seat was too high for her, so I put a telephone book at her feet to serve as a footstool. She said, "You are looking at an old woman, but how long has it been since I've been young? In one of your articles you mentioned a poet—I have forgotten his name—who said, 'Old people die young.' Golden words. This old person who sits before you will die a young girl. The soul does not age. In a way my memory becomes younger from day to day. What happened yesterday I forget, but things which occurred sixty years ago linger before my eyes. I have an unbelievable story for you. A story like this happens once in a thousand years."

"Do you want to tell me a story, or seek advice?" I asked.

"Both. But you must be patient."

"Do me a favor and make it short," I said.

"Short, huh? How can someone make fifty or sixty years short. But I will try. I am not just a nobody. My father was a scribe. He transcribed Torah scrolls, phylacteries, mezuzahs, and we girls—we were four daughters and one son—tried to copy his script, not on parchment, but on paper. I whittled the goose-feather quills for him and lined the parchment sheets. Our mother was a learned woman and she taught us the Bible. I could sit with you seven days and seven nights and still not tell a fraction of what I lived through, but today people have no patience. I also was quick when I was young. What's the rush now? I won't be late for the grave.

"Our father, Reb Moshe the scribe, as he was called, was a saintly Jew. His father, Reb Yerucham—also a scribe—was of such piety that before he transcribed a holy name he went to the ritual bath. In certain sections of the Pentateuch, God's name is mentioned in every line, and he went from the parchment scroll to the ritual bath and back to the parchment scroll. It took him twenty years to transcribe a complete Torah scroll and weeks to write sections of the phylacteries. He and his family would have died from hunger, but our grandmother Tirtza Perl had a small store. She was married at fourteen and had seventeen children in her lifetime. I remember her being pregnant even when she was a grandmother. She and my mother always went around with bellies. Of the seventeen children my grandmother bore, eleven died. This grandmother was the type of housewife one doesn't find in our time. She worked in the store, cooked, baked, did the wash, and even chopped wood if necessary. She prepared for the Passover while carrying a child in her arms. I will never understand where these people found the strength. That was my maternal grandmother; the other grandmother died young.

"Being the oldest, I had to help my mother carry the burden of raising the younger children. There was no time to develop friendships. I was an ardent reader of literature. My brother Shmuel Chaim had secretly read Isaac Meir Dick and Mendele Mocher Sephorim, and along with older boys had subscribed to a Yiddish newspaper from Warsaw; I read it, too. Here in America I read your works and I know that you understand the human soul. I want to tell you something that I never told anyone before. I was secretly very passionate and I began to think about love very very early. I understood a great deal but I didn't want to worry my parents. We sisters read Shomer's novels. There was a maid in our town, the daughter of a watercarrier, who was impregnated by a Cossack. There were many Cossacks in the village and they often went to a nearby brothel behind the Russian cemetery. Boys went there in the dark when the moon wasn't shining. There were nights when I would lie awake and break out in a cold sweat musing about these things.

"In America people have forgotten what went on in the old country. The younger generation doesn't know how good they have it here. Every year after the Feast of Tabernacles, an epidemic spread through the town. We had a gravedigger who was nicknamed Gehenna's Beadle. When the little children began to die, he went and collected the corpses, wrapped each one in a piece of linen from a torn bedsheet or a shirt, and buried them himself. I'm sorry to say it, but he was a drunkard like all the members of the Burial Society. On the way to the cemetery he used to stop off at the tavern. Once, he left a sack of tiny bodies on a bench. There was such a hue and outcry in the town that he was dismissed.

"Both my parents died before their time, within the same year. After they passed away, the younger children, our brother Shmuel Chaim, and my three sisters scattered in all directions. One went to serve as a maid in Lublin, another married a Litvak who took her to Russia. Eventually Shmuel Chaim ended up in America. They are no longer among the living. Look at what I've become—a broken shard. I was once a pretty girl. In those times a girl had to have a dowry. My aunt Chaye Gutshe had taken responsibility for me. When people proposed a match for me, she went to examine the man. My dear writer, she married me off to a tailor—a widower who was over forty years my senior, a father and grandfather. He already had a gray beard when we stood under the wedding canopy. I thought to myself, He's a man, it's better than having nobody. I'd rather not mention his name or the town we came from. When you hear the whole story you will understand why.

"We married. He was a pious Jew, a decent man, but nothing else. I had hoped to have a child, even a few children, but a number of years passed and I did not become pregnant. With us Jews, what is a woman worth without children? The thought that I was a barren woman, or wombless, as they say, was a blow. Perhaps my husband became sterile in his old age."

"A man doesn't become sterile in his old age," I said. "He may only become impotent."

"Huh? This he was not. But he was nothing to rave about, either. He waited for me to go to the ritual bath every month and only then did he come to me. He was a men's tailor and mostly made long gaberdines. He was unusually observant. Six o'clock in the morning he went to pray. They made him a trustee in the small tailors' shul. He also led the congregation in prayer. His only worry was that my matron's wig would slip somewhat and men would see my hair and fall into sinful thoughts. His one worker was also an elderly man. I cooked for both men and carried water from the well. My life was as good as over, but I made peace with it. My husband constantly spoke of saving money. In order to live honestly, one must always have something saved for hard times. We saved what we could. I was only a spendthrift when it came to books. When a book peddler came to town I bought whatever was available in Yiddish: storybooks, a novel by Isaac Meir Dick, Solomon Ettinger, Mendele Mocher Sephorim, Sholem Aleichem, Peretz, Sholem Asch. A small Yiddish library was established in our village and I could secretly get books there. My husband spat on worldly books, calling them heretical. But reading was the only pleasure left to me. My brother Shmuel Chaim sometimes sent me books from America: Zeyfert, Shomer, Kubrin, Libin. I cannot describe the satisfaction I got from reading these books. They literally saved my life.

"Now the real story begins. Once, my husband brought home an apprentice called Motke. He was a boy of thirteen from a nearby shtetl. I say thirteen because I remember when he put on phylacteries for his bar mitzvah. The other tailors kept their apprentices like slaves. They ran errands, brought water from the pump, poured out the slop pail, and rocked babies in their cradles. These boys were given only food and a night's lodging on top of the stove. The contract was signed by the boy's father, or by a relative if he was an orphan. Many tailors cheated the boys. Months went by before they taught them to cut out a hole or sew on a button.

"Motke was an orphan and I don't remember whether my husband wrote out a contract for him or simply made a verbal agreement. My husband was honest and immediately began teaching Motke the trade. This Motke was clever and had golden hands. He grasped everything quickly, and my husband praised him to heaven. What did he look like? He was dark with black eyes, clever, with a sense of humor like none other in the world. Little jokes poured out of him. He could read and soon indulged in my books.

"My husband always protected him, warned me not to overwork the boy or take advantage of him, God forbid. Who wanted to take advantage? I cooked the meals he liked and treated him like an only son. He said that I was like a mother and my husband like a father to him. The other tailors complained that we pampered him, and that if other apprentices heard of the comfort he enjoyed with us, they would rebel and demand higher wages.

"Times were changing. Strikes had begun in Russia. Workers were beginning to revolt, carrying revolvers and throwing bombs. The Tsar had been murdered only a few years earlier. We were a little town in the hinterland, but there were already those youths who sought equality for all. They met in the woods after the Sabbath meal and organized what they called a circle. A few apprentices secretly joined the group but Motke said he would never join. How could he complain when we provided him with the best of everything? He made fun of their petitions to the government and revolutionary proclamations. He boasted that when he learned the trade he would himself become an employer. He wanted to be a ladies' tailor, to sew jackets and dresses for pretty girls, not gaberdines for Hasidim. He was a big talker."

"You fell in love with him, huh?" I asked.

The old woman was quiet for a long while. "One should not eat kugel with you," she said.

"Why not?"

"Because you grasp things too quickly. Yes, you are right. I saw that he looked at me constantly. Once in a while he stole a kiss. I pleaded with him not to, but he listened to me like Haman listens to the grocer. He was ready to sow his wild oats. He often behaved like a fully ripe man. I considered telling my husband, who surely would have chased him out in disgrace, but I had grown attached to him. My dear man, since you are guessing things, what's the use of trying to deny them? Yes, he became my lover."

"When did it happen? How?"

"One summer, on a Sabbath. It could never have happened in the middle of the week, since my husband worked at home. But on Sabbath afternoons he used to go with the tailors' group to study the *Ethics of the Fathers*. Later, the congregation recited the evening prayer and ate the third meal, which consisted of stale challah and herring. Afterward they recited the Havdalah and sang valedictory songs. By the time he came home, it was already late in the evening. I used to read in bed after the Sabbath meal. That day I had fallen into a deep sleep. I opened my eyes and Motke was lying beside me in bed. I wanted to scream in alarm, but he closed my mouth with his hand like an experienced rascal. This was a devil, not an apprentice."

"Is this the whole story?" I asked.

"Just the beginning."

•

We sat in silence for a long while. It seemed to me the old woman's face had become younger and less wrinkled. Something of a smile appeared in her eyes. Only her head, with its black hair—dulled from the dye—trembled like an old woman's.

Then she said, "It happened and it's too late for regret now. I acted like a mother, but he treated me like a wife. At times our conduct seemed utterly sinful and ugly to me—a humiliation beyond words to me and to my parents in Paradise. He also had parents in the other world and I felt terribly degraded before them, too. I tried with all my power to drive him away, but he wouldn't hear of it. Although nobody visited us during the day on the Sabbath, still, what would I have done had the door opened and someone come in? I would have died on the spot. How I wish this had really happened, because what followed was worse than death."

"You became pregnant, huh?"

The woman's face became harsh and hostile. "God in heaven, I'm afraid of you! What are you? A mind reader?"

"I simply understand."

"Yes, it happened. But not immediately. He remained with us over two years. I had gotten so accustomed to him that I could no longer live without him. The entire week I looked forward to the Sabbath. A holy day, and I defiled it with such abominations. In the meantime, he became taller, broader, a real man. I cannot describe how good he was at tailoring, how adept at sewing on the machine which we later acquired. He helped my husband cut out material and take measurements. He held a piece of chalk in his hand and did everything with speed and precision like a master tailor. The tailors became my husband's blood enemies. It was against the rules to train an apprentice so quickly. Their notions dated back to King Sobieski's time—to keep an apprentice for three years without pay and afterward begin paying him half a ruble a month. I will make it short. The day Motke said that he was planning to leave and go to Warsaw, I knew I had lost him. For me this was a black day.

"Where was I, eh? Yes, said and done. My husband tried to talk Motke into staying with us, but with him a word was a deed. I yearned for him. The weekdays were still bearable, but when the Sabbath came I felt the pain. He promised to send a card, but it never arrived. This is what men are, egotists, young and old. Excuse me for speaking this way about your gender. It is not their fault, it's their nature. Weeks passed, months. Suddenly it dawned on me that I hadn't gotten my period, or the 'holidy,' as we called it, for some time. When this occurred, I knew I was going to become a mother and who the father was."

"How could you have known?" I asked. "You lived with two men."

"I knew. Normally I would have rejoiced at becoming a mother. My aunt always said, 'A wife without children is like a tree without fruit.' But to have a child out of wedlock, and with a young boy at that, was a sin God would not forgive and a woman, unless she is a whore, cannot bear. I seriously considered suicide, but I could not bring myself to do it. I had compassion for my husband, who became helpless after Motke left. His old age descended on him suddenly. He seemed sick to me. He had become half deaf and I had to repeat every word I said to him. He had difficulty threading a needle. His customers began to complain that their gaberdines were too long, too short, too narrow. You should excuse my frankness, but he made a pair of pants and the crotch came out too high or too low. In the middle of all this, I had to tell him the news that I was pregnant. He was a devout Jew and he took it as a gift from God, but I could see very well that he didn't feel this way. Who wants to become a father in his old age? Nobody, God forbid, suspected anything. In that time such a disgrace never happened, even among the lowest. What a crime to deliver a bastard to a husband! God in heaven, my days were hell, and at night I shook in bed as if in a fever. I begged God to let me miscarry. I had heard that if you drank vinegar or jumped off a table, a miscarriage would follow. I tried this at every opportunity, but to no avail. It was already too late. The baby was a girl. Usually people want a boy, but in this situation it's better to have a girl: she can get married and no longer carries and defiles her father's name.

"My husband lived only four years after her birth, and he loved her more than his other children. I know what you want to ask: 'How could I be sure who the father was?' From the beginning I knew, because my heart told me so. After she was born, I didn't need to rely on my heart: she looked exactly like Motke—his eyes, his ears, the shape of his mouth. I shuddered with fear that people would notice the resemblance and there would be a terrible scandal. But, thank God, no one suspected anything. Only I, the debased mother, could see the bitter truth."

"How old is your daughter?" I asked.

The woman was taken aback. "What? She is forty-five years old, but you wouldn't take her for more than thirty. A beauty, and educated as well. She is a teacher of mathematics in a high school, and they wanted to make her a professor in a college."

"When did you come to America?" I asked.

"Thirty-seven years ago, a few years before Hitler's slaughter. My brother Shmuel Chaim, or Sam as they called him here, saved me. He had become rich in America and sent me an affidavit. When I came here, he was better to me than a father."

"Is your daughter married?"

"Was. Twice. She is divorced."

"And did you marry again?"

"Yes, also twice, here in America. Both my husbands died. With one I lived only two years. With the other I lived thirteen years and he was close to ninety when he died. He left me a lot of money, but what good is money to me at this age? It is all for my daughter."

"Is that everything?"

"Wait, my dear man, this is still not the main thing I wanted to tell you. As I said, what happened to me can only happen once in a thousand years, or possibly a million."

"What happened to you?"

The old woman did not answer. Her lips quivered. She tried to speak, but she choked on the words. Finally she cried out, "My daughter lives with her father! He is her lover. They are planning to marry!"

Some time passed before the woman found her tongue. She looked at me with wrath, as if I were somehow to blame. She called out, "I alone am the cause of this abomination! Only I. Nobody else!"

"Your daughter . . ."

The old woman interrupted me. "She knew nothing and knows nothing. I had mentioned to her that we once had an apprentice, Motke, and that's all she ever knew. She came to America with me when she was still a young girl. She didn't know a word of English. I sent her to school. My brother, may he rest in peace, helped me, and she immediately took to her studies. She was the best student in her class, and it continued in this way every year. She finished high school at seventeen. She remembered my husband as her father. She had a fantastic memory, and what she couldn't remember, she asked about. She wanted to know every detail about him. Such love from a child to a father, who died somewhere in the old country before she was even five years old, always struck me as strange. Here in America children have little feeling for immigrant parents, especially if they are brought up without a father. But Sylvia—this is the American name my brother gave her, her real name is Sarah Leah—often investigated and questioned me. We had only one photograph from his Polish passport and she persuaded me to make a large portrait from it. This she framed and hung over her bed. I didn't want to talk about him too much and I didn't actually have that much to tell, but she simply exhausted me with her inquiries, year in, year out. When I remarried, she was angry with me; when

I married again, she became my enemy. What could I do? In the old country I was dead. Here I came back to life. I went to night school and learned English. I went to the Yiddish theater and later to the English theater as well. I loved my child more than my own life, but she had waged war with me and I knew this was a punishment from God. We had relatives, all living in Brooklyn. I once had a job with Abraham & Straus —I became their first saleslady. When I married the second time and gave up my job, they made a banquet for me.

"Now about my daughter. She is clever, pretty, educated. She resembles her father—her real father—like two drops of water. But she had no luck with men. She was married twice and it was wrong both times. Neither of these men wanted children. She was dying to have a child, but it was just her bad luck that men were always coarse with her, even brutal. My dear man, there is a lot to tell. At times I thought that her body was from her real father and her soul was from my first husband. You frequently write about dybbuks, mysterious things. Can it be that my first husband's soul entered her after his death?"

"Everything is possible."

"Ah, the world is full of secrets. I have to tell you something which has to do with your writing. When I came to America, I began to read the *Forward* and this opened up the world to me. I was hospitalized twice, and my daughter had to bring the *Forward* to me every day. She also learned to read Yiddish and wrote an essay on Yiddish literature in college. My daughter listens to you on the radio and . . ."

"When and how did you meet Motke?" I asked.

"It happened suddenly, like all misfortunes. We were shopping for bargains on Orchard Street at the pushcarts. We didn't find what we were looking for, but we got hungry and went for supper on Second Avenue at Rappaport's restaurant.

After we had been sitting and eating a while, a man approached our table. He was tall, well dressed. He came over and said, 'Ladies, excuse me, but I must ask you something.'

" 'What do you want to ask?' I said. And he asked, 'Aren't you from . . .' and he mentioned the name of our town.

"In New York we have a landsman society, a cemetery, and all the rest of it. But for some reason I never joined. God should not punish me, but I hid from our landsmen. Many of my acquaintances had died and the younger generation perished with the Nazis. My two husbands here were Litvaks and they were members of their own societies. When the man mentioned the name of our town, I wanted to say no, but I am not a liar by nature and answered yes. My daughter became all ears. She often confronted me about avoiding my landsmen. For her it was a sign that I was trying to forget her father. The man told me he came to America many years ago and became a rich garment manufacturer here. His wife died of cancer. I will tell you something and you won't believe me. I took one look at him and at my daughter and I knew that I had fallen into a trap from which one cannot emerge."

"Why didn't you tell Sylvia that he was her father?" I asked.

"Because I knew then, and I know to this day, that she would never have forgiven me for having deceived her. It would have been her death," the old woman answered. "I fear God, but I didn't want to lose my daughter."

"Why didn't it occur to him, since she resembles him so much?" I asked.

The old woman did not answer. She lowered her head and was silent. Then she said, "Who knows if it occurred to him or not? He made it clear to me that very night that he was an atheist. When my daughter was washing her hands in the ladies' room, I made him swear to me that he would never say a word to her about what had passed between us, and he promised me. He took the whole thing lightly. He sat with us three hours and talked only about his successes in business and with women. He had a son from a previous wife. He had a house on Long Island and an apartment on West End Avenue. People knew him well in Rappaport's, they even called him to the telephone. He wouldn't let us pay for supper and left a big tip. He made a date with my daughter on the spot. When we entered the restaurant, my daughter seemed tired, pale, and old for her age. But when he drove us home to Brooklyn in his Cadillac, my daughter looked and spoke like a young girl. A mother understands such things. It was, as they say, love at first sight. She sat next to him in the front, and I sat in the back and saw how he drove the car with his left hand. His right hand he had on her lap. She turned her head to me and said out loud, 'Mama, I found my father.'

"Those were her words. She didn't know that she was speaking the truth. My heart tightened as if a fist had clamped down on it with all its strength. I thought my end had come. But those who want to live, die, and those who want to die often live to be a hundred years."

"My dear lady, with such problems one goes to a rabbi or to a psychiatrist, not to a writer," I said. "You know yourself that I cannot help you."

"Yes, I know. But who can help me? I had one comfort: she was already too old to have children. At least she would not give birth to a bastard. But lately she began to say that she is prepared to risk everything in order to become pregnant. I have only one hope, that I will not live through the shame and the degradation."

"The world is full of illegitimate children," I said.

"Not from a father with his own daughter. People didn't commit such iniquities even in the time of the Flood," the old woman said.

She made a gesture as if to leave, and I brought her the cane. She leaned on it heavily, wobbled, and balanced herself in order not to fall.

"Come, I will lead you," I said as I held her by the shoulders.

"Please wait a minute. When I sit too long in one place, my legs get stiff," she said. "The blood no longer flows easily through my veins. My limbs are all sick, but my mind is clear. I thought that since she reads everything you write and worships you, maybe you could discourage her from this man."

"I would not be able to, nor would I want to. If God wants a kosher world, He will have to create one Himself."

"I am afraid He, too, would not know what to do in this case," the old woman said.

She smiled, and for a split second her face became young again.

Translated by Deborah Menashe

A Nest Egg for Paradise

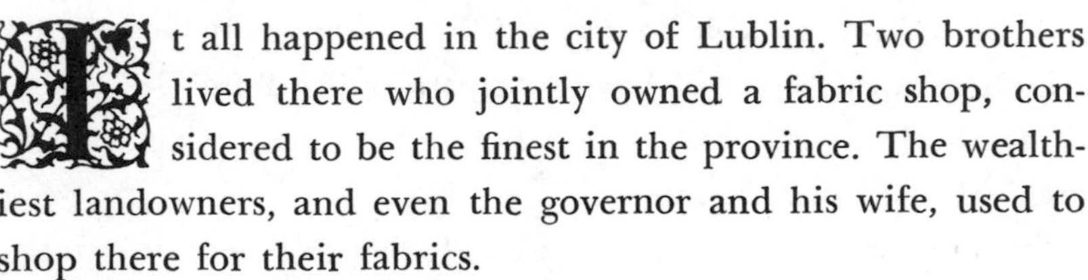

It all happened in the city of Lublin. Two brothers lived there who jointly owned a fabric shop, considered to be the finest in the province. The wealthiest landowners, and even the governor and his wife, used to shop there for their fabrics.

The older brother, Reb Mendel, had the reputation of a scholar. He was also a follower of the Hasidic master Reb Bunem of Przysucha. Because Reb Mendel was always absorbed in study and in Hasidic lore, he had little time left to devote to business. Both in his appearance and in his character Reb Mendel resembled his father, Reb Gershon of blessed memory: tall and broad, his beard and sidelocks black, his manner always gentle. The younger brother, Joel, was small, not given to learning, and a clown by nature. Joel had flaming red hair, a little red beard, and no hint of sidelocks. Whatever Joel did, he did in a hurry. He didn't walk, he ran. He spoke in a hurry, ate in a hurry, he rushed through his prayers. One minute he rose to recite the Eighteen Benedictions, the next he was done. He put on his prayer shawl and phylacteries, then promptly took them off. Because Joel had a flair for business, and because he liked to travel to all the great fairs, where he met buyers and traders from every corner of Poland and sometimes from other countries as well, Reb Mendel had drawn up a written agreement allotting sixty percent of the profits to Joel and taking the remaining forty percent himself. Basha-Meitl, Mendel's wife, fretted a good deal over her husband's agreement. Basha-Meitl had borne her husband three girls and a boy, while Lisa-Hadas, her sister-in-law, had borne Joel no children. Since the couple was childless after ten years of married life, Jewish law required Joel to divorce his wife. But Joel refused. When people asked him why he did not heed the law, Joel would answer with a joke, "I already expect a good lashing in hell. Let there be a few lashes more."

Another time he said, "If I divorced Lisa-Hadas, every widow, spinster, and divorcée would be after me to marry her. I'd never know which one to choose. Staying married is the best protection for a fellow like me."

By the time he was forty-five Reb Mendel had married off all his children. He could not provide large dowries for his daughters, but because they were pretty and well brought up, they found themselves good husbands. Basha-Meitl often complained to Reb Mendel that had he not been so immersed in Hasidic lore and practice—often spending more time in Przysucha than at home—he could have found himself more prosperous sons-in-law. But Reb Mendel would answer, "When a man reaches the world to come and is required to render accounts, the angel does not ask him how rich or poor his sons-in-law are. He asks instead, 'Did you study Torah? Was your business honorable?' "

It was the custom for Joel to send Reb Mendel his portion of the week's profits on Friday. Joel never offered to show Reb Mendel his account books and Reb Mendel never asked to see them. Although the shop had grown steadily larger and Joel had taken on additional help, and although the shelves had been stacked floor to ceiling with the finest merchandise, the earnings, it seemed, remained more or less the same. Basha-Meitl often nagged her husband to demand a precise accounting of expenses and profits. But Reb Mendel refused, saying, "If I can't trust my own brother, whom, then, can I trust? And if, God forbid, he is a swindler—what's to prevent him from falsifying the books?" And he made Basha-Meitl promise never to bring up these ugly suspicions again.

"What do they want with so much money?" Basha-Meitl would ask. "To whom will they leave their fortune?"

And Reb Mendel would answer, "With the Almighty's help, they'll live to a hundred and twenty."

As different as were the two brothers, so also were their wives. Reb Mendel's wife, Basha-Meitl, was the same age as he. A pious woman, she wore a double bonnet on her shaved head, so that when the hair on her head began to grow out again it would not be seen, God forbid, by a stranger's eye, because it is written, "A woman's hair is akin to her nakedness." Basha-Meitl fasted not only on Yom Kippur and on the Ninth of Av, as the other women did, but also on the Seventeenth of Tammuz, the Fast of Esther, and the Tenth of Tebeth, as well as the eight Fridays of the Shovavim Tat in the winter—which was only a custom and not a commanded law. Every Sabbath she read the weekly portion in the Yiddish Pentateuch, and she often read (in Yiddish translation) *The Good Heart, The Rod of Punishment, The Lamp of Light,* and *The Right Measure*. Frugal by nature, she had managed to put aside a small nest egg, so that come what may, neither she nor her husband should have to come begging, God forbid, to their children, let alone to strangers. Both she and Reb Mendel had written a will leaving one half of their savings to the children and the other half to various charities—to the poorhouse, for marrying off poor or orphaned brides, to the old-age home, and to the orphanage.

Joel's wife was ten years younger than her husband. Spared

the pains of childbirth and child-rearing, she looked younger still. Lisa-Hadas indulged herself in every luxury. She did no housework at all, employing instead two maids. She had a sweet tooth and was forever nibbling cookies, cakes, strudels, sipping sweet liqueurs or cherry brandy. Instead of a bonnet she wore a wig, whose hair she combed so that it blended with her own. Lisa-Hadas was the same height as Joel, and as quick and nimble as he. She flew about on her high-heeled shoes, darting here and there like a bird. As many dresses, blouses, robes, and coats as filled her closets, she always complained of having nothing to wear and spent long hours with her tailors and seamstresses. She had a chest filled with shoes of every color and another with hats topped with silk flowers, with ostrich plumes, with wooden peaches, pomegranates, bunches of grapes. Whenever Joel traveled, he returned with a piece of jewelry for her: a necklace, a brooch, a ring, earrings. Lisa-Hadas attended the synagogue only on the High Holidays, or on those occasions when she happened to escort a bride to her wedding. Like her husband, Lisa-Hadas was forever ready with a joke. Her high-pitched laughter often ended with a squeal. When she went to the ritual bath at the end of her menstrual periods, the other wives had much to envy her for. She'd come all decked out in silk lingerie edged in exquisite lace and long stockings which reached up to her thighs. Her breasts were firm and pointed like a girl's. The younger women showered her with compliments, but the older ones acidly asked her, "What is it with you, Lisa-Hadas, not getting any older?" And Lisa-Hadas would answer with a wink, "I have a potion which keeps whoever drinks it young till ninety."

•

There had been a time when Reb Mendel spent several hours in the shop every week, so that he might not become completely estranged either from the business or from Joel. But that time had long since gone. Joel had taken on clerks to help him wait on customers and to run the shop for him when he traveled. Women's fashions and styles were constantly changing. One year dresses hung loose, the next they clung to the body. One year lapels were narrow, the next they were wide. There was no sense in paying attention to such vanity. Besides, Reb Mendel was glad to avoid running into his sister-in-law. Lisa-Hadas had become a fashion expert. She subscribed to magazines which came to her from far-off Paris—that bit of Sodom whose women were forever occupied with finding new ways to titillate men. Napoleon, who was said to have been the vicious Gog, or perhaps the Magog mentioned in the Bible, had been defeated in one of his battles and had died on some bleak and forsaken island. But still the world craved nothing better than to ape the French, to speak their language, to imitate their whims and caprices. In the larger cities pious Jews had their daughters taught to prattle in French and to play on the piano. The Enlightenment, which had begun in Germany with the heretic Moses Mendelssohn of Dessau, soon drifted over to Russia and even to Poland. In Vienna and Berlin and Budapest reform synagogues cropped up, where rabbiners delivered their sermons in German, and where an organ was played on the Sabbath and holidays. Secular writers repeated in their Hebrew magazines every blasphemous theory put forth by the philosophers. They denied the miraculous nature of the Exodus from Egypt, as well as the divinity of the Torah. Reb Mendel suspected that secretly Lisa-Hadas belonged in their camp. He did not even trust the kashruth of her household, because she let it be run by Gentile servants.

After he stopped going to the shop, Reb Mendel studied the Talmud and Hasidic books at the studyhouse in Lublin every afternoon after his nap. Lublin was a city of Hasidim. When the Seer, Rabbi Yaakov Yitzhak, was alive, Hasidim from every corner of Poland flocked to Lublin. After the Seer's death, his disciple Bunem of Przysucha had taken his place. Reb Bunem did not perform miracles, as had the Seer. Reb Bunem's way in Hasidism was the way of wisdom. He assembled around him a select circle of scholars, keen minds, young men in search of a new way in Hasidism. Reb Bunem was fluent in Polish, even in Russian. He had been a pharmacist at one time. His adversaries, the Mitnaggedim, denounced him. Even among the Hasidim there were those who thought that he was too clever, too blunt, and that some of his utterances smacked of heresy. But those who understood a thing or two could glean layer upon layer of mystery from his words.

One summer afternoon, as Reb Mendel sat alone in the studyhouse poring over the same sacred volume, the door was pushed open a crack. Reb Mendel looked up, and standing in the doorway he saw his sister-in-law, Lisa-Hadas. She was dressed in a cream-colored suit topped with a straw hat and a ribbon. In one hand she carried a handbag and in the other a white parasol like the ones carried by the wives of the rich landowners to shield themselves from the sun. So startled was Reb Mendel by her presence that he dropped the book to the floor. Something's happened to my brother was the thought that raced through his head. He stood up and said, "Do my eyes deceive me?"

"No, Mendel. It's me, your sister-in-law, Lisa-Hadas."

"What brings you here?" he asked, with a tremor in his voice.

"I looked for you at your house, but the maid told me you were here."

"What happened? Is something, God forbid, wrong with Joel?"

"Yes. Something is wrong with Joel. But don't be alarmed. He's alive."

"Taken ill, God forbid?"

"I can't talk here."

"Where, then?"

"Come home with me."

"Home, with you?"

"Yes, why not? It isn't far. I'm not a stranger to you, Mendel. I am still your brother's wife."

"Is Joel back in Lublin?"

"Joel is still in Cracow."

Lisa-Hadas spoke to Reb Mendel with a mixture of impudence and mockery, born of familiarity. Reb Mendel had never walked with a woman in public before, not even with Basha-Meitl. When once it had happened that they went somewhere together, he had walked in front and she had followed behind him. He had always been mindful of the words in the Gemara: "Better follow a lion than a woman." He had also remembered the words "Manoach was a simpleton, as it is written: 'And Manoach walked behind his wife.' "

"Can't you tell me here what has happened to my brother?" he asked.

"No."

Reb Mendel hesitated before he followed Lisa-Hadas out of the studyhouse, and then he walked half beside her and half in front. He cast furtive glances at passersby to see whether they noticed him or pointed their fingers at him.

He muttered, "What's keeping Joel in Cracow?"

"You'll soon know," Lisa-Hadas answered.

Before long they arrived at his brother's house. Reb Mendel had not been to the house in years. Lisa-Hadas had had a garden planted in front, and as he approached, Reb Mendel saw large sunflowers in bloom. She had also had a balcony added to the second story. Lisa-Hadas grabbed the large brass ring which hung on the door and knocked several times. A Gentile maid in a white apron and a starched bonnet appeared to let them in. Real squires, Reb Mendel thought to himself. An Oriental carpet covered the floor of the front foyer. Two bronze figures holding lanterns stood facing each other. Lisa-Hadas led him into a living room crowded with sofas, stuffed chairs, paintings, chandeliers, pots filled with plants such as Mendel had never seen and for which the Yiddish he spoke had no names. She showed him to a sofa upholstered in black velvet, then sat on a chair opposite him and propped her feet on an embroidered stool. She said, "Mendel, I hate to be the bearer of bad news, but your brother has become a goy."

Reb Mendel turned pale. "Not converted, God forbid?"

"I don't know. Perhaps not yet. But he's got himself a Gentile mistress."

Reb Mendel felt his mouth turn dry and his stomach tighten. For a moment he was short of breath. "How can this be? I can't believe it," he stammered.

"I found a whole stack of her letters to him. He supports her. He showers her with gifts and money. It's been going on for over five years."

"Somehow I can't bring myself to believe all this."

"I'll show you her letters. You understand Polish, don't you?"

"A little."

"When your brother and I were first married, you used to come to the shop every day, and as I remember, you spoke with the landowners and their wives in rather fluent Polish."

"*Nu.*"

For a while both sat silent. Reb Mendel glanced at his sister-in-law and wondered why he had taken in her news without a greater show of grief. He was not a whiner by nature. He had not cried even at his parents' funerals. He had often seen Jews sobbing on Yom Kippur during the Kol Nidre or on the Ninth of Av during the Lamentations, but it was not in his nature to shed tears. He always kept in mind the verse: "I stand ever ready for adversity, and my woes are always on my mind." He prepared himself for whatever might befall him. The children, God forbid, might die; he, Mendel, might suddenly be taken ill or Basha-Meitl might be taken from him, leaving him a widower. How did the saying go? "There is not a moment without its woe." And yet, that his brother, Joel, their parents' youngest born, should sink to such depths—for that he was unprepared. He heard Lisa-Hadas speaking to him: "Mendel, since we are in the midst of speaking the truth, let me confess the whole truth."

"And what is that?"

"The truth is that Joel was not honest with you. You were supposed to receive forty percent of the profits, but in all these years you've received not forty, not thirty, not even twenty percent. He is your brother while I am only an outsider—what, after all, is a sister-in-law?—but I confronted him with this I don't know how many times and his answer was always the same: you are an idler, impractical, old-fashioned, and stubborn; you don't lift a finger to help, and so on and so forth. I told him: 'Mendel could do plenty, but you drove him out of the shop, you kept things from him, you excluded him from everything.' A wife should not denounce her husband, but if he's taking up with a shiksa and makes a fool of me, I owe him nothing. Am I right or am I wrong?"

"*Nu.*"

"All these years I have been faithful to him. I could have had more lovers than I have hairs on my head. Men lose their minds over me, but I've always believed in one God and one husband. Now it's all over. He is no longer my husband and I am not his wife. Let me tell you something, Mendel. You may not believe this, but you are closer to me now than he ever was. You are honest while he is a thief. When he and I were first married, you were the accomplished merchant while he was nothing but mama's pampered little boy. I was barely fifteen then, but I remember: from the very beginning he tried to take everything over and to push you out. I know, Mendel, that you disapprove of me because I'm not one of those overly pious matrons and I like to comb my wigs in the modern way. But I've always had the greatest respect for you. Don't laugh, but even as a man I preferred you to him. When my father, may he rest in peace, used to recite the Havdalah at the close of the Sabbath, my mother would hand me the Havdalah candle and say, 'Hold it high, and you'll have a tall husband.' When I became engaged and the people gathered to draw up the marriage contract, I thought it was you I was marrying. I was a child then, not more than fourteen. But when I saw that my bridegroom was short, shorter than me, a mere boy and not a young man—my heart sank. Why am I telling you all this? Because my heart is heavy now, and because I have no children, no heirs. I want you to know, Mendel, that it is Joel's fault that we are childless, not mine. I could have had a dozen children if I had married a man instead of a barren tree."

"How can you be so sure?" Mendel asked.

"A doctor told me. An obstetrician, that's what they call themselves. He examined me head to toe. 'You, Lisa-Hadas, are a healthy female,' he said to me. Those were his very words. 'It's your husband's fault, not yours.' What shall I do, brother-in-law? What shall I do now?" Lisa-Hadas cried out in a singsong voice.

Reb Mendel wanted to answer, but his tongue refused to

obey him. A lump rose to his throat. He made an attempt to swallow the lump, then he heard his own voice saying, "For the time being do nothing. Wait until Joel returns."

"His return frightens me. I won't be able to look him straight in the eye. He'll be coming to me from the arms of that whore, from her unclean body. Mendel, what is the matter? You're as pale as a ghost. Wait, I'll get something for you."

She sprang out of her chair, ran up to a cabinet, and flung open its glass doors. She pulled out a bottle half filled with a reddish fluid and poured from it into a polished glass. In a moment she was back at his side. "Here, drink this," she said. "It's sweet liqueur, for women. Let me get you something to nibble on."

Reb Mendel held the glass tightly in his hands, but they shook so violently that it was several minutes before he could touch it to his lips. He poured the liquid into his mouth and felt a sharp burning in his tongue, his palate, his throat. Lisa-Hadas returned, carrying another glass and a plate heaped with cookies. "Drink, Mendel," she said. "I know what a shock this must be for you. I had misplaced a ring of mine, and I thought I might have hidden it in one of his drawers. I opened the drawer and saw her pack of letters bulging out from under his papers. That night I didn't sleep a wink. I lay in my bed and shivered as if in a fever. I thought of hanging myself, of taking poison."

"God forbid. You'd be committing a grave sin." Reb Mendel could hardly pronounce the words.

"How grave can it be? I considered it all very carefully. There is no God."

"What are you saying? This is blasphemy!"

"Let it be blasphemy. Don't worry, Mendel. It's I who will roast in the fires of hell, not you. Come, let me show you those brazen letters of hers."

Reb Mendel wanted to rise, but it was as if he were paralyzed. Lisa-Hadas took his hands in hers and helped him to his feet. His knees struck against hers. A shudder ran through his spine, and for a moment he was overcome by lust such as he had not known since the days of his youth. Lisa-Hadas pulled him along by both his hands, she stepping gingerly backward and he stumbling forward half-blind, shaky and trembling in a sort of drunken minuet. "Master of the Universe, help me!" a voice within him cried. Suddenly Lisa-Hadas lurched backward and fell, pulling him down to the floor. Reb Mendel had no time to grasp what was happening. He tried to tear himself away from her; he had fallen into something like a swoon—an instant of sheer drunkenness and utter helplessness. She did something to him and he could not resist. He shuddered and it was as if he had awakened from a deep sleep, from a dream, from an evil force that robbed his freedom to choose. He felt as though his body had separated itself from his soul and had committed an abomination of its own accord. So dumbfounded was Reb Mendel by what had happened to him that he could not manage to shout out his grief. He lay there on the floor consumed with one wish—never to rise again. She helped him stand up and he heard her say, "He rightly deserved it." It was the voice of a Lilith: one of those female demons sent by Asmodeus to defile yeshiva students. Verses from the Book of Proverbs crowded his head: "She eats, then wipes her mouth, saying, 'I have done no wrong . . .' " "Her feet point to the grave, her footsteps lead into the chambers of death."

Evening came, and then sudden darkness. Lisa-Hadas grasped his arm and he allowed himself to follow her like an ox to the slaughter. What was the difference anyway? Lower than the deepest abyss one couldn't sink. His knees buckled under him and his feet were unsteady. Lisa-Hadas hung on to his arm and pressed her bosom to his ribs. "Shall I have the carriage harnessed to take you home?" she asked. "First I'll have to find the groom."

"No, no."

"It's not far to your home, but it's dark outside. You could slip and fall, God forbid."

He wanted to say, "Fall still more?" but instead he said, "No, I can see."

"Basha-Meitl will wonder what's become of you," Lisa-Hadas said with a chuckle.

Reb Mendel wanted her to let him go, but for some reason she clung to him. She said, "The darkness of Egypt is out there. I'd better go with you."

"I beg you, no."

"Mendel, forgive me."

"*Nu.*"

"We both must have been out of our minds," Lisa-Hadas blurted out to him and to the night. "Be careful."

Hesitantly she let go of his arm, and he set out on his way, unsteady like a drunk. "I've lost the world to come," a voice within him murmured. Everything happened in quick succession as in the Book of Job: "Even as one fellow was speaking, the second fellow arrived." Scarcely two hours ago Reb Mendel had been an honest, upstanding Jew. Now he was depraved, a Zimri ben Salu, a betrayer of God, a lecher. If at least a Phinehas arose to avenge the Lord of Hosts. His, Mendel's, vision had always been adequate. He could even read the small letters in Rashi. But now it was as though he had gone blind. "*Nu,* my iniquity surpasses my endurance." Words from the Gemara came rushing back to him: "May it be God's will that my death atone for my sinfulness." Someone came walking toward him, and Mendel halted. It was a young man, a Przysucha Hasid whose name was Hershel Roizkes. Recognizing Mendel in the darkness, the young man asked him, "And where might you be going at this late hour, Reb Mendel?"

Mendel didn't know what answer to give. He felt himself literally speechless.

"May I accompany you home?"

"*Nu.*"

The young Hasid took Reb Mendel's arm, the very arm that Lisa-Hadas had earlier held, and said, "The city pays some Gentile to keep the lanterns lit, yet the streets are always dark. God forbid, a person could break a leg or even his neck. In the summertime one can tolerate it, but when winter comes with its snows and frosts and the streets become slippery, a person risks his life every time he leaves his house. You're probably planning to spend Rosh Hashanah in Przysucha, Reb Mendel, eh?"

Again Reb Mendel had no answer to give. That he, Mendel, should present himself at the rebbe's in Przysucha? It was sacrilege even to mention that saint's name in the same breath with his, adulterer that he was, an outcast to his people, disgraced and polluted. But he had to answer the young Hasid's question and he murmured, "It's too early to say."

"Since you go to the rebbe every year, why not this time? Zeinvil the beadle predicts more disciples than ever this year," Hershel Roizkes said.

Despite his sorrow Reb Mendel couldn't help but smile to himself. Hershel was trying to engage him in Hasidic talk. How could he know that he, Mendel, was no longer Mendel but a villain seven times over, a man steeped in the Forty-nine Gates of Uncleanliness? And how would he, Mendel, greet Basha-Meitl when finally he arrived at his home? How would he look her in the eye?

Hershel Roizkes was speaking of Rabbi Bunem now, repeating a saying of his, quoting a witticism; but although Reb

Mendel could hear his voice, he could not make out what Hershel was saying. The Torah and he, Mendel, had grown estranged, one from the other, forever. The young man spoke up: "I see, Reb Mendel, that you are a bit impatient tonight. Are you, God forbid, ill, or what?"

"I do have a touch of heartburn."

"Ah! Right away I knew that something was wrong. You shouldn't be walking the streets at this hour. It turns quite chilly in the evening and one could easily catch a cold. Go home and get into bed. Your soulmate will give you something for it. A glass of tea with honey will cure anything. Here we are, Reb Mendel, here's your house. Good night, Reb Mendel, and may you recover soon."

"Thank you, Hershel."

When Reb Mendel opened the door to his apartment, he saw Basha-Meitl standing in the middle of the room, a kerchief wrapped around her forehead. Before he had time to wish her a good evening, she began to scream, "Where have you been? Where did you run off to so late in the evening? And why are you so pale? Did something happen, God forbid? You always come home immediately after the evening prayers, and here it's already ten o'clock! The worries I've had—may they fall on our enemies' heads. The frightful disasters that came to my mind! Mendel, what is it with you? I've even developed a headache from worry."

"I lingered at the studyhouse longer than I meant to."

"Mendel, I myself went to the studyhouse to look for you. The beadle told me that you had not been there for the evening service."

Reb Mendel stood and stared at his wife, utterly stupefied. Heavenly Father, he had forgotten to recite the evening prayers! In all the years he'd been saying them, this had never happened to him before. *Nu,* apparently I'm entirely in the hands of the evil host. He saw a chair and all but collapsed into it. I'm no longer a Jew, Reb Mendel thought to himself. It's better this way. It's better if those sacred words did not pass through my unclean lips.

"Where have you been?" Basha-Meitl shrieked at him. "You're as white as a corpse!"

Reb Mendel considered how to answer his wife. Should he make up a story? What sort of story? Fabrications and lies were not in his nature. Besides, someone might have seen him with Lisa-Hadas, walking in the direction of her house. At last he said, "I was with Lisa-Hadas."

Basha-Meitl clapped her hands together. "What? Lisa-Hadas? For such a long time? Is something wrong with your brother, God forbid?"

"Yes."

"What happened? Heaven help us! Such a young man."

"He's alive, he's alive."

"What is it, then? Don't keep me in suspense!" Basha-Meitl screamed.

"Joel is having relations with a Gentile woman."

"Relations? A Gentile? I can't believe it. I can't believe it!"

"It's the truth."

"When? Where? What sort of relations?"

It occurred to Reb Mendel that he should not have spoken the word "truth." According to the Gemara, truth was the Almighty's Seal. A sinner such as he ought not to let the word cross his lips.

Man and wife talked late into the night, until finally Basha-Meitl fell asleep. Reb Mendel lay in his bed fully awake. He had wanted to recite the Shema, as he did every night, but he could not bring himself to pronounce the sacred words and all the more not the Divine Name. How could a vile sinner such as he was proclaim: "In thine hand, O Lord, I entrust my soul"?

He had but one request of the Almighty: to be done with this world, its lusts, its temptations. What a bizarre transition: one moment he was poring over the sacred book, and an hour later he found himself ensnared in the net of incest. "It's a fall, a punishment," Reb Mendel murmured to himself. Somewhere he had read that temptations were sent to bedevil great saints—like the Patriarch Abraham, or the Righteous Joseph—or else they were sent to the worst of sinners, putting them on the road to Sheol. Lisa-Hadas had made him drunk, just as Lot's daughter had done to Lot. Well, and how did it happen that a brother of his, a son of God-fearing Jews, should take up with a Gentile woman and shame his parents in Paradise? And why had he deceived him, his elder brother, and held back his money from him? Reb Mendel recalled the verse in the Book of Psalms: "And I, in my haste, cried out: 'All men are deceivers.' " Even a saint like King David despaired of all mankind.

Yes, King David. He, the author of the Book of Psalms, had had his own share of troubles. One of his sons, Absalom, had plotted to seize the throne from his father and had openly copulated with ten of his father's wives. Another son, Amnon, had raped his sister, Tamar. Yet another, Adonijah ben Haggith, had sought to wrest the kingdom from his brother Solomon. And that event with Bathsheba and Uriah the Hittite! Well, but all these things belonged to ancient times. What did the Gemara say? "Whoever claims that David sinned is nothing but mistaken." Every word in the Holy Book was full of secrets.

Reb Mendel himself did not know who in his brain spoke to him now: Satan or an angel of mercy? But of one thing he was sure: he needed to do penance. Even a brute like Nebuzaradan, a murderer of Jewish children—when later he regretted his deeds, heaven accepted his atonement. But how could one atone for so heinous a deed as his, Mendel's, was?

For the most trivial of sins the sacred book demanded hundreds of fasts, self-flagellations, rolling the body in the snow in the winter and in thorns in the summer. An abomination such as he had committed was not even mentioned in that Holy Book at all.

Reb Mendel was too restless to remain lying down and so he sat up in bed. Basha-Meitl awoke and asked him, "Mendel, aren't you sleeping?"

"No."

"Mendel, if what Lisa-Hadas told you is true, then Joel stained the family's honor. But it is not your fault. The Patriarch Jacob also had a wicked brother: Esau."

"Yes, I know."

"Mendel, perhaps she lied. A woman like Lisa-Hadas is capable of bringing false accusations even against her own husband."

"No."

"Well, whatever happens—don't take it to heart. May God not punish me for saying this, but I never thought much of either one of them. I always told you that I had no faith in their honesty. But you ignored me, even scolded me. He stuffed his pockets with money and to you he doled out pennies. You know that is the truth."

"Go back to sleep."

"It will be a black day when word of this gets out in town."

"It's already a black day."

"When is he coming home?"

Reb Mendel didn't answer. He was reminded of the words in the Gemara: "Very good is death." That phrase had always puzzled him. The Torah was a teaching of life, not death. Only now did he understand what the words meant to say. Sometimes a man could become so hopelessly entangled that death was his only deliverance. And as if she could read his thoughts Basha-Meitl spoke: "Take care of yourself. Your life comes before everything else. Good night."

Basha-Meitl fell silent, but apparently she was not asleep. A cricket which had lived for who knew how many years behind Basha-Meitl's stove suddenly began its eternal chirping; a creature who with one haunting note could say all that it had to say night in and night out, generation after generation. In a coop near the stove slept a hen and a rooster. Basha-Meitl was raising the pair to serve as sacrifices for herself and for Mendel on the eve of Yom Kippur. Every now and then the hen clucked in its sleep. Although Basha-Meitl and Mendel possessed a clock equipped with weights and chains which chimed precisely every hour and every half hour, it was the rooster with its cock-a-doodle-doo that awoke them every morning at the break of day. A kind of envy swept over Reb Mendel for those innocent creatures. True, the Almighty had not granted them free choice, but the turmoil of breaking His commandments also didn't trouble their days. They fulfilled their mission simply and faithfully.

Although he was convinced that the night was lost to sleep, Reb Mendel finally dozed off. He slept for several hours without dreaming, or perhaps without the memory of having dreamed. When he opened his eyes the room was still dark. He awoke with a heaviness in his heart and a bitter taste in his mouth. He remembered that some dreadful event had taken place, but what it was he couldn't say. "Why am I feeling so low?" he asked himself. "Have I wronged someone—or has someone wronged me?" Basha-Meitl was sleeping now; he could hear her steady breathing. The cricket had stopped its chirping; perhaps it, too, had fallen asleep. Through the window Mendel saw the heavens thickly strewn with stars. He had once heard somewhere that each star was a complete world. So many worlds had the Almighty created that every righteous man was rewarded with three hundred and ten of them. Reb Mendel shivered. All at once he remembered the disaster that had befallen him in his old age.

•

Days and nights passed and Reb Mendel could not sleep. He would doze off, then wake up with a start. Although the nights in Lublin were quiet, his head throbbed with noise. Sometimes he heard the wheels of a carriage clattering across the cobblestones. Another time he heard a hammer striking loudly against an anvil. "Have I become another Titus that God should send a gnat to gnaw at my brain? Am I going mad? If so, I'd rather die." Reb Mendel considered doing away with himself. But how? Should he hang himself? Drown? Take poison? Since he had already lost his share in the world to come, what was the difference what he did? In the midst of his turmoil Reb Mendel took pains to keep his condition from Basha-Meitl. But she saw it just the same and tried to comfort him. She pleaded with him: "Mendel, he is your brother, not your son. Even when a son strays from the righteous path, one mustn't torment oneself."

Reb Mendel stopped going to pray with a minyan. He could not look the other Hasidim in the eye. He could not enter a sacred place where a Holy Ark stood filled with Torah scrolls. He put on his phylacteries in his study, but he could not bring himself to recite the benediction. He did not dare to kiss the fringes of his prayer shawl. Reb Mendel knew perfectly well that a Jew was forbidden to pray for death, but what, then, was left for him to do? He planned to leave a will requesting that he be buried not among those who died virtuous but behind the fence, where suicides and other sinful Jews lay buried.

Like all other Jews, Reb Mendel used to go to the bathhouse on Fridays, but no longer. How could he undress himself and bare to other Jews that organ, the sign of God's holy covenant, which had broken the injunction against incest? And how could he pray in the Hasidim studyhouse? What if he was called upon to read from the Torah? How could he pronounce the benediction over the Torah? Basha-Meitl informed the beadle of Przysucha that Mendel was ill and that he wanted no visitors.

In order to spare Basha-Meitl grief, Reb Mendel pretended to pray in his study. Friday evenings he put on his satin gaberdine and his fur-lined hat; he recited the "Woman of Valor"; he blessed the wine—all in a hurry, without chants, without joy. He swallowed no more than two spoonfuls of the soup, touched neither the sweet stew nor the meat, barely tasted a morsel of challah. When Basha-Meitl asked why there was no singing of hymns at the Sabbath table, he said, "I don't feel like singing."

"Mendel, you've let yourself slip into melancholy. You are committing a sin."

"*Nu,* what's another sin?"

"Mendel, you frighten me."

"I won't make you suffer much longer," Reb Mendel said, against his will.

Twice a year, on Shevuoth and then again on Rosh Hashanah, Reb Mendel was accustomed to travel to the rebbe in Przysucha. Although he was not a wealthy man, on those occasions he hired a coach and took along a number of the poorer Hasidim, those who could not afford the expenses of the trip. He paid for their lodgings in inns along the way, as well as their stay in Przysucha. The drive itself was one long celebration. The Hasidim crooned melodies, poked fun at the Mitnaggedim, regaled each other with tales about the Rabbi of Lublin, the Maggid of Kozienice, Reb Melekh of Lizhensk, and about his brother Zusya. Reb Bunem was not an explicator of Torah, neither was he a miracle worker. He did not accept payments for advice. He did not admit women into his study, and he did not give out amulets. On weekdays he did not wear a fur hat and a satin gaberdine, or even the white coat and trousers which Rabbi Menachem Mendel of Vitebsk and Rabbi Nachum of Chernobyl had worn. Instead, he went about in boots and a cloth coat, the same as the other Hasidim. But such was his greatness that scholars from every corner of Russian Poland had flocked to him, even from far-off Galicia. His disciples—Reb Yaahov of Radzymin, Yitzhak of Worka, Mendel of Kotzk, and Itche-Meir of Warsaw—were all about the same age as he, and each addressed him by the familiar "thou." They kidded him, and he in turn kidded them. They debated with him and good-naturedly contradicted him. Because few of Reb Bunem's Hasidim were elderly—mostly they were young—Reb Mendel of Lublin occupied a special place in Przysucha.

That year Reb Mendel startled the other Przysucha Hasidim in Lublin. Instead of waiting—as he had always done—for the week before Rosh Hashanah, he rented a carriage immediately after the first of Elul and departed for Przysucha alone, unaccompanied by other Hasidim. He did not even stop to take leave of anyone. "Did he suddenly become a miser?" the younger Hasidim wondered. Was it a sudden show of arrogance? Word of his illness had spread around the town, and it was concluded that that was the reason for his abrupt departure. Those Hasidim who could not afford to travel by carriage would have to travel on foot. Why all the fuss? If the Patriarch Jacob could hoof it all the way from Beersheba to Haran, healthy and young Hasidim could walk from Lublin to Przysucha.

It was a rare Hasid who arrived in Przysucha some three weeks before the holidays. Mendel was virtually alone. The large studyhouse was empty. Unlike other men in his position, Reb Bunem was not one to require the services of a beadle or a gabbai. Mendel opened the door to the rebbe's study and simply walked in. Reb Bunem—a tall man with a pointed black beard and flashing black eyes—stood at a lectern and scribbled with a quill on a slip of paper. Seeing Reb Mendel, the rebbe wiped off his pen on his skullcap and asked, "Am I seeing things, or is my calendar wrong?"

"No, Rebbe. Your calendar is not wrong," Reb Mendel answered.

"*Nu,* welcome, welcome."

The rebbe stretched out his hand and Mendel barely touched the tips of his fingers, so as not to defile the saint's hand with his own. Reb Bunem glanced at him and knitted his brows. He moved a stool toward Reb Mendel and sat down on the edge of a bench. "Reb Mendel, what's troubling you? You may speak openly."

"Rebbe, I've forfeited my share in the world to come," Reb Mendel blurted out.

The rebbe's eyes filled with laughter. "Forfeited, huh? Congratulations!"

"What does the rebbe mean?" Reb Mendel asked, alarmed.

"Those who pursue the world to come are engaged in a trade-off with the Almighty: 'I will observe your Torah and commandments, and you'll give me a larger portion of the Leviathan.' When a Jew forfeits his share in the world to come, he can serve the Almighty for His own sake, expecting nothing in return."

"I am not worthy of serving Him," Reb Mendel said.

"And who, then, is worthy?"

Reb Mendel hoped that the rebbe would ask what he had done, and he was prepared to make a full confession. But the rebbe did not ask him. He probably knows already, Reb Mendel thought to himself.

"Where are you staying?" Reb Bunem asked.

"I was given a bed in the inn. What more do I need?"

"Reb Mendel, take good care of yourself. The Master of the Universe has plenty of paid servants, but of those who would serve Him for nothing, He has hardly any at all."

"Rebbe, I want to do penance."

"The wish itself is penance."

Reb Mendel wanted to say something more, but Reb Bunem motioned with his hand as if to say, Enough for now. Before Mendel was out of the room, the rebbe called out to him, "Everything is permitted, except fasting!"

•

A fit of sobbing shook Mendel's body, and at the same time he was overcome with joy. He was not alone. The Almighty knew, and the rebbe also knew. He, Mendel, was sure to roast in the fires of all seven hells, but he also recalled a saying of the rebbe's: "Hell is for men, not for dogs." As long as there was a God and as long as there were Jews, what was the difference where one lived? Reincarnation? Let it be reincarnation. Purgatory? Let it be Purgatory. The rebbe had once said, "Among men there is justice and there is mercy. But for the Master of the Universe justice itself is mercy." Reb Mendel walked into the studyhouse. Until that moment he had carefully avoided touching a holy book. He had not even dared to kiss the mezuzah with his unclean lips. But now he felt his strength returning to him. "No, I have no use for Paradise, I have no need for a reward." He walked up to the bookshelf and pulled down the tractate of Berakhot. He sat down all alone at a long table, and he began to chant the holy words and to interpret them to himself: " 'At what time may one begin to recite the Shema in the evening? From the hour in which the priests gather to eat of their tithes.' " Rashi had inserted an explanation: " 'Priests who had become defiled and had immersed themselves in water . . .' " Yes, Reb Mendel no longer hesitated to peruse the holy letters with which the Almighty had created the universe.

A sinful Jew was still a Jew. Even a convert, according to the Law, remained a Jew.

Days went by. Once again Reb Mendel was able to pray with fervor. It struck him that in all Eighteen Benedictions the prayers were written not for the individual Jew but for the Jewish people as a whole. The plural form was used throughout. How could he, Mendel, pray for himself alone, for his own body, his own lost soul? But to pray for all the Jews—that even the most wicked man on earth could do. Even the evil Balaam had been granted permission to praise the Jews and perhaps to pray for them.

Soon Reb Bunem's disciples and students from all over Poland began to gather. They were all there: Reb Mendel of Kotzk, Yaakov of Radzymin, Itche-Meir of Warsaw, Yitzhak of Worka, Mordecai Joseph of Izbica. Several of them had in the meantime themselves become rabbis, had students and followers of their own. Hasidim had also arrived from Lublin, some by horse and wagon, others on foot. Before Reb Mendel had hurried out of Lublin, it had been rumored that he was gravely ill. Some of the Hasidim had believed that he had wanted to end his days with Reb Bunem in Przysucha. Now, heaven be praised, he seemed to have come back to life. Although he had later on been given a private room at the inn, Reb Mendel had cots brought in for poor Lublin Hasidim who would otherwise have slept on a bench in the studyhouse, in an attic somewhere, or wherever they could find a place to put down their heads. Reb Mendel paid for their meals as well.

Yes, once again Reb Mendel became what he had always been: a Hasid among Hasidim. It was thought that after the holidays he would return to Lublin, but Succoth came and went and Reb Mendel was still in Przysucha. Somehow he learned that his brother, Joel, had converted and had gone off to live with a squire's wife. Lisa-Hadas had sold the shop without offering Basha-Meitl a share of the profits. Although according to the Law a Jew, even if he converted, remained a Jew, and although his wife could not remarry without a proper divorce, Lisa-Hadas married some "enlightened" Jew, a lawyer by profession, and the man who had helped her to perpetrate her swindle. It was rumored that the two were living in some city deep in Russia. Reb Mendel wrote to Basha-Meitl informing her that he had made up his mind to stay in Przysucha and urging her to sell the house and join him there, because a wife's place was at her husband's side.

All these events unsettled and puzzled the Jews of Lublin, let alone the Przysucha Hasidim. That a Jew should fall in love with a Gentile and abandon Judaism was not unheard of. And besides, Joel had always been thought to be frivolous, a pleasure-seeker. For a long time it had been whispered in Lublin that he made the rounds of the big cities far too often, more often than his business required, and that he hobnobbed too closely with Gentile landowners. But that a merchant, well off as Reb Mendel had been, should forsake everything in order to sit at his rebbe's feet—that was something new. Basha-Meitl traveled to Przysucha to persuade her husband to return with her to Lublin. "Is it your fault," she pleaded with him, "if your brother strayed from the righteous path?" But Reb Mendel was adamant: "It is written: 'All Jews are responsible one for the other.' If even perfect strangers share in this responsibility, how much more so should a brother."

It took a good deal of argument before Basha-Meitl agreed to settle in Przysucha. Miraculously she had managed to save up a small nest egg. She had also inherited several good pieces of jewelry from her mother, her grandmothers, and her great-grandmothers. She rented an apartment on Synagogue Street, not far from the rebbe's studyhouse, and the couple began their new life. Reb Mendel did exactly what Reb Bunem told him to do: he served the Almighty without expecting any rewards. He rose at midnight, and he recited prayers and lamentations that had been printed in older prayer books. He prayed with fervor; he studied the Mishnah, the Gemara, other sacred texts. Although the rebbe had forbidden him to fast, Reb Mendel fasted every Monday and Thursday. From the day he had sinned, his appetite for food had diminished. He went to bed satiated and woke up feeling full. One meal in the morning, or in the evening instead, satisfied him. He no longer ate meat, except on the Sabbath. The *Reshit Chochmah* required those who committed a sin as grave as his to torture his body and to fast from Sabbath to Sabbath. But Reb Mendel did not want to distress his wife. The truth was that she, Basha-Meitl, was also eating less and less, even though her household duties did not diminish. Of what little money the couple possessed they gave tithes. There was a small yeshiva in Przysucha and Basha-Meitl undertook to feed several of its students, to wash their linen, to patch up their socks and shirts. Basha-Meitl did not want to arrive at the world to come without good deeds to her credit.

As for Mendel, he did not occupy himself with thoughts of the world to come. True, it was far better to sit in Paradise with a crown on one's head and to bask in the glow of the Shechinah than to wallow in thorns or to turn into a worm, or a frog, or a monster. But the pleasures of living year round in Przysucha more than made up for the torment which might be his later. A day did not go by when the rebbe did not speak a few kind words to him. Merely to gaze upon the rebbe's saintly countenance was a joy. Rabbis and scholars flocked to Przysucha from Poland, from Volhynia, and occasionally from more distant lands as well. Reb Mendel became the rebbe's gabbai, a service he performed without pay. When Reb Bunem was consulted on matters of commerce and worldly affairs, he always called Reb Mendel in and conferred with him. Reb

Bunem himself was also well versed in those matters. It was no secret that he had once been an adherent of the Enlightenment, and a pharmacist. He himself was actually a penitent.

Why dream of Paradise when Przysucha itself was Paradise? Instead of being flung into the depths of Sheol, as he deserved to be, Reb Mendel was surrounded with Torah, with wisdom, with the love and the warmth of fellow Jews. Reb Mendel never spoke of his sin to Reb Bunem, but it was clear that through the divine spirit which rested on him the rebbe knew what he, Mendel, had done. Once, on Simchas Torah, when Reb Mendel was striding behind the rebbe with the Torah scroll in his arms, Reb Bunem suddenly stopped, turned his head, and said, "Let the Mitnagged save up a nest egg for Paradise. We here in Przysucha are up to our necks in the glory of God and the radiance of the Torah right here and now."

Translated by Nili Wachtel

The Conference

They came together in Warsaw for a cultural conference. Actually, it was an attempt by the Party hacks to create a united front with various leftist groups. To the conference came Party members, radical Yiddishists, actors, educators, and people who always attend conferences—permanent delegates. This took place in March 1936. The organizers used every means to deceive the *Defensywa*, the Polish political police, but the police knew all about the conference.

The Party delegates came prepared with long speeches filled with doctrinal clichés. They wore thick horn-rimmed glasses, smiled shrewdly, and seemed pleased with their intellectual superiority. In the name of Yiddish culture they tried to attract to Communism some petit-bourgeois and neutral members of the intelligentsia. Every Communist was sure that Moscow would appreciate his merits; each thought that the day after the revolution he would be appointed to a high position in the proletarian government of Poland. The non-Communists seemed confused and bellicose. They had come to the conference with instructions from their factions to win all sorts of compromises and privileges. The conference was supposed to last for three days and end with a momentous banquet. The kitchen of the hotel was stocked with all kinds of provisions—fish, meat, soups, delicious pastries, and special dishes for the occasion. The management knew that no matter how much these intellectuals might haggle, they would eat in unison at the banquet tables.

Among the eighty-two delegates there were only three women, one of whom, Comrade Flora, was relatively young. She was a delegate from Lublin, part actress, reciter of poetry, singer of folk songs. Flora was small, fat, with a round face and the eyes of an owl. She tried to speak modern Yiddish, laughed loudly, garbled names. She was in possession of a few phrases which she used at every opportunity. One of these was: "Let us not scatter our progressive forces."

Almost all the male delegates developed a crush on Comrade Flora. They treated her to cigarettes and lozenges for dryness of the throat. They all attempted to arrange private meetings with her. They all wanted to confide in her. They were not understood by their wives, who were too busy with their children and households, or were too old and too frigid. Would Flora join them after the day's session? It would be nice to discuss Party matters over refreshments. Comrade Flora never said no. The first night it would be impossible; she had not slept the night before, because of work and excitement. Perhaps tomorrow . . .

At the first session the debates lasted until two in the morning. The delegates battled over various social problems, but concentrated mostly on the meaning of historical materialism. An anti-Marxist historian took three hours to prove that materialistic theory does not apply to Jewish history. Comrade Flora sat in the first row, across the floor from the dais, and the speaker did not take his eyes off her. He beat the table with his fist and screamed, "Can a materialistic point of view explain two thousand years of Jewish exile? Is it possible to use Marxist theory to explain the survival of the Hebrew language, the yearning for Zion? No, a thousand times no!" In her confusion,

Flora nodded and applauded. The Communists interjected cries of "Saboteur, reactionary, liar!" The historian became hoarse. He drank one glass of water after another and wiped his glasses with his handkerchief. He attempted to support his arguments by quoting Marx, Engels, and Moses Hess, but the Communists interrupted him and mocked him. Flora soon realized that she was badly oriented. Instead of nodding agreement, she now shook her head and cried, "Comrades, let us not scatter our progressive forces."

After the historian had finished, a Communist went to the podium to answer him. He smiled cunningly, his eyes gleaming behind his glasses. He proved that the so-called historian had knowledge neither of history nor of sociology. Flora applauded and cried, "Bravo!" This speaker had already approached Flora, who had promised to meet him later. He smiled triumphantly, showing a mouth full of gold teeth. He moistened his lips with the tip of his tongue and ran his fingers through his hair. He spoke directly to Flora and watched her every movement. He asked, "What did the Jews in the ghettos eat, bread or ideas?" and Flora shrieked, "Bread! Bread!"

The second day, Flora was again the center of attention. Almost all the men flirted with her and tried to arrange a date. The moment one man began to talk to her, another broke in. The delegates openly quarreled about her, half jokingly, half seriously. They gave her hints about jobs and trips. They offered her cigarettes and cookies. They touched her naked arm with their sweaty fingers. The more daring even tried to kiss her. They all told jokes, mimicked certain delegates, and made fun of some provincial speaker. Their eyes glittered, their gorges rose and fell rapidly. Comrade Flora began to think she wouldn't be able to escape this time. Luckily, the debates became especially hot that night. The anti-Communists became highly aggressive and lashed out at Stalin's worst crimes. A number of fellow travelers began to speak like full-fledged Fascists. The Communist speaker poured scorn on every social-democratic slogan, and warned that even one step away from Stalinism would lead to reactionary darkness. One delegate shouted, "We will hang all of you from the nearest lamp post." The chairman good-naturedly reproached him for this non-parliamentary outburst. The hall reeked with the smoke of cigarettes and echoed with shouts. Foreheads became wet with perspiration, ties hung limp, pince-nez slipped from noses. Comrade Flora fanned herself with a program and cried, "Forgive me, comrades, open a window!" One of the delegates brought her a glass of seltzer water.

About one in the morning there was such pandemonium that Flora managed to steal away without being noticed. A leather manufacturer from Lublin, her lover, had taken a room adjacent to hers. Flora made sure that the delegates were unaware that she had brought her capitalist paramour with her. She locked the door, bolted it, and warned her lover to make no noise. A few minutes after he entered her room, someone knocked at the door. It was the historian.

"Miss Flora, Miss Flora, please open!" he whispered in the hallway. Flora barely managed not to burst out laughing. She lay in bed and giggled into the pillow. The manufacturer pinched her behind, calling her "harlot" and "slut" in a low voice. She bit his earlobe and whispered, "Let them knock, the shmegegges. What do you care? I'm yours."

The third morning, Flora awoke with a headache. The manufacturer had left early to meet several traveling salesmen. Flora took an aspirin, but it did not help. She went down to the conference hall only after lunch. The conference was about to erupt again in turmoil, but slowly the delegates composed themselves because of a speech delivered by a writer who had the status of an immortal. He had come from faraway America.

He was the only delegate who had not made a pass at Flora—a man in his sixties, small, broad-shouldered, with a head of gray hair, with bags under his eyes and gold-rimmed glasses. He was reading a lecture from a sheaf of papers. Like a professor he went through the whole history of Yiddishism and socialism. He spoke in a monotonous, sleepy voice. Many of the delegates yawned and dozed. Others were stealthily reading newspapers. The delegates turned to look at Flora, but she pretended she was listening to each and every word of the famous writer. After he had finished, Flora approached him and said, "Thank you for a most interesting lecture."

The immortal took off his misty glasses. "Were you really interested?"

"Immensely."

"I noticed you, I noticed you—we should get better acquainted."

"It would be a great honor for me!" Flora exclaimed.

Soon the conference began to fall apart again, because both camps had become extremely unyielding. But a neutral group made a last effort to patch things up, and came up with a new compromise resolution. In the banquet hall the tables were already set. In the kitchen the cooks roasted chickens and ducks and poured gravy from one pan to another, but in the conference hall the war raged on. The delegates began to insult each other personally. One delegate had his ears boxed. A Stalinist threw an inkwell at a Trotskyite. They hurled such words as "Fascist dog," "betrayer of the masses," "provocateur." But the peacemakers did not let the conference explode. This would have been a victory for the Zionists. The delegates either had to decide on common action or to part like enemies. The Communists began to give in on some points, and the opposition became softer. A three-page resolution was put together, demanding that the great powers make an end to imperialism.

Greetings were sent to the comrades in China, Manchuria, and Mongolia. The United States was asked to put an end to its imperialistic greed, bloodsucking exploitation, pro-Fascism. However, the secretary who transcribed the resolution was a Communist and he altered the text. When his deception was discovered, there was an uproar of protest.

At that moment the delegates were summoned to the banquet. The waiters had to begin early; they had their union regulations. At the banquet the warring factions became friendlier. Everyone was hungry. They were given fresh rolls, carp with horseradish, vodka, wine, chicken soup with noodles, and stuffed derma. Flora sat between a Stalinist and a leader of the left labor movement. One put a hand on her knee, the other tickled her ribs. Flora drank liqueur and laughed loudly. She put a cigarette to her lips and both men lit matches in competition. Many of the delegates were angry with her for failing to make a rendezvous, but when someone proposed that she sing, there was general approval.

Flora was more than willing. She had come prepared, with a pianist. First she sang "The Day of Vengeance," and received a warm and lengthy ovation. Then she sang "On the Barricades." After a while, the delegates had had enough, but Flora had planned a long program and followed it to the end.

The last speech of the conference was made by the immortal from America. It was already after midnight. He had promised to be brief, but he became so involved in his speech that he could not finish. Just when he seemed about to come to an end, he entangled himself in a new topic. Outside, dawn was breaking in the sky. Some delegates snored, others made jokes, others winked and passed written slips to one another. Flora had to leave to rejoin her dangerously impatient manufacturer. The secretary who kept the minutes put away his pen. He yawned once and fell asleep. Only one delegate continued to write—an agent from the secret police posing as a leftist, who could not leave because he had to deliver a complete report.

The next morning, Flora slept late. When she finally went down to the conference hall, the chairs had been removed and the dais dismantled. The hall was now being prepared for a wedding. Leaning against the wall were a folded canopy, a huge brass trumpet, and a drum. Two men knelt, shellacking the floor. When Flora poked her head in, one of the workers whistled and said, "Miss, it's all over." The other said, "Comrade, come again next year, the revolution won't turn sour."

Translated by the author and Lester Goran

Miracles

I receive many telephone calls from my Yiddish readers, and often, when I place the receiver against my ear, nothing can be heard but a tense silence. Then a stammering and hesitating voice might follow which soon gains in strength. At other times, I lose patience with my caller and hang up. And sure enough, the phone rings again. On this particular occasion, the telephone rang twice, and hearing no voice, I hung up both times. The phone rang once again. After a while, I heard a stuttering voice. I am accustomed to this type of behavior. I even imagine that I can tell a person's character by his procrastination before speaking. It was a man's voice. It sounded muffled. Then the caller asked in provincial Polish-Yiddish, "Are you the writer, N.?"

I replied, "Yes, I am he—don't be embarrassed. Please feel free to speak to me."

He coughed loudly once, and then added a softer cough. "What I wish to tell you cannot all be said on the telephone. I know that you are a busy man, but—if it's possible—it is a strange tale—one of those things which the heart does not trust to the mouth, as the Talmud says—"

I set up an appointment with him. I told him what I usually say in such cases: that there is no reason for anyone to fear me; I take pleasure in listening to human experiences and one can confide in me. Immediately he became more trusting and his words more coherent.

He continued: "I have read all your writings. It is a sin to take up your time; however—"

Exactly at the appointed minute, the door opened to admit a small man with ruddy cheeks and a round gray beard. From under his yellow eyebrows peered a pair of green eyes, both piercing and gentle. Though his hair was gray, his face appeared youthful and even boyish. His head was bent and he shuffled as he walked. One shoulder seemed higher than the other. He was dressed like a modern man, yet his entire appearance was that of a Hasid from the old country. Hanging loosely from his body, his jacket looked to me like a shortened caftan. After many apologies and preliminaries, he began.

•

"I know that you are from the Lublin region of Poland, and if so, you must have heard about the Rabbi of Mechev. You haven't? I am amazed. I am the great-grandchild of Rabbi Abraham Malach and of the Holy Jew. My grandfather was a disciple of both Rabbi Bunem and the Rabbi of Kotzk. He had a small following and was not well known. Fame was not his goal. By nature he was a man of mystery. Every summer he visited a fair in the town of Naleczow and even traveled as far as Leipzig. It was rumored that in these towns he met the Thirty-six Saints. On Mondays and Thursdays, he fasted. The disciples of Kotzk did not believe in fasting, but my grandfather had ways of his own. He died at the close of Yom Kippur, shortly after the *Ne'ila* prayer.

"Before I continue, let me tell you that I am not pious in the usual sense. I am religious in my own fashion. However, I have seen with my own eyes how a sick man immediately regained health after my paternal grandfather had touched him. Grandfather had the gift of soothsaying. He could see what was happening scores of miles away. Don't ask me how—I give you facts, not explanations. My father, Rabbi Jachiel Mayer, had the same power. My mother, peace be with her, once visited her father in the town of Zelechow in order to celebrate a family wedding. It happened on the Sabbath of Song. My father and we, the children, stayed home. We were observing the custom of tossing kasha to the birds. Suddenly my father announced, "It's a pity that your grandfather has died. At least your mother will be able to attend the funeral." To come to the point, my maternal grandfather died the very minute my father had uttered these words. He had collapsed in the middle of the Sabbath chants. I read somewhere that clairvoyance is hereditary. It may very well be so.

"Our family was small: two daughters and myself, the only son. After my father's demise, I was to become the Rabbi of Mechev. But first of all, my father had no following to speak of. The old Hasidim had died. The young men had gone to other rabbis or had become enlightened. Second, I myself had lost faith. The Enlightenment came about a hundred years late to Poland, but when it finally arrived, it did more in a few years than it had in an entire millennium elsewhere. In the year 1913, there were only a half-dozen so-called enlightened Jews in the whole village of Mechev. In 1918, almost all the young men had shaved off their beards and had become Zionists, Bundists, and Communists. The studyhouse was deserted. The young women turned to smuggling. Mechev was occupied by the Austrians. Girls smuggled food into Galicia and returned with bags of tobacco. A library opened in Mechev and there I began to read secular books. Truthfully, I neither wanted to be a rabbi nor was there a need for one. After my father's demise, the entire rabbinical court crumbled. Only a half-ruined studyhouse containing a few hangers-on remained. My mother had gone to live with my married sister. I sat in my father's study and learned Polish and German from dictionaries. I studied algebra from a book eighty years old. Nobody was there to supervise me. The Austrians had brought the cholera to Mechev, and almost half the villagers died. Grass sprouted in the marketplace. Because most members of the Burial Society had perished in the epidemic, the dead lay unburied for many days.

"I put aside my books and became a gravedigger. I also went from one house to another massaging the sick with alcohol. The doctor had issued strict orders against drinking unboiled water and eating raw fruit. However, I did not listen to him. Not because I wanted to commit suicide. Far from it; I cherish life, even though at times I hate it. Some inner knowledge made me sure that I would not get sick. The people of Mechev were astonished. I was perplexed by my own behavior. Already I was a full-fledged emancipated skeptic. I even neglected to put on phylacteries. I had read Spinoza's *Ethics* in Hebrew. But still, I relied on mystical powers. I also discovered that I was praying—not aloud, but silently. It was a denial of all my convictions. I somehow knew in advance who of the sick would survive and who would die. I thought of myself as being fanatical, crazy, and superstitious. Then I was not as yet familiar with what today we call parapsychology. I fully realized that secular enlightenment and the belief in miracles were contradictory. Today one might say that I suffered from conflicts and complexes. Yet at that time Freud's theories were not popular, certainly not in Mechev. After the epidemic had ceased, I was to be appointed Rabbi of Mechev by the community elders. However, I ran away to study philosophy at the University of Warsaw."

•

"I said that I would make it short. But I could sit with you three days and three nights and not tell you a tenth of what happened. I came to Warsaw with about fifty marks in my pocket; this was before the zloty came into use. With no formal education, I depended on what I had absorbed from some old books. Any day I would be drafted into the Polish Army. Life in the barracks would be a catastrophe for me. I am sure that I wouldn't have lasted for more than a few days; I would either have collapsed or committed suicide. But what were my chances to be rejected? It's true that I was weak, but I was not sick. Shlemiels worse than myself were taken. Maiming oneself to escape the draft, as was done in the Russian epoch, was useless. The Poles were familiar with all these tricks, and besides, the army doctors were ardent patriots. Before entering the recruiting office, I recited a prayer: "Lord of the Universe, save me from brutal hands." Immediately after setting foot in the hall, I was surrounded by a mob of wild peasants. They were hitting the Jewish recruits. A roughneck approached me and shouted, "Jew, go back to Palestine." The Jews huddled together in a corner. How can you sacrifice your life for those who spit on you? I was ordered to disrobe, and this also was an ordeal for me. In the doctor's office, two of the physicians who examined me were about to give me a clean bill of health. One doctor even said to me, "The military will make a man out of you." But an elderly doctor, who I believe was a colonel, disagreed: "Why do we need such a misfit? It's a pity to waste the bread on him." The two younger doctors tried their best to persuade the old man to change his mind, but he had the final word. I was rejected. The two young doctors looked puzzled. I would have to be blind not to see that some higher power had interceded on my behalf. But who could it have been? Perhaps my deceased father. I certainly had no merits of my own. I had committed all manner of transgressions. I even smoked on the Sabbath.

"From that time on, miracles occurred one after another. All sorts of explanations could be given for these events—coincidence, chance, and so on. But what happened to me was not in accordance with the laws of nature. I prayed and my prayers were promptly answered. I began to act spoiled, as though I was the Almighty's only child. It is written: "Ye shall not tempt the Lord." Still, I kept on tempting Him. It was almost impossible to get an apartment in Warsaw unless one could pay a large sum of money to both the departing tenant and the superintendent. Yet I was able to obtain a rent-controlled apartment without any additional costs. I met a beautiful girl whom I liked. At first I did not dare to ask heaven for sensual pleasures. But, sooner or later, I prayed that she would fall in love with me. On the following day, she came to me under the queerest of circumstances. She later admitted that some unknown power, which she could not resist, drew her to me. She had even heard a voice.

"I had no chance whatsoever to pass the entrance examination into the University of Warsaw. Yet I received a passing grade and was accepted. The miracles continued to occur after my admission to the university. One of the professors, who was known to be an anti-Semite, became my ardent friend. The professor lectured only once a week to a small group of graduate students. He taught Spinoza, who at that time was my beloved philosopher. I was sitting in the library browsing through Orgelbrand's *Encyclopedia*. Suddenly a hand touched my shoulder. It was he, Professor Chrabowski. He asked me, "What are you searching for, young man?" I could understand him questioning me if he had seen me reading Spinoza or Descartes. But I happened to be glancing through an essay about Wyspianski. Professor Chrabowski was known to be an angry man and a misanthrope. He had a biting humor which could cut to the bone. Everyone feared him as though he were the Devil. But there he stood beside me, an old man of eighty years, trying to enter into conversation with a freshman. That same day, he invited me to his home. I think I was the only student in the university to be granted such an honor. And remember, I was a Jew and not even his student. He took a great liking to me. He even got me a fellowship. I was baffled by these episodes. The students spread rumors that I was a hypnotist or a warlock. Chrabowski himself mentioned that he couldn't explain why he was so gracious to me. This is only one example of hundreds."

"Why didn't you pray for a million dollars?" I asked.

"I was a fool. I was afraid to ask for too much. But actually, money was never my passion. At that time, I became interested in Kant and the so-called Marburg School. Hermann Cohen was my idol. I went to Berlin and then to Bonn. There new miracles began to occur. I didn't really know German; I brought nothing with me except a letter of recommendation from Professor Chrabowski, who was not known in Germany. I could have died from hunger and nobody would have cared. It was the time of the inflation and the despair which finally led to Nazism. As a matter of fact, Hitler had already attempted his famous *Putsch*. What could be worse than to be a poor Polish Jew, an *"Ostjude."* Nevertheless, they made me a lector at the University of Bonn. And I was invited into homes where the sons of the best houses had no entrée. At a lecture, I met Fräulein Annelisa von Freihoff, a famous beauty and a girl of the highest nobility. What happened afterward between us, I cannot tell you. You can see I am not the most handsome of men and yet she fell in love with me in a way that was most mysterious. Please don't mock me. All of this may sound ludicrous, but I have no reason to lie. I could even show you letters to prove that what I am saying is true. Yes, Annelisa von

Freihoff! To live with a shiksa is one thing, but to marry one is another. I could not forget that I am a descendant of Rabbi Abraham Malach and of the Holy Jew.

"Let me tell you that, in spite of all these events, I was at that time, and still am, an agnostic. Not as far as the existence of God and Providence is concerned, but in relation to dogma. I can't believe that each paragraph in the *Shulhan Arukh* was handed down to Moses from Mt. Sinai. However, as God created man, man's creations are also divine. I know what you are going to ask me: In that case, the works of Feuerbach and other atheists also should have a touch of divinity. Well, it is a question for which an answer does not exist in this world. If you still have a little patience, I want to continue with my story."

"Yes, tell it."

•

"You have written somewhere that every human being has a number one passion. My passion was women. It may seem funny for me to be playing the role of Don Juan. Actually, women are the passion of all shlemiels. Otto Weininger was right: the hundred percent male has no patience for the female. The hundred percent male is a warrior, not a romantic.

"I am not a sick man, but neither am I particularly healthy. Much of my time is spent in bed, and since this is my main occupation, I like to have someone with me. Of course the woman must be willing. But females in their own way can be the most unpredictable and spiteful creatures. It sometimes looks as if their only ambition is to discover a man's weaknesses. Once they succeed, they scorn their victim. I have seen giants reduced to flies in this eternal struggle. I had one weapon: prayer. I guess you read the story of Rabbi Joseph della Reina, who tried to bring the Messiah, and when his attempt failed, because he granted Satan a sniff of tobacco, he became a lecher. Through incantations, he was able to make the wife of the

Grand Vizier come to him. I became a Joseph della Reina. I expressed the will to have a certain woman and almost immediately she came forth. It happened like this so many times and under such strange circumstances that rational explanations have no place here. If I did not care about your time, I could tell you many such cases. Naturally, I also had a passion number two—a career. Even though I hadn't learned German thoroughly, I became a full professor in Germany. And not really knowing philosophy, I even wrote for philosophical magazines.

"Why are you smiling? I do not lie. To know philosophy—actually the history of philosophy—one must read profusely, and for this I have no patience. Regardless of how great a philosopher is, he has only one small if inflated idea, and sometimes not even that. When I pick up one of their books, all I do is glance through the pages. This is sufficient to quench one's curiosity but not to be a professor. I was constantly in danger of exposing my ignorance. But the years passed and my reputation never suffered. When I needed to quote a particular philosopher while writing my essays, I simply opened one of his books and found the right passage. I became known as a man of erudition, while in reality I was an ignoramus. Whenever a student asked me a question involving philosophical knowledge, it just so happened that the day before while browsing through a book I had come across the answer. It may very well be that such things happen to other people who just don't pay any attention to them. Also, Providence does not like to reveal its techniques and wears the mask of causality. If one could see its work, free choice would cease. By the way, even an insight into the ways of Providence would not lead to absolute faith. The brain is constructed so that a man can simultaneously be a believer and a non-believer. The Talmud's statement that the wicked do not repent even at the gates of Gehenna is a deep psychological truth. One may roast in hell and still remain an atheist. Sometimes I suspect that even God doubts His own existence.

"In the early thirties Germany was becoming a very dangerous place for one of my kind. The only country I could escape to was France. But I didn't know French. I was a Polish citizen and a Jew to boot. There was no reason for the French consul to give me a visa. I said my prayer and went to the French consulate. I was granted a visa immediately. I arrived in Paris almost penniless. I am not thrifty and I had spent all my little earnings. I took a room in a cheap hotel and figured out that at best my money would last me four weeks. But what would I do afterward? I was not permitted to work. After all my triumphs, I remained with nothing. True, I was accustomed to miracles, but the rationalistic part of me argued, "Better people than you have starved to death." I knew no one in Paris. The German Embassy crawled with Nazis. I took a walk in the streets and came to the Place de l'Opéra. I saw an outdoor café and sat down at a table. I ordered an aperitif, not because I wanted it, but because I saw someone else ordering it. The waiter brought it to me, and I then sat and waited for a miracle to happen. I sat for three hours and nothing happened. I became tired and decided to go back to the hotel. Well, even manna did not fall for more than forty years. From past experience, I knew that if there was no immediate answer from On High, no answer would come. In the dramas of my life, whatever was going to happen could be seen in the first scene of the first act. I lost my way to the hotel and became exceedingly tired from walking on the boulevards of Paris. On a side street I noticed a little café with a few tables outside. I was hungry and thirsty. I sat down and a waitress came out in a dirty apron. The menu she gave me was illegible. I ordered one of the items not knowing what it was. She muttered something and went inside. After a few minutes, she returned from the kitchen and began talking to me quickly with typical French verbosity. I understood that they were out of the item that I had ordered and I decided to order something different. At a table a few steps from me sat a couple. I barely noticed them. However, it seemed that they had sensed my predicament. The lady asked me, *'Sprechen Sie Deutsch?'*

"To make it short, they were refugees from Germany, and since they knew French, they wanted to help me. I thanked them and the young woman translated the menu for me. I looked at her and I was amazed. She was a copy of Annelisa von Freihoff, only a little older. She appeared more aristocratic, even though she told me she was a Jewess. She asked if I was from Germany. Her husband moved over to my table, so finally we all sat together. He was a giant of a man, six feet or perhaps taller, handsome, an athlete with a round face, red cheeks, and brown eyes. It was summer and yet he wore spats. When he heard that I had been a professor in Bonn, he became quite excited. He had studied there and graduated as an electrical engineer. Even if his wife hadn't been wearing a ring with a huge diamond, I would have guessed that they were wealthy people. They introduced themselves: Mr. and Mrs. Eggschwinger—a strange name for Jews, but they seemed completely assimilated. The husband, Hans, told me that he owned a factory that made electrical appliances. He'd left it in the care of his cousin and planned to go with his wife to Brazil, where another cousin of his had a coffee plantation. He boasted that he had managed to bring over the greater part of his fortune from Germany. His wife Gretl smiled just as Annelisa used to smile. I asked myself, 'Is this the answer to my prayer? Did heaven send me a married woman?' After a while the pair went back to their own table and began to converse in French. I saw that he reprimanded her for something, and in response she smiled coyly, like a schoolgirl. There was a nobility in her face which cannot be expressed in words. She was blond with blue eyes, and was above average in height. She looked more Nordic than the Nordics themselves. One thing astonished me: why did a rich couple choose to dine at such a low-class restaurant? On the other hand, there are in Paris small restaurants which are famous for their cuisine and are frequented by gourmets."

"Did you fall in love with her?" I asked.

"She was the greatest love of my life."

"What did they quarrel about?"

"He was pathologically stingy. He had come with her to this restaurant because meals were a few centimes cheaper here. This was only one of his idiosyncrasies. He was also a hypochondriac and slept with her only once every three months. He took many pills and fasted one day a week. She gave me a whole list of his peculiarities; naturally, later on.

"I realized that I had stumbled into something which I couldn't cope with. Until then, the Ten Commandments had been sacred to me. But a God who helps a man steal another man's wife is like a God who helps one kill somebody. Hitler was about to take over the German government, and in his speeches he babbled about the Almighty, who would help the Nazis enslave the world. A God who helps a man commit adultery may also help the S.S. men drag the innocent into concentration camps. But the passion aroused between us was stronger than all convictions. Hans Eggschwinger was not one of those who would tolerate such doings. When he learned of our affair, he took out a revolver and placed it at my temple. He swore that he would kill both Gretl and me. He denounced me to the police and said that I was attempting to destroy his family life. I could easily have been deported. France already had an overabundance of Polish Jews. I had gotten a job as a teacher in a Talmud Torah, but according to the law a tourist was not permitted to earn money in France. Every day miracles occurred to save me, and these miracles perplexed me. I couldn't accustom myself to the idea that God could be on the side of evil. A vicious God: this is something for the Ancient Greeks or the Teutons, not for a great-grandchild of the Holy Jew. On the other hand, two Jewish philosophers believed in an amoral God —Spinoza and Shestov.

"Much took place in the years 1935–1938. Our affair turned into a kind of sickness. We tried parting, but we could not detach ourselves from each other. Telepathy and clairvoyance were daily occurrences. When I awoke one morning, a voice commanded me to go to some exhibition. When I arrived at the destination, Gretl was there. Once we met by 'coincidence' in the strangest of circumstances, at the horse races located many kilometers from Paris. Both of us went there by taking the wrong autobus. I also became a master of conspiracy. The moment Hans left the house, I was there to take his place. Many times Hans and I would miss each other by seconds. Under such circumstances the senses become unusually sharp and all thoughts revolve around one goal. I became a lurking beast.

"And then there was always trouble with money. Though we were cautious, Gretl became pregnant and we had to pay for the abortion. Hans was so stingy that if she bought a glass of soda, he knew it. If I have something against Spinoza, it is his belittling of the passions. They are stronger than anything else in the universe.

"I still lived in the same little hotel in Belleville, a five-story walk-up full of whores and of idealists who tried to create a better world. War broke out in Spain and young Jewish men ran to defend democracy. I've long been convinced that there is a hidden Messiah in every Jew. The Jew himself is one big miracle. The hatred of the Jew is the hatred of miracles, since the Jew contradicts the laws of nature.

"One day, when I was staying home from my teaching, someone knocked on my door. I asked who it was and it seemed to me that I heard Gretl's voice. I opened the door and there stood Annelisa von Freihoff. She had married an officer who had later become a Nazi. He had come to Paris on a diplomatic mission and took his wife along with him. While her husband negotiated with the politicians, Annelisa came to visit me. How she found my address I never learned. I had nothing to offer her, not even a drink of water. She was an anti-Nazi and wanted to remain in Paris. All her plans depended on me. After I told her about my relationship with Gretl, she returned to her husband. Years later, I heard that Annelisa's husband was implicated in the plot to assassinate Hitler and was shot. Annelisa died soon after.

"In 1938, Hans Eggschwinger presented his wife with an ultimatum: either she returned to him or he would shoot all three parties involved. He swore to it on his German Bible. Neither of us had any funds. He had taken away her jewelry. She didn't even have her passport. We had to part. Hans had no business and he did only one thing—keep watch on his wife. After a while, he forced her to move with him somewhere on the French Riviera. Only a German woman would allow her husband to terrorize her to such a degree. I was now alone in Paris. It was difficult for Gretl to write to me. War was imminent. I tried to comfort myself with other women, but my yearning for Gretl did not cease for a moment. I prayed to God to help me forget her. But I must not have prayed in earnest, because I could not forget her for a minute. From time to time, she managed to write a letter, and each line exuded her passion. I understand that you are wondering what she could have seen in me. But you know the answer: love is really between the souls and not the bodies.

"Here I come to the essence of my story. I began to realize that I wished Hans dead. Until then, I had never wished death on anybody. The idea of murder made me shudder. Even as a child I was shocked when I read in Samuel II of King David's ways of getting Bathsheba and Abigail. The Jewish part of me, the *Talmud-Jude,* as the Nazis call someone like myself, could not tolerate such deeds. I can easily understand why the Hasidim looked askance at those who studied too much Bible. There is something primitive in the Bible which the Jew of the Diaspora —the real Jew—cannot swallow. I even had pity for Goliath. When I discovered my wish that Hans die, I began to pray for him. I recited a special prayer for his life, his health, and his well-being. But as I prayed for him, some tiny section of my brain—you may call it the subconscious—asked for the opposite. I stopped sleeping at night. Meanwhile, the year 1939 arrived. The Hebrew school where I taught was closed down. I had a little money, and although I knew I shouldn't, I took a trip to southern France. I deceived myself into thinking that I traveled this route to reach Palestine. But it was really Gretl I went to see. According to her last letter, she was living with her husband in Nice. However, when I arrived there, I learned that they had moved away. I asked the neighbors where the Eggschwingers had moved; nobody seemed to know. Once again I was left without any money, and again I awaited a miracle. I took a room in a fifth-class hotel and began to look at the ads in the employment section of the newspapers. Someone like myself was not needed anywhere. In my despair, I wrote a letter to the concierge of the hotel where I had stayed in Paris, asking him to forward any mail which I might have received. I could have requested the post office to do this, but I did not know my destination when I left the city. Besides, everything I do is on the spur of the moment. The concierge was lazy and a drunkard. In his house, I had seen heaps of letters which belonged to past tenants and which were never forwarded. After I mailed the letter to the concierge, a melancholy and a heaviness overcame me. In the past, whenever I was at an impasse, I prayed, but this time my lips were sealed and my thoughts turned away from prayer. I decided that my utmost desire was to die.

"A week passed, perhaps two. The little money I had was gone. I might have applied to the Jewish community for relief, but begging always revolted me. I remember it clearly: I was left with nothing but a package of crackers and half a bottle of sour wine. I owed rent on my room. I lay down on my bed and waited for death, no longer for miracles.

"Suddenly someone knocked on my door. It was a messenger with a special-delivery letter. The letter was from Paris and the address had been scrawled by my former concierge. I opened the envelope and inside I found a telegram. Hans Eggschwinger had died of pneumonia. While reading the telegram, I realized two things. First, that I was responsible for Hans's death, and second, that I would never be able to pray again."

"Where did he die?" I asked.

"In Switzerland, in St. Moritz.

"In the telegram, Gretl asked me to come to Switzerland. But I didn't have the fare. Besides, I could never have obtained a visa. The telegram had been sent on the very day I left Paris. If I had remained another hour, I would have received it there. I had no money to telegraph Gretl, but I still had a few centimes to buy postage stamps for a letter. But what could I write? As Nathan the Prophet said to David after the death of Uriah the Hittite, 'Thou hast murdered a man and also inherited his wife.' I knew that my fate rested with the Nazi hangman. Just the same, I wrote a letter to Gretl and she sent me five hundred Swiss francs. She asked that I try to obtain a tourist visa to Switzerland. But when the people at the consulate saw my Polish passport, they refused even to talk to me. Gretl made an effort to come to France, but the Swiss government refused to guarantee her return trip. It was a time when hundreds of thousands of exiles tried to find refuge in Switzerland. All the hotels were packed. I cannot tell you all the details. Many of them I have forgotten. In 1939, Gretl's return to Switzerland was assured. She went to Paris to meet me. By this time, everything appeared to me of little importance. The powers of the universe had severed communication with me. I knew that they had even begun to spite me. There is no such thing as neutrality in heaven. I had abused a privilege and it turned into a curse. Millions of people were condemned to exile, starvation, and death, and I was one of them. Until that time I had never suffered from impotence. The opposite—I was extremely virile. The women with whom I had had relations were always amazed, because this prowess did not match my physical appearance. Hans Eggschwinger was an athlete, but at love he was weak. But that evening, en route to Paris, I was assailed by a fear of impotence. The nearer the train approached Paris, the greater my fear grew. When I stepped off the train in the morning at the Gare de l'Est and saw Gretl standing on the platform, I knew for sure that I would be at a loss with her. She had never appeared to me so beautiful and elegant as she did that morning. She wore a hat with a wide brim and a black veil. As for me, I felt ugly and shrunken. Before the train stopped, I had seen myself in the washroom mirror. I looked emaciated, wrinkled, and aged. The little hair I still had was now gray. My clothes hung on me like rags. I was terribly embarrassed, and I did something only a madman is capable of doing. I glimpsed Gretl for the last time and got lost among the crowd of passengers. I didn't want to see the disappointment in Gretl's eyes, and I was also afraid of her pity.

"The result of that sudden decision, or call it impulse, was another year of starvation in Paris and then on to German concentration camps and all the horrors that went with them. The little man who sits here beside you was in Dachau, Stuthoff, and Majdanek. Even now I weigh no more than one hundred and ten pounds. When the Americans liberated the concentration camps, I weighed exactly sixty-six pounds. The doctors never believed that I would live. Just before the liberation, during the last days, I had fallen into a coma. I have already tasted death. I want to tell you now that there is nothing sweeter. All the pleasures of this world cannot compare with the peacefulness of death. How strange that man fears most what brings him the greatest bliss. Apparently this fear is necessary, since without it man would not clutch at life. I want to tell you that during the years 1941–1945 not a single miracle happened to me. I suffered through all the tortures and agonies of this period."

"When did you come to America?" I asked.

"In 1950."

"Did you marry here?"

"I'm all alone."

"Do you work?"

"I was a Hebrew teacher for some time. Now I do nothing. I live off my compensation money. Those who had a higher education are getting a higher allotment from the Germans. In addition to my pension, I received an extra thousand dollars. Somehow I manage."

"With what do you keep yourself busy all day?" I inquired.

"Nothing. Well, almost nothing. In the summer I rent a small bungalow in the Catskills. It costs me no more than one hundred and fifty dollars, and I stay there from June until after Labor Day, sometimes even until the end of September. I prepare my own meals and read the newspapers. Once in a while I pick up a book. In the winter, I do the same things in the city."

"No more love?"

"No more love."

"What happened to Gretl?"

"Gretl married the owner of the hotel in Switzerland where she stayed. He is not Jewish."

"Do you hear from her?"

"I met her in Munich in 1948."

For a while we both were silent. Then he continued: "I didn't tell you even one thousandth of what transpired. One time I went out into the street with the intention of finding money. And on the pavement amid all the passersby I found a fifty-franc bank note. My legs had directed me to this very spot. For some time I actually supported myself this way, even though I'm nearsighted and half-blind."

"Didn't this lead you to any conclusions?" I asked.

"What conclusions? There are powers up above which play with us. Lately it occurred to me that this earth is ruled by a divine prodigy who toys with little soldiers and dolls. When he tires of them, he rips off their heads. It is even written in the Book of Psalms: 'There is that Leviathan, whom Thou hast made to play therein.' "

"A prodigy has a father."

"He may be an orphan. And besides, the father may be occupied with other worlds."

He was quiet for a while. Then he said, "You, too, are playing. This is the reason I read your works."

"How does this all tie in with your miracles?" I asked.

He grimaced, clutched his beard, wrinkled his forehead, and shook as though he were studying the Gemara. "Life, play, and miracles are identical. Death, too, is a miracle, but not a game."

"What is it?"

"The very essence of being," he answered.

Translated by the author and Judy Beeber

The Litigants

There was talk about lawsuits, and old Genendl, a distant relative of ours, a woman learned, as they say, in the small letters, was saying, "There are people who like this kind of legal wrangling. Even among us Jews there are those who at any opportunity will run to the rabbi for a *din torah*. In olden times, duels and trials were a madness among the Polish squires. Not far from our town there were two squires, Zbigniew Piorun and Adam Lech, small landowners, not like the Radziwills or the Zamoyskis. Piorun had a few hundred serfs. It was before the peasants were freed. He owned fields, forests, and a stable with race horses. In his younger years he was a hunter and a rider, and he used to attend all the races. There was still the Sejm in Warsaw and Piorun attended its sessions every year. It was in the constitution of Poland that when the nobles tried to vote for a certain law or impose a tax, if only one delegate vetoed it, the whole project came to nothing. This was called *vetum separatum*. They could never come to any decision. Because of this wild situation Poland was finally torn to pieces. Piorun was almost always among those who used the veto. He loved making long speeches and made mincemeat of all the programs anyone introduced. At home, every few weeks he challenged someone to a duel. He had a court Jew named Reb Getz, who was in charge of the whole estate and, among other things, of milking the cows. It was Piorun's permanent ambition to prove to Reb Getz that Jesus was the real Messiah. Once, when Piorun began a debate with Reb Getz which lasted until evening, Reb Getz said, 'Your Excellency, whoever the Messiah is or will be, he is not going to milk your cows.'

"Piorun and his wife had sons and daughters. They were all good-looking and they married into the high aristocracy. Every year he gave a ball and people of high rank came from the whole of Poland. The other squire, Adam Lech, was small and black like a gypsy, with no wife or children. He had a neglected little estate with some hundred serfs. He had no court Jew. He managed everything himself. He was an angry man, and when a peasant did something he didn't like, he whipped him with his own hands. There was an old enmity between Zbigniew Piorun and Adam Lech. Their estates had a common boundary and for many years they quarreled about a piece of land which Lech claimed as his property. Piorun had included it in his territory and had fenced it in. The dispute came to a trial, and like all trials in Poland it went on for many years. One judge issued one verdict, another judge a different verdict. Each petition had to have costly tax stamps affixed. All the clerks had to be bribed with money or gifts. Piorun could afford all this, but not Lech. How does the saying go? 'Before the fat one turns lean, the lean one dies.' Neighboring squires tried to effect a compromise. Both sides remained stubborn. In time Lech lost everything. His hair became prematurely white. From too much grief and perhaps from drinking he became emaciated as if he had consumption. Gradually he sold all his fields, his forest, and even his serfs. People expected him to die any day, but some power kept him alive. Adam Lech was supposed to have said he could not leave this world until the courts gave him back what Piorun had stolen, since the truth must come out like oil over water.

"One day both squires, Piorun and Lech, received notice from Warsaw that on a future date they had to appear before the highest tribunal, where a final verdict would be handed down. Piorun didn't care anymore about the whole business. His wife had died, his children had dispersed. He barely remembered all the details of the litigation, but since the Sejm would be convening in Warsaw, Piorun had the desire once more to set forth his veto. He had an old carriage and an old coachman by the name of Wojciech. Piorun's old-maid servant gave the squire provisions for his trip, as well as a few bottles of vodka. The carriage had traveled only a short distance when suddenly it stopped. 'Hey, Wojciech, why have you stopped?' Piorun asked, and Wojciech said, 'Adam Lech is standing in the middle of the road and doesn't let me pass.' 'What? Lech, that old corpse!' Piorun said. At once he understood why. Lech had threatened many times to shoot Piorun like a dog, and now he was about to do it. 'It's good that I haven't forgotten my pistol,' Piorun said. The sun had set and it was twilight, as Piorun began to shoot his rusty pistol. He barely saw where he was aiming. His hand trembled. Wojciech alighted from the coachman's seat and began to scream, 'Your Excellency, Adam Lech is without weapons. He is waving his empty hands.'

" 'No weapons, what kind of duel is this?' Piorun shouted.

"Why drag the story out? Lech had also received a notice to come to Warsaw, but had neither carriage nor horses and, after long brooding, had decided to ask his longtime enemy to take him to Warsaw.

"You're laughing, huh?" Genendl asked. "This is what really happened. What does a squire do who is called to a trial and has no horse and carriage? Lech came up to Piorun's carriage and began to bow and scrape, to stutter and beg Piorun to do him a favor and take him to Warsaw.

"When Piorun heard these words and saw his archenemy bent down, wrinkled, and shriveled like a skeleton, dressed in an old worn coat, with a bag on his shoulders like a beggar, he forgot all their conflicts. He began to laugh and cry, and said, 'My dear neighbor, my friend, why didn't you come to me first? By a hair I almost shot you. It is true that we were once enemies, but we are Poles, brothers of one nation, and I will not let you go to Warsaw on foot. Come in, sir, to my carriage.' The two squires seized each other and began to kiss and embrace like old chums. Piorun took out a bottle of vodka and they drank each other's health and good-humoredly drank toasts to each other's success in the trial. Then Piorun said, 'Why do I need your piece of land? To whom will I leave it? My heirs are all richer than I am. All one needs at our age is a grave.' Lech spoke in the same manner. 'The whole war between us was nothing but a mistake, a caprice, a silly ambition,' Lech said. 'Perhaps the Devil himself, who always lurks behind God's children and tries to befuddle their spirits, has corrupted us. Your Excellency, why do I need the land? I don't even have anyone to take care of my flower pots.'

"Both squires traveled together to Warsaw, talking about old times, making fun of the Polish courts, their lawyers, their accusers, the false witnesses each litigant had hired, the court language written in a Latin no one could understand. Lech said, 'My friend, I don't believe anymore that the Warsaw parasites and vampires are about to come out with a final verdict. No litigant in Poland has ever lived long enough for a trial to be finished. The end comes to the litigants, not to the trials.'

"Adam Lech was right. In Warsaw both litigants learned that the court was far from ready to hand down a final verdict.

They were asked to hire land surveyors once again to measure the land, which over the years had become overgrown with weeds and teeming with snakes, field mice, porcupines, and all kinds of vermin. These measurements were going to cost a lot of money. They were to be compared with other measurements in archives, which only God knew if they still existed. Both Piorun and Lech scolded the court officials and called them thieves, plate lickers, rats, and scavengers. Then together they went to a tavern to drink.

"There was a lot of talk about this extraordinary settlement in the corridors of the Sejm, and when both squires came to the session in the Sejm, they received an ovation from all the benches. In honor of this peacemaking, Piorun did not use his veto on this occasion. For the first time in his life, he agreed with the other lawmakers as a sign that the Poles should from then on act like a united people.

"Too late! Not long after, the Kings of Austria, Russia, and Prussia divided Poland among themselves. Piorun and Lech died, and were buried not far from each other. For many years afterward the tale of these two friendly litigants was told among the squires and landowners all over Poland."

Translated by the author and Lester Goran

A Telephone Call on Yom Kippur

I often receive telephone calls from readers who assure me that they have a true story that would shock me. Usually I get rid of such propositions with any kind of excuse: I'm about to leave town, I'm not well, I'm working on a piece with a deadline. When I do surrender to my curiosity, I'm almost always disappointed. The stories are typical recitations of treacherous husbands, unfaithful wives, ungrateful children. This time a man called who swore he had a fantastic story to tell—a piece of reality with all the elements of fantasy. After some hesitation I made an appointment with him. On the telephone his voice sounded like that of a middle-aged man, but when he came to my office I saw that he was in his seventies, tall, with a head of white hair and a wrinkled face. Only his eyes expressed youthful eagerness. He told me that in Warsaw, where he was born, he had belonged to a circle of students who considered themselves Yiddishists. In the early twenties he emigrated to America—already a grown man. Here he practiced as a dentist and a dental surgeon for over forty years. I asked him about his family and he answered, "I'm sorry, I don't have any close relatives. I've never married. In Warsaw they used to say that when an old bachelor dies he is buried without a prayer shawl, but I never had one. I've always considered myself an atheist. However, when you hear the story

I'm about to tell, you will see that a full-fledged atheist has never existed. Somewhere we all believe in the supernatural. Who was it who said, 'When you scratch an unbeliever, a believer will emerge'?"

After a while my visitor began his story: "As I said, I'm not religious. This may be the reason I never wanted to marry. I doubted not only God but also women. In my youth I had affairs with a number of married women and I came to the conclusion that the saying 'Every woman has her price' is true. I'm not an anti-feminist. All I can say about women is that they are neither better nor worse than men. Our grandmothers were faithful wives because they believed in God and in the Torah, and were afraid of being roasted on a bed of nails in Gehenna. For the same reason, our grandfathers were devoted husbands. When the fear of punishment is gone, what can restrain people from deceit? I'm an old man now, but I still have a lover. When I was young I was what they call a playboy. I was successful in my profession. I even taught orthodontics in a university. I made a lot of money; I had an office on Park Avenue and a comfortable apartment. Although I had no confidence in women, I loved them, and I am not boasting when I say that I was a success with them. What is so difficult about it?

"Yes, I had affairs—juggling a number of women simultaneously. My rule was never to take any of them too seriously. Of course I did not always succeed. There were cases in my life when my love for a woman became so intense that I was about to take her to City Hall or stand with her under the wedding canopy. But at the last moment I had the strength to say no, and still they never left me. I possess huge albums with photographs of my sweethearts, and I have boxes of love letters.

"The most important of all these women was Helena. She was from Warsaw, where she had studied in a Gymnasium—something rare for a Jewish girl in Poland in those days. We met in New York—as a matter of fact, in my office. Someone recommended me to her as a dentist. She was a beautiful woman, intelligent, well-read, and with good taste. Her husband was an optical-instrument salesman who traveled all over America and made a good living. When we began seeing one another, she had an eight-year-old daughter, Mildred. She brought her to me to be fitted for braces. Even today it is not clear to me why her husband chose a business that kept him away from home most of the time. He was sometimes absent for weeks—even months. I have always thought that traveling salesmen and sailors cannot be jealous by nature. Who knows? Perhaps they are born with an exaggerated faith in the opposite sex. Maybe they subconsciously like to share their wives with other men.

"I'm coming to the point. Yes, the husband traveled a lot and made good money. He sent his daughter to private schools. And meanwhile, a tremendous passion developed between Helena and me. We often fantasized about her leaving her husband and marrying me, but I knew that I would never do it. I had no desire to bring up another man's child, or even a child of my own. Women often reproached me, and said that I was a cynic. Maybe I was, but what were they? Men of my disposition should remain unattached, and this is what I did. I am by nature as far from monogamy as heaven is from earth. I think it was Maupassant who said, 'Why a man should get up one morning with a decision to get married I will never understand.' He also said that he could not see why two women aren't better than one, three better than two, and ten better than three. It's possible his biographers ascribe words to him he never said. I certainly accepted his view.

"My affair with Helena went on for years, and it seemed to become stronger with time. In order not to get overly involved, I tried my best to have others on the side. Helena knew about them, and it made her bitter. Sometimes she threatened to make love to other men, but I knew it was not in her character. We had many quarrels. Whenever we separated both of us almost expired from yearning. I heard her calling me telepathically, and I answered her in the same manner. When one of us could not stand it anymore and surrendered, we fell upon each other with a thirst and an enthusiasm that almost killed us. She always said that only death could end our love. At the same time I knew that Helena never made peace with my betrayals. Her rebellion became even sharper with time; our quarrels lasted longer. We waged what they call today the battle of the sexes.

"The unavoidable happened—we parted. Mildred had already grown up and was in college. The reason for our parting was the husband's decision to move to California. Whether this had some connection with me I could never learn. It all came unexpectedly, and everything happened quickly. One day she told me that she was leaving, and a week later she was ready for the journey. They sold their furniture for next to nothing. Today people fly, but then people went by train. Helena had a phobia about flying. She once told me that her fear of flying was so great she was sure that her anxiety could cause the plane to disintegrate in midair. Helena believed in all the superstitions you write about—ghosts, premonitions, clairvoyance. I have forgotten to mention that Mildred never approved of me. She became my enemy when she grew up and understood our game.

"When Helena packed her luggage and prepared for the trip, she insisted that her moving would be a form of suicide. I had to swear that I would come to visit her soon in California. She cried so much that I could not be angry with her. She had lost weight, and I did not like the color of her face. She had written a will, in which she asked to be cremated after death. 'I don't want to rot in the earth,' she told me. 'It is my wish that my ashes be thrown into the ocean. I don't want you to visit my grave with one of your whores.' She spoke as if she had lost her mind. I suffered terribly myself, and there were nights when I lay awake and planned to run away with her. She said that if I was ready to go with her, and if I promised to marry her after she was divorced, she would live with me even in the jungle! But where could we run? Here I had my office, my patients. I lectured in the university. I had other girl friends and was in my own way attached to them, too. Helena was not young anymore, and in my late middle age I had begun to develop a taste for young ones. The woman who is directly connected with this story was a student then, about twenty-five years old. Her name was Martha."

"Not Jewish?" I asked.

"Yes, Jewish. But wait, the story is only beginning. Helena and I parted in love and in hatred. I knew that her husband was aware of me. You cannot conceal an affair like this forever. Almost immediately after she left, wild letters began to arrive from her. She hinted, then actually stated, that she was dangerously ill and that her days were numbered. Since I considered her a hypochondriac, I didn't take her too seriously. Then, in the middle of the night, the telephone rang and it was her daughter. 'My mother is dead,' she screamed. 'Her ashes are already in the ocean. Murderer!' She abused me with the most terrible words. She wailed so that she almost burst my eardrum. She threatened to come to New York and shoot me. I tried to answer but she wouldn't let me say a word. Mildred's last words were 'To me you are already dead. You can't hide for long.' She assured me that her father, too, was out to get his revenge.

"After that night I seriously considered leaving the States—running to Europe or the Land of Israel. The Jewish state had already been proclaimed. Who knows what hysterical people can do? Still, I remained in New York, and as you can see, I am still here. What could I do? Helena was dead, and I was certainly not religious enough to say Kaddish for her. I don't need to tell you that I was shattered. I don't know how it is with others, but I can never forget anything. If you ask me, the word 'forget' should be erased from the dictionary. A day did not pass when I did not think about her. All her words, all her caresses, and all her resentment were engraved in my memory. I had told her that she was the greatest love of my life and it was true."

•

My visitor went on: "After some years I began to fantasize about seeing Helena's daughter again. I could not hate her forever. I said to myself that as women get older they are more likely to understand the complications of love and to forgive. In a way, I had taken part in Mildred's upbringing. When I visited I often brought her chocolate and other little gifts. I hoped I could meet her again one day. Maybe she was already married and a mother. You know what takes place in a mind that is possessed with the illusions of love. Those who love money would like to grab all the capital from all the banks, and those who love women would like the entire female sex to belong to them. As I grew older I had saved a part of my earnings, and it occurred to me to leave Mildred some money in my will. However, between thinking and doing is a far cry in my case. By nature I postpone things. It may sound like a paradox, but although I doubt God's existence I trust his providence, or call it destiny. The whole phenomenon of man is a paradox—biologically and in other ways.

"Now the real story begins. My young lover, Martha, was working then on her doctorate. She had a sister, Sheryl, ten years older, the wife of a professor of philosophy at the University of California at La Jolla. The professor, who was much older than his wife, had taken a sabbatical and gone to England. His wife, Martha's sister, was supposed to visit him at Oxford some time later. Suddenly a cable came saying that he was dead—he had been killed in a car accident. After a short visit to England the widow decided to go on a long trip to Israel. She knew that Martha and I were planning a vacation, and she persuaded us to live in her house in La Jolla during her absence. She didn't want to sublet to a stranger. Martha and I were more than willing to take care of the house. We were supposed to stay there the whole month of September and three weeks into October. The house was on a hill, and many of the windows faced the Pacific. If you have ever visited there, you know that it is one of the most beautiful places in the world —even more splendid than the Riviera. This was my first trip to California. I had never wanted to go there before, because of Helena.

"Rosh Hashanah was over and Yom Kippur was approaching. Neither Martha nor I ever celebrated the High Holidays, and it never occurred to us to look for a synagogue out there. But for some reason I always fast on Yom Kippur—perhaps just to keep some contact with my parents and with earlier generations of Jews. A day before Yom Kippur, Martha received a telegram from a cousin in New York saying that an uncle of theirs who lived in a suburb of Los Angeles had died and left his old wife alone, a woman in her eighties. They had no children. The old woman was sick and helpless, and the cousin asked Martha to stay with her until the funeral. I disliked being alone on Yom Kippur, and I had hoped that no one would disturb our vacation. Martha suggested that I go with her to Los Angeles, but there was a chance that other relatives would show up and I wanted to avoid such complications. Martha prepared a pre-fast meal for me, and then she left. The death of her uncle had dampened my mood. It reminded me that the

Angel of Death has jurisdiction over California, too. Everything I read in the newspapers or heard on the radio was about death, death, death . . . The professor in whose house I was staying and in whose bed I slept was dead. His portrait hung in the living room and stood on his desk. My own relatives had perished in the Holocaust. I ate the cold meal by myself, thinking about my dead parents, my brothers and sisters and their in-laws. Some of them had died a natural death, others were destroyed by the Nazis or died in exile in Russia.

"Night fell quickly. As beautiful as the sight of the Pacific is in the daytime, everything becomes gloomy and melancholy after sunset. You look out into infinite darkness. The sacred night of Yom Kippur is always connected in my mind with ancient Jewish somberness; the Kol Nidre melody and other liturgies were humming in my mind. When I was with Martha, the evenings always seemed too short, but without her the hours dragged on. A cool wind blew from the ocean, and a dense fog covered everything. I tried to read a book, but after the first few lines it began to bore me. I don't know why, but I opened one of my valises and I began to search there—for what I didn't know myself. In a side pocket I found an old notebook with addresses and telephone numbers from years back. I was overcome with a need to call someone and to wish that person a Happy New Year—an impulse on that holy night to make peace, as was the custom in Poland, with someone I had quarreled with or become estranged from. I looked over the names. Quite a number of those whose addresses I had written down were already in the other world. After poking around for some time, I found Helena's telephone number in Los Angeles. It seemed that I had never given up the idea of getting in touch with her daughter. Perhaps Mildred is still living in her mother's house, I thought. I knew that the chances of that and of the phone number's being the same were small. In America things change constantly. Nor was I sure that I really wanted to renew a relationship with someone who had called me murderer and threatened to kill me. Still, I felt an uncontrollable need to call the number, even though it is forbidden to use the telephone on Yom Kippur, when God sits on the throne of glory and signs the decrees for life and death.

"Now comes the unbelievable part, the frightful thing, which brought me here to your office. I called and someone answered. It was the voice of a woman, but not Mildred's. It was the voice of an elderly person, and she spoke in a foreign accent. God in heaven, it was Helena's voice! I realized that it could be nothing but my overwrought nerves, or else my never-extinguished love. I wanted to hang up, but my hand clung to the receiver as if from an electric shock. I heard myself uttering my name, and the voice on the other side said, 'Yes, I recognize you.' I must have been mad with fear in that moment, because I asked, 'Where are you?' And the voice replied, 'You know where.'

"I made a strong effort and threw down the receiver. My heart was beating like a hammer. It became dark before my eyes, but miraculously there was a chair nearby into which I could collapse. In a second I was soaked with perspiration. I sat there shaking and waiting for my heart to quiet down. I saw the receiver on the floor and I barely managed to lift it and hang it up. Ten minutes later when I put my fingers to my pulse it was still beating one hundred and forty times a minute. I hobbled over to the sofa and lay down. Only then did I remember that I had said the words 'Where are you?' in Polish, '*Gdzie jestés?*' and she had answered me, '*Ty wiesz*'—'You know.' Helena came from an assimilated family and we always spoke Polish to one another, not Yiddish. But her daughter, like most children of émigrés, had no interest in the old country and didn't know a word of Polish. My heart, which had begun to subside, started hammering again. A new fear befell me—that I would have a heart attack. I lay there feeling mortally sick. 'It's an illusion,' I said to myself. 'Something is the matter with my brain.' Helena's answer, *'Ty wiesz,'* kept repeating itself in my ears. 'Could it be that I have heard a voice from the other world?' I asked myself. 'Is this an omen that I don't belong anymore to the living?' I could not remain alone in that forsaken house, but where could I go? I became cold. Martha had promised to call me when she arrived in Los Angeles, but the telephone was uncannily silent. In all my terror I decided not to mention a word of what had happened to me. Martha would be frightened to death and would rush me to a psychiatrist. I'll take this secret to my grave, I decided.

"After a long while I dragged myself into the bedroom and got into bed with my clothes and shoes on. I covered myself with whatever I could find, but I was still cold. I lay there numb and bewildered. I must have fallen asleep. The telephone on the night table rang, and I awoke in a tremor. I could hardly lift the receiver. It was Martha. She excused herself for calling so late. Her trip had taken longer than she expected, and she had found her old aunt sick and broken. None of the family, which was scattered all over the world, had appeared so far. Martha asked me how I had spent the evening and I tried to answer as calmly as possible. I recognized from her voice that she, too, was shaken by our unexpected parting. She said to me, 'This is my first direct encounter with death. It took a long time until the train reached Los Angeles, then I had to wait for a taxi. My aunt fell upon me and cried without stopping. The funeral will take place the day after tomorrow. My uncle belonged to a *landsleit* society, and he has a plot in their cemetery. I'll come home as soon as I can. I will call you tomorrow morning.'

"My hand was trembling and I had difficulty hanging up. I stretched out again on the bed, but I did not turn off the light.

For the first time since I was a child, I was afraid of the dark. If an accident had happened that night and the electricity had failed, I wouldn't be sitting with you here now. I would have been buried long ago in the Jewish cemetery in La Jolla—if there is one."

•

My visitor became silent and wiped his forehead with a handkerchief. His hand was shaking and I worried that something might happen to him in my office. I said to him, "Rest a while, Doctor. Shall I bring you a glass of water?"

"What? No. I'm all right."

He sat there, pale, pondering his own tale. I said, "Helena was alive, eh?"

"Yes."

"The daughter was lying?"

"With her mother's knowledge."

"Why couldn't Helena have just let you know she was finished with you?" I asked.

A frail smile appeared on my visitor's lips. "If you can lie, why tell the truth?"

He was silent again for a minute. Then I asked, "When did you learn that she was alive?"

"Not that night. I found some sleeping pills in the medicine cabinet and I swallowed at least a dozen. This threw me into a lethargy, in which I remained the whole night. I was awakened by the sun. One window in the bedroom faced east. It seemed that although I had been lying in a daze, my brain was working and seeking a solution to the riddle. If the dead want to reveal themselves, they don't need the telephone. Suddenly I grasped the truth: Helena was still living. I had become so weak that there could be no more thought of fasting. I went to the kitchen and drank a few cups of strong coffee. Only then did I find the power and the courage to ring the same number."

"Helena answered again?" I asked.

"Yes, and we spoke for over an hour. How weird it was to talk to someone whom I once loved so strongly and whom I considered dead for years. I spoke to her and shuddered. Was it true? Was I in a coma, and the whole thing one long nightmare? I won't bother you with too many details. Helena was alive, but she told me that she suffered from leukemia. Her husband had died a few years before. Mildred had married an Australian, who demanded that she convert to Christianity. She lived in Melbourne with her husband and two children. I asked Helena why she had entered upon this kind of deception, and she said, 'I wanted to chop off our affair with an ax. I knew that if you wrote to me or called, I would never get any rest. Only death could have parted us. And if not real death, then it would have to be the death that Mildred and I pretended. I knew that it was not in your nature to probe or to brood. You had others before me, and you forgot them quickly. One remarkable thing is that yesterday I thought about you all day and all evening. I wasn't just thinking. I had fallen into a sort of trance. You won't believe me, and I cannot even ask you to believe me, but when the telephone rang last night I knew it was you. I have no reason to lie to you anymore. I've reached a state where my lie will soon be the truth.' "

"Did you meet Helena later?" I asked.

"No. I wanted to, but she categorically forbade me to see her. She said, 'I want you to remember me as I was, not as I am now—a ruin. I don't even want my daughter to come to see me. She doesn't know how sick I am. It has been my fate to live all these years alone, and I intend to die alone. I hope that you will respect my wish. Don't come and don't call. If there is such a thing as life after death, we will meet in the other world.' "

"You never spoke to her again on the telephone?"

"No, but I saw her. In reality—not in dreams."

"How did this happen?"

"After that conversation I was again assailed with doubt. I could not stay alone in the house anymore. I was in fear of the coming night. To be sure that I was still there and not in my grave, I called up Martha. She cried out, 'I've been trying to call you for an hour, but the telephone was busy the whole time.' And here again is something unbelievable. Martha asked me, 'Who were you talking to for so long? Your dead lover?' She said it because she knew that Helena had lived in California. But the shudder those words brought to me I will never forget. 'Why did you say that? What was the idea?' I cried out.

" 'I'm only joking,' Martha said. 'Tell me the truth—who was on the phone that long?'

" 'It really was my dead lover,' I said.

" 'You will never know what I went through last night,' Martha said. 'It's true that my uncle is dead and my aunt's situation made me jittery. Just the same, I never knew my uncle and hardly knew my aunt. They are old people and they lived their lives. After my aunt managed to drive me crazy with crying her heart out, she went to sleep. I telephoned, as you know, and went to bed, tired from the trip and all the rest of it. I slept two hours or so. Suddenly I woke up with the feeling that someone or something had pulled my hair and whispered in my ear. I woke with a heaviness in my chest and with a terrible yearning for you. I told myself that it was silly. We have often parted for days or weeks without making much of it. Besides, I had spoken to you before I went to sleep. But I couldn't calm myself. I felt like crying, and you know I'm not a crybaby. I had a strong desire to call you again, but I didn't want to wake you. Now I hear that you, too, had a miserable night. Come and stay with me. None of the relatives has arrived yet. I have told my aunt about you. She won't make any trouble.'

"Some hours later," my visitor said, "I was sitting in the

train that goes from San Diego to Los Angeles. Once there, I asked the taxi driver to pass by Helena's street on the way to Martha's. I wanted at least to see the house where she lived. Perhaps I tried to find an excuse to see her, too. I should not say it, but many things have happened in my life just because I wished them to happen. How such things occur I don't know. My theory is that causality and purpose are two faces of the same coin. If you want something very strongly, the causes and the effects begin to adjust themselves and to cooperate. The fact is that we entered her street, a little alley with old houses, and I asked the driver to stop. It was twilight already. The taxi stood there some five minutes. I was about to tell the driver to continue when I saw an old woman come out of Helena's house, and it was she. I would never have recognized her if I had seen her by chance in the street. But I am a hundred percent sure that it was she. Some trace of her former self remained. She glanced at the taxi and sharply turned away. Maybe she recognized me, too. This is the whole story."

"You never heard from her again?" I asked.

"How? No one would have written to me about her death or called on the telephone, unless she herself from the hereafter—"

The last words seemed to slip from the old man's mouth of their own volition. He looked both frightened and ashamed. I heard him say, "Don't laugh at me. I'm still scared when I must make a telephone call late at night."

Translated by the author

Strangers

It all happened secretly. Even Reb Eljokum's daughters didn't know until the last minute what went on between their father and their mother, Bleemele. Suddenly the strange news came out: the old couple was getting a divorce. Reb Eljokum, an old man of seventy-five, wanted to live out his last years in the Land of Israel and to be buried on the Mount of Olives. Bleemele simply could not leave her daughters, her sons-in-law, her grandchildren and great-grandchildren, the large apartment with its furniture and rugs. Husband and wife planned the whole thing quietly. The whole fortune would go to Bleemele: Reb Eljokum took only his personal clothing, a few rare books which he might not find in Jerusalem, and enough money to suffice even if he lived until ninety.

The divorce took place in our house. Reb Eljokum had a beard as white as milk, a ruddy face and high forehead, blue eyes below white brows. He imported tea from China and owned some buildings. He was known as a scholar and an intimate of the Rabbi of Alexandrov. Bleemele was on her father's side a granddaughter of the famous philanthropist Reb Samuel Zbitkover.

Reb Eljokum had five daughters, all of them well married.

None of the girls was spoiled by modern thinking. It is true that Reb Eljokum and his wife regretted not having a son to recite the Kaddish after their death, but keeping the Torah and good deeds were even better than Kaddish. Reb Eljokum supported yeshivas and each year gave a thousand rubles to the Rabbi of Alexandrov.

As the scribe was preparing the divorce papers and the witnesses were practicing the special Hebrew script they would have to use in signing their names, Reb Eljokum was leafing through a Hasidic book. He wore a silk cap with a high crown in the old Hasidic style. From time to time he took a gold watch from his vest pocket to see what time it was. Only a few days earlier I had heard him say to my father, "I've had enough of business. I want to spend my last years with the Torah and prayer. If I move to the Land of Israel now, my bones won't have to travel underground to get there when the Messiah comes. I want to breathe holy air."

"You're a happy man, Reb Eljokum," my father said. "I hope you live to see the redemption."

"Everything is from heaven."

My father wondered why, since husband and wife had each passed the age of seventy, they needed a divorce at all. But Reb Eljokum replied, "Bleemele is younger than I am. A woman alone is helpless. If she wants to remarry I won't stand in her way."

"*Nu.*"

It was not an easy thing to leave a family, good friends, the Rabbi of Alexandrov, and to travel across the seas to a country under the domination of the Turks, but not a single sigh came out of him. Hasids of Alexandrov believed in silence. Bleemele, small, round, in a satin bonnet with ribbons and an old-fashioned cape, sat on a bench and wiped her tears with a batiste handkerchief. Her face was yellowish and looked to me as if made up of pieces of clay glued together. She shook her head, affirming a truth as old and sad as the female race. I had heard her say to my mother, "My dear lady, I wish I were dead."

"God willing, in Paradise you'll be together again," my mother comforted her.

Now in my father's study everything went according to the law. My father looked into a large volume and addressed Reb Eljokum in the second person singular. "Listen thou, Eljokum son of Eliezer Zalman. Hast thou uttered any words to negate this divorce?"

"No."

"Art thou willing to divorce thy wife, Bleema, daughter of Nathan Meir, in thy name, her name, and in the name of the Law?"

"Yes."

When my father told Bleemele to come over to the table and to cup her hands so that Reb Eljokum could place the divorce papers in them, the old woman began to collapse. My mother and another woman helped her to stay on her feet. After Reb Eljokum placed the papers in Bleemele's wrinkled hands, my father said what he always said in such cases, "You two are not permitted to remain under the same roof. If the woman wants to remarry, she must wait ninety days."

A maid and Bleemele's youngest daughter took her home in a droshky. Reb Eljokum went to the house of a former partner who was a follower of the Alexandrov Rabbi. A few days later Reb Eljokum left for the Land of Israel. I went with a few other boys of the street to watch as his luggage was loaded onto two droshkies. The rabbi came especially from Alexandrov to accompany Reb Eljokum to the train. The street was full of Hasidim. Bleemele had become ill. The daughters were angry with their father; only the sons-in-law and the male grandchildren came. The first droshky was occupied by Reb Eljokum, the rabbi, and two beadles. They were followed by a procession of droshkies packed with Hasidim. The young men sang Hasidic songs. We boys ran as far as the Vienna station.

Many weeks passed and I heard nothing of Reb Eljokum. My father remarked that he had probably arrived in the Holy Land. He had gone by train to Rumania, where he was supposed to board a ship for Jaffa. Bleemele had regained her health. I saw her often in the strictly kosher butcher shop across the street from our house. She walked with mincing steps and her maid walked behind her carrying a basket.

One day my father received a letter from Reb Eljokum. He wrote in Hebrew mixed with many Yiddish words that, praise God, he was already in Jerusalem living in the neighborhood of the Mea Sharim. He prayed every day at the Wailing Wall. He had already visited Rachel's grave and many other sacred graves. Jerusalem is filled with rabbis, scholars, Hasidim. Of course the poor suffer privation, but for money one can get everything. There are not many followers of the Alexandrov Rabbi there, but those who have come stick together.

A few weeks later we received a package from Jerusalem. It was a gift from Reb Eljokum. Inside, there was a prayer book bound in wooden covers with a carving of the Wailing Wall on the front and on the back the Cave of Machpelah. My father gave it to me. I lifted it to my nose and imagined it smelled of gopher wood, cloves, nard, myrrh, and other spices which are mentioned in the Pentateuch.

•

More time passed and I had almost forgotten Reb Eljokum. One evening I heard my father's hasty steps on the staircase—always a sign that he had heard some interesting news in the studyhouse. It was snowing outside and his red beard had turned white from the snowflakes. His velvet hat and his long robe were also trimmed with white. My mother warned him to wipe his half-shoes on the mat. In the reflection of the kerosene lamp his blue eyes seemed bluer than ever. He said, "Can you believe it? Reb Eljokum married in Jerusalem."

My mother became indignant. "That's what men are."

"He took a virgin. It looks as if he still wants a son to say Kaddish after him."

"It looks as if a young virgin is better than an old woman," my mother corrected him. Whenever she was angry her wig became disheveled by itself. I often imagined that my mother's wig was a living thing. Her sunken cheeks, usually pale from anemia, flushed. My mother had always feared that she would die prematurely and that my father would take a young woman in her place. My mother even described her. She would be small, round, with pink cheeks and a sugary smile. My mother believed that this was my father's taste. She was saying now, "I don't believe that the Holy Land was what he was looking for. That was only an excuse to divorce Bleemele. It wasn't the fear of God, only lust. Phooey."

"Since they are divorced and he has no son, what is so wrong?" my father asked. "The book says, 'In the morning sow thy seeds, and in the evening let not thy hand rest,' which the Talmud interprets as meaning that marriage may be a virtue of old age as well as youth. And . . ."

"I know what the Talmud says," my mother interrupted. "The truth is that women are faithful, attaching themselves to their husbands, but men are heartless. For over fifty years to live with a wife and their children and their children's children, and now he marries a strange wench. And why did she marry him? She's probably waiting for him to die so she can get his money."

My father shrugged his shoulders. He couldn't understand my mother's wrath, or the talk about love and an inheritance.

She was too worldly for him. She read the newspapers and the impious novels which were serialized in them. In my father's sacred books love was never mentioned. As for an inheritance, according to the Mosaic Law the sons inherited, not the wife. After a while my father went to his room for his evening studies. It was not in his nature to brood about such matters.

Since the older children weren't at home, my mother spoke to me: "One is not permitted to malign anyone. Since God created men and women it must be this way. Besides, you are a man, too, and when you grow up you won't be better than the others. But this kind of hypocrisy sickens me. That Reb Eljokum acted like a saint. When I heard that he gave away most of his money to Bleemele to be able to live in the Holy Land I had a lot of respect for him. But now I've lost all my faith in him. And can you imagine what your father would do if I were to disappear? Immediately after the prescribed thirty days of mourning he'd stand under the canopy with someone else. For him I'm too skinny and too outspoken. He loves honey, but I am horseradish. I take after my father, and your father takes after his mother, who was all smiles and a do-gooder. God should forgive me for my sinful talk. If I'm fated to die . . ."

"Mother, don't speak that way!"

"What's the matter, one doesn't live forever. Once I'm buried, what do I care what he does? Do the matchmakers have any sense? They make the silliest combinations. In my case all they knew was that I was the daughter of the Bilgoray Rabbi and your father was the son of the Tomashov Rabbi. The truth is that the in-laws also didn't fit. My father was a lion and your paternal grandfather was a lamb. All day long he sat in the attic and studied the cabala. Weeks passed and he never spoke a word. If your father had more sense we wouldn't be sitting here on Krochmalna Street. Other rabbis are ambitious. They have big careers. When your father was told that he had to study Russian and be examined by the governor he exclaimed, 'Never in my life could I speak to a governor.' This is why you're wearing torn boots."

"They're not torn."

"Patched. Well, one is not allowed to speak like this. I don't have any luck in this world and I will most probably lose the world to come."

"Mommy, when I grow up I'll give you a lot of money!" I exclaimed.

My mother smiled ironically. "Where will you get so much money?"

"I'll find a treasure."

"Well, you are your father's son. Enough of that."

•

My mother picked up the newspaper. For a while she read the large type on the first page about Prime Minister Stolypin and the anti-Semite Purishkevich who drove the Jews from the Russian villages. Then she began to read the local news. Her eyes became sharp and sad. There were always stories about people who were run over by trams, murders, suicides, tinsmiths who fell from rooftops. There was a recurring headline, A MAN—A BEAST, which always told the same story of a janitor who came home drunk and raped his own daughter. I did not know exactly what this meant, but I understood that it was better not to ask too many questions.

One evening when my mother was reading a Hebrew book, Zelda, the wife of our neighbor Wolf the tailor, opened the door and said, "My dear lady, I have news for you."

"What happened?"

"Bleemele got married. The former wife of Reb Eljokum."

My mother's eyes were full of mockery. "Is that so? With whom?"

"With Reb Shaya Peltes from the dry-goods store. His wife died only a few months ago."

"Can it really be . . . ?"

"They were married the day before yesterday. She's already selling in his store."

"If he could do it, why not she? I don't blame her."

"In Jerusalem Reb Eljokum's new wife is pregnant. Friends of his got a letter. They might have a dozen children together."

"It wouldn't bother me."

"Oy, my dear lady, what's happening to the world? My mother became a widow at twenty-seven and she never wanted to hear about remarriage. Every time a matchmaker came to her she had one answer: 'God willing, with my husband in Paradise.' "

"There are all kinds of people."

"How can you begin to live with a stranger after being together fifty years? Reb Eljokum was such a clean man. Reb Shaya is such a dirty one. Also a miser. He took her for her money."

"At her age you can't be choosy," my mother said.

"What does she need him for? I hear that her daughters are beside themselves with grief."

The women kept on talking, shaking their heads. Zelda had begun to hint at things which I could not grasp. She slapped her mouth with closed fingers and said, "I'd better keep silent." My mother nodded. "What are husband and wife?" she asked. "Strangers. They are born strangers and die strangers."

"So who is near?" Zelda asked. "Children grow up and go their way."

My mother threw a side glance at me. "Let them go. It's not our world."

•

The next day after breakfast I went to Reb Shaya's dry-goods store to see Bleemele. She stood behind the counter showing spools of thread to a customer. She wore a plain weekday dress and a bonnet without ribbons. She looked as if she had always been there. She spoke to the customer through her sunken mouth. On a high stool in front of a cash drawer sat Reb Shaya, his once white beard now browned by tobacco. His skull-cap was spotted and his gray coat was torn. He counted bank notes close to his myopic eyes. His eyebrows protruded like two brushes. I felt disgust for Reb Shaya, Bleemele, Reb Eljokum in Jerusalem with his pregnant wife. All grownups are liars, I thought to myself. I remembered Shaya's wife, Deborah Itta, from whom I used to buy buttons, needles, cotton. Where was she now? Did she know that Bleemele took her place? No, she didn't know. She was in Paradise. I suddenly decided that if my mother should die, God forbid, and if my father should marry that round little woman with pink cheeks, I would run away from home and become a cabalist and a recluse.

Translated by the author and Herbert R. Lottman

The Mistake

It was a hot, summery Sabbath afternoon, and Aunt Yentl sat on the porch with her cronies, gossiping and telling stories. She wore her arabesque dress and her bonnet with the colored ribbons and beads. She was saying, "It's easy to say 'I made a mistake.' But a mistake is not always a trifle. God protect us, one little mistake can ruin a life, especially of those who are proud and conceited. In our town, there was a Jew, Reb Shachne—a rich man, a learned man. He used to travel to Belz, not to the present rabbi but to his father, to ask for a blessing and offer a contribution. The rabbi himself would draw up a chair for him. Reb Shachne had a hardware store—locks, keys, nails, hammers, pliers, and other such things needed in a household or workshop. You could get goods from him that were hard to find even in the big cities. If he didn't have something in stock, he ordered it from Lublin and even from Warsaw. I was told that a tenant farmer had bought a strongbox from him with locks on it that even the most accomplished thief couldn't have picked open. Reb Shachne had in his store copper and also brass objects: mortars and pestles, chandeliers, all kinds of pots and pans. Landowners came to buy from him, and he never charged more than a fair price. Neither did he allow bargaining. I can see him now—not a tall man, of stocky build, with a red beard that fanned out from his chin. It was said about him that he was more learned than the rabbi. His wife, Lifshe, was distantly related to us.

"Lifshe bore Reb Shachne four sons and three daughters, but only two survived and the couple were left with one son and one daughter—Tevel and Gneshe, two cherished children. Tevel was known as a decent boy, willing to study and devoted to his parents. At sixteen he became a son-in-law of a rich man in Kielce, far from our region. He rarely came home for a visit. At that time there were few trains, and a journey by wagon took days. When Tevel got married, Gneshe was thirteen years old. Already she was known as a beauty: tall, with two blond braids. Girls were seldom sent to cheder, but we had one teacher who took girls into his school. His wife was a learned woman who taught the girls to pray and to write a line of Yiddish greetings. Gneshe helped her parents out in the store and spoke Polish and Russian. The Gentiles who shopped at the store would praise her beauty and refinement. There was talk that a Polish count had fallen in love with her, and had sent her a note saying that he wanted to marry her if she would convert. I wasn't there, but that's what I was told.

"Gneshe was still quite young when proposals for a match began to pour in. At Tevel's wedding, in Kielce, a wealthy woman spotted her and spoke to Lifshe openly—she wanted Gneshe for a daughter-in-law. Lifshe told her to send a matchmaker, and the woman said, 'I'll take your daughter as is. I won't bargain for a dowry.' Possibly her son had noticed the girl and had become infatuated with her. People fell in love in those days, too. Nothing came of that, but afterward our local matchmakers were always at Reb Shachne and Lifshe's door. Young as she was, Gneshe quickly showed herself to be choosy.

Whoever was proposed to her she found fault with. One wasn't smart enough, another was too short, a third shuffled his feet when he walked. Lifshe would come to my mother and complain. 'I pray to the one above,' Lifshe said, 'for her to come to her senses and stop looking for perfection. Even the sun has spots.' My mother comforted her: 'Don't worry, your Gneshe won't remain an old maid.' The girl was then all of fifteen years old, but she was well formed and had a knowing look in her eyes. She liked to joke and often made fun of people. Someone said that if she lived in Warsaw she could have become a stage actress.

"When Gneshe turned sixteen and was not yet engaged, Reb Shachne also began to worry. He called his daughter into his study and had a talk with her. 'One shouldn't think too highly of oneself,' he said. 'We are all no more than flesh and blood.' Gneshe supposedly answered, 'It depends on *what* flesh and what blood. I can bear anything, but to live out my years with a fool—that I cannot abide.' Every time a match for her was proposed, Gneshe would demand to see the young man and to be allowed to speak with him. In those days this was considered scandalous. A bride was not supposed to see her intended until the wedding, when the groom lifted her veil. However, an only daughter gets her way. She could have asked for the moon.

"Now, here's a story for you. One day Gneshe had an encounter with a young man from Lublin. He was from a wealthy household and, as it turned out, quite enlightened, wearing a short caftan with a slit, a small cap, a starched collar, a necktie, polished boots. The matchmaker had brought him from Lublin just to meet Gneshe. As he passed through Zamość Street, all the girls ran to the windows to have a look. They all agreed: handsome as a prince. When Gneshe had an interview with one of her prospects, she would usually leave the door open a crack to prevent anyone from peeking through the keyhole or listening from behind the door. For an hour the two were left alone, and the whole time the sound of Gneshe's laughter was heard. He was, it seems, a joker. So much laughter was seldom heard in a Jewish household, and Reb Shachne didn't approve. He said to Lifshe, 'What's all the merriment? The Holy Temple still is in ruins and the Jews are in exile. But what do the young care about what happened in the Holy Land?' After an hour Gneshe came out to her mother in the kitchen, all radiant, and cried out, 'Mother, this one is smart, bright as the day.' Those were her words.

"I'll make it short. Right then and there the match was decided upon and a telegram was dispatched to Lublin to the groom's parents asking them to come for the signing of the engagement contract. They were well-to-do and refused to stay at Reb Shachne's but asked to be put up at a hotel. We had only one hotel in town, and it was mostly used by Gentiles, but there the groom's parents settled themselves. Reb Shachne and Lifshe threw an engagement party for their daughter almost as elaborate as a ball. A large number of guests were invited. Wine, mead, and liquor were copiously served. The groom was given a good-sized dowry and a gold watch to boot. The groom's mother was all decked out in a hat with ostrich feathers and a hoopskirt. The groom's father owned, I think, a brewery. The groom's mother presented Gneshe with a string of pearls as an engagement gift. Many young men came to the party. The groom—his name was Mully, probably derived from Shmuel—passed out cigarettes to everyone. He himself smoked a cigarette in an amber holder. He signed the engagement contract in a flowery script. It was customary at an engagement party for the groom to debate some passage from the Talmud, but Mully rattled off jokes. Again and again, the girls and women burst into laughter. Later, Lifshe told us that after the engagement Reb Shachne said to Gneshe, 'Daughter, whatever else he is, a brooder your groom is not. But remember, my child, that the world is not a joke.' And Gneshe answered, 'What is it, then?'

"Both sides were eager to have the wedding soon. Gneshe had turned seventeen, which in those days made her almost an old maid. Mully was already twenty-one. He had just been exempted from military service and it had cost plenty to keep him out."

•

Aunt Yentl paused and then went on: "Since both sides agreed and there was no haggling about the dowry and the presents, there was no reason for postponing the wedding for too long a time. Yes, the wedding. Such a wedding I never saw before or after. Lifshe invited everybody. A long table for the poor was set up in Reb Shachne's yard. Everyone from the poorhouse came, and those who couldn't walk were carried in. The wedding took place on the thirty-third day in the Omer—the only day between Passover and Shavuoth on which weddings are permitted. It was a warm, sunny day. Later, there was talk that Reb Shachne had spent a fortune on the wedding and almost went bankrupt. It didn't come to that. Two bands were hired to play at the wedding. For weeks before, the tailors and seamstresses and shoemakers were up all night. The girls gathered in the evenings to dance and break in their new shoes. The hairdressers combed out who knows how many wigs. Gneshe's wedding gown had a train four lengths long. People began to grumble that such goings-on provoked the Gentiles. That's how Jews are. When times are bad they lament. When times improve, if only for a minute, they get out all their finery—and those who despise us grit their teeth. But we don't always listen to reason. Lifshe's maids weren't enough for the occasion, and she had cooks and waiters brought in from Lublin. Gneshe's mother gave her all the family chains and brooches and rings she had inherited and acquired.

"Anyone who didn't see Gneshe in her white silk gown as the veil was lowered over her face doesn't know what grandeur is. But somehow there was no joy in her eyes. The girls asked her why her face didn't glow with happiness, and Gneshe answered, 'A face is not a firefly.' That was Gneshe for you—shrewd as a fox and sharp as a razor. The wedding went on all night: the dancing and the hopping, the polkas, the mazurkas, the angry dance and the scissor dance. Two jesters outdid themselves with their mocking praises, wordplay, and witticisms, and the groom himself also threw in a joke or two. For a groom to make jokes at his wedding was unheard of, but still there was handclapping. I danced at that wedding till dawn. I was there when the bride and groom partook of the golden broth. When it was time for the seclusion of the newlyweds and just before the two mothers took the bride away, Mully must have cracked a joke, because there was a burst of laughter among those who stood nearby.

"I was quite young then, but still I thought, Enough is enough. What does the Holy Book say? 'A time to weep, and a time to laugh.' Children, I wasn't present, but my mother—may she intercede for us—told me that the day after the wedding or maybe the next day Gneshe came into Lifshe's chamber, pale as death, and said, 'Mother, I made a mistake.'

"Lifshe began to tremble. 'Daughter, what are you saying? Why?'

"And Gneshe answered, 'He is a fool.'

"Lifshe said, 'Of all things, a fool? All this time you've been telling us how brilliant he is.'

"And Gneshe cried out, 'My life is ruined.' "

•

"It didn't take long for the whole town to realize it. All through the seven days of benediction, Mully did nothing but clown around. He turned out to be insolent, too. He was disrespectful to Reb Shachne, to Lifshe, to the rabbi. He made fun of everyone, mimicked people. When he was served meat, he said that it was half raw or overcooked. He wanted to teach the cooks their trade. Gneshe sat there white as chalk, her eyes blazing with fury. She couldn't restrain herself any longer and spoke out: 'Mully, you are overdoing it.' Later, she told her mother, 'He has a silly smile. Where were my eyes? I must have been blind.'

"The cat was out of the bag and now everyone saw the truth. Reb Shachne was dumbfounded. He called in Gneshe and said, 'Daughter, from when I first saw him I didn't like that husband of yours, but since you were so entranced I kept quiet. What do we of the old generation know about today's world? Let me remind you, daughter, that there is such a thing as divorce among Jews. To err is human.'

"Gneshe heard him out, and answered, 'Father, there will be no divorce.'

" 'Why not?' Reb Shachne asked, and Gneshe answered, 'It was my mistake, not his. It seems I am a fool, too.'

"As was the custom, Reb Shachne had undertaken to support Mully for a number of years and to let him study as other young men who boarded with their in-laws did. But Mully was not a scholar. He was drawn to the marketplace. He stood among the shopkeepers, surrounded always by a ring of loafers, and jabbered away. He asked for the dowry money, which had been kept by his father-in-law, and went into business. He was no good at that, either. There was a toll bridge in our town, and the squire had leased it to a thickheaded youth, Leibush Cudgel. The peasants and wagon drivers who crossed the bridge had to pay two groschen each. It was considered a lowly way to earn a living. The peasants would look for ways to get out of paying. There was another bridge, at some distance, and many went across there. Leibush was dishonest; he cheated the squire, and was finally dismissed. Suddenly the news got around that Mully had taken over the toll bridge. It was a disgrace. Lifshe stopped going out in public and turned into a recluse. Reb Shachne said to the rabbi, 'I must have done something wrong to deserve such shame.' The whole thing was bizarre. When peasants looked at the young city slicker, all dressed up, they became abusive. One tried to get out of paying altogether, another said he'd pay tomorrow, later. One ruffian lashed at Mully with his whip.

"Everyone waited for the couple to divorce. But you never know what goes on inside someone else's head. All of a sudden word spread that Gneshe, in her blond wig, was sitting in the toll booth and collecting the tolls. I couldn't believe my ears, and went to see for myself. My dear people, Gneshe, already big with child, had put on a heavy vest with a deep pocket, like a market woman's, and had come out to help her husband at the toll booth. The peasants yelled at her and she yelled back. They cursed her and she cursed them. A small crowd had gathered. Some laughed and some pinched their cheeks in dismay. Someone said that a dybbuk had entered Gneshe. A woman ran to Lifshe with the bad tidings, and Lifshe said, 'I'm already dead and buried.'

"It wasn't long before she did breathe her last. Reb Shachne suffered on for another two years, but he became so emaciated that his clothes hung on him. Gneshe had already picked a fight with her parents, and had moved out of their house. She seldom came to see her mother during her illness. This was not the same Gneshe. Her eyes were always angry. Her child, a boy, was born after Lifshe's death. My mother had gone to see Lifshe when she was ill, and tried to comfort her. After all, she said, Gneshe had not killed anyone. But Lifshe said to my mother, 'This is not my daughter, it's some kind of transfiguration.' A few days before Lifshe's death, her son, Tevel, came to visit her, and he stayed until the thirty days of mourning were over. He said openly that he didn't recognize his sister.

"I forgot the most important thing. Gneshe had become a devoted wife to Mully, or so it seemed. He tried his hand at all kinds of businesses and she was always there at his side. The truth is, by himself he failed at everything. When she said buy, he bought, and when she said sell, he sold. He spouted mindless jokes and she laughed and asked to hear them again. If she, Gneshe the wise, had made a mistake, then she had to prove that it was right. It's an arrogance of sorts. She didn't let anyone say a bad word about Mully. She bore him four children. Except for the firstborn, all were girls, and they all took after their father: good-looking but silly. Gneshe bragged about how smart they were, but when she scolded them she would shriek that they were nitwits like their father. A neighbor of hers, who liked to eavesdrop at night from behind the shutters, told it to me. The children were petrified of Gneshe. If they didn't do exactly as she ordered, she'd whip them.

"Gneshe was a good businesswoman, and she soon began to do well. It was said that Reb Shachne had left three-quarters of his fortune to charity, but it seems that Gneshe had found his will and burned it, and what remained was a previous will, in which Reb Shachne left almost everything to her. All her brother got was books, a scroll, a spice box, and other such things. There is a saying: Husband and wife sleep so long on the same pillow their heads become the same. In later years, Gneshe began to make jokes, too—not as foolish as Mully's but too many, and in the same manner. She even began to look like him—still handsome but cheap."

•

"I had already moved away when Mully died—struck down like a felled tree. Gneshe wailed and lamented, bought a plot for him in the most expensive part of the cemetery, even intended to have a tomb built, but the community would not allow it. A tomb is built for a holy man, not a buffoon. Gneshe denounced the head of the community to the squire and the Russian authorities. The elders of the community came close to being imprisoned. The way she carried on, you would think that for her there would always be only one God and one Mully. Nevertheless, one day Gneshe went to Kielce—supposedly to see her brother, whom she had robbed of his inheritance—and returned with a husband, a short fellow with a gray beard. His name was Reb Fishele, and he was thrice a widower. Reb Fishele was supposed to have been at one time a successful businessman and an arbitrator at rabbinical lawsuits. He was called in to negotiate, he claimed, from as far away as Warsaw. Somewhere he had sons, daughters, grandchildren. He talked of nothing but his own cleverness; he babbled and boasted. People saw immediately that Gneshe had made the same mistake all over again. He bored everyone with tales of how he had outsmarted the most learned rabbis and the shrewdest merchants. He considered himself a healer, too. He had his own remedy for every ailment. He labeled all doctors quacks.

"My dear people, everything had turned upside down. In the few months that Gneshe lived with Reb Fishele, she wasted away as if from consumption. Her hands trembled and she began to walk with a cane. Reb Fishele went to the rabbi to complain that his wife wouldn't allow him in her bed. She openly—in front of the maid, and even in front of strangers—called him a good-for-nothing. She tried to evict him from her house, and he summoned her to rabbinical court. She had lost all shame. It turned out that she used to beat him, too. One morning he came to synagogue with only half a beard. People asked what happened to the other half and he answered, 'My bitch tore it out.' They advised him to run for his life, and he said, 'Not without a settlement.' But she had her way after all. One day he went to hire a wagon in order to leave her. People stopped him in the marketplace, and he declared, 'She's not a human being, she is a demon. It's forbidden to live under the same roof with such evil.' The wagon drove up to Gneshe's house and from the threshold Gneshe threw out his belongings. Still, he wanted to say goodbye to her, but she shouted out to the wagon driver, 'Take him away!' "

"A vicious one, wasn't she?" said one of the women who were listening to the story.

"When you're fed up with others and yourself, you lose all dignity," Aunt Yentl answered.

"What happened then?" another woman asked.

Aunt Yentl winced. "She died in spite. Took to her bed and never rose from it. The maid would bring her food, but she barely touched it. Her son lived far away. Two of her daughters came to see how she was, but she forbade the maid to let them in. She said, 'I've had enough of fools. I want to live my last days without them.' She didn't allow the doctor in, either. She told the maid to close the shades and she lay in the dark. The women from the burial society came to her to recite the confessional with her, but she sent them away."

"She died without confessing her sins?" a woman asked.

"Without a confession and without a will," answered Aunt Yentl.

"What became of her inheritance?"

"What usually happens with an inheritance? The daughters fought over it and became enemies. The son did not attend the funeral. The burial society asked an immense sum for the plot, and the daughters refused to pay. She was buried close to the fence, among the paupers and the suicides. Only the gravedigger said Kaddish over her."

Aunt Yentl lapsed into silence. Her bonnet, with all its ribbons, shook. Its beads reflected the flames of the setting sun. Aunt Yentl raised her index finger and pronounced, "A little mistake turns into a big mistake, and a big mistake can be an open door to Gehenna, may we be spared, Father in heaven."

Translated by Rena Borrow and Lester Goran

Confused

In the taxi from Kennedy airport, I dozed and mused simultaneously. I was returning to New York after a series of lectures in universities and synagogues. I had even spoken in a Catholic college for girls. I felt worn out from the steady moving around, lecturing, meeting people whose names and faces I forgot immediately, and from many sleepless nights.

In the apartment thick dust covered everything. I had left the light on in my clothes closet, shining away for the moths to eat my suits and coats. But do moths have eyes to see the light? I decided to look this up in the encyclopedia. Meanwhile, without taking off my coat or rubbers, I stretched out on the sofa and tried to rest. I hadn't turned on the lamp, but light from a tall building on West End Avenue shone into my living room. I took from my breast and trouser pockets the half-crumpled checks I had been given after each lecture. I must deposit them before they become illegible. I would soon have to turn over a good half of their total to the federal, state, and city governments. But what should I do with the rest of the money? As the years went on, I ate less and less. I had no desire for new clothes. Actually, I worked for the tax collectors.

The telephone rang, and even though I had taken an oath not to accept another lecture for this year, I heard myself saying yes to my agent for lectures as far away as San Francisco and Winnipeg. Then a woman called and she said to me in Yiddish, "You don't know me, but I know you through your books and stories. I know you are a busy man, but since I found your number in the telephone book, I can't resist the temptation of telling you how I admire you and also asking if perhaps you could meet me. Let it be just for a short while. I'm sure you get many such demands and if you refuse me I won't be insulted."

"No, I won't refuse you."

"I knew you were a man with a heart. When can I come over?"

I was silent and tried to figure things out, but without my engagement book (where was it?) any date I might give her would be wrong. I asked, "What are you? What do you do?"

"Oh, I used to be a teacher in a Yiddish school in Chicago. I'm deeply interested in psychical research. This especially has attracted me to your writing. Like you I believe that telepathy, clairvoyance, and premonitions are gifts that everyone can develop and . . ."

"May I ask how old you are?"

"Forty-two. Day before yesterday was my birthday."

"Congratulations. Where do you live?"

"Here on the West Side. I'm actually your neighbor."

Another crackpot, I thought. I am not going to bother with her. Instead, I said, "Come over right now. But I'm telling you in advance, not long. I'm just back from a lecture tour and I must go to sleep early."

"I will knock at your door in fifteen minutes. I thank you with all my being. It's not for nothing that I worship you."

There have been times I've tried to make a little order in my apartment when someone was coming to visit me, especially a woman, but now I had neither the strength for it nor the ambition. All I did was get out of my coat and rubbers and lie down again on the sofa. I closed my eyes and fell asleep immediately.

In the last few years my dreams have become strangely vivid. I dream almost exclusively about the dead. The following dream has repeated itself many times in variation: I come to visit my dead lover Ethel in Brooklyn on Ocean Avenue. It is twilight. She opens the door for me, and in the corridor I ask, "Is Leon here?" Ethel murmurs, "Yes, he's waiting for you." We enter the bedroom and Leon is already in bed. In my dream I remember that both Ethel and Leon have gone through mortal sicknesses but not that they have died. Even though the bedroom is dark, I can see Leon's face—lean, pale, with white eyebrows. He looks at me in a mixture of gratitude and reproach. I hear Ethel say, "Men, I'm yours."

The later parts of the dream I invariably forget when I waken. The dream always ends as if the Lord of Dreams decided to turn the whole adventure into a joke. Sometimes Leon starts to sing a liturgic melody that ends in cacophony. Ethel recites rhymes, like a wedding jester, in a mixture of Yiddish, Hebrew, and Polish, and she laughs hilariously. This evening, as always, I clung to the fading images until nothing remained but the solemn beginning and the mad ending—and an urgent need to urinate. My toilet, like all the utilities in this old house, has its own caprices. Sometimes when I flush it, the water begins to pour in a stream that I cannot stop and I have to call the janitor. At other times, it does not flush at all. It only squeaks, gurgles, and whines, as if a living creature were imprisoned in the pipes. This time, my shower suddenly began to run, although I hadn't touched it. When I stood on the rim of the bathtub to shut it off, something fell out of the medicine chest—a saltshaker that I did not remember having brought in there (what for?). Inanimate objects were playing spiteful tricks on me.

2

My doorbell rang and I ran to open the door. There stood a little woman who looked younger than forty, in a shabby fur jacket and boots, a kerchief over her black hair. Her face was light, small, girlish, with high cheekbones. She wore no make-up. In her dark eyes a mixture of provincial shyness and big-city knowingness gleamed. Under her arm she held a little basket. I had a feeling that I knew her, but from where? The moment she entered, she began to tell me that she attended all my lectures in New York and even in the suburbs. She called herself my female Hasid. I helped her take off her jacket. Her figure was also girlish. She had come to America, she told me, in 1948, from a German DP camp. She lived through the war in Soviet Russia. When she entered my living room she opened the basket and took out three of my books, two in English and one in Yiddish. She said, "You have inscribed these books to me—of course you don't recognize me. Knock on wood, you look the same. Here is one of them. See for yourself."

She opened one of the books and I read on the inside cover, "To charming Pessl with friendship and with the hope to see you again." She said, "This was actually an invitation, but I was in Chicago then and in my situation it was not easy to take a trip to New York. My name is Peshe but they called me Pessl. Here in America people are ashamed of such an old-fashioned name. Even in Poland they were ashamed of such names. But to me it is a good Jewish name. My great-grandmother was called Yente Peshe. She was rich, and she gave the Rabbi of Rizin a golden goblet as a gift when I was born."

"My apartment is a mess," I said. "I hope it doesn't upset you."

"Upset me? Nothing upsets me anymore. Besides, if you need someone to clean the place up, I will do it."

"God forbid."

"Why God forbid? Here in New York I became a cleaning woman and a babysitter. In Warsaw I graduated from the Gymnasium and I even began to study at the university, but then the war broke out and I became what the Germans call '*Gleichgeschaltet*.' I came to America with a sick daughter. It's a long story."

"Do you have a husband?"

"My husband perished in the Polish uprising in 1945. Don't be shocked, he was not a Jew."

"You are not upset by anything, and I'm not shocked by anything."

"Halina is almost twenty years old. She's emotionally disturbed. I have to keep her in a clinic. All my energy and almost all my earnings go into this daughter. She was brought up by her aunt, my husband's sister, while I vegetated in Russia. She never knew that she was Jewish until I came back to Warsaw after the war. The story of what I went through in Russia is too long to tell you now."

"In what way is she disturbed?"

"My sister-in-law, Stasia, is an anti-Semite, and she brought Halina up to hate Jews. I cannot tell you what a trauma it was for her to learn that her mother was Jewish. She even attacked me with her fists. In all the years that have passed since then, she has not made peace with her Jewish blood. This is not all. Days pass—sometimes weeks—and she doesn't utter a word.

She's always depressed. In addition, she stopped growing. When I found her in her aunt's house in Warsaw, she was quite tall for her age, but then something happened to her and she did not develop as a child should."

"Perhaps she needs hormones."

"Oh, they tried everything, even shock treatments. With what I earned I couldn't do much for her. But I found a lawyer who specializes in getting reparation money from the Germans and he was able to get a pension for her as well as payment for her medical treatment. My coming from Chicago to New York is also connected with her. Here I found the right clinic and a most wonderful doctor. I would like to do something for you."

"What would you like to do for me?"

"Oh, anything. I could clean your house once or twice a week. I'm even ready to wash your linen. I want to tell you that this doctor has arranged that my daughter can come home once in a while and stay with me a few days. Because of this I stopped teaching, since I never know when she may be sent home. Now my real occupation is babysitting. I can take my daughter with me when I babysit. For her it is a kind of relaxation. She hates me, but she loves children. She would never harm a child. Oh, my life is so crazy that no matter what I tell you, it is only a small part of what I'm going through. I have gotten quite a name as a babysitter. Young couples rely on me when they have to leave town. I taught in a nursery school in Warsaw and I worked for some time in the hospital for children on Slizka Street. Many couples have bars in their homes and they leave them open for me. I shouldn't tell you, but I became a drinker long before I left Russia. I wouldn't have lived through the Holocaust without alcohol. I never get drunk, only sleepy, but if a baby utters as much as a peep, I'm alert in a second. Why do I bother you with all these details?

It's your own fault, you ask questions. Since I'm here, I'm going to make a little order in this house."

"Absolutely not."

"Absolutely yes."

3

I dozed on the sofa and Pessl prepared supper for me. I wanted to take her to a restaurant, but she insisted on shopping for food and on cooking.

I had to force her to take money. I was so tired that after she went to the supermarket I fell asleep. When I opened my eyes, I didn't recognize the apartment. The dust was gone. She had made order of the piles of letters, books, telegrams that had gathered in my absence. How she managed in about an hour and a half to do what had been done I could not understand. We sat at the kitchen table and we ate like an old couple. I questioned Pessl and she told me that except for her late husband, Piotr Trapinski, and one lover in Russia, she had had no other men. She had been living ten years without a man, not out of modesty, but because her daughter drained away all her strength. Besides, the men she knew in Chicago, teachers of Yiddish, never aroused any desire in her.

After supper Pessl washed the dishes. Then we lay down on the sofa. We kissed and Pessl swore that she had been in love with me from the first time she met me at that lecture in Chicago. She solemnly promised to love me not only in this world but in the world to come and in all her reincarnations as well. Such enthusiasm from a woman over forty who had been through the Hitler hell and the Stalin terror seemed to me somewhat strange, but I had experienced enough in my life not to be surprised by any human behavior. Suddenly she cried, "What time is it? I have to leave!"

"Where to?"

"Come with me. It's ten to ten."

Pessl told me in her rush that she had a babysitting job that night only a few blocks from here. It was for a woman separated from her husband because of a lover. Her husband had hired a detective to spy on her and she had to sneak away to a place where he couldn't follow her. She always left her two-year-old with Pessl. "Come with me," Pessl said. "It will be the first night of our honeymoon."

I told Pessl that I could not come and introduce myself as an assistant babysitter, but after some persuasion I agreed to come to the apartment after the owner had left. I would wait for Pessl in a nearby restaurant and telephone her to learn if the mother of the child had gone. While we were hurrying to the restaurant Pessl told me, "You can call in ten minutes or even before. She's just waiting for me. I was supposed to be there earlier and she will be angry, but who cares."

In the restaurant she stopped just long enough to write the telephone number and the number of the apartment on a napkin and ran on. I sat down at the counter, ordered a cup of coffee, and read an evening paper that someone had left on a nearby stool. After fifteen minutes I telephoned and Pessl shouted, "Come right now!"

The building had no doorman and the elevator was automatic. I went up to the fourteenth floor. Pessl was waiting for me at an open door. I entered an apartment carpeted in red from wall to wall, with wallpaper to match, and modern furniture. The living room had a television set and a bar disguised as a bookcase. A cage with a parakeet hung in the window. In the bathroom there was a picture of a boy urinating and a little girl pointing and wondering. It was all cheap, petit bourgeois. Pessl opened the sham bookcase door with the names of Shakespeare, Milton, and Edgar Allan Poe on it, and she began to drink and smoke. She forced me to take a drink. She led me by the wrist to the bedroom and showed me the sleeping boy, Nicky, and his toys, among them a teddy bear almost as big as a real bear. The child had curly blond hair and flushed cheeks. He had a pacifier in his mouth.

Back in the living room we lay down on the sofa. I felt that I had known Pessl for a long time. With drinking she became cheerful, and she assured me that this was the happiest night of her life. She told me stories about her wanderings in Russia. She had been sick with typhoid fever and pneumonia. She had traveled on railroads that stopped for days in the middle of nowhere and that were so crowded one had to take care of one's needs in a chamber pot the passengers carried with them. She starved, went around in seedy clothes, smoked cigarettes made of dry oak leaves. She lived with death for years. But here she was, in a warm home, drinking cognac, smoking American cigarettes, and with whom was she? With her beloved writer. Could there be anything better? While she was saying all this, she kissed my face, my throat, even the sleeves of my jacket. I struggled with her and she cried, "When I kiss the man I love, don't you interfere."

After a while I was overcome with fatigue. Pessl, too, began to yawn. She brought a blanket and covered us. She embraced me and cuddled into me. I was lying still, about to fall asleep, when the dream of Ethel and Leon returned to me. I heard Ethel say, "Men, I'm yours."

4

I had slept long and soundly. I was awakened by a clamorous pounding, ringing, men's voices.

Pessl sat up in bewilderment. "Woe is me. Something has happened to the child!"

She ran to the bedroom, but we soon grasped that the commotion was at the door. Pessl rushed to open it. Firemen told her that there was a fire on our floor and ordered us to go down the staircase to the lobby right away. Pessl ran back to the bedroom and caught up the sleeping boy, and she shouted to me to take the cage with the parakeet. It was a miracle that we were both dressed. In the corridor we stepped over a huge hose. The air was full of smoke. The child awoke and cried. Pessl called out, "They will steal everything! Beatrice will accuse me!"

We started down the steps. In the cage the frightened parakeet jumped back and forth, trying to get out through the bars.

"Where is my watch?" I asked. I began to search in my pockets. "Where is my fountain pen?"

We walked down so many flights that I began to suspect we had gone astray in some underground labyrinth. But finally we reached the lobby, which teemed with the awakened tenants. The sofas and chairs were taken over by women and children. Men walked around in their pajamas, bathrobes, dressing gowns. Some had managed to put on slippers, but others were barefoot. Hoses were stretched across the floor. Firemen in black helmets ran to and fro, carrying axes, poles, gas masks, objects for which I had no name. Some of the apartment residents seemed angry, others laughed. I had put the cage with the parakeet on the floor and found a place on the sofa near Pessl, who rocked the little boy in her arms, trying to put him back to sleep. At the same time she spoke to me: "I knew that some calamity was bound to come. People like me are not permitted to enjoy even one good minute. My dearest, why did I have to drag you into this mess? Go home. I will find anything you have lost. You mustn't suffer because of my bad luck."

"Pessl, don't take it so tragically. They will soon put out the fire."

"If not this fire, there will be other fires. Just on the night when I could say with a full heart that I'm happy, crazy from happiness, this had to happen. *Nu,* it's a joke. Fate laughs at me and my illusions. When Beatrice comes back and sees the jumble, she will hang herself. Beatrice, Mrs. Klapperman, is the owner of the apartment. She leaves a child and runs around all night with a charlatan. She trembles over each of her trinkets. Sleep, little treasure, sleep. Mama will soon be back. Close your sweet eyes!" Suddenly she cried out, "My purse, where's my purse?" She handed me the child and screamed, "I must find my purse; everything I possess is in there. My God. Oy, my misfortune!"

I sat there holding a heavy little boy wrapped in a blanket. I saw Pessl running to the door that led to the steps. She stumbled and almost fell over one of the hoses. The child squinted and soon was crying with all his might. Women attempted to calm him. They put him on the sofa, rocked him, blew on him, called him babele, angel, sugar, but his rage only grew. He showed his teeth like a little beast. Pessl did not appear for a long time. The women began to ask who I was and in what apartment I lived. I had to admit to them that I had been visiting a babysitter. They asked me the number of the apartment, but I could remember neither the floor nor the owner's name. The women looked at one another, murmured, winked. I searched in my pockets. I had written down the number of the apartment, but the piece of paper had vanished. My God, I was stuck here with a strange child. Why, I could be accused of kidnapping. I wanted to search for Pessl, but with whom could I leave the child, who did not stop screaming?

A small woman with a head of fiery red hair cut short, wearing a green nightgown and slippers of the same color, came over to me and said in a tone of surprise, "Are you living here?"

The women around me became quiet. The child ceased crying.

I said, "I was visiting a babysitter and she left to find her purse."

"You don't remember me, I see, but we had lunch together one time when you spoke to our group. I introduced you."

"A speaker?" one of the other women said.

At that moment Pessl returned. "My purse is gone! Here's your wristwatch. I had everything with me, my money, my reading glasses, my bankbook. *Nu*, it's really a comedy."

"Maybe you left your purse at my house," I said, realizing at once that I shouldn't have said it.

"I never go out without my purse. Well, it's one of those nights."

"Firemen are not thieves," the little redheaded woman said. "You most probably left your purse somewhere else or—"

"Where is it written that firemen are not thieves?" Pessl said. "When they see a purse with money, they take it. If German officers, men who went through universities and read Goethe and Schiller, were not ashamed to tear the shirt off a poor Jew, to rob a child of its last bite of food and then cut off its head, why shouldn't some simple fireman steal a purse? Everyone grabs. They wouldn't let me into the apartment, making believe that they wanted to protect me from fire. But there is no fire in the apartment. They just destroy—"

Pessl did not manage to finish the sentence. A stout woman came over carrying two purses. "Miss, is this your purse?" she asked.

Pessl's eyes rolled. "Where did you find it?"

"It was lying right there near the wall." The woman pointed to the place where Pessl had been sitting. Pessl opened the purse, glanced inside, and closed it immediately. She said, "Somehow I came out alive from all my ordeals, but my nerves are shattered."

In all this tumult the boy had fallen asleep. A fireman called out, "Ladies and gentlemen, you can go home to sleep. Just don't break the elevator."

Everyone ran to the elevator, pushing and shoving, the little redheaded woman among them.

"Who is that redheaded creature?" Pessl asked. "I leave you alone for five minutes and you are surrounded by all kinds of pests. You know her or something?"

"She says that I had lunch with her years ago. She belonged to some ladies' auxiliary I spoke to. She was supposed to have introduced me."

"I know, I know. They look for any excuse to make acquaintances. She has the eyes of a hawk. Men work hard, get heart attacks, and these harlots have one occupation—taking men away from other women. From today on, you belong to me. I wanted to die, not once but a hundred times. But a voice inside me ordered, 'Pessl, wait!' I'm sure you don't believe in such premonitions, even though you write about them. Writers are split souls. They go on and on about love and believe only in sex. They tell stories about spirits and they themselves are the worst materialists. You probably thought that I dumped the child in your lap and ran away. Isn't that so?"

"I never knew that a child could make such a racket."

"What is a child? It has all the qualities of an adult. It is impatient to grow up and do its share of evil. I am a fool. That's what I am."

"Why do you say that?"

"What did I need the purse for since I have you? I would give away a hundred such purses for your tiniest nail. Don't look at me like that. It's all my cursed nerves. The slightest thing throws me off balance. One moment I am the happiest person in the world and then there is a fire, and to me a fire is not just a fire but the Nazi ovens. By nature I am very courageous—how could I have survived without courage? But I am also filled with fear. I had a husband and they killed him; I have a daughter and she tells me that I'm not her mother; you come to me and suddenly there is a fire. It's not an accident. Evil powers work against me. Look! There she stands, the red-haired slut. She's coming back."

The red-haired woman was approaching us. She said, "I live on the highest floor and it was impossible to enter the elevator. They push and jostle like mad. I don't intend to disturb you, I just want to tell you that meeting you under such circumstances was a surprise."

"May I introduce you?" I asked. "This is my friend Pessl. And this is—"

"I am Terry. Terry Bickman." She made a gesture to shake hands with Pessl, but Pessl backed away.

"You seem not to remember me." The redheaded woman addressed me. "You spoke to our group and afterward you took me to a vegetarian restaurant. My husband was with me then. We are divorced now."

"Yes, you refresh my memory."

"You don't live here?"

"No, I was visiting this lady and I stayed later than I realized."

"I understand. Our group would like to invite you again. I am their president now. Can you give me your address and telephone number?"

"I am in the telephone book."

"Really? That never occurred to me. Most writers have unlisted numbers."

"I don't hide from my readers."

"Good. I will be calling you. Good night."

Terry Bickman nodded to Pessl. She had barely taken three steps when Pessl said aloud, "*Nu,* am I right or wrong? She lurked there like a wolf for its victim. She wriggled like a snake. You may be sure that she will call you and you will again eat with her and who knows what else. So far as you are concerned I don't have any rights—we met today for the first time. You told me to come and I came. Just the same, let me tell you that if you are thinking of meeting this red-haired bitch, everything between us is finished. I have instincts and I receive vibrations. You'll never know how far they reach."

5

After all the tenants had returned to their apartments and the elevator was empty, Pessl and I went up, together with the sleeping baby and the cage. The moment the elevator moved, Pessl slapped her forehead with the hand on which her purse hung. She had no key to the apartment. Her face became distorted. Her eyes expressed despair and a kind of masochistic triumph: her prediction of imminent disaster had come true. The corridor still smelled acrid. She handed me the baby and began to pound at the door as if she suspected that some fireman remained inside. She even took a few steps back to get a running start and lunged at the door. I told her that we must go to the superintendent and ask for a key, but she said, "Where would I find him? Besides, I doubt that he even lives in this building. The dark powers have not given up on me. They plot new catastrophes every moment."

"You wait here with the child, and I will go look for the superintendent," I proposed.

At that instant the redheaded woman appeared as if from nowhere. She wore a different housecoat and different slippers. "What's going on here?"

"Do you live on this floor?" Pessl asked her in a hostile tone.

"No, one flight higher, but I heard the banging and thought a new fire had broken out."

"They locked the door, those stupid firemen, and I have no key."

"One could get a key from the super, but he lives in the next building. He's a drunkard and never gets home before dawn. You had better come up to me. When I am awakened, the night is lost. I have a bed where no one sleeps since my divorce. I will put the baby there and we will have a cup of coffee or tea. You are invited, too, my writer. I hope your friend won't be jealous. It seems to have been destined that you pay me a visit. It will be both an honor and a pleasure to have you."

"When Beatrice Klapperman comes home and doesn't find us in the apartment, she will become hysterical," Pessl said.

"Oh, she will know that there was a fire. Leave a note on the door that you have taken the baby to Mrs. Bickman's on the top floor. She knows me, the tramp. Does she always come home this late?"

"Sometimes she comes in the morning." Pessl's eyebrows tightened and she seemed to ponder the situation. The baby began to whimper. There was no choice. We walked up one flight. I lifted the cage. The parakeet stood on his perch congealed in an avian version of Nirvana. Terry Bickman let us into an apartment similar in layout to the one where Pessl was babysitting but more elegant, with Oriental rugs, silk wallpaper, original paintings. Both women busied themselves putting the baby to bed. I walked over to the window, pulled the curtain, and looked out to the street. I could see the Hudson aglow with the lights of New York and New Jersey. Behind me there was some discussion about writing the note. Pessl had difficulty spelling in English and finally she asked Terry Bickman to write the note for her. From a drawer Terry took a golden fountain pen, a sheet of pink letter paper, and eyeglasses outlined with rhinestones. She wrote every word with a curlicue in the final letter. She gave the sheet to Pessl with a piece of Scotch tape to fasten it to Mrs. Klapperman's door. Pessl's eyes were saying, 'I understand your sly tricks, but I cannot help myself.' The moment she left, Terry Bickman gave me a knowing look. "A refugee, I take it?"

"Yes, from the Holocaust."

"Why is she so afraid? I'm not going to eat you up. How long have you known her?"

"Not long."

"I shouldn't say it, but she doesn't look to me like much of a bargain. What kind of a job is babysitting? And why does she drag you into such a situation? It certainly doesn't add to your prestige."

"I'm not looking for prestige."

"What are you looking for?"

Pessl returned. "I taped the note on the door, but if she telephones and no one answers, she will have a seizure."

"Where do they crawl around the whole night? A mother should stay home, not hang out with gigolos. What would you like to drink?" Terry asked Pessl. "I can offer you everything—even champagne. If you drink *L'Chaim*, you forget your miseries." She turned to me. "How about you? American writers are all drinkers, but you don't look like one to me. Would you like some cherry brandy? A screwdriver? A Bloody Mary? I have all kinds, as in Noah's ark. It's for others, not for me. When I feel wretched I bake a cake. A good book helps, too. But where do you get good books? I often go to sleep with you, I mean with your books. For each night I spend with you in bed, I would like to have a million dollars tax-free. Suddenly you appear in person, and when?—in the middle of the night, in a fire! Fate has strange ways of bringing people together. What did you say, miss, you would prefer to drink?"

"Vodka, whiskey, whatever you offer me, perhaps poison."

"On ice?"

"No ice. The ice is in my heart," Pessl said.

"Don't be so dramatic, you will drink and warm up. Since this woman runs around all night, she's in no position to complain. Do you have a family?"

"A daughter."

"I have nothing. A daughter is better than a son. A son, when he grows up and begins to play around with girls, forgets his mother. A daughter stays attached. I have a mother, she is in an institution—senile. I visit her every week. I say to her, 'I'm your daughter, Tirzah, Terry,' and she asks me, 'Are you the nurse or the doctor's wife? They don't give me to eat here. They steal everything from me.' Suddenly she starts to speak to me in Russian. I say to her, 'Mother, I don't understand you,' but she continues to talk Russian. They give her plenty to eat. She's gained twenty pounds there. Nobody steals her linen or her few dresses. I look at her and think, Is this the old age everyone wishes to reach? But what do I accomplish with my relatively young age? I'm dying to find a man, I don't sleep nights, but when I meet one and hear his silly babble, I am disgusted. I cannot go to bed with a fool." She turned to me. "What did you say you drink?"

"Do you have some Coca-Cola?"

"Anything you desire. The days pass by somehow. I go here, I go there. I go to department stores and try on dresses and fur coats I would never buy. I have stocks, and once in a while I visit my broker to see how the market is doing. But the nights are horrible. I sleep two hours and I'm through. I brood over matters that can lead only to insanity. When they knocked at my door to announce that there was a fire in the building, I was happy. A fire is better than nothing."

Terry Bickman went into the kitchen to get me a Coca-Cola. Pessl drank half a glass of whiskey. She grimaced and said, "She will take you away from me. It's been this way all my years. *Nu*, I must laugh."

6

For a whole month I was once again on a lecture tour. I traveled in so many planes, trains, and buses that everything became blurred. I gained hours and I lost hours. I was continually adjusting my watch. In almost every place, a female admirer attached herself to me and took me around in her car, invited me for breakfast the day after the lecture, and later drove me to the airport or station. For some reason they all told me their secrets. They wrote my address and telephone number in their notebooks, and in my notebook they wrote their addresses and telephone numbers. Often I had one-day love affairs with these women. We kissed when we said goodbye and I promised to write. But the moment the plane or train or bus took off, I couldn't distinguish one from the other. I arrived home in a cool evening in May, exhausted, and stretched out on the sofa. I feel asleep and awakened four hours later because the telephone was ringing. My wristwatch showed 12:35. I hesitated about whether to answer. I expected the ringing to cease, but when it continued I picked up the receiver. The voice I heard was that of a woman—a strong voice.

"This is Mrs. Bickman."

I had not the slightest idea who Mrs. Bickman was. But I did not admit that the name meant nothing to me. Instead, I said, "Yes, Mrs. Bickman."

"I have been calling for three days. This night my heart told me that you would be home. You have unwittingly thrown me into a situation where I don't know if I should laugh or cry. If I awakened you, my excuse is that I haven't been sleeping for three nights because of you."

"Because of me? How could that happen?"

"Mrs. Trapinski attempted suicide. She did it in unbelievable circumstances. Mrs. Klapperman had gone away with her lover on a vacation or on a honeymoon—call it whatever you like—and Mrs. Trapinski was supposed to remain a week with the little boy, Nicky. I want you to know that we have become quite friendly lately even though we are as different as two women can be. One thing we share, however—we are both insomniacs. The fact that you went away for so long and you didn't find it necessary to call or even to write her a card shattered her. I wanted to tell Mrs. Klapperman that to leave a baby for so long is a risk, but it's not my nature to mind other people's business. It so happened that a day after Mrs. Klapperman left, Halina came home. She found the door locked and she stayed the whole night on the stairs. How the girl found her mother the next day is a chapter in itself. I will make it short. When finally she did, she spat in her face and beat her up. She called her a leprous Jew and said that Hitler had been right. Mrs. Trapinski asked me to come to Mrs. Klapperman's apartment, so I saw what the girl had done. By the time I got there, she had disappeared. Nicky is a sweet little boy and I had fallen in love with him. But I had to leave for half an hour because a handyman was coming with a ladder to put a bulb in my hallway. When I returned to Mrs. Klapperman's, I found Mrs. Trapinski lying in the bathtub with her wrists slit. I had to call an ambulance, and the police came also. Mrs. Trapinski is in the hospital and I have had to take over as babysitter. Halina came back the next day, and believe it or not, she's also with me. I hoped that Mrs. Klapperman would call, but she hasn't, and I have no way of reaching her. This Halina is not only crazy but also full of spite. I speak to her in English, which I know she knows quite well, and she answers me in Polish. That I haven't lost my mind shows I'm stronger than iron. But I'm telling you frankly that if you do not come and rescue me from this madhouse right now, I will call the district attorney. Too much pressure can lead people to anything. Do you hear?"

"Yes, I hear. Where are you calling from?"

"From my home. As I told you, the baby and Halina are with me."

"My dear friend, I am in such a state I cannot go anywhere. I've been away a whole month. I haven't slept many nights. You must call me tomorrow morning."

"How can I believe that tomorrow morning you will not be gone again? I have done my best to defend you to Mrs. Trapinski, but I am going to tell you straight out what I think of you. Wait a moment, someone is ringing at the door. Don't hang up."

I stood with the receiver pressed to my ear, too tired to feel insulted or guilty. I have always considered that stories about amnesia have been invented by writers of filmscripts, but I was experiencing it now. Not one of all these names—Trapinski, Bickman, Halina, Klapperman—sounded familiar. I put my hand into my breast pocket, where I kept my notebook, hoping to find some clue there, but the notebook was gone. Instead, I found a special-delivery letter I had never opened. It must have come before I left on the present lecture tour. From outside I suddenly heard the sirens of fire engines. As always when I hear fire engines, I thought of the miserable situation of the victims. Instantly all the women were identified: Mrs. Bickman, the redheaded little woman; Pessl; Halina, Pessl's psychotic daughter; and Mrs. Klapperman, the mother of the baby whom Pessl took care of. It bewildered me that I had not recognized these names at once. I waited for a long time, but instead of hearing

Terry Bickman's voice I heard a dial tone. I hung up and waited for the telephone to ring again, but it remained silent. I didn't have Terry Bickman's number. I must have written it down somewhere, but to look for it would have been hopeless. I returned to the sofa and lay there numb with fatigue.

7

I woke up at dawn. The lights were on in both the foyer and the living room. I remembered that someone had telephoned me before I slept and there had been talk about a scandal, a crisis, a suicide, but who had called me and who had committed suicide I could not recall. I put my hand into my breast pocket, took out the special-delivery letter, and opened it. The postmark showed that it had come from Chicago five weeks before. A Carol Brill wrote that she was leaving her husband and was coming to New York to look for a job. The tone was intimate. "Don't be afraid, my dear, that I will become a burden to you," she wrote, "but since you complained to me that you are in need of a secretary, I want to tell you, immodest as my words may sound, that you could never get a better secretary than I am. I'm ready to accompany you on your lectures and take care of you and your business as a friend and more than that."

Who is this Carol Brill? I asked myself. According to the letter, she had taken me to the airport after a lecture. Like the others, she had disappeared from my memory. At the end of the letter she asked me to answer immediately. All her plans depended on my prompt reply (underlined three times). But the letter had been in my pocket more than five weeks. There was no return address, only the number of a post-office box in Chicago. I had read somewhere that all our experiences remain in the archives of our memory. With the help of willpower, concentration, and relaxation, one can bring them back to consciousness. But no matter how I tortured my brain, I could not recall this particular lecture in Chicago. If only she had had the sense to send me her photograph!

I should have undressed and gone to bed instead of lying on the sofa in my clothes, but it was too late now to bring the night back. I looked out the window onto Broadway. All the stores were closed. The only lights were in the Chock Full O'Nuts across the street, where someone was preparing the counters for customers who came early for breakfast. At the newspaper stand near the subway entrance, a short man was untying bundles of the morning newspapers. A single passerby was walking from uptown. I could not see his face. He stopped at the entrance of the Chock Full O'Nuts and the man inside gave him a sign that the place was not yet open. What would happen, I thought, if he were to take out a gun and shoot the man through the glass door? Would I volunteer to be a witness? America is a country where murderers are let out on bail and the witnesses languish in prison. I suddenly remembered that there is a sky and I lifted my eyes to it. It hovered without a moon, without stars—a part of the space that according to Newton has no limit, and even according to Einstein is not less than ten billion light-years in every direction. The light from the Chock Full O'Nuts had already traveled millions of miles since I went to the window and would continue to travel long after there was no Broadway, no New York, no people, no earth, and perhaps even no sun. What a mystery! I turned and glanced at my desk. To my amazement I noticed that Carol Brill had sent me two other letters written later. In one she expressed her astonishment that she hadn't heard from me. She said that she had a friend in New York, a woman with whom she studied at Washington University in St. Louis. She intended to live with her in the Bronx. She gave me the telephone number of this friend. The second envelope contained a photograph. The moment I saw it I remembered my lecture, the hall where I spoke, even the fact that the next morning Carol Brill had breakfast with me in the coffee shop of my hotel. She had told me then that her husband, a lawyer, was a coarse fellow and that she had never had a moment of happiness in all the nine years of their marriage. I made up my mind to answer that letter that very morning. She was young and pretty. Let her come to New York. She didn't look like the kind of a person who would become a parasite. Well, but who had telephoned me late at night? Why did the call leave me with a feeling of such uneasiness? I resolved from today on to write down in my notebook everything I did, the name of every person I met. I was not going to allow Purah, the Angel of Forgetfulness, to swallow me up.

I decided to go to the bedroom and undress. I owed a huge debt to sleep. My wristwatch showed half past five. If the telephone would leave me in peace, I could sleep another half hour. Perhaps I could take the receiver off the hook. At that second, the telephone rang. I was sure it was Carol Brill. I lifted the receiver, said hello, and heard the words "This is Terry. Terry Bickman."

The voice seemed familiar as well as the name. But I could not place her. "Yes, Terry," I said.

For a while she was silent. Then she said, "I know that it's bad to call you so early. However, I have no choice."

"Yes, I understand."

"I have woken you up, but I didn't sleep a wink—that makes the fourth night."

"Why?" I asked.

She was silent again. "You don't know who I am, do you? You sound confused."

"Yes," I said. "You are speaking to the most confused creature who has ever walked this earth."

•

A few days later I had a vegetarian lunch of spinach and raw mushrooms with Pessl Trapinski and her daughter, Halina, in the apartment of the red-haired woman, Terry Bickman. Mrs. Klapperman had come home from her trip with her lover and had taken her baby. Pessl had just left the hospital. She showed me the scars of her slit wrists. As far as I could see, her daughter, Halina, was not stunted in her growth, as Pessl had said. She was just short. Neither did she show any signs of morbid anti-Semitism. I couldn't believe it, but she said she would like to study Yiddish in order to read my books in the original. I had written a letter to Mrs. Carol Brill in Chicago. I told her to come to New York and become my secretary. Her friend in the Bronx answered it by calling to tell me Carol had decided to stay with her husband, since he agreed to see a psychiatrist.

I am in need of a psychiatrist myself, but since I believe neither in Freud nor in Adler or Jung, who could be my healer? I will muddle through, one way or another. I have developed my own theory: Not all maladies must be cured. Often the sickness tastes better than the remedy. I am forty percent deaf, thirty percent blind, sixty percent senile, but I can still read my lectures, repeat my old jokes, discern a beautiful face, listen to the many secrets that women tell me on the morning after my appearance while we drink coffee and munch toast with jam. And when they kiss me before I board the plane back home or to another lecture, I kiss back and tell them all the same words: "When you happen to visit New York City, come to see me if I'm still alive."

Translated by the author

The Image

The women came to talking about divorces, broken marriage agreements, rejected brides-to-be, and my Aunt Yentl said, "One is not allowed to shame a Jewish daughter. There is a saying, 'It is better to cut parchment than to tear paper.' You probably know what this means. Marriage agreements are written on paper, but divorces are written on parchment. It's less of a sin to divorce than to break a marriage agreement."

My mother was present, and she said, "Forgive me, Yentl, but divorce, too, is written on paper, not parchment. It's a strong kind of paper and it's written on with a goose quill and an ink called *galish*."

"This I hear for the first time," Aunt Yentl said.

"I know. In our courtroom many divorce papers have been written," my mother said.

"If you say so, it must be so, Bathsheba."

There was a neighbor woman present, Chaya Riva, and she asked, "Why is it less a sin to divorce than to break a marriage agreement?"

"Really, I don't know," Aunt Yentl said. "You tell her, Bathsheba."

My mother pondered for a while and then said, "When a couple decides to divorce they know one another—they've had many quarrels, learned about each other's faults—and it may very well be they've both made up their minds that they can't live together. But an engaged couple don't know one another. The party who wants to break the engagement does so because of money or because of gossip about the other, and this is why the one who wants to break the agreement must pay a fine of half the dowry."

"Yes, yes, yes, where there's Torah there's wisdom," Aunt Yentl said.

"Weren't you about to tell a story?" Chaya Riva asked.

Aunt Yentl rubbed her forehead, as if she had forgotten that she had a story in mind. "What? Yes. This happened in Krashnik. We lived there for a time. My grandfather was the court Jew of the local squire, and my parents were still boarding in his house. They were boarders so long that my mother managed to have five children there. I was the youngest, and I must have been about seven years old when this event happened. Today children remain children for a long time—boys until thirteen, when they begin to put on phylacteries, and girls until twelve, when they are required to fast on Yom Kippur. In those times children ripened early. My mother, peace be with her, used to call me Old Spirit. I wanted to know everything. I listened when the adults spoke and I swallowed each word. We had a maid my age, and we could completely rely on her with soaking and salting meat, cooking, and even baking. She took care of my little brothers and sisters like a devoted mother and all she got for it was two guldens a half year. When she turned fourteen she married a shoemaker—a widower, the father of six motherless children—but this is a story in itself.

"At that time there was a small yeshiva in Krashnik—not more than a dozen students, mostly poor boys from other villages. As a rule, the head of a yeshiva is the rabbi, but our rabbi served as a judge in many litigations out of town and was often employed as an advocate for a rich businessman in Lublin. The head of the yeshiva was a talmudic scholar, Reb Pinchos. He had one son, who was already married, and two daughters. He was exceedingly poor. Reb Pinchos's wife, Greena Chasha, used to bake pretzels, and the boys would buy them from her, a groschen apiece. She also went to wealthy houses to knead dough, and sometimes even to wash linen, because to support a husband, a scholar, is a good deed and in those days Jews were still eager for good deeds. The two girls were separated by seven years. Probably some other children had died in between. The older one, Zylka, was a beauty—dark and charming, like Queen Esther. She had large black eyes and chiseled features. If one has daughters, one wants to marry them off, but girls must be given a dowry, and where could a pauper like Reb Pinchos get money for a dowry? But a miracle happened. There came from Lublin a young man, the son of a rich house, named Yakir. Why should a rich young man from a big city like Lublin be willing to study in little Krashnik? There was talk that he had developed a passion for card games when he was very young. Cards can be a passion like any passion. It's the custom to allow children to play dreidel, and even cards, on Hanukkah. For most of the youngsters it's nothing but a diversion, but in some cases it becomes an addiction. This Yakir became so involved in cards that he began to gamble with squires and Russian officers, and they play for big money. I know of a case where a squire lost all his fortune in card games, and his wife to boot, but this is another story. Yakir caused his parents great embarrassment, and they sent him to Krashnik, where there were no Russian officers. Besides, Reb Pinchos had a reputation as a scholar and a saint. He not only taught Talmud but preached morality sermons every day.

"Yakir did not come to Krashnik like some wandering orphan. He came into the village in a carriage, like a count. There was one hotel in Krashnik, where mostly Gentiles stayed, but Yakir engaged for himself the most spacious room. He brought with him many precious possessions—for example, a music box that played 'I Thank Thee,' a magnifying glass that could light a cigarette, cuff links made from gold coins—and fancy clothes. Everybody went to look at this guest from Lublin. I'm an old woman now but, God forgive me, I've never seen in my life such a good-looking man—slim, tall, dressed like a prince. I was still a child, but when the older girls saw him they were stunned. He was clever, too. He stood in the marketplace and made jokes with everybody—men, matrons, girls, even cheder boys. There was no lack of beggars in Krashnik and he dispensed alms right and left. The yeshiva students had heard about him and they came to meet him. He was not much of a scholar, but he quoted here and there from the Bible and the Gemara. They asked him why he happened to come to Krashnik and he said, 'I owe a general ten thousand rubles and he is threatening me with a revolver.' He laughed, as if he had told a joke.

"From the market Yakir went straight to the house of Reb Pinchos and there he saw Zylka. Such men do everything grandly. He looked at the girl and immediately fell in love—as they say, head over heels. She took one look at him and it seemed the same thing happened to her. My dear people, it was an instant match. Zylka's mother, Greena Chasha, became so overwhelmed that she lost her tongue.

"Yakir asked not more and not less than that there should be a wedding right away, but Reb Pinchos would not allow this kind of nonsense. First, he began to examine the young man, and it turned out that he didn't know enough to become a yeshiva student. What he needed was a tutor. Reb Pinchos taught his pupils from large volumes with small letters. One had to be prepared for these scholarly lessons. He also told the young man that this world was not a place where everyone did as he pleased. There is a God in heaven and He gave us the Torah.

"When Yakir demanded an engagement date, Reb Pinchos said, 'You don't do such things without a matchmaker and without the knowledge of your parents.' He told the fellow in strict language never to visit his house unless he was invited. Greena Chasha was frightened that everything would be spoiled between the young pair, but she knew quite well her husband was right. Zylka became white as chalk. A great fortune had fallen into her hands and her father had plucked it out. I was not there, but there were no secrets in Krashnik. People peered into keyholes and listened behind doors. If a woman burned her grits, they spoke about it in the butcher shop. Yakir became so enamored of the girl that he hired a tutor to prepare him for the yeshiva. He paid attention and he turned out to be a diligent pupil. Neither Reb Pinchos nor his wife would allow their daughter to speak more than a few words to the young man or take a walk with him, as young people do nowadays, but Reb Pinchos invited Yakir to eat in his house on the Sabbath and on holidays, and before long it became clear that the in-laws would come from Lublin and an engagement would be signed.

"I remember Zylka from that time. It was summer and we children used to go to the forest to pick mushrooms and blueberries. We often saw her walking along on the way to the forest and sometimes in the woods. She strolled around as if she were in a dream. We had heard about love. When a tailor and a seamstress got married without a matchmaker, people said, 'Love was the matchmaker.' Among better people this kind of marriage was considered a disgrace.

"His parents soon arrived. They were not just rich—they acted like Jewish squires. They came in two carriages and took over the whole hotel. Reb Pinchos had a small house but still the engagement ceremony took place there, in the house of the bride-to-be, as was the custom. The dinner was served in the synagogue yard, and this was nothing less than a royal repast, paid for by Yakir's father."

•

Aunt Yentl began to cough and clear her throat. She went to the kitchen and came back with a glass of water. "Yes," she said, "the engagement party took place late in the summer, and the wedding was arranged for a Sabbath in Hanukkah. As a rule, they write into the engagement papers how much the bride will give as a dowry, but in this case the bridegroom was supposed to provide the dowry. All the time one could hear Zylka's mother murmuring, 'May no evil eye strike us, Father in heaven. People are envious. They eat us with their eyes. Such luck, such good fortune—it should not be spoiled.' The day after the engagement, Yakir's parents went home. One could see that this match was a blow for them. But what can parents do when a son is stubborn? He threatened to commit suicide if he didn't get his Zylka.

"After his parents left, Yakir returned to the yeshiva, but the other boys saw that his mind was not on learning. Yakir was allowed to see Zylka only on the Sabbath. He complained it was too long until Hanukkah. One day he let his future in-laws know that he had to go to Lublin for a week or two. My dear friends, it took him longer than a week, longer than a month, two months. He didn't even write a letter. Zylka used to go to the post office every day. They told her that if a letter came they would send it to her. Waiting for letters is a terrible ordeal. My mother once said that the wicked in Gehenna lie on their beds of nails and wait for mail.

"The summer passed, and the rain and snow began. Hanukkah was approaching, but not a word from Yakir. What

Zylka went through you can't imagine. She was a solitary person by nature. She didn't have a single girl friend. People said she read her father's books. Sometimes when the yeshiva boys came to Reb Pinchos's home and discussed the Talmud, Zylka listened. She was supposed to have taught herself Hebrew. She had signed the engagement papers with a scholarly flourish. Someone in Krashnik joked that when she married she would not know how to bake a kugel.

"One winter day—outside the snow was deep—a sleigh came to Krashnik, and from it emerged a lady in a sable coat. The lady was none other than Yakir's mother. She went to the rabbi and told him that her son wanted to annul the match—he was asking for a written forgiveness paper from Zylka. His parents were ready to pay Zylka the agreed-upon fine of half the dowry. Half the dowry in this case was a sum of thousands of rubles. The rabbi sent for Reb Pinchos and gave him the bad tidings. Reb Pinchos listened and replied, 'We don't intend to drag an unwilling man to the wedding canopy. If he changed his mind, it is his privilege. A Jewish daughter should forgive when she is shamed, and we are not going to take any reward for forgiveness, God forbid.'

"The rabbi reminded Reb Pinchos that the fine had been written in black and white on the engagement papers, but Reb Pinchos said, 'There is no law that we must accept the fine. Since the young man is canceling the match, this means it was not destined. Probably the Angel decided on someone else.'

"When Greena Chasha heard the dismal news she fainted away, but Zylka took the same position as her father: if Yakir didn't want her it was unfortunate, but she would accept no payment. Yakir's mother went to Reb Pinchos, and there she stopped acting like a fancy lady and wept and bemoaned the lot of her son. He was a charlatan and had humiliated the family. He had fallen in love with the daughter of a doctor, an unbeliever who shaved his beard and didn't go to the synagogue even on Yom Kippur. The wench ran around with Russian officers. Yakir's mother pleaded with Zylka to accept the fine. She could have a large dowry and be able to find the kind of husband she deserved. Yakir's mother foresaw that her son's new madness would ruin him and them. She asked again for written forgiveness and Zylka said, 'I will give it to him but with one condition—that you take back the ring you gave me for signing the engagement agreement.' The woman did not believe her own ears. 'I gave it to you,' she said, 'and I'm not going to take it back. This is a slap in my face.' Zylka said, 'I can't keep it.' She took the ring out of a pocket in her apron. It had a huge diamond, worth a fortune.

"To make it short, the woman was forced to take back her gift, and Zylka wrote the forgiveness papers herself in Hebrew. Those who looked in through the keyhole maintained that the woman fell on her knees and begged Zylka not to return the ring, but to no avail. Zylka was supposed to have said, 'I cannot keep it. I cannot sleep at night if this ring remains in our house.' "

"A haughty princess," Chaya Riva said.

My mother remarked, "Some people are ready to disgrace themselves for a few pennies. They cheat, beg, swindle, they go bankrupt, they are always greedy to grab something for nothing. Others are so gentle they will refuse even what belongs to them. Well, she was the daughter of a scholar."

"If I were she, I would have taken everything—half the dowry and the ring. With such a treasure she could have got the best fiancé," Chaya Riva said.

"Yes, every person has her calculations," Aunt Yentl said. "She didn't want anyone else."

"What *did* she want?" Chaya Riva asked.

"Who knows? The lady from Lublin climbed into her sleigh

and left—a little sleigh, with two large horses. The coachman covered her feet with the fur of a bear or some other animal. He cracked his whip and the sleigh shot off like an arrow from a bow. Krashnik had plenty to talk about. Hanukkah came and there were other weddings. Zylka's mother, Greena Chasha, had become ill. Her face was yellow. The neighbors said they heard her crying at night. It is not a small matter. First a stroke of fortune, then such a misfortune. She kept insisting that enemies had given her the evil eye. As for Zylka, she did not thrust her problems on anyone. To whom could she talk? She walked a lot and always alone. In winter, in the deepest snows, one saw her walk into the forest or toward the road that led to the watermill. People said that she could not be in her right mind. She didn't want any company. When she was spoken to, she didn't answer.

"Now, here's something. In her father's yeshiva there was a student whose name was Illish. He was supposed to have been a prodigy. He came from the town of Kielce. He was an orphan. Why he went to a yeshiva so far from his home I don't know. Since no one told him what to do, probably he had taken to the road on foot and on the way learned about the yeshiva in Krashnik. All he brought were his phylacteries. He immediately went to the yeshiva, and when Reb Pinchos examined him, he saw that the boy had the brain of a genius. He took him into the yeshiva and arranged for six patrons to feed him—each for one day of the week. On the Sabbath he ate all three meals in Reb Pinchos's house, and I think on Saturday night the valedictory meal as well.

"He was a good-looking boy, blond, with long sidelocks and blue eyes. I remember him because he ate at our house every Tuesday. The other yeshiva students were not shy. If they didn't get enough to eat they asked for more. They transacted all sorts of business between themselves: 'I give you my Thursday, you give me your Wednesday.' They knew who prepared a fat soup—a soup with gold coins, as they called it—and who prepared a lean soup. They knew which matron was stingy and which was lavish. Some women liked to question them and find out about everyone's private affairs, but my mother disliked gossip. Tuesday was a holiday for her. She cooked a sumptuous meal for Illish, but he was a small eater. He nibbled—gave a smell and a lick and he was finished. He always carried a book with him, and while he ate he looked at it. He never forgot to say 'Thank you.' A quiet boy, and bashful. When a female spoke to him he dropped his eyes. We girls loved him as if he were a brother. The matchmakers tried to arrange a match for him. Why should I deny it? My oldest sister, Zyvia, liked him. But in those days a girl would rather burst than let fall an affectionate word to a man. I was the youngest and I, too, liked him in my childish way. My sisters fought about who should serve him the meat, who the soup, and who the dessert. Yes, my mother prepared dessert for him, even though it was a weekday. She would say, 'Who knows what he gets in other houses? Let him have one good meal in the week.'

"Suddenly we heard the strange news that Illish had gone to Getzl, the matchmaker, and had sent him to Reb Pinchos with the message that he wanted to marry Zylka. He did it all secretly, but there were no secrets in Krashnik. There was an uproar in town. Our rabbi had a daughter and also two sons, but the sons had no desire to study and there was talk that Illish might marry the rabbi's daughter, Feigele, and after the rabbi's demise inherit his position. Who could have expected a quiet person like Illish to send a matchmaker to Reb Pinchos and ask for his daughter's pledge? Zylka was older than Illish. Besides, when an engagement contract is canceled, the girl is considered damaged goods. However, since Illish had no parents to take care of such matters, he had to decide for himself. I remember all this as if it happened yesterday. When the news arrived at our house all three girls cried. My mother said, 'Why are you howling? It's not Yom Kippur,' and my sister Zyvia cried out, 'If Illish marries he'll stop eating in our house on Tuesdays.' 'Nothing is forever,' my mother said. 'A boy is not born to eat at other people's tables for the rest of his life.'

"We all thought that from this dough there would be no bread. A poor boy needs his wife to bring a dowry and Zylka didn't have a penny. In the other houses where Illish ate, the women tried to dissuade him from marrying Zylka. Reb Pinchos was a pauper, his wife was sick, and Zylka was unbalanced. Why put a healthy head into a sickbed? They tried to match Illish up with other girls. He listened to everyone and answered no one. Everybody was sure that Zylka would reject him. He fit her like a square peg in a round hole. She was taller than he, and more mature. But no one really knows how a match comes to be.

"When Reb Pinchos heard that his best student, Illish, wanted his daughter, he was more than willing. He later admitted that he had wanted him for a son-in-law from the very beginning. Yakir had always displeased him. When Greena Chasha learned that Illish wanted her daughter, she became healthy again in a minute. Reb Pinchos spoke to Illish openly. He could not provide any dowry but he could keep the newlyweds in his house for some time. Greena Chasha said, 'When I cook for four it can also serve five.' Everything depended on Zylka. With a girl like this one had to be careful. Reb Pinchos spoke to her and she said she'd give him an answer. 'When?' Reb Pinchos asked, and she said, 'Tomorrow.' The next day she said yes, and they drew up a preliminary contract. They had to be cautious with her. The engagement party with Yakir had been like a ball, but the signing of the contract with Illish was attended by only a few yeshiva students. Since Illish ate in Reb

Pinchos's house every Sabbath, Zylka knew him well. She was supposed to have told a neighbor, 'He never looked at me, and suddenly he wants me for his wife.' Whether she really said it or not I don't know. It was not in her nature to reveal her feelings. Perhaps her mother said it.

"There was no reason for envying the newly matched pair, but still people did envy them. Many girls in Krashnik had wanted Illish. He was considered a serious young man. Feigele, the rabbi's daughter, walked around like a chicken without a head. The fact that first Yakir and now Illish wanted Zylka meant that men desired her. 'What do they see in her?' the girls asked, but who knows what men see in a woman? They look with different eyes.

"The wedding was set for the thirty-third day in Omer. The pair didn't have long to wait. Reb Pinchos could not give his daughter a trousseau. They said in town that her mother ordered for her a single dress. Reb Pinchos did not permit Illish to eat in his house, because it was considered loose conduct to let an engaged couple see each other at the table. Illish had to find another house to dine in on the Sabbath."

•

Aunt Yentl paused for a moment to fix her bonnet, and then went on: "A few months passed and it was spring again. I've seen poor weddings in my life, but a pauperish wedding like Zylka's I never again experienced. Greena Chasha did not have the strength to make preparations. Zylka was supposed to have said, 'As far as I'm concerned the guests can be fed nothing better than potatoes in their skins.' She was clever in her own way, but to be too clever is not good. It was the custom in Krashnik for the wife-to-be and two of her friends to go from house to house a week before the wedding and invite women to the ceremony, but Zylka refused and people were furious. Her mother told Zylka that she had made everybody her enemy, but

Reb Pinchos sided with his daughter. He said that the bride's going around to invite people was nothing but a Gentile observance.

"On the day of the wedding I went with the other girls to look in the window and see how Zylka sat in her bridal chair. It was a broken chair and Zylka was sitting on the edge of it, not in the dignified way a bride usually sits, and she looked impatient and harried. I shouldn't be punished for my words, but the whole wedding seemed like a joke. It was the custom on the night before the wedding for musicians to play a good-night melody as the bride was led into the ritual bath for her ablutions, but Reb Pinchos had no money to pay the band. The elders wanted to give him a subsidy, but he refused to take it. He took charity for the yeshiva, not alms for himself, he said. There's a saying, 'The apple doesn't fall far from the tree,' and the Krashnik wedding jester was supposed to have said, 'The apple tree is not far from the apple.' Reb Pinchos was a saintly man but overly honest. The daughter was too proud. Everything that is exaggerated does damage.

"They put up the wedding canopy in the synagogue yard, and even though few were invited, the whole town came to witness the happy event. Greena Chasha and another woman led Zylka to the canopy, but she walked too quickly and almost dragged them. Some toughs joked that the bride was in a rush. They called names after her and whistled. The rabbi recited the blessings in a hoarse voice. Illish had always been short, but that evening he appeared no taller than a cheder boy. The few guests who went to the supper reported later that they left hungry.

"Now, listen. It was a tradition in Krashnik that at dawn after a wedding a bunch of matrons dashed into the bedroom, tore away the sheet under the bride, and went outside with it to dance a kosher dance celebrating the bride's virginity. They did it this time, too, but there was no blood on the sheet. The matrons later complained that Zylka had screamed at them and scolded them. My dear people, heaven and earth conspired that no secret should remain unrevealed. Some women said that Illish was such a shlemiel he didn't know what a man should know, and others contended Zylka was not a virgin, that Yakir had skimmed off the cream. When the seven nuptial days were over, the rabbi summoned the young pair to his courtroom and began to ask questions. What was the matter and why? Illish stood there frightened and pale as a corpse and he couldn't utter a word. The rabbi had told the beadle to cover the windows, but the synagogue street was black with curious people. The rabbi continued to interrogate the pair, until the needle came out from the haystack. A man had been lying between bride and bridegroom and would not let them approach each other.

" 'A man?' the rabbi cried out. 'What do you mean "a man"?' And Zylka replied, 'Yakir, his image.'

"What went on in Krashnik that day and the days and weeks thereafter one could not describe even if we sat seven days and seven nights. It was clear that it was not the real Yakir. Yakir chased around with women in Lublin, not Krashnik. It could only be a demon, but how could a demon get hold of the young pair? The rabbi told Reb Pinchos to examine the mezuzah on the door, but not a letter of the parchment had faded. Greena Chasha, the grieved mother, began to suspect that some enemy had bewitched her daughter, perhaps made a knot in her wedding dress, in the fringes of her shawl, or in the lace of her bloomers, or perhaps in a sheet or a pillowcase, but she found nothing and there was no one she could suspect.

"The rabbi and the yeshiva boys questioned Illish on whether there had really been an image lying between Zylka and him when he came to her bed, but he could not give a clear answer.

He mumbled, 'Yes, no, maybe.' They looked over his phylacteries, his prayer shawl. Everything was as it should be. Zylka stopped leaving the house altogether. She lay in the dark bedroom sunk in gloom. When Illish came home for supper his mother-in-law served him his meal. Reb Pinchos did not belong to the Hasidim, but nevertheless he went to a wonder rabbi and brought home a bundle of talismans. Greena Chasha went so far in her anguish that she asked advice of an old Gentile woman, a witch, who gave her all kinds of incantations and herbs. Nothing helped. Zylka remained a virgin."

"Are you sure she was a virgin?" Chaya Riva asked.

"What else? There was no one in Krashnik with whom she could have misbehaved. There was no hiding place in Krashnik. A hundred eyes lurked in every nook."

"Were they finally divorced?" my mother asked.

Aunt Yentl did not answer right away. She said, "One day Greena Chasha went to Zylka in the dark bedroom and said, 'My daughter, you cannot stay separated forever. There is no such thing as a Jewish cloister.' Zylka said, 'There should be. I wish there were.'

"Her mother thought this was just one of her sharp sayings, a spiteful answer. But a few hours later, when Greena Chasha came to her daughter with a glass of tea, the bedroom was empty. The mother screamed and called and went to look for her daughter, but there was no more Zylka in Krashnik—neither that day nor the days and years after. Zylka had gone to the Catholic priest and told him she wanted to give up her faith."

"She converted?" Chaya Riva asked.

"Became a nun and went into a cloister."

"When and how did they learn about it?" my mother asked.

"Not immediately, but after some time," Aunt Yentl said. "The community tried to save her, to redeem her with money, but the priest refused to hear of it. When they take captive a Jewish soul they never relinquish it."

"What happened to Yakir?" my mother asked.

"I don't know. Sinners never end up well," Aunt Yentl said. "As for Illish, he married Feigele, the rabbi's daughter, and after the rabbi's death he took his chair."

For a long while the women were silent. Then my mother said, "This image was not a demon."

"What was it?" Aunt Yentl asked, and my mother said, "A mirage, a figment of madness. You get something in your head and you cannot drive it away. It keeps on boring day and night like the gnat in the brain of the cursed Titus."

"Wasn't it a dybbuk?" Chaya Riva asked.

My mother pondered for a while. "No, Chaya Riva," she said. "A dybbuk talks, screams, howls, wails, and therefore he can be exorcised. Melancholy is silent, and therein lies its uncanny power."

Translated by the author and Lester Goran